Rosa's

DISTRICT 6

ROZENA MAART

We acknowledge the support of the Canada Council for the Arts for our publishing program.
We also acknowledge support from the Ontario Arts Council.

 Canada Council for the Arts **Conseil des Arts du Canada**
ONTARIO ARTS COUNCIL
CONSEIL DES ARTS DE L'ONTARIO

Cover designed by David Drummond

"No Rosa, No District Six," was previously published in *Fireweed: Feminist Journal* (Toronto: Spring 1991) and in *The Journey Prize Anthology 4* (Toronto: McClelland and Stewart, 1992).

Library and Archives Canada Cataloguing in Publication

Maart, Rozena, 1962-
Rosa's District 6 / Rozena Maart.

ISBN 1-894770-16-1

I. Title.

PS8576.A29R68 2004   C811'.6   C2004-905349-3

Printed in Canada by Coach House Printing

TSAR Publications
P. O. Box 6996, Station A
Toronto, Ontario M5W 1X7
Canada

www.tsarbooks.com

To my sister Sharon,
who blossomed in District Six

Contents

No Rosa, No District Six

mummy and mamma orways say dat I make tings up and dat I have a
lively emagenation and dat I'm like der people in der olden days dat jus
used to tell stories about udder people before dem das why mummy and
mamma orways tear my papers up and trow it away but tis not tru I
never make tings up I orways tell mamma what happened and mamma
doan believe me and I tell mummy and mummy doan believe me too
and den I write it on a piece of paper or on der wall or behind Ospavat
building or in der sand at der park and Mr Franks at school he doan
believe me too cos he says dat I orways make trouble wi der teachers and
I talk too much and I jump too much and I laugh too much and I doan
sit still too much and I orways have bubble gum and I orways have
pieces of tings and papers and my hair orways comes loose and mamma
toal Mr Franks dat I'm under der doctor and dat I get pills cos I'm hyper
active like mamma say "someone who is restless all der time" but Mr
Franks doan believe dat I'm under der doctor cos I make too much
movements and today Mr Henson gave me four cuts cos he say dat I was
disobedient and dat I cause trouble in der class but tis not true cos you
see last week we celebrated Van Riebeeck's day on der sixt of April wit
der flag and we sing "uit die blou van onse hemel" on der grass for der
assembly and four weeks ago Mr Henson teached us Van Riebeeck made
Cape Town and built a fort and erecticated a half way station for food
and surplies for der Dutch people and der European people so dat dey
could rest at der Cape after a long journey and den Mr Henson also toal
us dat Van Riebeeck's wife was Maria de la Quelerie dis is true I dirint

make dis up like mummy and mamma orways say I make tings up and den Mari der big girl in my class she has her periods oready she toal us she wondered where Maria put her cotton clot wi blood on it in der ship from Holland cos Mari's mummy told her not to tell her daddy her broder or her uncles about her periods cos men mus never see or know dees tings and den we all laughed cos Mari's very funny and today we had to give in our assignments on Van Riebeeck and Mr Henson ga me four cuts on my hand cos I drew a picture of Maria and not Jan and Mr Henson say dat der assignment was about Van Riebeeck and not Maria and I say is der same ting cos it was part of der same history lesson and Mr Henson screamed at me to shut up and his veins was standing out and he say dat I was not paying attention and dat he is going to write another letter to mummy about my bee haviour and I ask Mr Henson if Maria and Jan had children and Mr Henson say dat I want to play housey-housey all der time and not learn history and I say dat if Maria was Jan's wife den dey must have had children and den Mr Henson took me down to der office to Mr Franks cos Mr Franks is der principal and Mr Henson tell Mr Franks dat I was causing trouble and Mr Franks believe Mr Henson and tells me dat I know I should not have been in school in der first place and dat I've made trouble since Sub A cos when I was in Sub A Mr Franks found out dat I was 5 and not 6 and Mr Franks sent me home and der next day mummy went to school and made a big performance and Mr Franks took me back cos mamma doan wanna look after me der whole day and cos I start to write when I was four and mamma say I make too much mess on der walls and on der tings and now der school doan want me back no more and Mr Franks say dat I mus bring mummy to school but I dirint do anything wrong all I wannit to know was if Maria and Jan had children, dat's all
April 9, 1970

A warm April afternoon greeted the child as she stood with her hands on her hips, her sticky fingers cupping the flesh around her cheeks. She eagerly observed the friendly wall upon which her writing spoke her truths. Her eyes scanned the written area, narrowing with approval whilst her mouth formed a severe pout. Rosa took the fringe of her dress and tucked it into her bloomers. It bubbled like a fluffy pancake as the Cape Town afternoon wind encircled her body; her brown cinnamon legs sweetened its appearance whilst also holding her rebellious posture together. She giggled as she saw her reflection in the sun. Rosa lifted her schoolcase and threw it across the gravel park. The stones were filing her case smoother and her shoes now had to suffer the grinding the brick wall was to put them through. The crevices between the stone bricks of George Golding Primary School knew Rosa well. She climbed with no difficulty. Once at the top she leapt like a grasshopper and knelt on the ground for a while pretending to sort out pebbles. Rosa unbuckled her black shoes and knelt forward to pick the thorns off her socks, throwing them one at a time at a row of marching ants. She removed the fringe of her dress still caught between her bloomers. Her plaited hair, tentacled in spider fashion, lay scrunched up between her legs. Its web of discomfort awaited the mystery that only Rosa could decide. The black balls of her eyes surveyed the area and alerted her to her peers some yards away. She saw nobody she knew; no one who would complain to Mamma Zila. Upon deciding whether to go home through Hanover Street or down Constitution, Rosa chose Hanover. Verbalizing her decision to herself aloud, she exclaimed, "In Hanover Street there are lots of busy people and nobody watches your feet, only your face!"

The shuffling of feet, the racing of pulses, the screams of little children being bathed by older sisters and brothers in the backyard, the green hose curling itself up among the plants, the sound of the toilet being flushed in the backyard, where its circular swashing motion competed with bundles of hair awaiting disposal, the sound of creaking floors as boys and men raised themselves from their place of sleep, the smell of the fire as the stove brewed its first round of morning tea, the ravenous chirps of gulls circling the street for breadcrumbs, the sound of peanut butter jars being emptied by eager hands clenching sharp knives, the smell of fresh tobacco as working women and men lit their first cigarettes, the aroma of freshly braised turmeric onions from homes already preparing the base for tonight's supper, the ripeness of tomatoes, onions, potatoes, Durban bananas, and Constantia grapes shining like jewels in Auntie Tiefa's cart, the disgruntled noises of dockyard men walking the charcoaled streets, their feet removing chips of wood and cigarette butts from the previous night's fire, their eyes looking ahead matching their place of work—the sea, with the sky above their heads—and spotless Table Mountain—gray with not a speckle of white on its top—these formed the backdrop of early-morning Cape Town. Rosa was searching for a place to hide until the streets were clear. She "morning Aunti"d everyone in sight as mothers took their children across the street and sent them on their way to school with older kids from the neighbour-hood and others carried their day's produce, bundled on their heads or packed in their carts for purchase, to Hanover Street. There was a regional meeting for teachers at George Golding Primary School. Mr Henson, Rosa's class teacher, was not attending the meeting and would be supervising their class the whole day. Mr Henson and Rosa had a his-tory of conflict, the former having asked that Rosa be expelled from school. The child recollected her thoughts and smiled to herself, remem-bering how Mamma Zila, Rosa's maternal grandmother, had asked politely that Rosa be readmitted. Mr Henson, being a rather stern man who, on many occasions, demanded far more respect than Mamma Zila thought he deserved, asked that Mamma Zila sign a written document for Rosa's conditional reacceptance and, in addition, state that Rosa was to behave and do as she was told. Resenting his authoritarian tone, Mamma Zila held Mr Henson by the the collar, lifted him out of his shoes, and insisted that Rosa be readmitted without conditions, men-tioned a few of her relatives' names—implying the threat of a larger, family fight—and upon stating these, Rosa was reaccepted. Mr Franks, the principal, warned that if Rosa was found doing anything unlawful, like writing on walls, engraving graffiti on wooden desks, influencing other female children, or throwing stones, she would be expelled perma-nently.

Deciding where to run and hide was not very difficult at 7:30 in the morning. The men from Ospavat factory were all outside waiting for the two sirens before the start of their working day, the wooden chips on their overalls still visible from the previous day's work. The women could usually be seen at 7:45 rushing towards the red-faced Mr Stowe, waving their sandwiches at the White doorman and supervisor. For many of the men, it was their first opportunity to look between their prepared sandwiches and bargain with Auntie Tiefa for some tomatoes or maybe some homemade mango pickle.

Motchie Tiema shouted at Wasfi and Ludwi to go to school. "Don't kick the bloody tins. You two boys better start walking before I come down with my stick. I mean right now you two devils."

"Morning Motchie, the children being troublesome again," three men shouted. "Ai, tog, you know when these boys start to grow hair on their balls." The men all laughed, shaking their heads in agreement and not wanting to disagree with Motchie Tiema. "See you men later, the beds are waiting for me."

"Salaam Motchie," Auntie Tiefa said in greeting. "Aleikom Salaam Tiefa. I'll give in my order on Thursday, the usual you know. Send Krislaam to Galiema from the Seven Steps."

"Okay Motchie," replied Auntie Tiefa. The two women waved good-bye.

Auntie Tiefa loaded the cart for the day's sales of fruit and vegetables. A few men gathered round to buy some fruit before Auntie Tiefa took off to Hanover Street. She hit their hands away and made sure that nobody was helping themselves to fruit.

"No focking hand-outs for anyborry, I dirint ask you to help, okay." Some of the men grumbled a bit and reluctantly moved away. "Are you talking to me or chewing a brick Boetatjie? Your father went with my father to the war, so don't try your kak here," Auntie Tiefa reprimanded one man.

"No, no, no, Auntie T, it's time to leave now and the siren is going off any minute and I jus wannit to save you der trouble."

"Gmmm! Okay, take der tomato and skoot." And so they did. The men were pleased when the first siren rang and they could move towards the big white building. Children walking past the factory automatically covered their ears; others yawned the full duration of the siren—some exercising their jaws, others competing with the loud factory sound.

Rosa, hiding in the lane, pretending to fasten the buckle on her shoe, saw the opportunity to run. Then she noticed a moving vehicle. It was the Free Dispensary van, which came to collect Uncle Tuckie. Mrs Hood and Auntie Flowers were standing at the door waiting for the driver to come to a halt and open the van. Both the women lifted Uncle Tuckie into the van, dragging his lame legs one at a time. Rosa noticed that the two women were dressed for visiting or shopping. Mrs Hood was not wearing her apron and Auntie Flowers had her stockings on. The elastic garters were visible to Rosa as she watched Auntie Flowers bend to lift Uncle Tuckie's legs. Hiding inside their house would be a wonderful idea, she thought. She could always leave, and since nobody locked their doors anyway, it would be as easy as chewing bubble gum. Rosa removed her shoes, held them in one hand, and entered the home of Mrs Hood without the two women noticing. At 7:45 a.m., the second siren rang. Now everybody would be inside attending to household chores. Auntie Raya was late, and so was Mrs Benjamin. Both women were shouting at Mr Stowe to wait for them.

"Meneer, we're coming now-now . . . Meneer."

Mr Stowe smirked in his usual arrogant manner. Auntie Raya folded her apron and tucked it under her armpit, nodding thankfully to Mr Stowe for waiting for them.

"Ai, Tuckie was really a handful dis morning, der man jus doan stop talking about der war."

Mrs Hood stooped to pick up Uncle Tuckie's plastic gun and shook her head, still communicating to Auntie Flowers. Rosa heard the two women coming into the house. She was at a loss for where to go to now.

She ran into Mrs Hood's bedroom. Both women were walking towards the kitchen, or maybe the bedroom. This she was not sure of as the two rooms were so close together. Rosa slipped under the bed. "Ai no! Mrs Hood didn't take the pee-pot out yet," Rosa thought, and cursed the sight of the urine-filled pot sitting boldly beside her. She fitted her shoes like gloves onto her hands and placed them, rubber facing downward, onto the floor. She soon realized that she would need both hands for protection. She wiggled them out slowly and stuffed the shoes in her unbuttoned bosom, placed both hands over her mouth like a mask and stared at the two pints of urine in the cast iron pot. She lay there immobile. When she lifted her head the diamond pattern wire from the bed caught her hair. When she tried to wiggle to either side, the shoes, boxes, and other stacked-away household goods prevented her from moving.

Auntie Flowers always dragged her feet, and when Rosa could not hear them any longer she knew Auntie Flowers was standing still. Auntie Flowers placed herself on the unmade bed, right in the middle of it. Rosa's inquisitive face fitted neatly between the impression of the grown woman's legs. Auntie Flowers raised herself from the bed and walked towards the mirror. The springs above Rosa's head gave a bowful bounce, as if saluting Uncle Tuckie's military boots.

Rosa's attention was fixed on Auntie Flowers, who slowly removed the pins from her circular bound hair. Rosa had never seen Auntie Flowers with her hair down. Although Auntie Flowers was quite fond of her, it seemed to Rosa that now would not be a good time to comment on Auntie Flowers' many hairpins, so she remained silent. She was mesmerized by the sequence of events, most of which she would never have observed had she not sought the privacy of a small space under Mrs Hood's bed. Rosa's mouth fell open as she counted to herself: Aaah 15 16 17 18 Detecting the urine stench against her palate, she closed her mouth instantly, covering it with both her hands. She continued counting, nodding and memorizing so that she could remember to tell Nita and maybe write it on one of her favourite walls. Auntie Flowers started singing, "Wait by the river, wait by my side," as she brushed her hair in long, silent strokes. She sang in a funeral voice, Rosa thought, the kind of voice that vibrates, makes waves, and causes everyone to cry. Auntie Flowers' voice was deep and passionate. "Wait till the moon is right, wait up all night, wait till it's morning, come hold me tight, wait till we kiss goodnight, come let's not fight." Opening and closing her mouth was more agonizing than Rosa had anticipated. She wished she had told Mamma Zila that she was ill and could stay home to watch Auntie Flowers under better conditions. Her excitement was hampered by the presence of the urinal.

Rosa watched carefully as Mrs Hood brought the metal bath into the bedroom. Mrs Hood moved towards Auntie Flowers and stroked her hair. It was not so unusual for Rosa to see Mrs Hood plant a kiss on Auntie Flowers' cheeks. This kiss was long and wanting. Auntie Flowers was still singing, "Wait till the birds are singing, wait till my heart is ringing."

"Flowers, gimme a hand wit der water please," said Mrs Hood.

"Wait for the morning sun, wait till the birds are done." Auntie Flowers wrapped a towel around her hands and assisted Mrs Hood with the pot of hot water from the coal stove. As Rosa waited for them to enter the room she was aware of something moving on her head. Rosa, for fear of missing out on the bathing, shook her head sideways until a small spider fell to the ground. It was a small spider. Its presence distracted Rosa immensely. Auntie Flowers hated spiders and seeing one now would cause for her to run out of the house and for Mrs Hood to go running after this harmless creature, only to find yet another under her bed—a more dangerous eight-year-old creature between her overdue urinal and her husband's military boots. Rosa grabbed the spider and tossed it into the urinal. It died instantly.

The two women had brought the big cast iron bath into the room. Mrs Hood kept pouring cold water into the bath. Rosa, in the meantime, found a pair of Uncle Tuckie's shoes and placed them over the urinal to block the smell. Auntie Flowers went into the backyard and came back with some lavender violets and yellow daisies. She gently removed the petals and threw them into the water. Although its floating glory was not visible to Rosa, the child smiled a pleasant smile, thinking that Auntie Flowers was finally going to announce the name of her love and ask, as female-children do, "He loves me yes, he loves me no, he loves me yes?" and at the pluck of the last petal, accompanying the positive answer with a scream of joy. Instead, Auntie Flowers placed the last petal on Mrs Hood's head. The woman exhaled from deep within her bosom and blew the petal until it floated on the air, coming to rest on her dress. Rosa watched attentively as Mrs Hood undressed. Her dress was the first garment she lifted over her head. It fell softly to her feet. As Mrs Hood bent to pick it up, Rosa saw Mrs Hood's kadoematjie. Unlike Rosa's, which was tied to her vest, Mrs Hood's was tied to her bosom. Her breasts were large and full and held her petticoat firmly. Mrs Hood removed her arms from the garment. She slipped it off her shoulders and wiggled around with both her hands between her legs. Without much ado, the full contents of Mrs Hood's underwear were removed and

Rosa's mouth gaped open at her nakedness. It was Mrs Hood's belly that fascinated Rosa most. It was similar to Uncle Tommy's. His had scars of war, physical fights, operations, and many other journeys he had been on. Rosa thought about her geography lesson and how Mrs Hood's stomach resembled a map, with mountains and all. Mamma Zila's flesh was firm for her sixty years and she had no scars of any sort. And like Mamma Zila, Mrs Hood had not cupped her breasts either. It was their resistance to White-settler colonial culture and the need to remain untainted by it which was not observable or understood by the eight-year-old female-child, since she had rubbed her breasts with onions—a local remedy—with the hope that hers could soon fit a commoditized, prepackaged cotton cup. Mrs Hood's breasts were darker and clustered around her nipples lay larger, orally celebrated protrusions. Mrs Hood's breasts hung flat against her belly and her warm fingertips gently soothed the clustered skin until the fullness of her nipple was visible to Auntie Flowers. It looked warm and comforting. Rosa was moving her hands around, thinking about how the long extensions of breasts reminded her of her winter gloves—the ones she wore during July and August when her hands were sore and stiff.

Auntie Flowers also unbuttoned her dress, and the two women faced one another naked, each with their own shape. They stepped into the bath together, Auntie Flowers embracing Mrs Hood from behind. Splashes of water fell to the floor and small lavender petals stuck to the outside of the bath. The two women remained locked in their embrace for quite a while, their silence perturbing Rosa greatly. Mrs Hood placed her head gently on Auntie Flowers' shoulder. Her long gray hair made big circles on the nape of her neck, sculpturing her clavicles in a some-what vivacious manner. The room was silent. Both women were breathing deeply. The release of their breaths shook the room. "Woooooow," they both breathed out repeatedly. It was not like the voice lessons Mrs Jacobs gave, Rosa thought, this was very different. Auntie Flowers broke the embrace, removing Mrs Hood's arms and hands. She stroked them rhythmically, like the voetvrou does with babies, whilst Auntie Flowers hummed a song. It was unfamiliar to Rosa. She had her eyes fixed on Auntie Flowers' knees, which were round and big like Mamma Zila's and told Rosa that it was Auntie Flowers who did the scrubbing and polishing of floors in the house. Auntie Flowers stroked Mrs Hood's hair and made rings with it, sprinkling water on the curly strands. Some of the droplets nestled onto Mrs Hood's lips. The two women placed their fingers in each other's mouth. Rosa found it exciting to see grown women exchange spit. She wondered whether they did the same with food. Although this was an exchange of water, Rosa thought of it as equally defiant. Mamma Zila had warned Rosa so many times about exchanging food already chewed and Rosa thought about telling Mamma Zila about this incident.

The thought left her mind immediately as the two women exchanged places in the bathtub. They sat facing one another now, and Rosa could only see Mrs Hood's back and some parts of Auntie Flowers. It was the way in which Auntie Flowers cupped her hands and poured water over Mrs Hood's breasts that fascinated Rosa most. It reminded Rosa of Father John and baptism at St. Marks, where the family attended church. Auntie Flowers did utter a few words—silent words, warm words, judging by the serene smile on Mrs Hood's face—although not exactly in the same tone as Father John. Both women's eyes were cast upwards at the ceiling. Rosa wondered if they were talking to God. The women embraced one another tighter. Water squirted out between their legs and the overflow ran under the bed to meet the unwelcome gaze of Rosa's shoes, both of which were still stuck in her bosom. Suddenly, like a stroke of lighting, Mrs Hood raised herself. Rosa closed her eyes for fear of what was going to happen to her. With her eyes closed and waiting for her punishment, Rosa heard Mrs Hood grab something, and ruffle its contents. A ray of sunlight shone on the side of Rosa's face. The sun, although not casting its fullest power, had enticed Mrs Hood towards the greater acceptance of its rays. Boldly she drew the curtains, wrapped them around her wet legs, and danced a childlike dance—a tantalizing, somewhat naughty teasing motion that enhanced the sharpness of her clavicles. Its wetness was bronzed like a medal, waiting patiently to be touched and admired. Mrs Hood's teeth met the temptation, sucking dearly at its warmth until blood filled the gaps between her teeth. Her kiss planted a red glowing print on Auntie Flowers' face and the woman's sparkling eyes made Dracula seem like a hopeless case for seduction against the wishes of frightened, chaste women. Both women ate graciously from the blood, their tongues curling with lust and their palates seeping with its nutritious contents. There was passion, love, admiration, and exchange of caring moments, stolen from the heavy load which the constraints of marriage bore. No body or blood of Jesus Christ could fulfill the spirituality of body, of being, that these two women felt and allowed themselves to indulge in. As the blood coloured the water, Auntie Flowers scooped a handful and poured it over her face. Rosa's tilted face and opened mouth allowed for the sun to shine on her palate, gulping the air from which these two love-drunk women breathed. Rosa's eyes were still; her body lay motionless. And like a mother feeds a child, Mrs Hood lifted her breasts from the waist up, holding onto their length with her knees whilst Auntie Flowers' mouth enveloped the quivering protrusions. Heavy breathing like a voice lesson, Rosa thought again, was the medium through which these two women communicated their desire. Mrs Hood's partner's desires were fulfilled and, slightly salivating, eyes closed, and fingers clenching the rims of the bathtub, Auntie Flowers moved her body forward, lifted her legs and feet out of the bath, and wrapped them around Mrs Hood. Auntie Flowers' feet, crossed one over the other, made a shape of a bow. Is this what Auntie Spider spoke about when she referred to White women being scared of Black women's powers and how our women can wrap men up like Christmas presents? It was no idle thought. Rosa lay watching every movement of Auntie Flowers' toes, each cracking joint succumbing to the vibrant touch of its beholder. She recognized the visual image implanted in her mind, one created by the words of Auntie Spider, also known as Auntie Legs, who regularly told stories about Black women's sexuality to girls in the neighbourhood, preparing them for their approaching womanhood. Is this like sex? she asked herself, having been told that that was when a woman allows a man into her vagina.

Slowly Mrs Hood moved her head back as her breasts extended themselves into the mouth of her lover. Auntie Flowers bore no resemblance to a child any longer. Her whole body was wrapped around Mrs Hood, who accepted its passionate, lubricious glory. The women held each other close and kissed every freckle, every inch, every part of the other's face. Rosa lay still, motionless, with a smile on her face. There were no hands visible to Rosa; but, to the women who each had their folds unfolded, stroked, and stimulated, the organs attached to their arms fulfilled every libidinal desire, transmitting their otherwise clandestine sexual appetite, their voracious tongues sweeping every morsel. Several soft cries were muttered, then louder ones filled the room, each with a distinctive sound and echo from all of the four flabbergasted lips; then, a cry of relief, accompanied by laughter and softer outcries, each one exhaling more joy than the one before.

There was a knock on the door. The women looked at one another. The visitor had decided to enter the house—a common practice—to see what was keeping the inhabitants of the house from answering. Remembering their arrangements for a ride to Hanover Street, both women gasped, looked towards the window to assess the brightness of the light—telling the time of day—and answered the caller.

"Just wait Peter, we're getting dressed." Rosa could hear the person stopping in his tracks.

"Okay, Mrs Hood, I jus wannit to know if you ladies were ready for Hanover Street."

It was Peter Jantjies, a neighbour who worked at the dockyard and sold fish to the vendors in Hanover Street. He was taking several women down to Hanover Street and offered women in the neighbourhood the option of selecting the finest pieces of fish and, on occasion, would give them a ride in his cart. The two women raised themselves simultaneously and silently hugged as the water ran over their firmly held arms. The towels brushed their skin lightly, and slowly, reluctantly, both women clothed themselves in silence. Mrs Hood opened her wardrobe, groped among the many items, removed her money cloth, and clutched it under her arm. It had several knots in it and the woman, feeling a bit of discomfort, removed the cloth and relocated certain portions. In the far right corner lay the rent money, knotted until the end of the month; in the far left corner lay the food knot, which did not include money for purchasing fish. Mrs Hood located the fish knot just below it, its proximity strategically placed so that, whenever possible, small transfers could be made, especially since Peter was a gullible peddler and known for his kindness, and sometimes, not often, the money scored on bargaining would be used for buying stockings and rose water. Peter left the

door open and Rosa could hear him calling women in the neighbourhood. The two women lifted their tub of passion and released it in the
backyard, where the water removed splints of wood and took them
down the drain. Auntie Flowers and Mrs Hood departed and met Peter
at the door. Rosa could hear them assisting Peter with calling of their
equally late peers.

Rosa was relieved that she was finally alone to make decisions about
the rest of her day. She removed herself slowly from under the bed,
looked about herself to absorb her surroundings since she had not been
able to enjoy them lying under the bed. She giggled softly to herself,
then louder and louder until the sound filled the room with panic. She
fell silent, bit her lip, pouted a bit, and nodded to herself. "It's a secret
and nobody knows anything," she uttered. It had dawned upon her to
speak to one of her many walls—her companions—and this event needed to be recorded. Rosa walked into the backyard and placed herself on
the concrete step, pulled her dress down so as to protect her body from
the coldness of the cement bricks, and sat down. She stared at the wetness of the cement floor seeing the reflections of the two lovers whom
she, like other people in the neighbourhood, had thought were cousins.
She unbuckled her shoes, removed her socks, and stuck her right toe
into the wetness. She pulled it back instantly, still staring at the reflection of her thoughts. Did she now partake in this event by placing a part
of her body into the water? Several thoughts occupied her mind, most
of which seemed to suggest that the events she had just witnessed were
secret. She raised herself almost graciously, in adult fashion, and found
a piece of wood at the back of the yard and took a splint from the dry
log. Having pricked her finger, as she usually did when writing on walls
and implanting her print, she swore to secrecy and vowed never to talk
about the events she had witnessed. She remembered Mamma Zila's
words: "Child, talk about everything, hide nothing." Then there was
also the statement which followed: "Child, when you grow older, you'll
find out that there are some things you just doan talk about. These
things take time to talk about." Rosa had always thought the latter a
strange saying since everybody exchanged stories and, as far as she knew,
there were no secrets—only ones not told to White people, if you
worked for them in their homes.

Touching her nipples and remembering the fullness of Mrs Hood's breasts, she climbed over the wall and rested herself among the wooden logs in Mrs Benjamin's backyard. There was nobody home and she could climb all the walls to the end of the street. When the sun shone way over Ospavat indicating that it was twelve noon, Rosa would go the Hopelots forest and play in the trees, where she could again see where the sun was, wait for the sirens to sound after lunch and return home promptly, as expected.

The Green Chair

A warm breeze was hanging over Table Mountain and extended itself to Devil's Peak, located to the right of the mountain range. The southeaster was now blowing its last few breaths and a cool, sometimes cold, northwesterly wind would take its place by the month of May. Devil's Peak is not visible to those seeking it out from the streets of District Six, yet it looms in the backdrop, with horns ready to draw the will of those who surrender to it. District Sixers especially refer to the mountain and mean by their reference Table Mountain, or rather the Tabletop, and sometimes forget about Devil's Peak; but it never forgets them. The wind which howls from its horns during moments when unsettled souls roam the streets capture the essence of that moment of weakness; once they gaze at the horns which seek them out on those weary days when shadows follow footsteps, they are overcome by its might. Imaginary hands push hard against strong winds, and they will drag you down so that your tongue too may touch that soil of forgotten sorrow. The horns lock the will of those who cannot lock their own. Devil's Peak often puffs balls of smoke over Table Mountain when it is angry, challenging the mountain to chastise her children and when she fails to do so, he claims the spirit of those who tamper with circumstance. But the church bells and the call of Islam, as prayers bellow into the hearts of worshippers, are often stronger than the will of horns that bellow untruths into the ears of evildoers ready to plunge to their doom. Winds speak, silently, and horns, by their very presence as they tower over Devil's Peak, ask to be worshipped, by the weak and the lowly. When all is said and done it is Signal Hill, on the far side of the mountain, that gestures, in the form of clouds, wherein lie the future of those who beckon at its feet.

It was 1970 and the middle of April; the long weekend was upon the residents of District Six. Auntie Raya's family packed their van. Its pregnant windows overflowed, there being no glass in their panes, and with great tenacity they held the loads which had been thrust into the van. Sheets were packed, clothes, pillows, toys for little children and lots and lots of pots and pans for making traditional dishes at their favourite seaside camping spot, Bordjies Drift. Rosa watched Auntie Raya pack and observed as the woman's husband smoked and passed the rolled cannabis weed to his friends who were all gathered around him on the balcony. Auntie Raya's husband gathered his drums together as Rosa imagined what a glorious time the family would have with campfires, barbecued halal sausage, home-made popsiclesand late-night music with drums and dancing . . . and no cleaning, because they would be living in a green canvas tent . . . and no school. Several families left that Thursday evening for seaside camping grounds whilst others stayed at their homes in District Six for the entire Easter weekend.

Pickled fish was a traditional District Six dish that was often eaten during the year but especially on Good Friday. On Good Friday, the smell of onions sautéing in oil and turmeric took over the streets; palm-sized pieces of fish would be fried then placed in the turmeric sauce, which contained not only tamarind and brown sugar but also vinegar as the extra, necessary ingredient to preserve the fish. The smell of freshly baked white bread, made by women, mostly, would waft in and out of homes as women got their knives ready, sharpened them against the paved step in their backyards and would cut bread to accompany the fish. The smell of oil, onions, fish and baked white bread enveloped District Six. Although the sun was not at its brightest, little children scurried along the streets taking plates stacked with food to each other's homes, and would cherish the moment when they received a sweet or two for their efforts. Christian families attended the three-hour mass in the morning, and returned home to eat their pickled fish. Muslim families went to mosque in the morning; they too would go home to enjoy their pickled fish and then would return to mosque at different times of the day. Food in District Six was not divided along religious lines. Many families kept halal homes because they had extended family that were

Muslim, and eating was such an important part of District Six life, everyone wanted their friends and families to be able to eat at their homes. Good Friday was usually a quiet, somber day with no music echoing from the long-player or the radio.

Saturday mornings in District Six brought their own charm and glory. There was washing to be done for those who chose it as a washing day, cleaning of backyards, cleaning of dogs for those who kept any, and for little girls like Rosa it meant visiting as many people as possible without having to go to school. After Good Friday, most residents resumed their normal day-to-day life. Since the shops were closed on Good Friday, Magda and Mrs Osman, her mother, took to the streets early on Easter Saturday morning. The air was crisp, and the smell of fresh cut grass blew across from Roeland street as the two women walked down DeVilliers Street, then down Constitution Street into the city centre, otherwise known as "town." Mrs Osman waved as she walked past the homes of her community members. Magda was a little less concerned with formalities and looked straight ahead. Magda's two daughters, Latiefa and Jasmin, were given strict instructions to clean the house. Magda was mindful of the magnitude of their tasks and wrote down every little detail, then placed her written instructions on the refrigerator door with a magnet.

Latiefa, seventeen years old, and Jasmin, fifteen, were dancing to local music. They thrashed about on their grandmother's bed and laughed hysterically each time they looked at one another. District Sixers had their own music because they made their own music. Composers and performers came from the streets they walked to work and to school. Their uncle Sid played the saxophone and music was played in their home mostly on weekends, when friends brought their instruments and neighbours brought their rhythms, their food and their alcohol, to partake in grooving to the beat of their labour, their leisure and the time they gave to one another to take pleasure. To outsiders this was township music, a blend of sounds and rhythms that reflected the hustle and bustle of District Six: of moving about and brushing elbows with the neighbours after the sweat of the day's labour had been scrubbed off, of borrowing sugar from your neighbours in the same cup which would later serve as a musical instrument, of women shuffling their feet on sandy shores, barefoot and pregnant, or not, and of little children making their own instruments from whatever was available and discarded from their homes. Bottle tops would serve as pipes for cannabis-smoking adults, and later as mouth organs, when necessary; drums and other instruments would be made from anything that children and adults could lay their hands on: spoons, water-filled glasses, stones and sand in bags or tins, pieces of metal and tin rhythmically rattled at the appropriate cue, and feet stamping daily delights into the ground upon which they walked. Latiefa and Jasmin imitated others in their neighbourhood and named their subjects each time they performed a different dance move.

"Do Mamma Zila, Jasmin."

The younger sister complied and the two young women hugged each other as they shared and compared their dance moves when their laughter drew them physically close to one another. They did the latest dance and their arms swung from side to side with their eyes following on. After their joint efforts at imitating their friends Latiefa hastily got into her mother's black skirt; her younger sister draped a wig on her head.

"Let's dance something else, Jasmin," Latiefa insisted.

Jasmin ran towards the long-player and put one of her mother's favourite records on. As the music played they bumped into each other with their bottoms rhythmically colliding to the sound of Peaches and Herb. Laughter and giggles could be heard some yards away. Their kitchen stove had a few logs on it and the heat of the house warmed their cheeks in a delightful way. They resembled the pinky powdery texture of the Turkish delight which lay tucked away in the sweets tin, without its lid on, left over from Eid Mubarak.

"You're meant to do it much slower," Latiefa said, gesturing her hands, whose gloves reached to her armpits. "I know, baby," her sister replied, almost mockingly, in her cool Americanized singing voice.

Peaches and Herb brought out a particular performance quality in the two young women quite unlike their own District Six music.

"This is probably how the old 'toppies' do it," Jasmin said, referring to the older generation, as she motioned slowly with her hips moving in the opposite direction to her shoulders.

"Give me the eye pencil," Latiefa requested.

"Nooooo!" Jasmin called out as Latiefa grabbed it from her.

Jasmin caught a reflection of herself in her grandmother's mirror and burst out laughing. She had a red-toned birthmark on the right side of her face, above her lip, much like her father, and was now becoming accustomed to lipstick. "I will have to find a colour that is close to this mark hey, Tietie," she remarked. Her sister glanced over at her without replying. "Tietie" was the term used in all Malay homes for the oldest girl in the family.

Latiefa now looked at her sister's face and the ease with which she handled comments related to the red mark on her face, which the young girl treated as part of her appearance and not a hindrance, as the comments of others often implied. Latiefa had grown accustomed to being told that it was she who looked like her mother and Jasmin who looked like their father.

"Come on. Mummy will be back soon. We'd better clean up here," Latiefa asserted.

Latiefa knew that her mother and grandmother expected the pair of them to clean the house on Saturday mornings. They did not question their duties but performed them as requested each and every time. The door stood ajar and the young women heard someone trying to reach the children's hook on the door. The hook was at least a meter high and not really meant to keep anyone out but rather used as protection for little children who frequented the house and who might wander off into the street if the adults momentarily placed their attention elsewhere.

"Jasmin, go and check at the door. It's probably Rosa."

"Tiefaaaa!" the young child called out.

Latiefa just looked at Jasmin and grinned. "No chance of her not being heard, huh?"

"I can't reach Tiefa," the young child called out again.

"Hold on, Rosa, Jasmin's coming now-now," Latiefa replied as she posed with the broom, filled with a performance mood, yet ready to complete her housework. She then moved into the kitchen and checked on the curry her grandmother had started. She stirred the contents in the pot a few times then moved it to a slower heat on the stove whilst Jasmin cleared a pathway, moving furniture about, in order to get to the door. As she lifted the lid, the aroma of lamb curry filled the entire house. "Mmmm," she murmured, almost achingly. "All this dancing has really made me hungry." Latiefa placed the lid back onto the pot and looked at her watch. It was almost twelve 'o clock. "Oh, I better get going because with Rosa here, I might not get anything done," she exclaimed. Latiefa looked down the passage towards the door and saw that Rosa had not entered the house yet. "Jasmin!" the older sister shouted in dismay with both her hands on her hips. "You're really taking your time. Come on, slow coach. Let Rosa in, kanala. You know what she's like when you keep her waiting." Jasmin smilingly lifted the hook from the door and let the young child into the house.

"Hi Jasmin. Where you going?" the young child asked in a slow but curious voice.

"I'm not going anywhere," Jasmin replied almost apologetically.

"So why you dressed like dat?"

"I'm being Peaches . . . argh, never mind." Jasmin waved her hand as if to suggest that she was erasing her comments from the air within which their conversation took place.

"I know Peaches and Herb. I not stupid . . . I heard der music outside," Rosa replied, as she gave Jasmin's outfit the full benefit of a look over that only her eyes could perform with such daring confidence.

"And look at you! Look at that dress! And that little book . . . you always have your little book, hey Rosa? . . . oh, you have it around your neck now . . . that was after you dropped it in the fire in the Hopelots, hey, and I heard Ludwi had to fish it out . . . but you have to keep it clean . . . oh, look, you have chocolate on it," Jasmin said all at once as she inspected the young child.

"Ludwi pushed me . . . and my book fell in der fire. It ormost burned, Jasmin," Rosa said, patting her book. She looked at her dress and smiled; her dark legs were visible quite close to her panty line because the garment was rather small and very short. Her dress was a burnt, faded orange, and it was one she inherited from one of Mamma Zila's family members from Mossel Bay. The music was attracting Rosa's attention and she placed her book, with the attached string, on the table as Jasmin inspected her appearance. Rosa started to click her fingers and sing along with the music.

"Teeeteee . . . ," Jasmin called out. "Come and seeeee!" she bellowed out again. "Rosa's singing." Latiefa ran into the living room. Both the young women were now clicking their fingers and bobbing their head to encourage Rosa. "Rosa, come on . . . on the table," Jasmin urged in a sing-song voice as she moved her body to match Rosa's moves. The child complied without hesitation. Rosa was now dancing on their grandmother's mahogany table. Jasmin shoved the flower arrangement in the glass bowl to the side of the table; it was clearly too dangerous left where it was. Latiefa indicated to Jasmin with her eyes and the younger sister turned the music up a notch without a care as to whether the neighbours would complain.

"What do you think? She's gonna be a helluva woman when she grows up, nuh?"

Latiefa regularly speculated on the kind of woman Rosa might turn out to be. It was a thought many young women in District Six indulged in as they observed the young child taking pleasure, unashamedly. Rosa was singing and miming to her heart's delight and carrying her body in dance moves she had learnt through observation of her mother and other women. She had a way of moving her arms as though she was performing in a circus, and considering that her hair was always tightly plaited and tentacled, she looked quite a spectacle. The two girls followed on and they waved their arms about as they imitated their mother's favourite music.

Rosa suddenly stopped. "When Auntie Magda coming back?" the young child asked.

"Mummy's out for a while. Doan worry. We have to clean the house," Jasmin answered whilst getting undressed. "Rosa, are you still speaking to Nita? I haven't seen the two of you together in a whilst. I was very disappointed with the two of you fighting like that on Roeland Street, like two fisherwomen." It was no idle question. Jasmin had observed the two little girls in a physical fight two weeks ago and reported it to Mamma Zila.. "So, are you still speaking to Nita?"

"Jaaaa, is Saturday and Nita Catholic. She orways go wit her Mummy to der church on a Saturday afternoon." Rosa did not look at Jasmin as she answered. She looked toward the kitchen to see what Latiefa was doing.

"Oh ja, that's right," Jasmin replied.

"Jasmin, lift Rosa off the table," the older sister ordered.

"Oh, we better get that polish out, Tietie. Mummy will go berserk, hei," Jasmin said when she realized that the table had footprints on it. The music was now turned off and the young child was swept for any threads of cotton that the clothes might have attracted.

"Rosa, show me your hands," Latiefa asked.

"No!" the young child exclaimed.

"Rosa, I just want to see. You can click your fingers now . . . So it's not sore then . . . or stiff?" Latiefa was speaking slowly so as to encourage the child to share the details of her undiagnosed condition. Rosa did not reply. "So Mr Henson doesn't bother you anymore, huh?" Rosa did not reply and stood with her hands behind her back. "Did Mamma Zila get you to wear the book around your neck so that you won't write on the walls anymore, Rosa?" Rosa still did not reply.

"What the doctors say, Rosa?" Jasmin asked as she bent down to Rosa's height.

"Nothing! . . . Is not contay . . . ay . . . ," the child stammered.

"Contagious, contagious . . . is that the word?" Latiefa asked.

"Yes, dat's der word. Der doctor say dat," Rosa replied. "It means dat noborry else can get it from me," she said, looking wide-eyed at both Latiefa and Jasmin.

"Rosa, we are not worried for us, we are just worried for you, sweetie," Latiefa said reassuringly. Rosa clenched her fists since she did not want the young women looking at her hands. "It's okay, sweetie. You know Jasmin and I love you, sweetie . . . we are just concerned for you. I'm glad Mamma Zila got you to wear your book around your neck," Latiefa said reassuringly to the young child, who held onto her hand as Latiefa's comforting words found their way to her heart.

They heard a gentle knock on the door. Jasmin frowned and realized that she had shut it after she let Rosa in. When they were cleaning they would leave the door ajar so that the air could circulate and also so that they could always be aware of who was walking past their house.

"Come in!" Latiefa called out.

Lester peeked his head around the door. "Morning," he said, his aftershave rushing towards the roofs of their mouths. His hair was combed back with Brylcreem, and the clash of aftershave and hair cream, although pleasant, was what he was known for. The young girls would often smell him before he even made an appearance.

"Morning, Uncle Lester," they all called out.

"Rosa?" Lester remarked, surprised by her presence.

"Morning, Uncle Lester," the young child replied.

Lester looked about the house. He was immaculately dressed in gray trousers and a powder-pink shirt. "Is your Grandma home?" he asked in a soft and humble voice.

"No, Uncle Lester, Grandma and Mummy went into town and Uncle Sid went into work today."

"Yes, I know Sid has to work Saturdays now. I only got a glimpse of your mother this morning, not your grandma," he remarked with a slightly tilted head.

"No, Uncle Lester, Grandma went into town with Mummy. Mummy does walk ahead sometimes," Latiefa remarked.

"Oh, yeah, of course," he said knowingly, as his eyes widened in recollection of their mother's habits. "You girls cleaning up then?"

"Yeeees, Uncle Lester," Jasmin replied in a singsong tone.

"You should clean Rosa's face as well. Give her a good polish too," he said as he chuckled. Rosa frowned at him and locked both her arms over her chest. She stood there looking at Lester, who had already shifted his attention. Lester looked at Latiefa long and hard with narrowed eyes. "You look more and more like your mother. Well, when you take that muck off your face," he said giving her one of his tormenting looks.

"Oh yes," she said as she rubbed her face. "We were just having fun with Rosa."

Rosa tucked at Latiefa's dress. "Tiefa, when you make me der sanwich wit fish paste . . . ?"

"Ah, Rosa, later," the older sister replied as she sighed.

"Has that boyfriend of yours been here today?" Lester asked, still wavering between being stern and being their uncle's best friend. "No, Uncle Lester. Jasmin was just making that up," Latiefa replied as she looked towards her sister.

"Well, I have seen him here a few times . . . standing outside. He's not our kind of people."

"Uncle Lester, Faiz is from Walmer Estate. What does Uncle Lester mean he's not our kinda people?"

Lester smirked as he spoke. "He's a rich boy. Born with a silver spoon in his mouth."

"No . . . no," the young woman replied, using her entire body to assert herself.

"Hey, I am just teasing," he announced, after realizing that he might be offending the seventeen-year-old. He extended his hand in order to shake hers. "No hard feelings, hey. I like to pull your leg," he said, with a smile on his face. "You should go out with whoever you want. You girls are still young and it's nice to know that you are still in school and making a change to this land. We never had your opportunities. So, hey, you girls take it. I'm very proud of you." He took two five rand notes from the inside pocket of his trousers and handed one to each of them. Rosa pulled her sad little face.

"What about me?" Rosa called out. "I sang too . . . and I don't get nutting"

"Did you hear something? Did someone say something?" Lester asked with a look on his face that Rosa could not quite make meaning of.

"What about me, Uncle Lester," she said again.

"Did you hear that, Jasmin? No . . . I heard it only slightly . . . someone speaking somewhere."

"Uncle Lester . . . it's me," Rosa called out, stamping her feet.

"Oh, its you. I thought I heard a ghost," he replied, rolling his eyes in imitation of one. "I'm not a ghost. Auntie Magda is der one who talk to der ghosts, not me."

"What is she talking about?" Jasmin asked with a frown on her face.

"Never mind. The child has an overactive imagination. I don't think your mother speaks to ghosts," Lester replied.

"Yeah, Auntie Magda do dat. Auntie Magda speak to der ghost, not me. He have a boy's name," Rosa asserted and nodded her head with certainty.

"Oh Rosa," Jasmin said patting her head. Latiefa just raised her eyebrows as she dusted the kitchen cupboards.

"Uncle Lester, what about me?" Rosa asked again.

"Okay." He stuck his hands in the outside pocket on the right side of his trousers. "Rosa, I have ten cents for you."

"Really, Uncle Lester?" she asked.

"Really," he replied. "You see when you grow older then you'll also get five rand because you have to buy all your womanly things. But for now, it's ten cents, okay?"

"I know, I know," she exclaimed, eagerly. "Like Mari . . . she have her period oready and her grandma also give her money to buy her womanly tings."

"Mmmf! This child, hey? Never a dull moment," he remarked as he closed his eyes and scrunched his mouth at the suggestiveness of her thought. He waved his hands about to show his reluctance to further engage Rosa, and the two young women laughed to themselves as they realized that Rosa had made him slightly uncomfortable.

"Thank you, Uncle Lester. We'll tell Grandma that Uncle Lester came to say hello," Jasmin called out as she observed Lester's move towards the door.

"Not in front of the ol' girl, hey," he reminded them.

They sniggered. "Yes, Uncle Lester, we won't say anything in front of Mummy," Jasmin responded as though it was a drill.

"Uncle Lester, where's uncle's whistle today?" Rosa asked.

Latiefa and Jasmin smiled.

Lester took his pennywhistle from his pocket and played a short tune.

Rosa was bobbing away again. Lester now began to use the large dining room table as a drum. He kept the whistle in one hand and drummed with the other. Lester stood still and laughed as he saw how easy it was for Rosa to dance.

"She's not shy, hey, Uncle Lester," Latiefa remarked.

"Oh no. Not at all," he added.

"I like it better wit all der udder people playing . . . wit der drums . . . I like der goema," she asserted.

Latiefa and Jasmin could not contain their laughter. The two young women were holding onto each other and laughed joyfully.

"Ja, you're District Sixer, Rosa," Lester asserted as he shook his head proudly. "No one in District Six can live without their goema, huh."

Lester was smiling from ear to ear as he held onto his pennywhistle.

"Ja, Uncle Lester. I love der goema."

"Show me how you dance to goema and I will play goema on the table."

Lester then used both his hands on the table and beat against it as Rosa bobbed up and down in full and rhythmical form. Latiefa and Jasmin sang along to the table drumming.

Lester chuckled again. He moved towards Rosa and rubbed her head.

"I have to go now. Bye-bye, hey."

The two young women looked at one another. "Bye, Uncle Lester," they called out as he left.

"I have ten cents . . . I have ten cents . . . I have ten cents . . ." Rosa sang and bobbed her head to go along with its rhythm.

"Rosa and her goema, hey," Jasmin remarked. The child was now in another world.

"Rosa, are you still going to help with the cleaning?" Latiefa asked as she observed Rosa's eyes surveying the house and seeking out playing areas.

"Mmmm, I doan really like cleaning. It make me feel a little sick, Tiefa . . . and, der doctor say is not so good for my hands."

"Ai, Rosa. You always do that, hey," the older sister replied.

"Is true. My hands doan feel so good after I do der cleaning."

"Ah huh, but not after packing your hands full of sweets, huh, or carrying Grandma's koeksisters to your house then into your mouth."

"Can I sing whilst you do der housework, Tiefa?" she pleaded.

"Okay," Latiefa replied. "Come and help me tie my head scarf, Rosa," Jasmin asked as the young child looked about the room. "Mmm . . . Tiefa, what about der fish paste, der Redro fish paste sanwich you orways make for me." Latiefa sighed again. "Ai, ja, Allahhh . . . Jasmin, go and make Rosa a fish paste sandwich, kanala. *Here ruh* Rosa, you never stop eating, huh?" The child followed Jasmin to the kitchen her eyes big and bright and almost as large as her appetite.

Jasmin and Latiefa were in the bedroom that their mother and grandmother shared.

"You know, Jasmin, I am so tired of cleaning and polishing this ridiculous-looking chair," Latiefa remarked as she looked at the cluttered room.

The room had two beds, two wardrobes, two chests of drawers, a trousseau chest, which had many purposes, and several boxes of linen, several boxes of household items, which also included family garments, all of which were stacked under both beds, and, of course, their mother's green chair with the mahogany legs.

"How long has Mummy had it now?" Jasmin asked.

"I don't know. Ever since I can remember," said Latiefa. "We should try and get another one at the market, nuh, don't you think, Jasmin? We can put our money together and see if we can get another chair. Grandma doesn't even like this chair. Maybe Mummy is just keeping it to fill up that corner."

Latiefa's eye caught the faded photographs of dead relatives on the walls, which were at first placed in cardboard frames then covered in a hard, tight plastic. So whilst the outside looked like glass it was actually hard plastic, a safe choice considering how much movement there was in District Six homes. She raised herself to her mother's bed in order to dust the photographs. She looked at a few of them and touched her favourite ones and the one of her great-grandmother. She bit her lip as she recalled the many stories she was told and in acknowledgment that she too saw a resemblance to the woman many in District Six still revered as a great historical figure. Her great-grandmother had died when she was four years old. She was tearful, only momentarily, then looked at Rosa.

"Oh, dat Auntie Magda's chair," said Rosa. "Auntie Magda say dat I should never sit in der chair or touch it."

"Oh, ja, Mummy always make a big fuss about that chair," Jasmin replied as though she was mocking her mother.

"Jasmin, do you really think we should take the chair?" her sister asked.

"Ja. Why not? I think Mummy's just a little silly. She has said before that we are the ones who were making the fuss . . . so we should just take it and see if we can get another one. Maybe if that guy is there at the market who does upholstery we can ask him if it is better to have it fixed." Jasmin made her intentions clear. Her sister stood still for a whilst then shook her head in agreement.

In an instant the twelve o'clock gong was fired from the City Hall, in the centre of town. This was an occasion for Rosa to count along with the clock. "One . . . two . . .three . . . four . . . five . . . six . . . seven . . . eight . . . nine. . . ten . . . eleven . . . twelve." She bowed after her performance and Latiefa and Jasmin both clapped. The older of the two sisters grabbed both of her helpers by the hand and led them to the outside tap.

"Wash your hands, a small lunch is coming up," Latiefa declared as two sets of eyes looked at her each with their own peculiar expression. After Jasmin and Rosa dried their hands Latiefa indicated for them to sit down at the table. Rosa was excited and had both her hands and arms almost caressing the table. "Off with your hands, my dear. This is not the park. Mamma Zila would be upset if she saw you now," Latiefa remarked as she pointed at the young child with the fork she used to fry daltjies. Latiefa fried six daltjies and six samoosas, all of which had been prepared the night before. Rosa was already chewing before the samoosas and the daltjies landed on her plate. "Two of each for everyone, okay." Rosa nodded with great delight. "Jasmin, get the tamarind sauce from the fridge," Latiefa requested and the younger sister eagerly complied. "I want to see if we can go down to Hanover Street . . . maybe with Uncle Peter. We can eat roti and curry when we get back, okay?" Jasmin certainly agreed and Rosa nodded her head at Latiefa, who usually took charge of meals when her mother and grandmother left her in charge. After their samoosas Jasmin and Latiefa got into their work. Latiefa, after cleaning the kitchen and sweeping under every crevice, then tackled her mother and grandmother's room. Rosa followed her throughout the house. She was dusting something and bent down to straighten the mat when she suddenly lifted herself and threw her head back.

"I can't stand the sight of this chair no more. Rosa, kanala tog. Go and see if Uncle Peter is at home. Ask Uncle Peter to come round because we need a favour." Latiefa asked this of Rosa whilst the young child was still bending over in the doorway but standing a safe distance from the green chair.

"Auntie Magda talk to someone wit a boy's name in dat chair," Rosa said.

"What?" Latiefa asked, as she frowned and looked at her sister.

"Is true. I was playing in der yard, over dere." She ran along as she spoke with both young women, who followed her. She pointed toward the far side of the yard where the wood was kept for the stove. She continued, "and den I hear Auntie Magda speak to someone wit a boy's name and Auntie Magda talk to him and say tings."

"What? Rosa, stop making up stories," Latiefa said sternly as she stared daggers at the young child.

"Is true. Auntie Magda say dat I shouldn't tell anyone dat she talk to der boy in der chair. You know I orways tell you everyting Tiefa. . . mmm . . . Latiefa!" She called out as she observed the young woman not paying attention.

"Did you see the boy?" Latiefa asked, with both her hands on her hips. Rosa shook her head. Latiefa sighed and rolled her eyes.

"Tiefa, I orways tell you everyting from der time I was so small." She gestured with her hand to indicate a size smaller than her present stature.

"Argh! Rosa, remember what we said about making up stories?" Latiefa said again.

"Ja. I know," the child replied.

"Well, so don't then. Go and call Uncle Peter, kanala, Rosa. We need to know what time he's leaving for Hanover Street." Latiefa took another glance at her watch as the Town Hall clock struck one.

"Remember what happened wit Faiz der other time . . . and you also said I was making up stories."

"Mmmm, ja, that is true," Latiefa said as she shook her head.

"Der policeman took him in der van . . ."

"Rosa, I don't want to hear about it anymore," she interrupted. "Go to Uncle Peter and ask him what time he's leaving and whether Jasmin and I can have a ride to Hanover Street. Rosa rolled her eyes in retaliation. "Go now, kanala," Latiefa asked, her arms crossed in determination. Latiefa had lectured the young child on manners before. Jasmin smiled as she observed her sister's eagerness to get Rosa to co-operate. Rosa stood motionless in her tracks still trying to provoke Latiefa. "Okay, chop-chop. Now, Rosa. Go!" Latiefa reiterated. Jasmin let the young child out of the house. She sauntered towards the door, pausing only to pick up her little book.

"I'm not leaving my tings in dis house . . . cos you will read all my tings," she uttered, mopefully. Rosa wore her annoying face now.

"Rosa, you're still my sweetie pie," Latiefa remarked. The young child's face bore a silent smile as she jumped off the step of the house.

"The things Rosa says. Mummy of all people who is so against people telling ghost stories," Jasmin commented, when the two sisters were alone and had their hands on their hips.

"Oh well, Rosa likes to entertain herself," Latiefa was quick to add.

"She does always tell you everything, Tietie. Her own mother has admitted this. She did tell Tietie what happened to Faiz and considering that you were running around going out of your mind trying to find out what happened to him . . . Ja, Tietie, and no one knew a thing." Jasmin reminded her sister of the recent past. Latiefa's face grew cold and hard. She remained silent and contemplative. Jasmin seemed keen to continue this topic. "People aren't afraid of the Boere . . . they just didn't see anything and Rosa told you what she saw even though she knows that Boer who drives up and down here might have even have seen her."

"Thanks Jasmin, I don't want to hear about that anymore. Faiz is okay now. It's behind us," Latiefa stressed, not looking at her sister.

"Hmm, I am not so sure," the younger of the two added.

"Jasmin, if I wanted your opinion on Faiz's state of mind I would ask you. Just stay out of it, okay?" Jasmin shrugged her shoulders and walked out of the room.

The two young women swept the entire house again, ensuring that every morsel and crumb had been collected and every fiber and fabric was erased and that the dishes were shelved, thus leaving no trace of their musical pantomime. Latiefa checked on the door of the refrigerator every so often, each time sucking the air through her teeth. She seemed annoyed at the lengthy note and the endless list of detailed descriptions of cleaning she and her sister had to do. They had accomplished these tasks many, many times, yet their mother still listed them, and wrote a new note every Saturday morning. After the sweeping was done, Latiefa and Jasmin both went on their knees, placing their usual kneecloth down on the floor and each with a basin of water: one filled with a homemade soapy mixture for dipping the cloth and cleaning the floor, and the other containing lukewarm water with lemon peels for rinsing. They then washed the floors of the entire house.

Whilst they were washing, there was a gentle knock on the door. "Just hold on," they called out. They looked at each other and smiled.

"It's probably Uncle Peter," Latiefa said, looking at her watch.

"Weren't you supposed to make rice?"

"Ja, Jasmin. Argh! It can wait. Go and open the door and put it on the hook so that the floor can dry."

Jasmin placed both the pieces of cloth on the floor then placed her feet on it and dragged herself towards the door without leaving footprints. "Hello, Uncle Peter."

"Hello, Jasmin. Busy with the housework, hey?"

"Yes, Uncle Peter."

Peter Jantjies was dressed in khaki overalls and a black beret. He rubbed his hands together and swallowed hard.

"Can we get you some roti and curry, Uncle Peter," Jasmin asked as she observed the man salivating.

"No, no. I was just tinking how I like Grandma Osman's roti but I eat oready, hey." He continued to rub his hands together and pursed his lips in an effort to taste the food that he could only smell.

"Uncle Peter, is it okay if we get a ride with you to Hanover Street?" Latiefa asked.

"Sure. Ja, okay. I was just coming to tell you girls I'm ready. I just have to go to Mrs Hood and Auntie Flowers and get Uncle Tuckie's paper for der chemist. I orways pick up Uncle Tuckie's pills you know." Peter Jantjies was inspecting their work. He looked about the house approvingly. "You girls really pull your weight, hey. Is nice you not too big for your boots yet." He chuckled as he rubbed his hand on Rosa's head.

"Uncle Peter, can you give us a hand with the chair? We also want to take it to the market and see if the upholstery man is there today," Jasmin noted.

"Is it okay if I go into your mother and Grandma Osman's room to have a look?" he asked.

"Yes, Uncle Peter," Jasmin replied.

Peter stood in the doorway of the room and looked at the chair from a few feet away, then turned his body and his head at different angles to give it his full consideration. "I tink you girls are better off taking it to Caledon Street. Dere is a man dere who do great work wit chairs," he remarked. "Get ready," he urged. "I'll wait for you girls outside in five minutes, okay?"

The two young women hurried to the back of their yard and turned the hose on their knees. The water splattered about and sprayed on their clothes. They patted themselves dry and giggled all the way to their bedroom. They brushed past each other in the small and cluttered room to take off their cleaning clothes and dressed in jeans and jerseys.

"Jasmin, you better wear a scarf, hey."

"Ja. I'll get one," the younger sister replied. "Don't want Daddy's family to wag their tongues if they see us in the street . . . oh, and then I am always so lucky to bump into Imam Moosa when I am looking my most terrible and without my scarf."

Latiefa as the older of the two knew that she had some responsibility towards the attire of her sister. Jasmin brushed her hair and Latiefa shrugged her shoulders at her younger sister.

"I don't think we have time for that right now. Just put the scarf on your head, not around your neck hanging like that. You look like a cowboy from those western films when you tie it up like that around your neck." Latiefa scrutinized every piece of her sister's attire. She also looked in the palms of her younger sister's hands. "Your ghienna has faded."

"Are you done, Tietie?" Jasmin asked in a rather aggressive tone. "I am tired of this inspection now."

"Rosa, you're very quiet," Latiefa said as she observed the young child standing quietly against the living room wall.

"No, I just watching. I doan wanna be here when Auntie Magda come home. I doan go wit you or Jasmin. Bye." The young child waved as she darted out of the house still clutching her little book. "I go home now," she said again as she jumped off the step and onto the pavement.

"Rosa! Rosaaa! You're being silly now," Latiefa called after her, but the young child did not even turn around.

"Auntie Tiefa . . . Auntie Tiefaaaa," the young child called out.

Auntie Tiefa had returned from Hanover Street and had some select produce on her cart. "Rosa . . . anerkind . . . put your shoes on properly. Come and get some grapes, hey." Rosa took off as soon as Auntie Tiefa offered her the grapes and did buckle her shoes properly. Auntie Tiefa shook her head as she observed Rosa's dress and shoes. Latiefa stood at the door and observed woman and child engaged in conversation. Latiefa had a smile on her face as she observed Rosa bringing both her hands together to accept the grapes Auntie Tiefa gave her. "And doan spit der skins off in der street like a skollie, hey . . . Here child . . .chht! You doan stop eating, hey." Auntie Tiefa observed as Rosa took such delight and curled her tongue around each grape without ever using her hands.

Jasmin observed the look of concern on her sister's face. "Just leave it, Tietie. Maybe we're better off because she knows everyone and there's always some little boy who's trying to bully her and then we'll end up in a fight . . . you know, the Rosa type things that we always get involved in. We're better off, really, and we can get things done a lot quicker." Jasmin seemed convinced that their trip would be trouble free without Rosa. Latiefa still looked towards the door expecting Rosa to come back into the house. The young child did not.

When Peter Jantjies came to the door the two young women had already polished the entire house. There was now a fresh wax smell in the air and the furniture showed evidence of proper care. In preparation Latiefa and Jasmin tucked four pieces of ragged cloth under the legs of the chair; in this way they could all drag it out of the bedroom, into the living room, then out of the house and onto the van. Peter Jantjies was quite amazed when he entered the house to see that they were so organized.

"Dis is a strange green colour for a chair, hey," Peter said almost breathlessly as he bent down to get a firm hold of it. "I got Allie's van so I can take you girls to Caledon Street first hey and den speak to der man dere."

"Thanks, Uncle Peter," Jasmin replied as she shifted her scarf back in its proper place.

"Is Rosa not coming?" Peter asked.

"No, Uncle Peter. She is behaving very strangely."

Latiefa was still looking about the street as she answered Peter, convinced that Rosa would make an appearance. Peter just sniggered and shook his head. Latiefa darted into the house again, and perused the entire piece of paper her mother had left. She read the instructions aloud, at times mocking the manner in which her mother had phrased them, at other times, simply waving her hands about to dismiss the precise detail with respect to cleaning her mother required them to perform. She hurried out of the house when she heard Jasmin calling her name.

It was after 1:30 p.m. when Magda and her mother returned home; it was a lot windier that when they had left in the morning. The southeaster was now affecting the composure of the women as it blew their skirts over their heads and undid hairdos. Unsightly underwear was the least of their worries, for their breath and stamina were taken by the wind, which they fought. Women like Mamma Zila, Auntie Flowers and Mrs Hood did not fight the wind; they allowed it to circle around them, engulfing their whims and their fancies, and they went with it, wherever it took them. Men were bewildered, and their moods were affected too, for they did not think quite clearly on days when there was more wind, legs and underwear than there was will. As Magda opened the door, the wind trapped her skirt between her legs. Her skirt stuck to her as though it had been glued to her legs. Magda grabbed her mother's arm and ensured that the older woman was inside when she straightened herself out.

"Latiefa! Jasmin!" she called out. "Well, at least they cleaned the floors. The floors are waxed . . . mmm, perhaps overly waxed. The vinegar smell is missing though." Magda's nose was sharp. She continued to sniff about the house.

Mrs Osman walked into her bedroom whilst Magda completed her inspection. "I don't like it when the girls don't use the vinegar in the washing basin."

"Shall I make a cup of tea, Mummy?"

"Yes, please," the older woman replied, placing her shopping bags on her bed. She curled the shopping bags around her forearm and did not once complain to her daughter about her arthritis. Magda followed suit

and she too placed her bags on her bed, which was on the opposite side
of the room. Mrs Osman would always check with her daughter to see
whether she needed privacy to get dressed or undressed.

"Arrrrgh! Arrrrgh!"

Mrs Osman stood dead in her tracks. She ran from the kitchen into
her room. She held her right hand close to her heart and her left hand
to her mouth.

"What happened. Is someone here . . . in your cupboard?"

Magda lay on the floor without uttering a word. She shook her head
fiercely.

"Oh my God, is someone under your bed?" her mother asked fear-
fully.

"Arrrgh!" Magda called out again. "My chair! It's gone."

"Ooooh! You gave me a fright. My God, child." The older woman
sank onto her bed still clutching her heart.

"My chair is gone . . . gone . . . gonnnnne!" Magda lifted herself then
threw herself onto the vinyl floor again, each time looking at the space
the chair had occupied.

"Magda! Magda! Magda!" her mother shouted hysterically. "Oh
God, child, shall I go and get some help? O God! O No! O God!" The
older woman called out clutching her heart and holding her breath.
With not a sound coming from Magda the older woman ran about the
house. "Magda! Magda! . . . where did she put the smelling salts?" She
was now speaking to herself. She ran about the house opening and closing all the kitchen cupboards with her aching, crooked, fingers. "Magda,
it was in that blue glass jar, hey? Magda! I'm going to get Auntie
Flowers." Mrs Osman could not open jars and certainly could not hold
many things in her hands let alone between her fingers. The older
woman was still wearing her long-sleeved jersey. She clutched her handkerchief and sobbed loudly in it. She could hardly open the door without being blown against the inside wall of the door. "Rosa! Rosa! Go and
get Auntie Flowers, child. Tell Auntie Flowers to come quickly." The
young child's eyes grew larger and her red toffee apple fell to the ground;
she did not attempt to pick it up. Mrs Osman leaned against the wall
with her whole body and held onto the knob of the door, her fingers
cupping her hand in a round stiff posture. She was sniffling and sobbing

at the same time when Auntie Flowers arrived with her feet bare and with her healing bag. Auntie Flowers held onto Mrs Osman, without uttering a word, and helped the older woman into the house. Rosa was holding onto Auntie Flowers' dress and allowed herself into the house as though she was an assistant to the woman who was known as a healer. Mrs Osman simply pointed with her hand. Auntie Flowers soon found her patient. Magda was lying stretched out on their bedroom floor. Auntie Flowers opened a jar and gave the lid to Rosa.

"Hold this, sweetie, " she said to Rosa whilst observing Mrs Osman wringing her hands. The child clumsily held the lid with her sticky fingers. Auntie Flowers placed the menthol smelling salts, her own mixture, into the palm of her hand, then lifted Magda's head and placed the woman's nostrils under it in order for her to inhale.

"Aah . . . aah," Magda murmured.

"It's okay, darling. Everything's going to be okay. Sit up for me, darling." Auntie Flowers lifted Magda's head then the rest of her body so that she could sit up. "Now sit, up for me darling," Auntie Flowers spoke in a gentle manner.

"Aah," she murmured once again. "My chair . . . my chair is gone."

"Did anyone break in here?" Auntie Flowers asked with a big frown as she looked at Mrs Osman.

"Latiefa and Jasmin were . . ." Rosa started to give her account of events. "Not now, sweetie," Auntie Flowers replied. "I'm talking to Mrs Osman."

"No, Flowers. I don't see anything missing. As you can see, the girls cleaned up. They did say earlier this morning that they wanted to go down to Hanover Street to that market . . . maybe also stop by to see their father." Mrs Osman was speaking with her hand placed over her heart. She breathed heavily as she spoke.

"What could have happened to the chair then?" Auntie Flowers asked. Rosa raised her hand as though she was at school. "Yes, sweetie," Auntie Flowers said as she closed her eyes and tried to be patient.

"Latiefa and Jasmin took der chair wit Uncle Peter to a man to fix."

Auntie Flowers stared at Rosa, then back at Mrs Osman.

Magda jerked her body forward then found her way to her feet. "That little witch!" she called out.

Auntie Flowers and Mrs Osman both appeared to be taken aback as Magda suddenly spoke with such strength and fervour. "Now, hold on, Magda. You're not saying that Jasmin took your chair because she was being mean, are you? Did the chair need repairing?" Auntie Flowers was still looking at Mrs Osman then back at Magda.

"That little witch!" Magda said again, this time walking up and down the small living room, contemplating the extent of her younger daughters' actions. The two older women followed her into the living room.

"Magda, dear, I'm sure the girls were only trying to do something they thought was a good idea." Auntie Flowers looked at Mrs Osman hoping that she would say something to Magda. The mother had no words for her daughter. Magda was pacing up and down and her arms were going in opposite directions to her feet. She walked towards the door, opened it, and looked about De Villiers street.

"I'm off then!" she shouted. "Magda! Magda! Come and talk to me. Don't leave like that. Have some water or some boiled buju before you leave."

"Thank you, Auntie Flowers. I have to go and find my chair," she said. Her mother was surprised that she even bothered to be courteous to Auntie Flowers.

Auntie Flowers tried one more time. "Magda, wait here until the girls get back."

There was no stopping Magda. Her eyes were darting to and fro and she looked as though someone had stolen her soul and tried to have it repaired without her permission. She was speaking to herself as she walked past Mrs Hood, and even when the woman greeted her she did not respond. Mrs Hood was carrying Auntie Flowers' shoes in her hand. Neighbours returning from town with shopping bags filled with groceries all looked at Magda. No one was quite sure whether to greet her.

"Magda! Magda! Is everything alright?" Mrs Hood called out. Mrs Hood now joined Auntie Flowers and Mrs Osman.

Mrs Hood handed Auntie Flowers her shoes but the woman's eyes were cast down as though she was mapping out an area in her mind upon which to draw her memories and tried to recall incidents which might give her some insights into Magda's behaviour.

"Afternoon, Mrs Osman." Mrs Hood added a nod to her greeting. The older woman was still holding her handkerchief. "Afternoon, Mrs Hood." She just stood there shaking her head. Auntie Flowers explained the short sequence of events to Mrs Hood, who frowned throughout. "Oh, I forgot to mention that Rosa told us that Latiefa and Jasmin took the chair to have it repaired. Apparently Peter took them in Allie's van." Auntie Flowers looked straight at Mrs Hood. She was concerned and looked towards Mrs Osman, who still held onto the comfort of her handkerchief. Rosa then began the telling of the tale and of how she had told Latiefa and Jasmin not to take the chair. None of the adults actually asked the young child why she had adopted that stance; they simply assumed, as they looked at one another with raised eyebrows, that Rosa must have been in on the decision and was now trying to underplay her role.

Magda's brow was sweaty and cold as she brushed past her neighbours without so much as a word to them. She did not return anyone's greetings nor did she look at anyone who looked in her direction. Her eyes were fixed on the road ahead of her. Young girls in their Saturday best parted from one another to make way for Magda. "Get out of my way!" she screamed at two little boys on a wooden cart with iron wheels who were clutching each other in order to stay on. "Bloody children!" she yelled as she tried to sidestep a group of young girls playing five stones. Two pregnant women with arms folded over their protruding bellies stood watching as people on the street and the pavement made way for Magda. "Breeders!" she exclaimed as she pushed past them too. Both women shook their heads and sucked the air through their teeth, almost rhythmically. A group of young men smoking cannabis and drumming on their balcony in Sackville Street bothered her too. If looks good kill they would all have been dead. "Dagga smoking no goods," she remarked, to herself as she crossed over to the shady side of the street. She ran hastily across Constitution Street, looking back at the shoemaker and recalling that her silver high-heeled shoes were still at his workshop since the day after the New Year's Eve party. The screeching of car tires alarmed her and she stood still as a car pulled up in front of her. It was her brother Sid and his taxi-driver friend, Jimmy.

"Hey, Sis. Remember Jimmy, huh?" He turned towards his friend who merely nodded. Magda could smell the alcohol on the driver's breath. She had a rule of not speaking to men who consumed alcohol. "What's going on?" her brother asked. His frown deepened as he closed in on her. "Magda, I'm talking to you," he said in reprimand when she looked the other way.

Magda was heaving. "I'm going to find the girls. Jasmin took my chair. I told that little red-spotted witch to leave my chair alone, but noooo, she doesn't listen. She has to spite me." Magda undid the thick black belt she wore on her long flowing skirt. The silver buckle shone like an ammunition piece, which is exactly what she intended for it.

"Come on, get in," her brother insisted as he opened the back door. Sid exchanged a few words with his friend. The back of the car was cleared of his jacket and other small parcels. Sid got out of the car to help his sister settle herself down then placed his parcels in the boot. Magda followed her brother to the boot of the car.

"He is sloshed. Pickled, I tell you. I am not getting into his car." Magda spoke with disgust as though Jimmy, the driver, was not present at all. Jimmy was listening to the racing at Kenilworth on his radio and could not hear what was being said about him.

"Don't perform. Someone else was in the car before we saw you. Jimmy hasn't had that much to drink." Sid looked at his sister as she draped the belt around her fist. "You're not using that on the girls. Not here in the open. We'll go and find them and take them home."

Both brother and sister moved from the boot of the car towards the back door.

"Light me a cigarette," she said looking long and hard at her brother.

Sid ignored her request. "Magda, you have to stop this thing with Jasmin. You're turning her against you."

Magda stared at her brother then grabbed the cigarette, which Jimmy offered through the front window. Sid opened the back door for his sister, who slid into the seat then aggressively shut the door. "Family drama, huh," she said as she took her first puff and looked into the eyes of the driver, reflected in his finger smudged mirror.

As the three adults sat in the car with tensions running high, they heard the two gongs of the town hall clock. It was now two o'clock.

Magda pierced her thumbnail under her fingertips, flicking under the nail of every one of her fingers. Her movements were that of a woman digging under her nails and swiftly, murderously, eliminating what she found, which was in fact nothing at all. She bit hard on her cigarette and drew long on it.

"What is this," she said to the driver as she caught his eye in the mirror again. She spat the nicotine puff she drew from her lungs right through the half opened window and pulled a distasteful face.

"It's Lexington," he said, rather timidly. "I know it's not a ladies cigarette, but it's all I have. You're probably a Rothmans' woman. Now there's a ladies cigarette, hey, Sid . . ."

"It'll do," she said, snapping at him as though his mere presence offended her.

Sid sat facing her and had his whole body towards Magda in order to communicate his desire for peacefulness. Magda sniffed and looked about the streets. The driver reached the corner of Hanover and Tenant and looked into his mirror again waiting to get his cue from Magda.

"Let's go to the Jewish chemist. I think Peter Jantjies gets Uncle Tuckie's medicine there. If he has not been there yet we can always wait for him." Magda had planned her course of action.

"Magda!" her brother called out, rather sternly. "I am not going to have my nieces beaten in the street." She scrunched her face and pouted her lips tightly together to suggest that she was indeed indifferent to his words and did not want to hear any of them. "Magda, I'm telling you. There'll be no hitting and swearing in the street. You'll wait until the girls get home. What is wrong with you? It's Easter. Yesterday was Good Friday . . . gee, it was Eid for the girls not so long ago. Control yourself."

"I want my bloody chair!" she snapped.

"What's the problem? You'll get the chair. You look as though you are out to get the girls, for what? For taking your chair in to be repaired, which is probably what they've done? So what if Jasmin knew you didn't want it done. Is it just not possible for you to believe that the girls wanted to have the thing repaired. I have heard them mention it—"

"So, you were in on this, huh?"

Magda jumped out of the car before Sid could respond. As soon as she slammed the door Magda ran into Mr Ruben's chemist shop. The man and his assistant were rather taken aback by her manner. She was not at all courteous and had no intention of being the least bit polite. The young woman at the till, who knew Magda by sight, tried to explain to her that she knew who Peter Jantjies was and that he had not been in the shop yet. She also explained that Peter usually waited for the tablets and other medication and unlike other customers he was usually prompt.

"We are open until five and Mr Jantjies usually comes here just shortly after two o'clock. I am sure he'll be here shortly, Madam."

The young woman tried her best to appease the rattled and impatient Magda, who, because she was well dressed, was addressed as "Madam" by most merchants and their assistants. She wrung her hands and nervously moved her engagement ring on her finger. Magda squinted at the young woman, who also looked familiar to her, and held onto her cigarette. She did not smoke inside the shop, but the older man's stares aroused a discomfort within her, which led her to wait on the pavement and lean against the bus stop post. Sid had his jacket draped over his shoulders and there was no taxi in sight. Magda looked at his hands.

"Jimmy took my stuff home," he said in anticipation of what he hoped might be her question. He stood close by and observed every move Magda made.

Several moffies passed by and whistled at Sid. "Hello Bokkie!" they called out, all dressed in their netball clothes. Sid smiled and exchanged a few words with one of them. He stood, momentarily, with a smile on his face completely absorbed in the long list of compliments he received.

"Those hands can touch this any time hey," said Miss Singana as she touched her buttocks.

Magda looked at them scathingly. "Oohh, Auntie has a sour face, hey," someone uttered. Magda was too absorbed in maintaining it to even hear anyone speak of her, let alone respond. Moments later Peter pulled up in the van. Before he could even reverse into the parking space, Magda had her hand on the driver's door handle. "Where's Latiefa and Jasmin?" she bellowed into his right ear.

"Aaah! You gave me a fright, Magda." Peter was nervous and his eyes stood back in his head as he yelled then spoke apologetically when he received Magda's cold stare.

"Where are Latiefa and Jasmin?" she asked, this time snarling at him.

Peter looked concerned but replied anyway. "I took der girls down to Caledon street . . . to der upholstery place . . ."

Magda slammed the door shut and scurried off. Sid crossed the street after standing in the middle of it; he waited until the cars had passed before he dashed towards Peter. They still hooted at him and he waved them down. He leaned into the driver's seat window.

"Hi Peter," he sighed.

"Hey Sid, what's going on? Did Jasmin and Latiefa do anyting wrong at der house? When I went to pick der girls up dey were cleaning house."

"No, Peter. They didn't do anything wrong. Where did you drop them off?"

Peter explained to Sid and the two men exchanged greetings and made a promise to enjoy a card game later that evening. Sid walked over to the chemist's and leaned against the door; he greeted the young woman at the till.

"I believe congratulations are in order."

She nodded and seemed to shift her eyes about as though she was trying to make a connection of some sort. When she finally did, as was visible by her raised brow and larger pupils, it was clear that she understood that Magda was Sid's sister. She smiled and nodded again and uttered a soft "Thank you," as she touched her engagement ring. Sid waved at her to indicate that he was leaving. Sid hastened his pace to catch up with Magda.

"Magda! Magda!" he called out after her again. Magda was running. She turned the corner of Caledon Street and started to take off her belt. "Magda!" Sid called out again.

Latiefa and Jasmin were walking arm in arm and suddenly started running when they saw their mother coming towards them. Her whole body carried her anger and there was no way they were going to wait for their mother to catch up to them. They kicked off their shoes and left them on the pavement as their uncle tried to grab hold of their mother.

"Where's the chair?" he asked, raising his voice loud enough for everyone on the street to hear. The girls were some meters away. Jasmin pointed toward the shop where they had left it as she tried to adjust her head scarf whilst her eyes bounced in her head and her breathing tried to catch up to her fears. "Go over to your father's until I come and collect you!" their uncle called out.

Latiefa had both her hands on her hips and stood upright waiting for her mother to make her next move. Sid still had his arms around his sister's waist and he kept her in a tight grip until the girls were out of sight. Most shops closed at one o'clock on Saturdays but many lingered on a little longer on Caledon and Hanover streets, which were not really part of the central business district although they tried to keep the same hours. Several little children who previously had their eyes cast on the sweets hanging in the popular sticky-fingered window now turned around to observe the spectacle in front of them. There was nothing sweet in the observation although the prospect of seeing two grown girls, young women as it were, beaten in public somehow aroused the taste buds of the little boys especially for they pushed past the little girls and stood, hands behind their backs, in an orderly row in order to get a better view.

"Control yourself, Magda," said Sid.

"Stop making a scene. The girls aren't children anymore, you know. Your days of hitting them are over. Pull yourself together, woman!"

Magda was breathing heavily and clawed her brother with all her might. She eased her grip and her tears flowed, spontaneously, as her brother held her tight. The little children who now held onto one another could almost taste one salt drop after another, for they swallowed the occasional one that dropped long and hard on Magda's neck.

Magda allowed her brother to hold her for a moment, then pushed him away. She straightened herself out, put her belt back on, and walked into the shop. Her brother followed dutifully and the group of young children scurried a few steps along in a pack.

Sid now grabbed her by the arm. "Let me talk to them," he asserted. Magda stood to one side and looked at her brother with contempt. Sid approached the man who he thought most likely the owner. "Good afternoon, sir." He began by giving a description of Jasmin and Latiefa and said that the two girls had brought a green chair in for upholstery and repair.

"Oh yes, I remember the lovely young ladies. The one had a little red birthmark on her face. They wore scarves on their heads. What well-mannered children you have," he remarked. Sid did not correct him. The man then began to describe the nature of their conversation.

"Where is the chair?" Magda called out, abruptly. The man put his spectacles on his face and held onto them with his left hand. He squinted in Magda's direction, shocked by the abrupt emission, quite contrary to what he experienced from Sid. He looked over at Sid and smiled. "I just got my son to put it on the van and run it down to our workshop off Buitenkant Street," he replied, looking somewhat bewildered.

"Give me the address," Magda said. "I need to get that chair back."

"I promised the young lady that the chair would be ready on Wednesday," he replied again, looking at Sid for some sort of explanation.

"Wednesday is too late!" Magda called out.

"Well, I'm afraid no one at our workshop is authorized to give out any furniture. All of the pieces we work on get brought back here." He took his glasses off again. He did not need them any longer.

"Thank for your time, Mr . . . er," Sid attempted.

"Kahanovitz," he said. "Or Mr Kay."

"Thank you, Mr Kay." Sid nodded then turned to his sister. "Let's go," Sid said to Magda. Magda resisted. "Stop making a scene. You're too old for this. You're coming home with me," he grunted in her ear.

Magda started running again. Sid tried to catch up but was impeded by the oncoming cars. The young children now scurried off in the opposite direction. Sid quickened his pace whilst holding his jacket in his hand. He tried to wave down a taxi despite the garment flapping about. The driver was not his friend, and the man just threw both his arms up to indicate that he could not be of service.

When Sid got to Buitenkant Street the wind, now strong, muffled his ears. He could see over towards the parade where the flower sellers were now packing their belongings. Magda was not visible in the crowd of women who walked about in such colourful attire and called out to their customers with such forthright speech, the content of which was barely audible to Sid. The whipping wind and dust obscured his vision. Sid paused a moment, mindful of the eyes on him. He gathered himself, straightened his shirt, then wiped his brow. He looked up at Table

Mountain and allowed his eyelids to bow to its beauty. There was still
no sign of Magda.

He walked slowly, staggering from side to side, pondering what her
next move might be. Sid observed that some of the buildings had been
knocked down at the end of Caledon Street and sighed aloud for he
knew why. There were chunks missing, like from a partly eaten loaf of
brown bread, and he looked at the surrounding buildings, wondering
how they supported themselves. He was now on Castle Street, and the
castle lay right before him, as a reminder of who he was and why he lived
in District Six. He held this thought, his face assuming a contemptuous
look, for a few seconds. His mouth curled with sorrow and he looked
behind him at the site upon which District Six was erected.

He was still looking about, observing the older brown brick buildings, their crevices, their black railings, so picturesque, the sculptured
detail which embellished them, and the flowery tops of the metal railings, where, upon close observation, you could almost see the sign of the
cross if you stood back to observe it closely, when suddenly he heard
someone banging and screaming. Magda had found the shop and was
standing there, with her hands shielding her eye from the sun's glare in
order to see the pieces of furniture. At intervals, she would bang her fists
against the glass window. She appeared to be calling the chair to come
to her. She started calling out. "My chair! There's my chair!"

Sid stood behind her with his right arm on her right shoulder, saying, "Magda, there's nothing we can do now. Just leave it until Monday
morning. The doors are locked, there is nothing we can do right now."

Magda pressed her face against the glass. She exhaled onto it deeply
so that her breath showed. As she stood back, Sid could see that her tears
had also left their mark. Magda was sobbing and her brother moved to
give her some room. Her sobbing grew louder and within minutes she
was crouched on the floor, right beside the door, sitting upright with her
head leaning against the iron bars.

"Magda, get up!" said Sid. "Come on, it's time to go now."

Magda did not stir. A faraway look now glazed her eyes as she stared
over the top of the government buildings into the clouds. The wind was
beginning to circle and dust particles were gathering. Sid looked about
and bent down to touch the sand; its texture and fresh smell of ancestral

blood told him that it had blown in from recently demolished buildings. He sighed, looked at his surroundings and down at Magda. Little papers blew about and cigarette butts were now being lifted as the wind gained fuller momentum, taking charge of the afternoon.

"Come on, Magda. The wind is picking up," said Sid trying again to appeal to his sister to leave.

Magda still did not move. Sid bent down and held his hand out to his sister. She did not take it. He then placed her hand on top of his, placing her fingers around his fist to ensure that she would be able to hold on as he prepared to lift her. Her body moved towards him reluctantly. She stood up as though she was not present at all. She simply stood straight up with no effort of her own and with no willingness either. Sid got hold of her arm and walked with her. Magda's body simply followed on in silence. Her mascara had smudged considerably and her hair was mussed. Sid barely glanced at his sister and remained silent. He looked about to see if there was anyone they knew or if she had left anything behind. When they took the Roeland Street corner, the wind hit them hard in their faces. Magda's eyes were, surprisingly, shut. Sid looked towards the northeaster and observed the horns of Devil's Peak; he looked at them openly, then looked straight up at table mountain and observed the clouds pouring over as if they had been whipped into a froth. The clouds descended into the streets of District Six and De Waal Drive. The aroma from the corner store, which sold rotisserie barbecue chicken, had Sid chewing his lips. The aroma was now on his palate and he swallowed reluctantly, hard, against his own wishes. He did not want to take the chance of going inside the shop with Magda. Magda was completely oblivious to food smells or oncoming cars; she was certainly oblivious to the weather. Sid held onto his jacket; whilst he desperately wanted to wear it as the wind wore him down, he was not going to ease his grip on his sister's shoulders.

By the time the two adults had turned DeVilliers Street onto Roeland Street, Sid was tired. He avoided walking through the Bloemhof flats, an important artery of District Six and usually his first choice since he jammed with several men from the flats, and took the cowardice route, up Roeland Street. The smell of petrol from the corner garage did not help either as it reminded him of smells he could have inhaled, like samoosas, daltjies, and slangetjies, which his tongue was aching for. He simply nodded at the young men in attendance and proceeded down DeVilliers Street. He was in no mood to greet anyone, let alone chat. Little children playing with skipping ropes greeted them merrily and he merely nodded. Magda did not look at anyone. Neighbours bustling in and out of their own homes and carrying food into the homes of others frowned and squinted in his direction, stammering their greetings, whilst gesturing with their hands towards Magda. They juggled their plates skillfully whilst his mouth salivated in silence.

"Everything oright, Sid?"

"Yes, Mrs Smith," he replied. He repeated his response each time a neighbour asked and looked puzzled at both he and Magda.

Spider was dressed in her Saturday best and winked at Sid. Spider ignored Magda since they were not friends. Sid motioned to her with his eyes and Spider pulled a face, pushed out her bum, waved her arm as though to suggest that she could not be bothered, and walked and mumbled with an attitude that only she could carry off. Sid did understand every one of her gestures. He sneered at her and she scurried off when she saw his face. By the time he got to his house, Mrs Osman, who had been standing at the window with a cup in her hand, leapt to the door. She called out to Latiefa, who stood rather sternly and refused to move. Sid walked into the door with Magda and stroked his mother's head and her hands. He noticed his parcels, which Jimmy must have dropped off. Latiefa glanced over at her mother and did not move from the dining room table. Sid merely nodded at her. He walked into his mother and Magda's room, then placed Magda down on her bed. Her body did not move at all; her eyes surveyed the area and she did not once look at her brother. He lifted her feet, then removed her shoes. He looked over and found a small shawl on his mother's bed, which he then draped over his sister. At that instant, Magda curled herself into a fetal position. Sid stood looking at his sister for quite a while, mesmerized by the position her body had now coiled itself into. After several minutes Sid tiptoed out of the room and shut the door. He was then met with two pairs of eyes; one worried, the other distant.

"Where's Jasmin?" he asked.

"She's with Daddy." Latiefa held her head high as she answered and looked towards the bedroom where her mother now lay. Her narrowed eyes seemed to shoot daggers. "I'm not afraid of her. Last year was the last time that she hit me. That's not going to happen again. I'm not a small child."

Her uncle breathed out heavily as she spoke. He nodded and looked at his mother. "All this over a chair, hey?" Mrs Osman glanced into her empty cup. "Oh, there's some food for you in the oven. Want a cuppa tea to go with it?"

"Yes, please, Mummy," Sid said.

Latiefa was standing with both her hands on her hips. "Sit down Mamma, I'll get it for Uncle Sid." Sid nodded at her. "Oh, Auntie Spider popped in. Auntie Spider wanted to know if Uncle Sid was playing in the BoKaap tomorrow."

"What did you say?" he asked, grinning.

"I told her to ask Uncle."

"Ja, I'm playing there tomorrow. Spider is supposed to sing with us. You know she and your mother don't see eye to eye and we can't practice here."

Latiefa raised her eyebrows, and sighed aloud, "Ah-huh!"

There was a knock on the door. Latiefa looked at her watch momentarily. Sid was on his feet in seconds.

"It can't be Spider," Sid said, hoping silently that it was. But it was Lester who appeared at the door and who entered the house reluctantly. "Come in, Magda's sleeping," Sid said, to ease the look of concern on his friend's face.

Lester rubbed his hands together. He greeted Mrs Osman and Latiefa. "I just spoke to Clifford and he said he saw you with Magda and that something was going on."

"Ja. Sit down. No, not here. Let's go to the kitchen." Sid was eager to eat. "I was just going to have my . . . lunch." He looked at his watch and shrugged his shoulders.

Sid and Lester walked into the kitchen. Sid moved towards the backyard and ran the tap over his hands. His mother took hold of the tea towel and passed it to him. Latiefa stood in the passageway behind the laced curtain. "Hi, Uncle Lester. I haven't had a chance to tell Grandma or Uncle Sid that Uncle Lester came by."

Sid looked at Latiefa and frowned. In this house children did not always join adults when the conversation was meant to be of a particular kind. Latiefa usually observed this etiquette, but at times would join her grandmother even though she knew her mother would object.

Sid now looked rather concerned. "You knew that the girls took Magda's chair down to Caledon Street to have it repaired?" Sid asked, as he sat down to eat.

"No. What are you talking about?" Lester asked as he looked at Latiefa and Mrs Osman.

The older woman just shrugged her shoulders and looked towards her bedroom door. Latiefa waved her hands about.

"Don't worry, Uncle Lester. Its just Mummy causing a scene," the young woman said as she lowered herself into a chair and sat around the kitchen table with the adults.

Lester tilted his head as he spoke to her. "Don't speak about your mother like that," he said slowly and with great caution in his voice.

"Uncle Lester, why do you even care? Mummy is so rude to you. She doesn't even speak to you except to insult you or order you to do something."

"Ai, Latiefa. You're young. There are some things that are between two people, a man and a woman, that you won't understand."

"I understand that Mummy treats you in ways which I would never dream of treating anyone."

The young woman was adamant. She wanted Lester to know what she thought. Mrs Osman nudged Latiefa with her foot. Latiefa looked up at her grandmother, jerked her shoulders and threw her head back, indicating that she was entitled to make her remarks. Her uncle observed that there was now an adultness to her. Her body language declared her status as a young woman and placed her contribution to the conversation as one of entitlement.

"Can I get you some roti and curry, Lester?"

"No, thank you, Mrs Osman."

Latiefa was determined to continue the conversation. "It's true, Mamma, Mummy is awful to Uncle Lester and no one says anything about it."

"Take you elbows off the table," her grandmother remarked.

"Argh!" she called out.

Sid was looking at the young woman and eating his roti and lamb curry with his hands.

"Are you sure you don't want a small bite, Lester?" Mrs Osman asked again.

"Yes, I am sure. Thanks, Mrs Osman."

Sid ate with delight. He placed the curry, which contained potatoes and butter beans, around his fingers then scooped it into his mouth. He would break off pieces of roti, hold it in his hand, all artfully cupped, then use the roti to scoop the curry mixture with sauce and all from his plate into his mouth.

During a moment's silence, they heard Magda's bedroom door open. Magda came charging out.

"What the hell is he doing here? You don't have a home to go to?" she asked, expecting Lester to remain silent. "You don't live here no more," she continued.

Magda walked towards the backyard and spat on the cement floor. Sid got out of his chair. He grabbed the wet cotton cloth beside the sink and wiped his hands from the curry.

"Magda, that is the last time that you speak to Lester like that!"

"Just leave it, Sid," his mother requested.

"No! I am not leaving it. Inside now!"

He motioned to Magda with his outstretched arm. Magda lifted her right hand as though she intended to strike him. He caught her hand just in time.

"You're out of order. Mummy had to put you straight a long time ago. Lester shouldn't have moved from here. You're completely out of order and everyone lets you have your way."

She struggled with him. Lester moved as though he was about to leave.

"Stay there, Lester. I am putting an end to this right now." Sid pointed to Lester as he spoke. "He is my friend. Yes, something happened between the two of you a long time ago and that is it. It was a long time ago. Then when things didn't work out with you and the children's father, suddenly everyone around you was to blame. You have hatred in your heart . . . pure hatred. If you're not trying to beat the kids to a pulp with your belt then you're giving Mummy a hard time. You need to come right." Magda approached her brother with a cold stare. "Get away from me," he said as he looked at her.

Magda looked at Sid long and hard, then turned her back on everyone. She went back into the bedroom she shared with her mother and slammed the door shut. The door rattled a bit but she soon kicked it into place, its silence evidence of her strength. Latiefa appeared stunned. She looked towards her mother's bedroom door, then back at her uncle. She had not heard her uncle speak to her mother like that before. Mrs Osman placed her hands over both her sons' shoulders. Sid placed his right hand over his mother's, to soothe her and to let her know that he was fine. Her fingers found their way around his, and his around hers. Mother and son held that position a moment in silence, their hands locked together on his shoulder.

Then Sid released his grip, and pushed his plate to one side. Neither his friend nor his family could now observe his illustrious appetite. He looked at the plate of food and shook his head. He had been robbed of his joy. He hung his head and shook it again, his eyes shut. He then took a deep breath of air to enable him to stand up and face the remaining part of his day.

"We should go and get Jasmin. There's no reason for her to be out of the house because of this."

There was a knock on the door. It was Mamma Zila. Sid let the woman in after greeting her then suddenly he looked down, and there, low and behold, looking rather glum but curious, and in an unusual costume, was Rosa. Sid enjoyed teasing the child and so tugged at her book. She pulled it away, moved the string on her neck and kept it behind her back. Sid smiled at her without uttering a word. Rosa's costume was suggestive of someone who walked along the coast, a vagrant perhaps, for she wore an old hat and had facial hair on her face which Mamma Zila, no doubt, had placed there. He pinched her cheeks and the child retreated behind her grandmother.

"Hello, Vera," Mamma Zila greeted. "Hello, everyone," she said as she looked about the house. "No sign of Magda," Mamma Zila asked, without apologizing for her forthright manner.

"She's lying down, Zila," Mrs Osman replied as she looked at Mamma Zila and squinted at Rosa.

"Is everything alright, Vera? Flowers said she was here earlier and Magda had fainted."

"Yes, everything is alright now, Zila," Mrs Osman replied.

Mamma Zila looked about the house again. "And Jasmin, where's Jasmin?"

"She's at her father's," Sid added quickly.

"We just had some people stop by from Mossel Bay."

Mamma Zila blinked her eyes as though she was now turning a page of a children's book she might read to Rosa. She spoke dramatically, moving her arms about, as though to suggest that she was now changing the subject. Sid did enjoy watching the woman.

"Well," she said as she placed her hands on her hips. "We all have to go down to Mossel Bay. Willie's oldest sister might just be on her deathbed. I had a funny feeling the other day. And with this weather, my knee hasn't been feeling right, and Willie's sister came to me in the middle of the night you know. I told Willie, is time for us to get a car and go down to Mossel Bay. Mmmf! But does the man listen to me?" She moved her body forward as she spoke with her arms still on her hips. "Peter is going to take us all down. We were wondering, because of the holiday and the long weekend, if Rosa could stay here with the girls. I'll bring Rosa's school uniform just in case we're back late on Tuesday."

Mamma Zila always spoke with a lot of hand gestures and expressions. She would move her hands on her hips and then wave them about when she spoke. She acted out every story she told with great passion. It was easy to see where Rosa got her colourfulness from.

Latiefa looked down at Rosa, then knelt. Everyone was still mesmerized and took a while to respond. "Er . . . yes, Mamma Zila. Rosa can stay here if she stops telling stories." Latiefa smiled and winked at Mamma Zila as she spoke. "Did you hear that, Rosa? No making up stories." The child frowned at Latiefa then pulled a sullen face. "And who are we today, Rosa," Latiefa asked.

Everyone now looked at Rosa, who was scrutinizing her clothes and trying to ascertain who exactly she was meant to be imitating.

"I'm a strandloper," the child said as she observed their eyes surveying her outfit.

"Yes, yesterday she was Vasco da Gama and today she's a strandloper," Mamma Zila said in a matter-of-fact way.

Sid looked at Rosa and smiled.

"I wish I had my camera here," he said looking at Rosa and smiling from ear to ear.

"I can be a strandloper again Uncle Sid, hey Mamma," Rosa asserted as she looked towards her grandmother to further acknowledge her statement.

"Yes, sweetie, you can be a strandloper again," her grandmother replied. "You can be whoever you want."

Latiefa giggled softly as she observed Mamma Zila's eyeballs.

"Actually, Latiefa, I want to check with your mother about Rosa staying here. I don't like making arrangements without Magda knowing about them."

"It's okay, Mamma Zila. Mummy isn't feeling too good," the young woman replied as she looked at her uncle.

"Don't worry, Mamma Zila," Sid replied. "Rosa has stayed here many times before. Magda will be fine with the arrangement."

Rosa was still looking curiously about the house. Lester came into the living room from the kitchen.

"Afternoon," he said, nodding in a gentlemanly sort of way.

"Afternoon, Lester," Mamma Zila replied with raised eyebrows, still looking about the house and expecting Magda to make a furious appearance.

"Afternoon," Lester replied.

"And Merem goema?" he asked, referring to Rosa by her choice of District Six music. "Where are you going?"

"She a strandloper . . ." everyone called out, then laughed heartily.

"Well, I'm off then. We have to pack. And with you looking after madam here, I need to pack a few things for her too. Sid, can you pop into the house from time to time?" Mamma Zila asked.

"Yes, of course," he said smilingly.

"Oh, child, we never lock the house and I will have to go and look for the key now. Argh, forget it. I don't have time now. Ta, hey." Sid nodded at Mamma Zila again. "Oh Latiefa, madam here needs to have a

wash, as you can see . . . and she knows the rules . . . all the rules, don't
you, Rosa?" Rosa nodded.

"It's okay, Mamma Zila. I can get Rosa ready for bed here," Latiefa
replied.

"Oh, Latiefa, if you see Mrs Jacobs, tell her not to worry. I am sure
we'll be back before Thursday and I will take Rosa up there myself in the
evening to her house for the child's voice lesson after Rosa attends Mr
Salie's Muslim school." Mamma Zila touched her head in an effort to
remember tasks she still needed to complete. "Did I remember everything, Rosa?"

Rosa nodded at her grandmother still clutching her little book and
keeping it safely away from Sid. The older woman blew Latiefa a kiss as
Rosa went towards her friend. Mamma Zila thanked her friends and said
her good-byes. She did not inquire after Magda, although she did glance
toward her bedroom door before stepping out.

As evening approached, Sid was starting to worry about Jasmin. He was
pacing to and from the window, each time looking in both directions
then up towards the mountain. Magda was still in the bedroom and did
not leave it, not even for dinner. Mrs Osman left her plate of food with
another covering it on the table, then later placed both plates in the bottom oven. She stirred and stoked the stove a few times, moving the coals
and wood about with the poker.

"Mummy, let me do that," Sid said as he observed the tiredness that
was evident on his mother's face. He looked at his mother's hands and
refrained from asking her how they were holding up. "Actually,
Mummy, why don't you get ready and I take you to Auntie Mary," he
said to his mother.

"You know I don't want to visit my sister when I have troubles here
at home."

"Mummy, you should go. I will go and check on Jasmin, and Latiefa
can stay here with Rosa. Is that clear?" he said as he tilted his head to
ensure that Latiefa was listening. Latiefa simply nodded. "Don't open
the door for anyone. I will make sure that Jasmin stays at your father's
house. It will be too late for her to come back here anyway. I will stay at
Lester's tonight after the card game. We also need to practice for tomor-

row. Alright?" Sid looked at Latiefa, then at Lester, both of whom simply nodded.

"So I guess with Peter going to Mossel Bay we're one man down for jamming . . . no drummer, hey . . . and one man down for the game, nuh?"

"We'll find someone," Lester said confidently.

Mrs Osman packed a bag whilst the two men chatted and proposed several men to one another as possible drummers and card players. Mama Zila and Rosa's mother said their good-byes to the young child, who had now received a warm-water wash in the backyard under Latiefa's guidance. They left her ironed school uniform, still on the metal hanger, hanging against Latiefa and Jasmin's wardrobe, along with a small bag of clothes. Rosa's mother also brought several tins of biscuits, a small jar of beetroot, two small jars of homemade mango pickle, a small box of apricots, which were Rosa's favourite fruit, and grapes, which Mamma Zila knew would be greatly appreciated by the two young women to whom she entrusted her grandchild. Rosa's mother and grandmother left without being tearful and Rosa bade them farewell. Latiefa then took Rosa to the toilet, which was in the backyard, to ensure that the young child did not have to get up in the middle of the night. Sid and Lester conversed merrily. Sid packed his saxophone and carried the large instrument in a black velvet bag, which he then placed in its hard black case. Lester had his pennywhistle in his pocket and he played a quick tune as Rosa and Latiefa looked on. When Mrs Osman was ready and had packed her small bag, her son and Lester joined her, arm in arm, on either side.

As soon as they stepped off the doorstep and shut the door behind them, they saw Spider. Spider, speaking with her eyes, asked Sid where the venue for the practice was, and Sid called out the name of the friend whose house they were playing at and the time they expected her to arrive, all of which was signalled with his hand. Spider raised her head, as though she was listening. Mrs Osman simply nodded at her. Spider was in and out of her house and the one beside her, to her right. Just as Sid was bidding her farewell with his eyes, since both his hands were occupied, Nana, one of their neighbours and a former singer herself, came to her front door.

"Evening," she said as she looked at Mrs Osman.

"Evening," they all replied.

Nana was a very glamorous woman and spoke with a cinematic voice, as many said. She had a Joan Crawford look about her, day and night, and asserted her presence even if it was not welcome.

"I see you have lowered your standards now," she said, as she looked up the road towards Spider's house.

The men just looked at one another. Before they could reply she had slipped inside her house again and slammed the door. Sid and Lester looked at one another. Young men and women greeted them and smiled when they saw Sid's saxophone in the case. There was rhythm on the streets and bodies jerking and moving about: it was a usual Saturday night, except that Easter brought out a particular festiveness among its residents. Music was already playing and young adults were getting dressed for the evening. Sid looked behind him as he heard hurried feet shuffle past him.

"Evening, everyone. Evening," Auntie Flowers said again, ensuring that Mrs Osman heard her and would turn around. Mrs Osman seemed surprised and greeted Auntie Flowers, who spoke hurriedly. "I'm off to Peyton Place, Vera. Gabieba's having her twins and Imam Moosa just came by to tell me on his way to Motchie Tiema. I'm in a rush. See you all tomorrow," she said, as she hastened her step.

"Ai, what would women do without Auntie Flowers, hey?" exclaimed Mrs Osman. The men beside her simply shook their heads. Sid and Lester greeted three young men who were part of a gang called Star Seventeen. Neither Sid nor Lester belonged to a gang and therefore did not risk being physically harmed. Mrs Osman knew one of the young men, knew his parents and family that is, and he lowered his head respectfully and removed his woollen hat.

"Evening, Auntie," he remarked as he lowered his eyes.

Mrs Osman simply nodded to acknowledge his greeting. The young men soon crossed the road with their rhythmical walk and with their jackets drawn up to their ears.

Sid and Lester walked Mrs Osman to Tenant Street, the extension of DeVilliers Street once it reached Hanover Street, to her sister

Mary's house. It took no time for Latiefa to get Rosa to bed; Latiefa placed the young child in Jasmin's bed, on the bottom bunk. The young woman had been tired out herself by the events of the day. Magda had still not moved. Latiefa turned off the big central light and then turned on the smaller light, which she moved from the small bedside table and placed on the floor. The small light was only visible on the floor if Rosa needed to go to the toilet in the middle of the night. She climbed the metal ladder to the top of the bunk bed slid into her tightly made bed.

The wind rustled against the windowpane and sang screetchingly in Latiefa's ear. She stirred and untangled her tousled hair with her fingers. She looked beneath her on the lower bunk bed and saw that Rosa was also stirring.

"Sssh, go back to sleep Rosa."

Rosa stirred slightly. Latiefa would have gone back to sleep herself if it wasn't for the sound of soft conversation. She stopped moving in her bed and listened again. She could hear her mother's voice. But it sounded too gentle to be her mother's. She looked about the room then slipped down from her bed. She held her wristwatch close to the window in order to tell the time. She shook her head in disbelief when she saw that it was 3:45 in the morning. She looked at the luminescent alarm clock and noticed that it too said 3:45. Who could her mother be speaking to? Her grandmother had left to stay with her sister on Tenant Street and Jasmin was at their father's. No one had entered the house since. She had bolted and locked the door herself after her uncle left. Sid often stayed with Lester on Saturday nights, and he had given her specific instructions that she was not to open the door under any circumstances. She looked over towards the settee, which served as Sid's bed when it opened up, and saw no evidence of her uncle's return. It was where her uncle had slept ever since she could remember. She now walked on the tips of her toes and was trying very hard for her toes not to crack. The floor was old and creaky, but she managed to walk a few feet without making a sound. She could still hear her mother speaking. The young woman was less interested in the sound of her mother's voice and more interested in finding out who had caused it to be altered in this manner. The frown on her face remained as she walked towards the door and listened for the other person's voice. There was still no sound. Her mother had paused occasionally and then continued to speak in a humble, subdued, and unusually loving tone. The young woman stammered at the door and pushed it open slightly.

There, to her amazement, stood a figure of a man. He was standing in the spot where the chair had been. He was leaning against the wall and did not utter a word. His eyes were directed at her mother. She gasped, then placed her hand over her mouth. She narrowed her eyes as the brightness of his presence was too much for her to bear. A shimmering light was beaming from his body, which enveloped him. She narrowed her eyes even further in order to get a good look at his face. "Huuuh!" she gasped, quietly and leaned against the inner wall of the door, breathlessly. The young man's presence was illuminated. He stood there in shining perfection like one would imagine a god would appear: silent, shining brightly, and beautifully composed, even regal. His eyes were silent too, silent yet calm and content. Her mother was speaking to him again. She could hear Magda referring to him as "Jake." The young man's eyes were serene, and they were so deep that they entitled him to a crown for he governed over her mother with such might. As Latiefa looked at him again, she could see the shining outer layer that covered his body almost beaming towards her mother. He had Lester's hairline . . . his strong chiseled nose, Lester's eyes, his height, his shoulders and his facial expression . . . when silent. She realized in an instant that the young man's face looked like a younger version of Lester. The young woman, upon her realization, could not contain herself any longer. She burst into the room. Her mother sat straight up in her bed.

"Get out! Get out, you little witch!"

"Who is he?" she screetched at the top of her voice.

The young man still did not stir. He looked at her mother as though no one else was in the room.

"Get out!" Magda called out again.

"Who is he . . . and why . . . does he look . . . like Uncle Lester?" Latiefa was stuttering and tears flooded her eyes. Her mother grew silent. "Why does he look like Uncle Lester! Answer me!" Magda stared at her daughter blankly. "Tell me!" She moved forward and grabbed her mother's feet, which were covered in blankets and shook them with both her hands. Young Latiefa was shaking. "Mummyyyy, he looks just a little older than me." She was sobbing uncontrollably now. "Mummyyyy," she called out again.

"You should consider yourself lucky that you can see him," Magda said. She now spoke in a monotone. "He doesn't show himself to anyone, except me. You should be so lucky to even come close to him."

Her mother's voice did not match the face or the character of the woman she knew as her mother. Latiefa continued to sob uncontrollably as her mother spoke to her without once looking at her.

"Why . . . why does he look like Uncle Lester?" she asked again between sobs.

"Why do you think?" her mother replied, still looking at the young man.

"Mummy," she cried out. "Mummyyyy!"

"He is my first born," Magda said, looking lovingly towards the man who stood there expressionless. "He is my first. I lost him at birth. What did Lester know about how a mother feels? How any woman feels when she loses her first born."

The young man now sat on the floor and crossed his legs. He looked only at his mother, not once at his sister.

"Mummy, the chair. Is the chair for him?" she asked, now almost in a childlike tone.

"For my Jacob," Magda replied. "The chair is only for my Jacob."

"Mummyyy!" the young woman cried out again. "He . . . he visits you and . . . and . . . you've never said anything." Latiefa was now developing hiccups. She stammered through her speech.

"Yes, my Jacob. He visits every night. My Jacob comes to me at night and we talk. He listens to me. My Jacob is twenty-one today. It's his birthday and he has no chair to sit in." Latiefa started doing the math with her fingers. She was nearing her eighteenth birthday. She looked at the young man again as she wiped her tears with the sleeve of her nightgown; he still only had eyes for his mother.

"Does Uncle Lester know?" Latiefa asked as she wiped her tears.

"Who? What?" her mother replied in a normal voice. "He doesn't know a damn thing. He wouldn't know if something hit him in the face. What did he ever know? What did he ever do?" her mother replied in a normal voice.

"Uncle Lester loves you," Latiefa said, almost pleadingly.

Her mother was quick to cut her off. "Don't you dare talk to me about love. I don't love anyone. I love my Jacob. I gave myself to that stupid bloody man and my child was taken away from me. Then I met your father, and look what good that brought me."

Latiefa burst out crying, now louder than ever. She could not control her tears and fell to her mother's bed, sobbing loudly into the blanket. She held onto her mother's feet. Magda pulled herself from under her daughter's grip. Magda still looked only at her son.

Latiefa lay there, her face covered with a woollen blanket and tears. Slowly, and without much fuss, she lifted herself from her mother's bed. She straightened herself out, pulled her sleeves down and did not look at her brother at all. She walked towards the door without looking at her mother. As she pulled the door close she noticed a tiny little figure of a child sitting crouched on the floor with her head hung as though she were asleep. Without uttering a word, she bent down and picked Rosa up. The child had clearly witnessed some of what had taken place. Rosa curled her legs around Latiefa's body. Latiefa held the child's head close to hers. She stroked Rosa's hair and the child, who had both her arms around Latiefa's neck, held on close too. Latiefa positioned her in order to have greater mobility. She lifted Rosa back into Jasmin's bed and rubbed the child's forehead in circular strokes, silently, just the way she liked it. Rosa's eyes were almost shut and she held onto Latiefa's hand. Latiefa only let go of her when she was sure that the child was asleep.

Latiefa then climbed the metal ladder to her bed. She was still shaking and sobbing. She reflected momentarily on Rosa's revelation earlier in the day. The young child was telling her the truth. She held her arm out towards the light of the window. Her watch said 3:45. It can't be right, she thought to herself. She tapped it gently a few times with her fingers. The arms on her watch did not move. She turned towards the illuminated alarm clock. It said 4:07. She tapped her wristwatch with her fingers again: there was still no movement from the arms. Latiefa took her watch off and shook it a few times. She sighed out loud. The hands on her watch did not move. She moved away from the window, wrapped her neck in her Hellenic Soccer scarf, which she kept under her pillow, and went back to sleep.

Money for Your Madness

April afternoons in Cape Town were always unpredictable, and never more so than in 1970. The afternoon clouds would hover over Table Mountain until the wind lifted them and sent them tumbling down the cliffs, gracefully and breathlessly. When the clouds tumbled down the mountain everyone in District Six would stand still to watch the event. In a matter of minutes, the mountain would come to life, take on a character of its own, transform its setting, and change the weather completely, which would in turn change the mood of those who observed it. Residents of District Six sat around Table Mountain, ate their meals around it, said their prayers around it. Muslims and Christians alike were its disciples, because Table Mountain determined their mood, their well-being, their livelihood, and was also a reminder of how the land shaped itself to suit the needs of people who lived to eat—and eat they did—with joy and passion. Some say Table Mountain was put there by a woman, millions of years ago, so that she could always feed her children and their children—who were born to be ruled by the mountain and live at its feet.

The mountain was not the only physical feature of Cape Town. There was the sea, the warm and wonderful sea, the cold and dangerous sea. At Cape Town two oceans came together, clashing warmth with cold, currents hurling against one another, in a blue profundity that could tempt you to curl yourself into a shell and sink into the surrounding elements of sand, sun and foam, and remain hidden forever. Cape fur seals swam gloriously in Table Bay Harbour, the southern right whale preferring to swim further along at Muizenberg. Some say it is the birds who call women to enter the sea and who whisper in the ears of those who hear voices as often as they hear church bells; others disagree, believing that the sea draws women in like it draws in the fresh Cape Town air, perpetually.

The fishermen were wary; their wives cautiously awaited the passing of their partners' moodiness, and dogs lying too close to the pavement's walkway knew to keep away from residents who appeared as though they were holding their breath, awaiting the decision of the clouds. Older, wiser dogs sniffed the pavements for Easter chocolate, and when a silver paper was spotted, an older dog would nestle his body right beside it. The electrical wires whistled their own high-pitched tune with tight, knotted tension. Birds gathered leaves in haste and built their meticulous nests hastily. They would scramble for little pieces of wood blowing in the wind, which they would not ordinarily have access to. Now in full windy bloom, the birds indulged themselves whilst young children were kept indoors by their grandparents awaiting the outcome of the mountain's decision. Curtains were partially drawn, and curious, frowning faces ran to windows eager to witness, firsthand, the decision the mountain made. Fishermen who sailed in and out of Table Bay and those who circled the waters as far as Lion's Head would shake their head, pout and stretch their mouths; this expression would be passed on to the entire community, and within minutes it would reach District Six. It was a good day for snoek, the sharp-beaked long silver fish, but not a good day for those who did not watch the descent of the clouds over Lion's Head.

It was Wednesday afternoon, and Clifford stood at the corner of DeVilliers and Sackville Street. He had attended the noon mass earlier that day and remained in his church clothes, a pair of black trousers with turned-up bottoms, and a stiffly pressed and starched white shirt. His trousers were neatly ironed and lined themselves up in fine horizontal form, giving him the appearance and composure of greatness, one he cultivated. He had removed his knee bandage earlier that day and there was no evidence of ointment on his body, not even the smell of it. A small red bow tie lay stiff on his collar, straightening him somewhat whilst giving his nervous face a gentle and desiring quality. A pair of his father's braces lay neatly over his freshly pressed white shirt, which was a little too big for him. As the wind circled close to him it gave off the whiff of Old Spice.

He waited anxiously and held a bouquet of flowers in his hand, which he kept close to his body whilst tapping his feet on the gray cement pavement. Clifford had contracted polio during childhood and his left leg never fully recovered, yet he kept it tapping, rhythmically, to ensure that those around him knew he had use for his leg and did not treat him as a cripple. He looked over both his shoulders at regular intervals, as if expecting someone to approach him from behind. His eyes darted to and fro and on each occasion he turned to face south, towards Hanover Street, and his whole body jerked as women shouted at their children, which was rather a common occurence in District Six.

Rosa sat a few meters away eating a red toffee apple. Her little book, which had a pencil with a string attached to it, hung snugly around her neck. There was no dance class for her to attend on this Wednesday afternoon since Mr Jacobs usually took an extra week for his Easter holiday. The young child was smiling and waving at Clifford. Rosa's hands were still sticky, and each time she clasped them together to see the effect of the sugary syrup on her palms, she laughed aloud.

As Clifford squinted in the full glare of the sun, he could see the stickiness on her fingers. Clifford was taken by her laughter, and at each turn of his head in her direction he straightened his bow tie. Once, having observed this clasping together of sticky hands, he shook his head then smiled at the thought of the pleasure the young child was indulging in. Mamma Zila was close by talking to several women. Rosa's mother, Maria, who worked the night shift at the hotel in the dockyard, must be sleeping, Clifford thought, as she usually did during the day. Clifford was waiting for Nana, Louisa's mother, to offer her a bouquet of flowers for Louisa. Perhaps this way Nana would allow him into the house to see Louisa. His head jerked twice as he saw Nana approaching. Rosa, uncertain as to whether Clifford had spotted his target, started calling out.

"Cliffie! . . . Cliffie! . . . Cliffieeeee!"

"Ja. . . Ja!" He waved with his left hand, ensuring her that they had both observed the appearance of the same person.

The young child persisted at the top of her voice: "Cliffieeee!"

He waved her down, turned around, then gestured with his hand that it was time for her to go. He shook his head and breathed out heavily a few times in realization of how loud Rosa really was when she wanted to be. Rosa had played an enormous part in his presentation of flowers to Nana as a means of getting to see Louisa. Clifford looked about him again; as Rosa had promised earlier that day as they locked fingers to seal the agreement, she had removed herself from the street where Nana and Clifford hoped to speak. There was no sign of her now, although Clifford did not for one moment believe that just because he did not see Rosa that she would not be watching from one of her many treasured spots. He rubbed his face with his left hand, smoothing out the creases of unease. He did not want Nana to see Rosa, let alone hear her calling him.

Nana was tall in stature and had a towering, forceful presence. She was a glamorous woman and dressed like a movie star. She wore a tightly fitting black dress with fishnet stockings. Her lipstick was a devilish red—a kind no one in District Six wore—and her lips were lined to form an "O." One almost expected her to utter the very expression and pout, for her lipstick covered the fleshy parts of her smaller upper lip too as though her mouth was dissatisfied with its natural boundaries. Nana's lips were full, and she thrust them out to the world, as though awaiting someone to kiss them. She carried herself as though an event of great magnitude was about to happen and she wore sunglasses to look mysterious. Nana had the appearance of someone whose body parts made love to one another; they were caressed by her vanity. She had a slow and casual movement, which was both alluring and seductive. Men would hang out of their windows, lean over their balconies, to watch her. Men would stop shaving to watch her, from any place they found themselves, completely oblivious to their scantily dressed state, their mouths salivating with desire as their wives and partners prepared to use the rolling pin or an old newspaper to beat them out of their trance. "Afternoon, Mrs Nana," Clifford said with the voice of a learned gentleman, one he thought she would best respond to.

"Aah!" she sighed. She rolled her eyes and batted her eyelids with the false eyelashes.

"Afternoon, Mrs Nana," the young man said again,trying not to stutter.

She raised her sunglasses into her curly mass of hair and placed her left hand on her left hip. "Aah!" she sighed again, as she perused his presence and scrutinized every piece of his clothing.

Nana was chewing gum and the chewing motion gave her a younger appearance. He could only see the white of her eyes as she posed, somewhat seductively, somewhat contemptuously, to listen to what he had to say.

"Boy, what is this?"

She pointed to the flowers as she spoke, still with one hand on her hip, and appeared somewhat agitated. "Afternoon, Mrs Nana. I was waiting here for Mrs Nana to give Mrs Nana der flowers for Louisa. I bought dem fresh dis morning in der Hanover Street market, Mrs Nana." Clifford spoke steadily without pausing as though he had been rehearsing for days. "I ask Mrs Nana to give der flowers to Louisa. I put a letter in der paper for Louisa. Dey say dat if a person have a mental problem is nice to have flowers. I'm sure Louisa can still read, she was orways very clever. I ask Mrs Nana to give for Louisa der flowers and der letter."

He was almost breathless from talking. Nana stood there and spoke with her eyes before she opened her red lipsticked mouth.

"Oh, child. I have told you before. She doesn't really remember much. She's not okay, you know." Nana touched herself as she spoke. She placed her right hand over the neckline of her dress as though she was caressing her own words and steered the gum in her mouth in many different directions. "She's in a world of her own you know," she continued. "Don't know why you bother, Cliffie."

At the end of her sentences her words, much like her eyes, seemed to go through hoops of fire. Clifford stood firmly and looked at Nana's mouth as she spoke. He was too afraid to look elsewhere in case she reprimanded him.

"But I ask dat Mrs Nana just give der flowers to Louisa. Mummy say dat even if Louisa doan remember many tings is still good to have der flowers," he said, ensuring that his voice also echoed the concerns of his mother.

"Look, Cliffie," she said in a long drawn-out tone. "I do my best, you know. I don't like people telling me what to do. She's nobody's problem but mine. People like to say things but they don't know anything. I do my best."

Clifford nodded to show just how agreeable he was. Nana was a singer and she would often break out in a tune, or sing something whilst she was speaking. She had not appeared on stage in more than twenty years and thus had not earned her living since. At times she would speak very slowly as though she was reciting a piece of literature.

"Yes, Mrs Nana . . . Mummy say der same ting . . . dat Mrs Nana do her best. I know Mrs Nana do her best."

Clifford bowed gracefully as he handed Nana the flowers. His face lit up, and he stammered as though he was about to say something else. The look on Nana's face gave him every indication that he had said enough.

"Thank you, Cliffie." Nana pronounced every syllable; she often overpronounced her words to mock those who were less fortunate in their articulation. Nana lowered her sunglasses again. She stroked her hair back in place and touched her small nose. Nana looked about the street; she was observing the Sackville Street neighbours, mostly men, who were leaning over their balconies. She was convinced that they were staring at her, and gave them every reason to enjoy themselves. The washing on the lines, strung across the buildings and hanging boldly between them like additions to the architecture, was beginning to flutter but the clouds appeared to be standing still over the tabletop. Nana smoothed her hair again and positioned herself slowly for a more seductive walk. There was now a vanity in her step as she carried the flowers close to her bosom. She looked over her shoulder occasionally to see if Rosa was following her. The young child had on many occasions followed Nana and imitated her walk. But there was no sign of Rosa anywhere.

Nana busied herself to admire the bouquet of flowers, mindful of those who were watching her. There was an assortment ranging from poppies to daisies, a few irises and gladiolas, small orange orchids placed sparingly, but best of all an abundance of red tulips, which were a particular favourite of hers. A woman as curvaceous as she seemed perfectly matched to carry tulips. Tulips seemed like the perfect accompaniment, an accessory even, for someone as sculptured as Nana. She used

her left hand to wave at the neighbours, who appeared to be looking in
her direction.

She could see Auntie Flowers perking up at the sight of her bouquet
of flowers as the woman stood in her doorway speaking to Auntie Tiefa,
who had already returned from Hanover Street with her empty cart.
Auntie Tiefa was not in the habit of greeting Nana; the woman grunted
at her and refused to converse with her. Peter Jantjies was further away,
still wearing his dockyard dungarees and covered in fish scales; he was
carrying logs of wood into Auntie Flowers and Mrs Hood's house.
Mamma Zila was swinging the rope attached to the electrical pole for
Rosa, who skipped to her heart's delight. Mamma Zila did, of course,
converse with passersby and updated herself, and the company she kept,
on all matters pertaining to District Six.

Nana spat the gum out of her mouth and stamped it into the paved
ground. She looked towards Rosa, but the child had no intention of
placing her attention elsewhere. Nana ground her heels into the pavement several times, not particularly focused on the gum, but there was
still no response from Rosa. She looked over towards Clifford, who was
now joined by Queenie. Queenie was very annoyed at him, as evidenced
by the manner in which she used her hands. It was not known whether
the two were lovers, since Clifford denied it so strongly, but Queenie
exerted great ownership over Clifford and took care of him. She fussed
over him, made him wonderful dinners, and did not mind that he had
affections for Louisa. It was seeing Clifford in the company of Nana that
drove her green with envy. Clifford was allowed to converse with women
freely; if he was seen with another moffie, her friends so to speak,
Queenie would take severe steps towards punishing him. Nana smirked
as she saw Queenie reprimanding Clifford. Queenie spat on the pavement when Nana gazed in her direction. It was clear the women detested one another.

As Nana held onto the doorknob of her house, she smoothed herself
over again. She pushed her sunglasses back over her hair. Nana sighed as
she brushed her shoes against the small prickly welcome mat, which read
"Wel" since the last four letters had faded. The hanging glass drapes
made a delightful sound, after she slid the key into the front door and

the wind caressed its way into the house, almost urging her cinematic entry. The wind was always referred to as a manly wind, especially the southeaster, to those who believed it lifts women's dresses over their heads and kept men alert. Nana's presence, especially her step, did have a musicality to it, and she stepped up her rhythm as the wind blew her into the house.

Her mother had the tea tray ready: stacked with selected biscuits. The three o'clock story on the radio had just finished and Grandma Naidoo was calling out, "Oooh, jai, jai, jai." Nana looked at the small radio on the kitchen table, paused, observed the tea tray momentarily, and then began to call out, "Sunny boy. Where's my Sunny boy?" No one answered. Nana cooed like a little bird and waited for a response. Grandma Naidoo's eyes were cast downwards and she spoke to Nana as though her daughter had noticed her and she was in conversation with her.

"I wish the weather would decide what it's doing. This is not weather, this . . . this is just the clouds playing with us, making us wait, and they can't seem to make up their minds. Where is the wind when you need him."

Her mother was a round woman with long hair, which she twisted, taking separate pieces as she piled them, intertwined them, much like a doughnut, on top of her head. She wore an embroidered apron over a black dress, and had worn black dresses for more than ten years now. Her husband's death had taken her by surprise. She still mourned his death and spoke of him on a daily basis to anyone who was willing to listen.

Nana walked right past her mother and into the backyard.

"How's my Sunny boy? How's Mummy's little baby boy?" Nana called out again. A small yellow budgie peeked out from beneath the stacked wood and flew into Nana's open-palmed right hand. "Come to Mummy. There's Mummy's boy. Yes, Mummy's little baby." The little bird lifted its head and placed its peak close to her mouth. She kissed him in the palm of her hand, a small yellow bundle, then placed her left hand in the pocket of her dress and fed him small little treats. "There's Mummy's little baby." The little bird nestled his head among the tidbits that were left for him in the palm of Nana's hand. Nana caressed him, stroked him gently whilst she hummed. "Okay, darling, okay, my love, off you go. Mummy will come now-now." She lifted him in order for him to take off then blew him a kiss. "Mummy's babyyyy," she cooed as she spoke. Nana grabbed a wet cloth from the washing line in the backyard and proceeded to dust herself. As Nana entered the kitchen and swung around, her mother suddenly jerked back.

"What is this?" she asked with surprise.

"It's flowers, as you can see," the daughter replied with a condescending tone.

"But who is it from?" her mother asked, accentuating her interest as her voice reached a higher peak.

"No one's business," Nana replied, shaking her head slowly and cautiously.

Grandma Naidoo was beside herself. Her eyes surveyed each and every one of the flowers. She kept her annoyance to herself.

"It's beauuuuuutiful. Shall I get a vase?" the older woman asked.

"No. Sit down and have your tea. They are my flowers and I will get the vase. Your story on the radio is done, isn't it? Don't you have anything else to do?"

Nana swung herself around the chair, her hips slightly challenged by the enormous effort she had placed on them. Grandma Naidoo was standing in the passageway, looking for a card or perhaps some sign which might reveal the name of the sender; but none was visible to her unspectacled eyes. Grandma Naidoo's eyes surveyed her entire memory bank, and as her eyeballs darted to and fro searching through her recollections she suddenly smirked rather smugly, then sucked the air through her teeth.

"Gmm, gmm, gmm," she uttered, the defiant snarl coming from the depth of her nostrils.

She wiped her hands on her apron and bent down at the kitchen cabinet to reach for her bread mixture. She placed the metal bowl, which was covered with a plastic bag in order to draw moisture, on the table. She reached for her glass jar of flour and stuck her hand in it and took from it a rather large handful, which she sprinkled on the table. Grandma Naidoo separated the pieces of dough swiftly. She tackled each one of them individually, still pondering whom the flowers might be from as she punched, stretched and kneaded thoughts of her dismissive daughter into the dough. She often spoke to her husband as she cooked and baked bread. Her daughter simply ignored her or shrugged her shoulders. She moved momentarily to collect her cup of tea from where Nana had moved it. She lifted it then looked at it. It was now cold. "Ssss," she exclaimed through her teeth, as her palate detected the difference to its earlier taste. She gulped it down anyway then moved very quickly towards the bread tin where she broke off a piece of crust and thrust the chewable wheat to where the tea had left its unsavoury mark.

Louisa sat in her chair with a white towel placed over her shoulders. She wore a yellow dress she had sewn herself. It was plain and not very stylish, but she liked the way she looked in it. She combed her hair, the towel catching dandruff and loose dead hairs; the brush was still in her hand as she stared in the mirror. She adopted this habit after her first hospitalization some twenty years ago now: everything she used on her body had to be white and clean and if they were not, she would bleach them until they achieved a whiteness she was satisfied with. Her room was small and compact and the bookcase, which filled most of the room, conveyed several areas of interest. The bottom section housed her wooden box wherein she kept her report cards; the whereabouts of the key were unknown. She stacked the report cards in the order of the years of her primary and secondary school education. Right beside the wooden box, she kept a white plastic container of all the armbands she wore for hospital. Small mementos were placed in this white plastic container, which also included prescription and several cards, which her school friends had sent her whilst she was hospitalized. On the shelf, second from the bottom, were stacks of papers which bore her writing and wrapped around them was a white ribbon and a neat, flattened bow. She had written various short stories whilst in hospital, none of which Nana or her grandmother knew anything of, and she read them to herself on days when she felt well enough to do so. To the left of this shelf, she had a stack of romantic Mills and Boons paperbacks, and many of them contained pieces of paper and bits of cloth from various events, which she used as bookmarks or memory sites.

Her room was immaculately clean and tidy and for every item she

had a place. She had photographs of her sister and brother on the wall
in glass frames, and these too were dusted every day. She hung the silver
chain Christina had given her around her photograph and placed Billy's
school medal for long distance running on her dressing table. On the
wall opposite to her family photographs she kept one of herself, seated
at the piano, with Mr Petersen, her former piano teacher. Mr Petersen
only visited occasionally now since he did not feel comfortable in Nana's
company. On the small bedside table to her left she kept a Bible, a small
dictionary placed on top of it and a small glass filled with water right
beside both books. All of her tablets were kept in her dressing table
drawer.

Her dark mahogany wardrobe was heavy and bore a mirror in its
centre; she would often sit facing it, and would converse with whomso-
ever appeared in it. When she closed the door and moved the robe
which hung behind it, she would stare at the photograph of her Aunt
Eva. Eva died a year before her grandfather. It is said that Eva walked
into the sea, and that she was kept as the mistress of the man she worked
for. Louisa remembered visiting her aunt when she was much younger
and had vague memories of Grandma Naidoo taking her Aunt Eva food
and clothes.

To District Sixers, Eva worked in service, that is, she worked as a
domestic servant and lived on the premises of her employer. It was said
that Eva was both his paid subordinate and his mistress. Louisa did not
speak of her aunt, and when engaged on the matter by her grandmother, she would venture an opinion but only slightly for fear that her
grandmother would cry. Nana forbade both her mother and her daughter to mention her sister's name in their house. Many in District Six
speculated on how Eva came to her madness. Many said it was a slow
insanity since she was kept inside the man's house for years and did not
go out into the streets; she did not accompany him to visit his friends or
family. Louisa sat on her bed, and pushed her door until it shut. She
then proceeded to speak with her aunt, who replied and told Louisa her
side of the story.

Louisa was fragile and pale most of the time. Her lips were dry and
her skin looked as though it needed the sun. Louisa's back was hunched
over and she kept all of her limbs close to her body, all crunched up as

though she preferred for her body to resemble a ball. She stuck her tongue out and looked at the colour of it in the mirror. She did this routinely, several times a day, diagnosing through the colour reflected in the mirror, whether she was well or not so well. Nana peered into the room.

"When are you going to stop using that towel. Use another piece of cloth. My God, when I was your age . . ." She stopped, but only for a second since another comment was already departing from her mouth. "You can try to look better you know . . . stop using that towel to comb your hair . . . and in the name of God, that yellow dress makes you look paler and sicker than you are . . . if that's possible." The latter she uttered beneath her breath. "Do you have to dress in the same colour as your pills . . . oh, why do I bother."

Louisa's mother's words were uttered with great rapidity and agitation.

Louisa, aged thirty-four years, stared at her mother in the mirror. She sat facing it and most times exchanges between mother and daughter would take place in this manner; not flesh to flesh. Nana looked as though she was going to open her mouth to say something, when Louisa prevented her from doing so.

"I don't want to. I like this towel." Her words were coarse and her manner cold. "Nothing in this house is clean. Everything is so dirty. I wash this towel every day because nothing that you wash is ever clean."

Nana had already left the room, after Louisa's first sentence. Grandma Naidoo called out, knocked, then entered her granddaughter's room upon her reply. Nana walked into her daughter's room without looking at her mother.

"Have you taken your pills?"

There was silence. Louisa did not answer her mother. Louisa's grandmother was standing behind her mother and gesturing towards her daughter.

"Leave her! Leave her!" she motioned silently with her hands. Mother and grandmother proceeded to the kitchen. "She is just responding to your difficulty," the older woman asserted.

"I know," Nana said.

"So stop provoking her," the older woman warned.

"I'm not provoking her. I just want to make sure that she's taken her pills," her daughter replied with agitation.

"She knows that you're checking on her and she's going to provoke you," the older woman responded sternly.

Louisa had her tongue out again. She thrust it out several times and moved it about, curved it, then examined its different shapes. Her face was mobile and she scrunched her nose as she lifted her tongue to examine it from underneath. She lifted herself from her chair and walked into the kitchen. Her face was stern and her body stiff. She looked about the kitchen and sniffed it.

"It smells like a funeral in here. Who died?" No one answered. "Oh, it can't be you. You're still alive." She looked scathingly at her mother. "It must be that bloody bird. He better be quiet." She turned around and observed the flowers, which Nana had placed in a vase. "So, you bought yourself flowers from my mad money. Nice hey!" Her mother did not respond. "What else did you buy? Stockings for those skinny legs so that you can go whoring again? Snacks for that little bird? He's your man, hey. All your other men don't give you money. You go whoring but they still don't give you money. You have no money. Nice, hey, living off your mad daughter."

Her grandmother closed her eyes, opened them then shut them again. She rubbed her eyes as though she was erasing the present. She shook her head and indicated to Louisa to stop the antagonism with her mother. Nana continued to arrange the flowers as though she had not heard a thing. She placed the tulips right at the front of the bunch and smoothed them out a little.

"Why do I bother to come back into this house," Nana said, still looking at the flowers. "It's not my fault that you are in this state. I'm going to speak to the doctor next time," she said sighing without looking at her daughter.

"Which next time? You hardly go and see the doctor, you only go and collect my money. Since when can you be around mad people? There aren't enough men to look at you." Her mother kept a safe distance from her. "Ha, ha," she laughed aloud, her vulgar outburst intent on bruising her mother's ego. "Yes, they drool, but only because they are loony, not because they fancy you. Imagine that! Huh!"

Louisa was standing behind her mother. Nana had still not turned around.

"Aren't you tired of the same old argument? Be original for a change," she replied, in a slow tone, her eyebrows and eyelashes still not moving as she busied herself in the kitchen.

"Original! Why don't you be original? I mean, Joan Crawford would laugh if she took one look at you," Louisa said as walked over to the stove.

Nana turned around and raised her eyebrows at her daughter.

"Oh, don't worry about what I'm doing. I'm only getting hot water. It's what us mad people do, you know, when our mouths are dry after talking to evil people like you."

Nana sighed again as Louisa proceeded to speak without looking at her mother. Grandma Naidoo fussed over her granddaughter.

"What about some tea, Louisa. Lemme make you some tea and the two of us sit in the backyard, hey . . . how about that?"

"No, I don't want any tea. I just want hot water."

The little budgie was crying out over Louisa's words. Nana left her chores to attend to him.

"This is not how Sunny usually calls. He is upset and I wonder why . . . mmm, some people just know how to make a scene."

Louisa just looked at her mother. "That bloody bird of yours better not come near me. I have hot water in my hand and you know . . . us mad people do strange things . . . not like the strange things you do . . . like sitting on men's laps to get attention. And where is Mr Petersen now? . . . Huh, where is he now? Too embarrassed to come near you even though you threw your legs at him."

Nana turned to her mother.

"Can you see? Can you see? . . . She's starting again . . . she's starting again. No, but I am the one who's to blame here and she gets to rule this house and my life."

Grandma Naidoo took Louisa by the arm and led her into her room. "Why don't we go for a walk to the park up on DeWaal drive, get some fresh air, huh, Louisa?"

Louisa looked about the room. She tidied as she spoke, most of the time, even when she was alone. She looked at herself in the mirror and smiled. She pushed her lips over the edge of her teeth and stuck out her tongue as though she was inspecting herself, much like a dentist would. Grandma Naidoo helped her granddaughter straighten out her room and collected the towels from the clothes hook behind her door.

"Go and shake these out in the backyard, Bokkie. Come on, the sooner we get out of here the better."

Louisa complied with her grandmother's wishes. She walked into the backyard and observed her mother in close, intimate, conversation with her little yellow bundle.

"Don't shake that out here! Go into the toilet. Those hairs will get stuck in Sunny's throat! Go into the toilet and shake your hairs and dandruff out there!"

Louisa opened her mouth wide and let out a scream so loud that Nana staggered. She screamed louder and louder until she was breathless. Nana placed both her hands over her ears.

"Oh, here we go again. The screaming routine is back now." Grandma Naidoo came rushing towards her granddaughter, and looked fiercely at Nana.

"Why don't you take the bird inside instead of telling Louisa to go into the toilet. Be reasonable." Nana was holding Sunny close to her bosom.

"Yes, take her side. Spoil her. Make sure that she disobeys me . . . that is what you want to do, isn't it?"

"Nana, I have no time for your nonsense."

Grandma Naidoo turned and walked into her bedroom, her chest heaving, as her granddaughter got ready. She conversed with her husband for a moment asking him for his guidance. Then she turned to face her daughter and she announced her decision.

"Louisa and I are going for a walk now," she said.

"Oh, you are going for a walk," Nana replied. "So you are her mother now, huh, you are giving her orders now? She can't go outside, not the way she looks. People will make fun of her . . . have you thought of that?"

"Will you keep your voice down?" her mother insisted.

Louisa was now getting ready and seemed determined to leave the house with her grandmother. Mother and daughter were locked in a look of anger. Grandma Naidoo sucked in the air right through her teeth and rolled her eyes in contempt. Nana simply held onto her bird and glared at her mother.

"That is why Billy and Christina left. You have no way of speaking to your children."

Nana shrugged her shoulders. She seemed unperturbed by her mother's comment.

"Children leave all the time. I am not a mother hen. If they want to live with their father with the peppercorn hair, then who am I to stop them? They can stay there in those small little towns in the Eastern Cape and live their lives with backward people."

"The only one who is backward is you," her mother replied. "Many of our people come from the Eastern Cape and there's nothing wrong with living in a small town."

"Yes, Gandhi, you would say that," Nana replied with a smirk. Grandma Naidoo made a fist, slammed it on the kitchen table, and then turned her back. She had struck her daughter once before, only to regret it the very next day. Nana looked at her mother up and down in disapproval. "That is why my Eva could never stay in this house," she uttered under her breath. Nana walked up to her mother and stood a few centimeters from her mother's face and stared at her fiercely, condescendingly, then whispered, "She was a nutcase. Just like that one inside. She's better off in the sea. That is where mad people go."

She turned around, walked away from her mother and whipped her buttocks into a mocking waddle. The older woman went into her bedroom and sat down on her bed. She held her face in her hands and felt the warmth of her anger reach her cheeks. Her breathing was heavy, and as she grew more and more aware of her husband's presence in the room, she let her hair down. He was there, watching her, and she delighted in his presence. She did not offer him a seat for he hovered about like he usually did when he returned from work. She brushed her hair, then oiled it slightly. She looked at the mirror and the small black and white photograph of her husband as he stood beside her. The photograph was covered with her prints, which seemed to cluster around her husband's mouth. She exchanged a few words with him and he stroked her hair and whispered in her ear. Grandma Naidoo smiled. Her posture had changed completely. She was now perky and she walked about her room with a smile on her face.

"I'm ready, Grandma," Louisa said in a soft voice.

The older woman sighed as she observed her granddaughter's outfit. She was not going to instruct Louisa on what to wear. Louisa still wore her yellow dress and had added a yellow crocheted long-sleeved cardigan to her outfit. She knotted the scarf to her head as her grandmother stood and waited for her to be ready.

In a moment, quite unlike her, Grandma Naidoo walked back into her room and shut her door. She called out to Louisa, "Gimme a few minutes. I'll be out soon." Louisa was stunned when her grandmother finally made her appearance. Grandma Naidoo wore a dark maroon sari, her husband's favourite, and had adorned herself with a maroon bindi, placed in the centre of her forehead. She wore no jewelry and little makeup, just a little lipstick she had not worn in years. She fingered the colour on her lips. It was dry and brittle, so she added a little vaseline to moisten it a little. Her lips stuck together. She went to her chest of drawers and got a piece of toilet paper, which she used to dab her lips.

Louisa stared at her grandmother with tears in her eyes. She bit her lip and did not say a word to her grandmother. Nana came from the kitchen and stood behind the dangling glass between the kitchen and the dining room. Her mother looked back at her.

"Oh, and what do we have here? Is it carnival time already?" Her mother did not reply. "So you've decided to get out of your mourning clothes. How nice. What a wonderful change of scenery. An old woman in District Six wearing a sari and showing her flesh." Her mother kept her eyes fixed on her granddaughter and did not utter a word. "I suppose that you expect me to be here when you get back, hey? You have no problem taking her out like that?" Her mother just looked at her and shook her head. Louisa did not look at Nana as she turned the handle of the door.

Grandmother and granddaughter walked arm in arm up DeVilliers Street. It was Rosa who came running to them when a beach ball bounced in front of Grandma Naidoo.

"Afternoon, Grandma Naidoo . . . Afternoon, Lulu," Rosa said in greeting. The young child looked at Grandma Naidoo and squinted, and then looked towards Louisa for an explanation. "Nita and I playing dodge ball with Ludwi. He gone now cos he afraid of Lulu," she said, breathlessly. Nita came running towards them too. She greeted the two women in a formal manner and also looked at Grandma Naidoo's sari. "Lulu, you look nice. Can Nita and me come wit Grandma Naidoo and Lulu?" Grandma Naidoo looked towards Louisa.

"Yes, it's okay, Mamma. I like Rosa. Nita's okay. She doan say much." Louisa knelt down to speak to Rosa.

"You have to go and ask Mamma Zila, hey, Rosa," Louisa said slowly.

The young child jumped for joy. "Ja, I go now-now to ask Mamma Zila and Nita's Mummy leave Nita wit us so Mamma Zila have to say yes for Nita as well."

"Does Rosa still have those winter hands, Nita?" the older woman asked as a means of generating some conversation.

"I don't know, Mrs Naidoo," the young child replied.

Louisa moved closer to her grandmother and whispered in her ear. "She speaks as though she's not from here. She never knows anything. She doesn't talk much."

Rosa was back and bouncing about.

"Ja, Grandma Naidoo, Nita and I can go." Rosa jumped up and down as she delivered Mamma Zila's verdict.

"I see you went to fetch your little book, hey? Oh, and that pretty little string, did Mamma Zila make that?"

"Yes, Grandma Naidoo, Mamma Zila make it with crochet. I orways take my book for writing all my tings," the young child replied as she placed the book about her neck. Her pencil had been sharpened, the rough edges showing evidence that it had been sharpened with a blade. Grandma Naidoo inspected the pencil and smiled. "No one is s'pose to see my book, Grandma Naidoo . . . is for all my private tings."

"Oh, Bokkie, I was just looking at your pencil. It's nice that you have your own private writing. Come on, let's go now."

Grandma Naidoo took Rosa's hand and asked Rosa to take Nita's.

"Can I hold Lulu's hand, Grandma Naidoo?" she asked.

"Yes, come over here," replied Louisa. The two girls moved places and rearranged themselves in order to take the walk up DeVilliers Street and then up Roland Street to the park.

"Rosa, have your hands started again?" Grandma Naidoo asked.

"Just a little bit, Grandma Naidoo, not a lot."

"Can you bend it, Rosa?" Grandma Naidoo asked.

"Yes, Grandma Naidoo . . . is not stiff no more."

Louisa clasped Rosa's hand and looked at her grandmother. She nodded to confirm the child's words.

"Rosa, what does Mamma Zila say about the weather? Is Mamma Zila feeling anything in her knee these days?"

"Mamma Zila say is going to rain tonight, Grandma Naidoo." The child did not hesitate to report on her grandmother's weather predictions based on the sensation the woman felt in her left knee.

"We always get a little bit of rain after Easter. It's meant to wash all the chocolate away in your tummy."

Grandma Naidoo looked at both the girls. Nita actually chuckled and Rosa was beside herself with laughter. When Rosa laughed, her arms, her legs, her fingers, every part of her body laughed. Grandma Naidoo smiled as she observed the child's joy.

"Grandma Naidoo, why Grandma Naidoo wear dat dress like der Indian ladies?" Rosa asked as she stood and inspected the woman's clothes.

Grandma Naidoo looked at Louisa, who was now standing and looking at her grandmother, for she too waited for a reply.

"I am Indian, my dear . . . and this is a sari. It's been a while since I've worn my sari. This is my heritage. It is what I am supposed to wear and what I enjoy. After my husband died, my dear, I did not wear my sari, and now, today, I feel I want to wear it again."

Rosa nodded and looked up at Louisa. Louisa looked at her grandmother and nodded; her face was calm and her gestures slow.

As they walked up DeVilliers Street, Grandma Naidoo greeted her neighbours; it appeared as though many more of them were now leaving their homes to witness the return of the sari. Some of the women still had their spoons in their hands since they were making supper, others had children hanging at their breasts, but a glimpse they wanted, and a glimpse they got. On these occasions Louisa often appeared shy; Grandma Naidoo was calm and walked as though she owned the street. Their neighbours greeted them with care and affection, not once commenting on Grandma

Naidoo's sari—although their eyes did all the talking.

Grandma Naidoo was always impressed by how well Louisa was treated by her neighbours. Ludwi stood on the balcony, covered in feathers from the chickens Motchie Tiema kept and watched as Auntie Flowers stopped to speak to Louisa and Grandma Naidoo.

"Oi! Coo-ee! Naidoo! Good to see you back wit der sari hey!" Motchie Tiema shouted. Motchie Tiema chuckled and waved at Grandma Naidoo and Louisa. Ludwi still looked from the distance but only half-heartedly. "Hey, Boetajie, you keep der hens on dat side, hey."

Motchie Tiema shared the long balcony with her sister, who lived beside her. The cocks and hens were separated for convenience and also as per their family arrangement. Ludwi looked down every so often and when his eyes strayed for too long, Motchie Tiema would whack him over the head with her feather duster. Many on Sackville Street called Ludwi "Eina," the Afrikaans expression for "ouch," since it was a word he used with such regularity, as he covered his head to prevent the blows handed out by Motchie Tiema.

Auntie Flowers smiled and Louisa stood with her grandmother and both waited for the woman to join them.

Auntie Flowers extended her hand to Grandma Naidoo. "You're back," she said. The two women smiled. Auntie Flowers and Grandma Naidoo held hands. Auntie Flowers looked at Grandma Naidoo and nodded. Auntie Flowers then shifted her attention to Louisa. "Nice to see you out, Louisa. You should come and visit. Mrs Hood and I were saying the other day that you'll be having your birthday soon and that we should have a little afternoon birthday party for you." Auntie Flowers was stroking Louisa's arm as she spoke.

"Thank you, Auntie Flowers. Yes, my birthday is next week," she replied, shrugging her shoulders shyly but taking great pleasure in her conversation with Auntie Flowers.

"Well, we'll have to get started then." Auntie Flowers looked at Grandma Naidoo and winked at her. This was suggestive of her willingness to arrange social events for Louisa despite Nana's assertion that Louisa stay indoors at all times. Auntie Flowers had opposed Nana on several occasions and Louisa saw Auntie Flowers as an aunt, someone in District Six who stood up for her. Auntie Flowers was also one of the few people who refused to comment on Nana's beauty.

Grandma Naidoo was smiling and looked pleased. She whispered a thank you to Auntie Flowers.

"Hey Louisa, I might even invite Clifford. He still holds a little flame for you."

Louisa was now embarrassed and hung her head. She giggled in a childlike manner and held her hand in front of her mouth. It was at moments like these when her age was hidden. She giggled much like a teenager would when confronted with remarks on how a young man took a fancy to her. Auntie Flowers moved towards Grandma Naidoo and said softly, "You look fantastic, my dear. It's not just the sari but your face. You look happy in the sari. I am so glad for you. How's your sweetheart today?"

"Thank you, Flowers. Oh, on days like today I have to ask him to give me strength. May he rest in peace. Flowers, Nana is impossible, you know. What did I ever do to deserve the treatment she dishes out?" Grandma Naidoo sighed.

"Anything you want to talk to me about?" Auntie Flowers asked. Grandma Naidoo shook her head. "No, Flowers, just Nana being difficult, you know. Her father must be so disappointed. He gives me strength. He always gives me strength." Grandma Naidoo took a deep breath.

"He was always your heart, wasn't he, your sweetheart? Zila and I always sit down and remember Alfie. Alfie was really a wonderful man."

"Yes, Flowers," Grandma Naidoo replied. Auntie Flowers stroked Grandma Naidoo's shoulder then bade the whole party farewell. "Oh, that smell of poultry . . . oh, I should have known Shaeffer's poultry would smell like this on such a day. The wind has picked up again. And the sea, what does Peter say about the men in the dockyard?"

"Oh, Bokkie, your Alfie would have known right away. I hear the sea is not so good today. She's a little angry, and you know what that means . . . not a good day for us women. So, Bokkie, watch your step as you take that corner to the park . . . you'll be standing right under the mountain . . . and you know, the old girl must be very cross herself too. Just look at that table top."

The two women held onto each other and laughed. Auntie Flowers was of course speaking of Table Mountain, and gestured towards it as though its presence warranted inclusion. Just then they heard the siren from Ospavat and the girls joined in. Grandma Naidoo glanced over at Louisa and shook her head with a smile on her face. The two women observed Rosa's every move and took great delight in watching the young child enjoy every activity, especially one where she sounded like a siren herself. Rosa was clearly trying to sound her siren louder than Nita's.

"The workers will be having their afternoon tea now. Come on, move it you two. I want to get to that park. I brought my crochet and I want to finish my tablecloth today. Come on, Rosa, why don't you race Nita whilst we watch."

It was an invitation Grandma Naidoo made knowing full well that Rosa would not turn down the opportunity. As they took the corner of Roeland Street, the wind hit hard against their faces.

"Oh, I forgot about this corner," Louisa commented.

"Yes, hold onto me, dear."

Grandma Naidoo was silent for a while.

Louisa looked about and stood still, staring at the cars which drove by in both directions.

"How long am I going to have to take pills, Grandma?" she asked. Her grandmother appeared struck by the question. "How long more, Grandma?" she asked again.

"I don't know, Louisa. Your mother seems to think that you need the pills all the time. She said that the doctor wants you to stay on the pills because that is how things are. You know, I try to interfere as little as possible. We all know what happened with Billy and Christina, and I don't want to interfere again. I so much want to go and see them, but I can't leave you here with your mother. Billy and Christina won't come here. You know, your own uncles, your mother's own brothers, won't come near the house. Oh, the trouble that Nana has caused. Your uncles both feel that I should leave and go and live with them . . . but I can't do that. I can't leave District Six. Your Pappa Alfie wasn't from here, he came here to work in the dockyard, but my family . . . oh, we go way back . . . I can never leave all of this."

Grandma Naidoo swooped her hands together, as if gathering

District Six in her hands. She looked up towards the mountain, then glanced adoringly at her granddaughter. Louisa cast her eyes ahead of her. The trees were swaying in the wind and the clouds were racing. Louisa looked ahead to see whether Rosa and Nita were safely on the pavement.

"But I want Grandma to come with me to the doctor. I don't think that Mummy tells the doctor everything," Louisa said almost pleadingly.

Her grandmother looked concerned and bit her lip.

"We'll see, child. We'll see."

Louisa held onto her grandmother tightly. Little boys on the opposite side of the road were throwing stones at Rosa and Nita. The young child did not hesitate to retaliate.

"Rosa, cut it out! The stones are not even coming close to you or Nita."

Grandma Naidoo tilted her head sternly as she spoke to the two girls. They skipped and hopped and kept their backs to the road, preventing them from witnessing the boy's planned actions. Grandma Naidoo called out at the boys, who then scurried off into one of the streets which led off Roeland Street.

"You know, I feel a little dizzy," Grandma Naidoo said.

"Did Mummy make the tea?"

"No, I made my own tea."

"Every time Mummy make Grandma tea then you feel faint."

"Don't be silly now. That is exactly the kind of comment your mother would make. Don't make your heart hard against her. Even if she has bad thoughts, don't you do the same." Louisa nodded then hooked her arm into her grandmother's again.

As they entered the park, Grandma Naidoo found herself a nice bench close to the merry-go-round. Louisa settled herself on the grass, close to her grandmother's feet. Grandma Naidoo was wearing her spectacles, and each time Rosa tried doing something acrobatic or what Grandma Naidoo considered to be dangerous, she peered over her spectacles at the child and gave her a fierce look. Louisa seemed entertained each time Rosa called out to her and asked her to watch what she was doing. Nita was occupied in similar activities but did not call out to either Louisa or

Grandma Naidoo.

Louisa patted her grandmother's leg to indicate that a visitor was approaching. Mr Martin crossed the park with his walking stick and waved at the children on the merry-go-round. He wore khaki trousers and a blue fisherman's jersey. His hat had a peak in the front and a stud, which kept its firmness down. It almost matched the colour of his trousers. His outfit made the older man look sporty even with his walking stick swinging between his eager footsteps.

"Oh, this man must be standing and watching from his window."

"Oh, Grandma, don't be like that. He's nice."

Mr Martin walked towards the bench and took his hat off.

"Afternoon ladies," he said. "Mmm, mmm, mmm, don't we look beautiful today?" he said, looking adoringly at Grandma Naidoo.

"Afternoon, Mr Martin." Grandma Naidoo kept her greeting formal.

"I was just saying to Zhara, I have to come and say hello. I have not seen you in your Indian dress in years."

Grandma Naidoo kept her eyes fixed on her crochet as Mr Martin spoke.

"It's not an Indian dress, it's a sari."

"Hello, Bokkie," Mr Martin said, as he bent down to touch Louisa's hand.

Louisa held her hand out to the man. And as expected, he paused, looked at both her hands and said, "Beeeaaautiful! Just beautiful. I like a lady with nice hands."

She giggled and held her hand over her mouth. Her body was still hunched over as she sat on the grass.

"May I join you ladies?" Mr Martin asked.

"Yes, you may," Grandma Naidoo replied. She did not move her crochet bag or the tablecloth, which clung to her crochet hook. Louisa seemed determined for Mr Martin to join them. She moved the bag of crochet wool and placed it on her grandmother's lap. The wind had nestled up at her grandmother's feet, lifting the colourful garment somewhat, and Louisa noticed that her grandmother had also changed her shoes, to accompany the sari. Mr Martin sat down and exhaled as though he had been waiting to do so for quite a while.

"This is real fisherman's weather," he said.

"Mmm," Grandma Naidoo replied, not quite as enthusiastic as he.

"On days like today, when der sea is so deurmekaa . . . a bit rough, hey . . . is good for der snoek."

"Mmm," was Grandma Naidoo's reply.

"Lulu . . . Lulu . . . Louisa!" Rosa called out.

Both Rosa and Nita were now standing on a mound in the park and wanted Louisa to catch them as they rolled down it.

"Those girls have to be careful, Louisa!" her grandmother called out. "Rosa gets out of hand, you know, so you better watch her closely." Louisa looked at her grandmother and sighed.

"Sorry, I know you can handle her. She just gets too much for me sometimes."

Nita was rolling away and chuckled as she reached the bottom. Rosa did not wait for her to stand up but rolled down the sloped grass patch soon after and landed almost on top of her. The two girls laughed joyously. Grandma Naidoo still looked over her spectacles at them.

Nita jumped up to return to the top of the mound and Rosa jumped into Louisa's lap

"Lulu, you get the flowers dat Cliffie give you?"

"What flowers?"

"Cliffie give flowers to your mummy to give to you. Remember I say you last week dat Cliffie is going to give you flowers."

"Are you making this up, Rosa?"

"No, is true. I saw Cliffie give der flowers to your mummy."

"When?"

"Dis afternoon when your mummy come back from Hanover Street."

"Did Cliffie tell you this, Rosa?"

"Ja. I told you orso last week, remember? Cliffie ask for me to watch when your mummy come back. Cliffie den give your mummy der flowers for you. On Saturday, last week, Cliffie gimme a letter and den your mummy see der letter in my hand and your mummy ask me . . . 'What's in your hand Rosa?'" Rosa imitated Nana to Louisa. Louisa chuckled. "Den your Mummy want to take it and I say is a paper from Mamma Zila and I run home."

"Where's the letter now?"

"I doan know."

"Rosa!"

"Is true. I put it in my book . . . but is not here now no more. Look!"

Rosa demonstrated to Louisa where she had placed the letter. "I think der letter fell out, Lulu. But you know, I hear Mamma Zila telling Auntie Flowers about your letter from Cliffie. Maybe Mamma Zila have der letter. Mamma Zila orways give you your stuff, huh, Louisa?"

Nita came down the mound again and came to stand beside Rosa. She put her arm about Rosa's neck. Her pose seemed to bother Louisa, who sneered at the child as though she was being precocious.

"Okay, Rosa, go and play with Nita."

Louisa looked over at her grandmother, who was now chuckling.

Rosa bent down, poised her head curiously beside Louisa and said, "What Mr Martin say, Lulu?" Louisa kept her gaze fixed on her grandmother.

"I bet Mr Martin is telling fisherman stories," she said to Rosa.

Rosa giggled. "Is Mister Martin saying der story about Van Riebeeck and der ships . . . and when der Portugeeze came to der Cape . . . or . . . or der udder story when der English people came . . . Mamma Zila say is not true what Mr Henson say cos Table Mountain discovered der people," she said all at once as Louisa looked on.

"Mamma Zila teaches you a lot, huh, Rosa?"

"Ja, when I tell Mamma Zila what Mister Henson say at school. . . and Mamma Zila say what is tru and what is not tru."

Louisa smiled and nodded at the young child. She patted Rosa on her shoulders.

"Okay, off you go."

Rosa then ran across the park to join her friend back on the mound.

Grandma Naidoo waved at Louisa and gestured for her to join them. Mr Martin urged her to do so too.

"Lulu, we're going to der slide . . . Lulu," Rosa called out.

"Yes, okay!" she said, waving at them with both her hands. Louisa pulled at her fingers one by one, waiting until each one cracked before she moved onto the next one. She held her ear close to her fingers and jerked each time she heard the crack. Grandma Naidoo nodded at the children and watched Louisa closely. She positioned herself in the bench to face the children on the far side of the park. Mr Martin brushed her leg with his hand so that she could have more room as she adjusted her body. Grandma Naidoo merely stared at him over her spectacles. Louisa came walking towards her grandmother.

"Hey, Louisa, I see Cliffie earlier with flowers standing on the corner. He's still trying hard, hey . . . still trying after all these years."

Grandma Naidoo took her spectacles off and looked at Louisa. Then she gave Mr Martin a stern look.

"Don't talk about things you don't know, hey? What do you know about any flowers?"

He threw his hands up in the air.

"Sorry, sorry, doan mean to offend anyborry. I saw Cliffie dis morning at der fish market. Saw my old pal there. Saw Flowers. She got some nice pieces of fish from Tuckie's friend. And den I turn around and I see Cliffie. Dis was after I got my snoek from my pal. I doan go down to der dockyard no more. So, dere was Cliffie talking to another chappie and he say he's buying flowers for Louisa."

Louisa was giggling but her grandmother had a stern, concerned look on her face. Mr Martin was at a loss as to what to say.

Grandma Naidoo scrunched her face. She folded the tablecloth, which hung onto the crochet hook, and put it in her crochet bag. She sighed a few times and folded her hands on her lap.

"So, no flowers den, Louisa?" he asked, despite the look he received from Grandma Naidoo.

"No, Mr Martin . . . I dirint get anything. Mummy always gets flowers. I dirint get anything."

"Well, why the boy tell me he's going to buy flowers for you? Gmmf!"

"Mr Martin, I think we've heard quite enough now. Thank you," Grandma Naidoo said, reverting back to her polite self.

"Get the girls, Louisa, its time to leave now." Grandma Naidoo seemed agitated.

Louisa walked across the park. She hunched over and hung her head. She looked at the grass and did not look up at the young girls.

"I dirint mean to offend anyone," Mr Martin said again.

"Oh, doan worry. I just wish you wouldn't say things like that in front of Louisa. You should have told me. She's so sensitive."

"I know Nana won't let Cliffie in the house . . ."

"Nana won't let anyone in the house for Louisa," Grandma Naidoo replied.

"But why?"

"Oh, it's complicated."

"And her other kids are gone too hey?"

"Yes. What can I say? Louisa is a nice girl. She's a woman. Nana has forgotten that she's a woman. I mean, I doan know about all dis mental business, but she look oright to me. I know dat all my girls, especially Zhara, my oldest, say dat Louisa used to be very clever before she got sick der first time many years ago."

"Yes. She was. But you know, we are not doctors and we doan know about this kind of illness."

"But she needs friends, udder people . . . I mean, der girl must get lonely sometimes. She needs udder people to visit and take her out."

"Ja. I am getting old," Grandma Naidoo added. "Nana is taking advantage of my age. I feel like I am letting Louisa down. I am getting old and I can't fight Nana no more."

"Nooo, you? You will never get old."

Grandma Naidoo paused for a moment. She did not speak but hung her head, slightly.

"Your other daughter, the one who died, now she was a good-looking woman . . . what a shame that was, hey."

Grandma Naidoo got up from the bench. "Okay, Mr Martin. Everyone's here now. We better leave now, it's getting late."

"I walk down wit you. Is dat oright?" he asked, almost expecting Grandma Naidoo to reject his request.

Louisa nodded. Grandma Naidoo looked at Louisa and smiled. There was no resistance from her. Rosa and Nita played with Mr Martin's hat. Rosa walked about performing a walk she had observed among local gangsters. Nita laughed as Rosa swung her arms and her hips.

"Rosa, come here you. So, you're a skollie now, hey? And walking like a little gangster even. Give that hat to Mr Martin this minute," Grandma Naidoo ordered as she sat down.

Rosa obeyed her order and took her time. Nita soon erased the look of spectator off her face.

"I still feel a little dizzy."

Mr Martin held out his hand to assist Grandma Naidoo. She did not take his. Louisa made sure that Rosa and Nita had no grass on their clothes. There were three boys standing near the slide and Rosa dashed towards them showing them her clenched fists.

"Come here, madam. You're not going anywhere and certainly will not be boxing anyone. I think Mamma Zila would want your little face back in one piece. Aai, aai, aai, Rosa. What is der matter with you?"

Rosa abandoned her little trip. She signaled to Nita with her eyes.

"No talking with the eyes. I am watching you, young lady." Grandma Naidoo gave both the girls her sternest look and threw her hands up in the air as she spoke.

Mr Martin smiled at Rosa and Nita. He gave each of them a sweet, which Grandma Naidoo took from them. She held both the sweets in her hand as she spoke.

"This is for after your supper. Little girls get far too many sweets. It makes them too active, and then they get hooked on other stuff."

Grandma Naidoo lowered her voice as she looked towards Louisa, who was some meters away.

"Go and walk with Louisa, Rosa. You too, Nita."

The two girls took off. Grandma Naidoo turned to Mr Martin.

"I just wonder whether you upset Louisa with this nonsense talk about Cliffie. I don't want her to be upset. She's very fragile. Her sister and her brother left for Port Elizabeth and there's no one for her to turn to," Grandma Naidoo said as she moved closer to Mr Martin's body.

"I tell you, Cliffie has always had feelings for Louisa," said Mr Martin.

"Yes, but you know what Nana is like."

"But Louisa's her own woman. I know Nana doan like me but . . . cos I not afraid of her and I doan compliment her. Never! I know she your daughter and all dat, but she gets too many tings in life because of her good looks. What about Louisa? She's a woman too."

"It's not that I don't think about Louisa. I can't anymore with Nana. Nana is almost fifity-five, you know . . . and me . . . you don't want to

know how old I am. My other children have also left because of Nana.
I can't even see my boys. They are all in Durban living their own lives
and they don't want to be around Nana." Grandma Naidoo held onto
her crochet bag tightly as she spoke.

"You still look as young as you did when you were twenty-one. Nana
may think that's she beautiful, but she's nothing compared to you."

Grandma Naidoo blushed slightly. She hit his hand, as though to
dismiss his compliment, which went straight to her heart.

Mr Martin stared at her long and hard. His eyes were focused on her
moistened maroon lips.

The two adults walked casually behind Louisa and the two little girls.

Grandma Naidoo looked about the street. Before Mr Martin knew
it, she had put her arm around his on the pretext that she was cold. He
smiled and held her arm closer to his body, going along with her. He too
gestured with his mouth, pulled the air into his mouth to give his body
more warmth, to suggest that he too was cold. He pulled his face in a
proud manner, as a peacock might, when befriended by a female who
had taken a fancy to him.

The cars were now bumper to bumper on Roeland Street; a few drivers
hooted. Mr Martin took full credit for all of the commotion, assuming
that those who hooted where envious of the company he kept. He had
a beautiful woman on his arm and he enjoyed every stare which drove
on four wheels. Grandma Naidoo even allowed strands of her hair to
blow in her face without attempting to push them back into the bun she
piled on top of her head. It was Mr Martin who stroked her hair up, as
he gave his eyes the benefit of a full and closer glance at her attire; she
closed her eyes each time he did. Mr Martin was about to take his leave
when a flock of birds descended over Louisa and the two younger children. There were several of them, all dark and gray, and they were squab-
bling, protesting their lack of food. There might have been forty or fifty
of them, and Mr Martin ran towards them, shooing them away. Two of
them flew towards him, causing Mr Martin to move back swiftly into
the wall. He shouted obscenities at them, and the flock, followed by
their two brave leaders, left in a flurry. The two young girls laughed for
the birds were all over them and did not offend them at all. Rosa held

her hands out at them and crouched. She emptied her pockets, and as little bits of bread and nuts soon found their way to the paved ground, Nita followed on and she too emptied her pockets. Mr Martin gasped and rubbed his head, using his hat to shoo them away. Louisa seemed unperturbed by it all. She grinned as Rosa and Nita ran after the birds, pretending that they could fly.

"We're fine from here," Grandma Naidoo said, without once looking at him. She held her hand to her mouth and looked towards the mountain, considering the direction the birds had flown. Mr Martin appeared to be tense and he breathed heavily a few times, as he braced himself for their departure. Louisa and the young children seemed oblivious to his anxiety.

"Okay," Mr Martin said as he tried to catch Grandma Naidoo's eye. "Bye, Louisa! Bye, Rosa! Bye, Nita!"

All of them waved at Mr Martin, the two younger girls holding Louisa's hand.

Mr Martin looked longingly at Grandma Naidoo.

"I'll go with you to the doctor at the free dispensary. This dizziness doan sound good to me. You jus let me know when you want to go."

"Thanks for the walk," Grandma Naidoo said hastily.

"Always my pleasure," he said, a generous smile on his face.

Grandma Naidoo turned her back and called out to the young children and her granddaughter.

"Wait up!"

Mr Martin lowered his head, tilting it to his right side. He, like many District Six men, always ended conversations by gazing upon the beauty of the women whose company he kept. She looked beautiful even from afar, he thought. He put his hat back on his head and walked briskly with his walking stick, leaning eagerly against the wind.

As they walked along DeVilliers Street, the Ospavat siren rang and the men, who had queued at the front gate, came rushing out.

"Just stand still. Don't move!" Grandma Naidoo ordered.

Mamma Zila was waving. She also gestured at them to stay where they were, away from the factory exit. Mamma Zila crossed the road to meet the group. Louisa and the girls were leaning against the wall and Grandma Naidoo stood close to them.

"Naidoo, you look smashing. I am so glad." Mamma Zila threw her hands in the air as she spoke. "I am glad it's all over. It would be nice to see you looking like this more often. Alfie was a wonderful man and he would want for you to be happy."

Grandma Naidoo grinned and nodded as Mamma Zila spoke. Mamma Zila then turned her attention to Louisa.

"I hear Cliffie sent you flowers, hey?"

Louisa looked at her grandmother.

"Where did you hear this, Zila?" Grandma Naidoo asked casually to ensure that Louisa remained at ease.

"Flowers told me. She said Cliffie was at the market and she helped him pick out a whole set of different ones. . . didn't he take it to you?"

Louisa was heaving. Her grandmother now put her arm over her shoulders.

"No, I dirint get any flowers, Mamma Zila."

"That's strange. Cliffie is a man of his word. I should think that he would have brought it over."

"Can we drop this now, Zila? I will look into it," Grandma Naidoo quickly added. Mamma Zila frowned. "We saw Flowers earlier and she didn't say anything."

Mamma Zila exchanged a few words with Grandma Naidoo as Louisa looked about.

Louisa walked away, suddenly, jerking her body. Her neck looked taut, as though she was about to have a nervous attack again. Her grandmother called after her but she did not look back.

Rosa and Nita followed her and Grandma Naidoo held her breath, but was soon relieved when Louisa paused and waited for the young girls. She took Rosa and Nita's hand and safely crossed the street.

"Nana up to her tricks again?" Mamma Zila asked.

Grandma Naidoo did not reply.

"You know, when Flowers and I brought that woman and her sister to Louisa last year, the woman who reads the cards, and her sister who reads the leaves, they both said that there's nothing wrong with Louisa. Nana is the problem. She gallivants all over the place with a different man every weekend and is besotted with that little bird of hers yet she begrudges her daughter a little bit of affection." Grandma Naidoo looked attentively at Mamma Zila as she spoke.

"I go and see you and Louisa; I'm not fooled by Miss Joan Crawford. Cliffie and Louisa are the ones who are suffering."

Grandma Naidoo did not say a word. She lowered her head and tapped her foot rhythmically on the paved ground as Mamma Zila spoke, as though she was tuned into something else.

"Naidoo, what's happened to you? You're okay when Nana isn't home . . . has she been up to her tricks again today?"

"I started to feel dizzy again in the afternoon . . . and I still have this headache . . .I know that Louisa thinks that Nana gets up to funny business . . . I don't know, Zila."

"Did you drink the rooibos tea with buju that Flowers left for you?"

"Yes I did. I had some of it this afternoon. Anyway, Zila, I better be off. I don't know if Nana made anything for supper."

"You can always come here. Always. I make do with the little I have but there's always a pot on the stove. I'll come over tomorrow. That daughter of yours doan fool me." Mamma Zila pulled a face then gathered her arms behind her back. The two women parted—one with raised eyebrows, the other with lowered expectations. Rosa and Nita were engaged in telling their friends of the birds, and exaggerating their number. Grandma Naidoo smiled, and as her smile subsided a worried look stole over her face again.

When Grandma Naidoo entered her house, mother and daughter were at it again.

Nana immediately turned to her mother. "You put ideas in her head about Cliffie? You're just like everyone here in the Six . . . don't mind your own business."

"Good evening to you too," her mother replied.

"Flowers? What flowers? All I get when I have been making food to feed the two of you is flowers . . . something about flowers."

Nana looked at her daughter. "You are not well. It's been twenty years and I would have thought that you would have gotten it into your head now. Nothing . . . is . . . going . . . to change." Her words were meant to leave an imprint on her listeners as she pointed to her head and hammered her words into her own skull.

Grandma Naidoo walked past her daughter into the kitchen. The flowers, which Nana had placed in a vase earlier in the afternoon, were still there—beautiful and speechless.

She filled the small black pot with water and placed it on the stove.

"I made supper," her daughter said. "I may be glamorous but I'm not useless." She pushed her hair back with her small finger.

Louisa was in her room dusting and cleaning. She remained in her clothes and talked to herself as she rearranged her bookshelf. She hastened towards the mirror again and stuck her tongue out several times. On each occasion she stared at it, almost expecting something to emerge from it. She flapped it around, curled it, straightened it out, made sure she looked at it as it reached the roof of her mouth, and then sat down and looked about her room. She took her books off their shelves, dusted them with a cloth, and then put them back. She touched the books with her fingertips but there was no dust visible. She used the same cloth to wipe the mirror. She straightened the rug on the floor and started cleaning her shoes, which were neatly stacked under her bed.

When the water boiled it was Nana who took it off the stove. Nana started making tea. Nana busied herself with taking out crockery and laying placemats on the table. She reached for the sugar bowl and prepared her mother's tea. She stirred it as she usually did, and whilst she was busying herself with getting something from her purse, Louisa crept up right behind her and called out, "Huh!" She was frightened and right off her feet. Cupped inside Nana's left hand was a yellowish bundle. As she lost her balance, her daughter hit her hand, and the contents of her hand flew out and rolled on the vinyl floor. Nana's whole body shook.

"What were you doing with my tablets?" Louisa screamed at her mother, her eyes larger than usual.

Nana stared at Louisa, who was now on the kitchen floor, trying to find her pills. She bent down and looked under the furniture as she counted. "Three . . . four . . . five . . . how many more that I can't see hey?" Nana stood there bewildered and afraid.

"You were going to put my tablets in Grandma's tea! All of it or just a little at a time? You evil witch!"

"I was doing no such thing. I was just counting them."

Her daughter moved towards her and grabbed the collar of her dress.

Her button came undone and one of them dropped to the floor.

"Mummy . . . Mummy!" the older woman cried out. Grandma Naidoo was lying down. She did not move at all.

"Let go of me! . . . You bloody psycho," Nana screamed, as she tried to rid herself from Louisa's grip.

Louisa still held on. She had both her hands on her mother's throat.

"Er . . . er . . . er," she exclaimed, and then gasped for air.

There was quite a struggle between mother and daughter. Nana was quite ruffled and her dress was pulled over her shoulders, as though she was about to be picked up by the collar of her dress.

"Twenty-rand notes in your bra, hey? You evil witch! Give them to me!"

Louisa did not relax her grip on Nana. She simply grabbed the notes, which were now sticking out of her mother's bosom. Nana's hands were not strong enough to compete with Louisa's. Louisa held the money in her hand and threw it on the table. Nana slackened her grip and Louisa tightened hers.

"So that's where you keep my money . . . witch! Witch!" Nana could hardly breathe. She held on and her arms slackened.

Grandma Naidoo was beside her daughter a few seconds later looking at the crumpled twenty-rand notes on the table. She looked at Louisa, then back at Nana. Nana's face was turned and her neck bent, as she struggled fiercely against the strength of her daughter. Grandma Naidoo did not call out or ask Louisa to let go of her mother. She simply stood beside Louisa without uttering a word. Sunny was now calling out too. Grandma Naidoo's eyes met those of her daughter. Nana's eyes were now rolling in her head, which was bending more and more to her right, as though it was about to snap. Her arms hung at her side and were becoming slacker. Grandma Naidoo looked at Louisa without uttering a word. Louisa loosened her grip and her mother fell to the floor.

"Mad people are strong, hey," she exclaimed, then held her head towards the ceiling and laughed mockingly at her mother. "You look like a real movie star," she said.

Nana did not look up at her daughter. "Er . . . ee . . .ee," she whimpered, and then took a deep breath.

Grandma Naidoo did not move to assist her daughter. Nana now lay breathless and almost lifeless on the floor, which was littered with the small yellow tablets.

Her daughter climbed over her and walked towards the backyard. Louisa was still dressed in her yellow outfit. She stood in the doorway of the backyard and observed her mother's little bird. She made a fist with her right hand, then held her thumb up, and moved it across her throat suggestively, as the bird watched. He was squeaking and Nana could not come to his aid.

Nana dragged herself slowly across the vinyl floor to her room. Her mother had still not taken her sari off and looked unperturbed by the present events. Grandma Naidoo stood there and watched her daughter as she tried to get herself into bed. Grandma Naidoo could not stand to be in the same room as her daughter and slowly, casually exited. She walked into the kitchen and collected the bunch of keys that lay on the floor beside the kitchen cabinet. Bending was difficult for the woman, but she performed it almost effortlessly now. She walked towards Louisa and held the keys in full view so that her granddaughter could see that she had taken possession of them.

She dangled them as she spoke. "I'm going to go to Mamma Zila to eat supper there. Wash your hands and face and join me, Louisa."

Her granddaughter nodded in agreement.

Sunny was still whimpering. He wanted to be held but his crying was not audible to Nana. Louisa walked towards him and he flew under a pile of wood to hide from her. She climbed over the logs and lay on top of them, her yellowness calling out to his. He did not make a sound. She continued to lie there, and minutes later she was cooing at him. The little bird may have been attracted to her colour, and for the first time he fluttered his wings and emerged from hiding. Louisa was still lying among the logs, her face turned up and her arms beside her body; her hands were open, palms facing up, and her legs were crossed. Sunny flew closer and closer to her. In a moment, Louisa caught him. She held him tightly in her hand as he squealed and fussed. She moved around and climbed over the wood until she could walk with greater ease. She held the little yellow bird in her right hand with only his head showing. The kitchen table had not been cleared of the utensils her mother used for making supper. Nana's favourite kitchen knife, known as a kitchen devil, was lying in full view. Louisa took hold of the kitchen devil by its black handle, observing that it still had remnants of tomato on it. She lifted the knife to smell it and inhaled the full aroma of onions. She pulled a face, then she cleaned it methodically, swiping it back and across the wooden block until there were no remains of onions or tomato. She held it in the sun and inspected it. She found a small speck of tomato on the knife and she swiped it back and across again, as if to sharpen it, until it was squeaky clean. Sunny's head was still moving about despite the tight grip within which he was held. In a swift and silent move she slit his throat. The little creature did not cry out. He stared at her . . . just stared at her . . . as the knife moved across his tiny yellow throat and he poised his peak as though he knew his assassin's

intentions. His tiny eyes did not narrow as he gazed into her larger ones. She held the knife close to her, not high against the backdrop of the blue sky still visible in the backyard, as she had many times imagined she would. She turned her wrist a few times; turned the knife to catch his reflection in it and even made a little trail of sunlight walk against the cool and shadowed wall at her side.

Sunny's head now rested on the counter, limp and severed from the rest of his tiny-feathered body. Louisa had no blood on her hands, none at all. She turned her head a few times, from side to side, as if she was asking herself something deep and personal. She placed the knife on the wooden block in the backyard and glanced at the blood on its edge. Louisa tilted Sunny's head up and down. Sunny would never chirp again. Her forefinger now had blood on it. She held it up to the sun, then moved towards the wall, where she made several marks with her finger. She walked over the logs of wood and looked over her shoulder to see if he was still where she had placed him, beside the knife on the wooden block. There was now a trail of death to where he had sat and chirped and sometimes hid. Louisa pushed the blocks of wood away to find the one at the bottom, where she left another bloody print. She had now touched and stained with blood almost every piece of chopped wood that he would sit on. She motioned her hand to resemble his shape and made his sound as he lay there lifeless on his back with his neck gaping open and with his eyes fixed on her. For a moment she stopped, almost convinced that she heard him, and then mimicked him again, and again, until her own sound convinced her that she had finally copied his chirp—and for once, he had to bear witness to her call.

She went to the outside toilet and pulled on the cut squares of newspapers hanging from the wire, which her mother had placed there. Of course, her grandmother had real toilet paper in her chest of drawers, which she hid from Nana, and Nana likewise. Louisa held the piece of newspaper in her hand and dabbed blood on it. She looked closely at the photograph of Ian Smith and the caption, which read, "Ian Smith facing rebels in Rhodesia." She rid herself of the small spot of remaining blood on her forefinger by smearing it on his printed face. She then scrunched the piece of newspaper, flattened it with her palms, and placed it neatly in the rubbish bin. There was a knock on the door.

"Come in, come in," she called out, confidant and assured that her grandmother would not have locked the door.

The doorknob turned and small footsteps sounded. It was Rosa.

"Lulu, I bring you der letter. You see, I found der letter. I put it under my pillow wit my book. Der letter fell down der side of der bed, at der back. So, I look dere orso and I found der letter under der bed. You see. I doan tell lies." Rosa handed Louisa the letter. "Mamma Zila and Grandma Naidoo are waiting for you to come eat, Lulu."

Louisa read the letter and smiled. Rosa stood by, her eyes begging for information. Louisa sat on the floor as she read the letter. Rosa huddled up close to her.

"Are you coming, Lulu?"

"Yes, I am coming," she replied. "I have a nice white dress, and if you wait with me, I'll go and change and go with you." Rosa looked at her and did not say a word. "After supper, I am going to visit Cliffie, Rosa. And you know what, nobody is going to stop me."

Rosa nodded and followed her friend into her bedroom.

Ai, Gadija

In 1970 the early May weather brought bursts of rain and thick, full, cumulus clouds, which hovered before sinking deep into the bosom of District Six. Many young toddlers stayed indoors in the afternoon with their grandparents. The homemade toys would be dragged from underneath beds. Pots were filled with water and fish heads then placed on the stove, and cut onions would follow, after watery eyes were dried, and would simmer in the spiced and flavoured currents created by the stirring of a wooden spoon, and bay leaves, peppercorns and allspice would swim warmly and gaily.

Pumpkin fritters were fried on days like this and with the smell of fishsoup, rain, grass and cinnamon, the streets of District Six brought together food flavours with the natural elements of the weather. The smell was mesmerizing. Between rainy periods the sun would pierce through the clouds, and when it did, in bright, lingering moments, it sought out the food smells and flavoured the paved grounds upon which residents walked, scurried and jostled. The smokiness lifted itself mysteriously from the gray paved ground whilst the water rushed along its gutters, destined for the underground drains. It was a day when toddlers walked barefoot and dragged themselves through the rain-filled gutters despite the stares from the evil lady—everyone had one on their street, or so they believed. That warm swashing sensation and the thrill of rainwater running over their feet was what District Six children enjoyed most. On days like this monkeys got married, according to District Sixers. When it rained in May with the sun visible in the sky, the colours of the rainbow would appear like celestial exhalations; they would shower District Six with little drops of magic that you could only taste on your tongue at the very moment when monkeys exchanged their vows and locked their hands together in earthly matrimony.

Gadija arrived home, placed all her parcels on the kitchen table and ran towards her room to collect her towel. She towel-dried her hair as she walked about the house and looked at her wristwatch momentarily. She kicked off her wet shoes and left them on the small mat where the kitchen met the backyard. Her stockings were wet too and she took them off, one at a time, and hung them on a chair in the kitchen near the wood-burning stove. Gadija had a couple of hours to do her university work, prepare dinner, cook it whilst she read and did last-minute touches to her essay, then leave for Belleville. The stove was low on wood, still the small smouldering remains of the morning; as was customary of homes in District Six, stoves received their rejuvenation in the afternoon, when supper was made and evening warmth was needed. She lifted a few logs from the wooden crate on the floor and placed them on the fire. She watched the small flame merge with the wood and smiled as the wood took to it. Gadija sighed as she looked into the refrigerator, her body still bent in the direction of the small light that glowed from it, as she tried to determine the extent of her cooking tasks. Her mother had left the ingredients for vegetable soup on the middle shelf, and a small joint of mutton leg lay close by, wrapped in the plain white paper she recognized from the local butcher. She filled the big soup pot with water then placed the leg of mutton in it. She absently hummed a tune, and walked about the kitchen collecting bay leaves, peppercorns, allspice and cloves from various glass jars stacked in small overflowing cupboards, then cut potatoes, carrots and celery, and put them all in the pot on the stove. She filled the kettle with water, placed it on the stove, and stood beside it to absorb some of its warmth. She rubbed her hands together and stroked her damp clothes as she moved closer to the stove, hoping that they would dry. She was caught quite unawares when the kettle suddenly whistled interrupting her thoughts. She scooped the tea leaves out of the usual tin with the wooden spoon that was placed inside it and made a pot of spiced rooibos tea; the ginger, cardamom pods and cinnamon sticks she took from the refrigerator, each in their own glass jar. She poured the tea, scooping pieces of fresh ginger and cinnamon sticks into her cup, and inhaled the overwhelming aroma.

Gadija looked about the house then took the teacup into her bedroom, cupping it with both her hands and sipping it. She was studying part-time at the University of the Western Cape in Belleville, otherwise known as Bush, hence the pile of books on the floor beside her mother's bed, which were stacked there almost permanently now. On Wednesdays her mother, Gafsa Ebrahim, known to her children as Oemie and to those in the neighbourhood as Motchie Gafsa, would collect the twin girls, Amina and Mymoena, aged eight years, from school and take them to the community hall for ballet. Gadija worked at Stuttafords, a large department store on Adderley Street in the center of town, and had every Wednesday afternoon off; she worked a half hour extra every morning to make up her expected working time. Wednesday afternoons she had entirely to her self. It was on these afternoons off that she did most of her studying and preparation for her weekly psychology class, which was the last she needed for her Bachelor of Arts degree.

Gadija was dressed in a stylish two-piece suit, the latest 1970 model. The black skirt lay soft against her body and its length just passed her knee. The jacket was short cropped against her hips, and its shape gave her body a delicate yet sophisticated look. Her long thick black hair, straightened with an ironing comb, hung in a glossy cascade down her back. She would cover it with a headscarf when she was in public, as was customary for respectable Muslim women. Gadija had thick eyebrows, a full mouth, painted with a dark maroon lipstick, and was considered by most to have the shapeliest legs in District Six. She wore black stockings to work and would take them off, both legs at once, and throw the elastic garters in the air as soon as they were released from her legs, which was, usually, the minute she walked through the door of her home.

Gadija walked about the room, sipping her tea. Her mother's bed, the lower one on the bunk as it were, looked tempting. She proceeded to lie on it after she first picking up a photograph of her husband, who had been serving time on Robben Island since 1964 for conspiring to overthrow the government. She gazed at the picture. It had been six years and her visits with him had been so brief that she could hardly remember what they had spoken of. She would return home, write in her diary, and then rewrite it the following day, each time correcting her first retelling of their most recent meeting. Her thoughts drifted. Finally she gathered herself together and got off the bed. She walked into the kitchen, the smell of the soup was calling out; she stirred it and added two cups of water.

Back in her room, she held the moistness of the broth to her nose and mouth, inhaling the aroma of her supper. She looked about the room at the pile of books awaiting her, then opened them to where they were last marked. Several pencils were used as bookmarks, and a piece of paper with writing on it lay stiff between the pages of one book. She noted that the sender was Ganief, one of the men in her study group. She scrunched it up and threw it in the bin behind the door.

Gadija paced up and down the compact room, caressing her fingers then cracking her knuckles. On the wall were family photographs. The two double bunk beds in the room and took up quite a lot of space. She occupied the top of one, beside the window, whilst her mother occupied the lower bed. Her two daughters, Amina and Mymoena, shared the other one. The room also boasted a big wardrobe, a chest of drawers, several boxes under the beds, shoes grouped in pairs, and a small table with two chairs. Gadija would sit there and study as often as time and duty permitted, and that was where her daughters did their homework each afternoon under the supervision of their grandmother.

Her mother, Gafsa Ebrahim, worked as a cook in a crèche, which closed at three o'clock in the afternoon, and her sister Galiema, the quiet and softspoken one, worked as a secretary at Chapel Street primary school. Gairo, the youngest, and considered the most manly of all Motchie Gafsa's children, worked at a printing press. Gadija's brother Rashied was regarded as the middle child since he was younger than Galiema and older than Gairo; he worked in a clothing factory close to the center of town. Galiema and Gairo shared the second bedroom and their brother slept on a mattress in the dining room; it was folded and stored under their mother's bed each morning. Their father, Gatiep, had died five years earlier from cancer, which had developed in his legs and feet due to the strain of working in the sea, at the dockyard, with little protection.

Gadija kept a photograph of her husband on the small table in the corner of the room and would hold it in her hand as she studied. During the early years of Abdul's imprisonment she would burst into tears when his name was mentioned. As time passed she grew accustomed to his absence and her girls stopped asking after their father.

Now, age twenty-nine, she had two children and an absent husband. She had met Abdul during her last year of high school, at Herald Cressy, and the year after their first meeting they were married. Abdul was her first love, and although he was considered far too possessive by most of her friends, Gadija, who had not enjoyed the pleasure of another man's company in an intimate way, simply tolerated his jealous fits because she admired him so. Abdul was a community leader, a man of strong convictions, and a man who knew how to be in the world, although many would say that he did not know how to be with her. She would observe other couples, note the intimate way in which they spoke to one another, and wonder why her relationship with Abdul seemed so matter of fact. After six years of visiting him, he had become more physical with her and urged a response from her that she could not quite provide because it had not been nurtured or nourished, but elicited through the need to sustain his manly lust. Gadija felt desired, for the first time, through barbed wire and plexiglass, more than the days when they had made love daily to fulfil their marital contract. On her initial visits, he would exhale his lust, its dampness still visible on the glass window when she left. The cleaner, who stared at her when she was not looking and walked about with his eyes cast down each time she entered, would then polish the windows to a luster.

Gadija lit a jasmine incense stick, as was common in most Muslim homes, and placed it in its holder on top of the window sill. She stretched her legs under the table and tackled the readings from the standard psychology textbook designed for third-year university students. The section was on sexuality. The readings were quite demanding and the case studies they were meant to read, study and discuss always left her wondering, a little more than other times, what her life would have been like if she had enjoyed some of the practises these cases studies cited, let alone discussed these readings on sexuality with her husband. Abdul had an answer for everything, she thought, as she glanced through the section's

contents and sighed. She brushed the neckline of her suit, caressing herself not out of boredom but out of necessity, and felt the jumpiness of her
own skin responding. She continued her reading, with little thought to
her own experiences, even though the readings demanded some self-
reflection and for her written responses to include her own experience.
She was meant to share these in a small group. She took out a sheet of
paper that bore the names of those in her small group and smiled when
she considered how they might respond to these questions. There was
Sarah, outspoken and outrageous, who wore the most eccentric clothes;
Shaheeda, her closest friend, who lived a few streets from her on Drury
Lane and who was thoughtful and cautious in every aspect of her life;
Irefaan, gregarious and daring, who worked at a children's home and
befriended every man and woman on the campus, and Ganief, the quiet
one, a high-school teacher by training and Muslim-school teacher in his
spare time, whom she had known practically all her life. Gadija had
attended primary school and high school with Ganief; they had been
close friends during adolescence and knew each other well enough to chat
casually and intimately if and when circumstances permitted. They
were as close as any Muslim girl and boy could be; he would walk her to
her gate, but never enter the house. He would be welcome only if and
when he made his intentions clear and when he was over the age of eighteen or, better still, over the age of twenty-one. Motchie Gafsa knew
Ganief by sight and would wave at him as she stood in the window waiting for Gadija to return from school. When Gadija met Abdul, he forbade her friendship with Ganief. Gadija did not protest her fiancé's decision and Ganief resented the fact that she went along with every demand
Abdul made. Her male friends always referred to her as Abdul's wife.
Ganief, on the other hand, did not even mention Abdul's name. She
often found herself thinking of Ganief in ways which made her blush.

Gadija moved about in her chair, inhaled the incense for quite some
time, and then went into the kitchen to pour another cup of tea. The
soup was doing nicely, she thought, and she replaced the lid on the pot
and moved it to the back of the stove to simmer. She also stoked the fire,
rearranging the wood before she shut the front door of the stove, ensuring that it would burn lightly and sparingly and that the soup would be
ready when her mother and daughters returned home.

Rain has a way of reminding you of what you have and what you don't;
of what you yearn for and what you are simply too afraid to demand of
yourself, let alone of others. When it rains, it pours, as many say of Cape
Town. People from the Eastern Cape say Cape Town is like a baby, it's
either wet or it has wind. And perhaps it is like a baby: demanding, joy-
ful and indulgent in the pleasures of the body, the pleasures of food, the
pleasures of singing and cajolling, which many say people do not cele-
brate in other parts of the country as they do in Cape Town. Cape Town
is a city of sea, mountain, wind and sun; the pleasures of eating, drinking and conversing are certainly celebrated in District Six as though there
is no tomorrow. Sayings like "Tomorrow never comes" is always on the
tip of the tongues of those who indulge in pleasures. Many would argue
that District Six represents six pleasures: eating, drinking, dancing,
cavorting, talking and rebelling—and that these are always accompanied
by music.

Gadija's jalopie, her old second-hand red mini, rattled constantly but it
took her where she wanted to go. The rain was streaming down the
front window, the wipers kept the windows clear with every stroke. The
three friends were now rather quiet as they drove home from university,
following their heated discussion in the seminar room. Ganief came to
sit beside Gadija after she dropped Shaheeda off. As Ganief took the
front seat, Shaheeda, who was walking towards the already opened front
door of her house, looked over her shoulder and grinned. Shaheeda's
mother greeted her, then waved at Gadija and Ganief as they took off.
They were now alone and Ganief looked at her without any concern for
her eyes catching his gaze.
    "I'm always amazed at how you do this, Gadija."
    "What do you mean?" she asked, looking at him rather sternly.
    "The full-time work . . . the children . . . your studies."
    "I have some help, Ganief."
    "But still, you have so much to do."
    "I have my mother, my sisters, and my brother."
    "I know. But you still have to do it yourself and keep everything
together," he said as he moved closer towards her in his seat.

"It's what mothers do, Ganief," she said.

"It's what you do. It is what you've done." He looked at her long and hard, positioning himself for his next attempt at conversation.

"I know what you're going to say but I'm going to ask you anyway Gadija."

"Go onnnnn," she replied, dragging her words.

"Come with me to the cinema," he said softly, as a lover might, once intimacy had been established.

"You know I can't," was her casual reply.

"I know your reasons, but what about you? Is it really doing you any good staying indoors all the time?" He had now resumed his normal tone of voice.

"I just cannot bring myself to go out," Gadija said, looking almost indifferent.

Once the words were uttered her eyes matched the glazed look she wore when she was alone with Ganief; a look she cultivated and one whose intention Ganief was not entirely convinced of. He stared at her eyes, smiling to himself since she pretended that she was unaware of his warm and loving gaze.

"When are you going to think of yourself?" Ganief asked, lifting his head and moving his right hand towards her hair.

"I am thinking of myself," was the reply offered.

"Are you trying to tell me that you would not enjoy my company outside this car, or outside our one class a week together?"

"I'm not saying that."

"Well, what are you saying?" he demanded.

"Oh, you know," she said, touching her face and stroking her hair.

"Know what?"

"Oh, so now you're testing your interviewing skills?"

She looked towards him as he narrowed his eyes.

"No? Your interrogation skills then?" she asked as he started to pout.

"No, come on, tell me?" he asked again.

"People will talk . . . you know," she drawled, weary at the mere thought of having to respond to gossip.

"People talk all the time," he replied, coiling her hair around his forefinger.

"Well, you know what I mean. I don't want people getting word to Abdul that I am going out in the evening . . . and with a man."

"So, you have noticed then," he said, pushing his chest out. He twirled her hair around his fingers, taking great pleasure in it for her scarf was not upon her head but loosely around her neck. He touched it, for its presence warranted some sort of comment. Muslim women who kept with tradition wore their scarves on their heads and did not display their shiny locks in public. If their scarves slipped off their heads they would hasten to adjust them in order to maintain their respectability.

Gadija had a vacant look on her face. Ganief remained silent. It was time for him to get out. The corner of Constitution and DeVilliers Street was always busy and she had to find a suitable place to stop since there were quite a few cars behind her. There were young men still selling fish on each corner most likely the remains of the last catch of the day. On all four corners and across the pavements, young boys, barefoot and with little plastic yellow jackets, were selling the evening newspaper.

"Argie! Argie! Argus! Read all about it! Read all about it!" echoed in the air as people scurried to get home.

Ganief got his books from the back seat, speaking to Gadija in close proximity.

"Tell me you have no feelings for me and I won't ask you again," he said, almost at her earlobe. Gadija jerked forward quite alarmed by the loudness of his voice and its content.

"I'm married," she replied, still moving her eyes about as though she had been hit and awaiting the next blow.

"Tell me you have no feelings for me," he said again.

"I'm married."

"So, this is the reason why you can't have feelings? Is it just an excuse for not answering my question or a standard response to everything in your life that you are too afraid to confront? Is it what you say to everyone when you are too afraid to ask yourself who you are and what you want? Is that a nice way of pushing morals into people's faces when you are too much of a coward to ask yourself what you want . . . so instead you say, 'I'm married,' like that is supposed to explain everything? Well, it doesn't."

Gadija held her breath and clenched her teeth. Ganief was sharp and she knew it; it is what she liked about him, and what she absolutely despised about him. Her mouth was open as she gazed at the wipers clearing the rain, beating down on her front window. She had her right hand on the wheel and her left hand on her head, her fingers touching her scalp through her thick hair. He continued and was clearly quite prepared for this moment. His stream of words gushed without a pause.

"Your husband has told you that you should get a divorce and you don't want to. You can't even touch him through that glass. Oh yes, don't look at me like that. I know all about it and you just don't want to know it. These things leak out. He knows there's nothing much to save, he's not the selfish one here. It is you who crave the pity from others and you who have turned yourself into a martyr because you don't know how to be yourself. You only know how to be a wife whose husband is on Robben Island. Be a martyr and see how far it gets you." Gadija's body was crying out and she breathed heavily in preparation for her response, but Ganief did not give her a chance. "I know that you and Abdul had major problems even before you were married. *Here ruh*, Gadija, you think I don't know? You were not so happily married, but suddenly you are because you don't have to be in the same room with him and can just play this role because that's all it is. You with your fancy ideas and all . . . after all the studying . . . all the philosophy . . . the psychology, what good has it done you but just made you see yourself as the community leader's wife. What liberation are you fighting for, hey, comrade?"

"Get out! Get out! Bastard!" She thrashed her legs about, putting the car in neutral with its hand brake up. Her blood was boiling. "I don't need this from you! I don't need this from anyone!"

She threw his things on the street and sat trembling. Several cars were honking, their passengers shouting atrocities at her for holding up traffic. Ganief stood with his left foot on the door whilst the rain poured down on him. Gadija was screaming and banging her hands on the steering wheel as he stopped to collect his belongings from the wet and busy street. He kept one foot in the door, not taking his eyes off her.

"If you, like all the men who try to bowl me over, just think you can push my buttons and use my husband's absence as your means . . . because you want to get into my panties . . ."

"Don't insult me, Gadija. If I want to get into a woman's panties I wouldn't have to beg or even go out of my way too much." He was now almost shouting since he was competing with the rain and the sound of the honking cars and their cursing drivers.

"Full of yourself, huh," she said, as she tried to push the door of the car against his foot; he had it firmly placed. He peered into the car again, to utter his final words.

"No, just telling you how it is. If that's what you think of me, then fine. I'll get out of your car, out of your group, find another ride to Bush, and I will go out of my way not to see you."

"Get out! Get out!" she shouted.

"Every time any grown woman sees you they say, 'Ai, Gadija.' Why? Because they feel sorry for you and they start to ask you about your husband on Robben Island and start to say how awful it must be for you to be without your husband." He was almost breathless now.

"Get out! Just get out!" she screamed.

"And you enjoy it!" He shook his head then bit his lip.

"Get out!" she shouted, her voice hysterical.

"Enjoy your life as a martyr. And thanks for the ride. Have a nice life. Well, why don't you go and . . . argh! No, you're not brave enough to do that. Being sexual with oneself requires a capacity for pleasure, as our discussion in class today revealed. But in your case, courage is the determining factor, and you . . . you have neither."

"You pig! You filthy pig!" she screamed. Ganieff was taken aback by the unutterable curse. A most savage look, like that of a desperate, cornered animal came over her. His eyes stared penetratingly at her and he slammed the door shut and shook his head.

Gadija placed her hand on her mouth, her eyes filled with apology, but the offensive word had already been uttered. He stood at the window, his palms open and his breath warm against it. "Its ten years today," he said, "ten years today when I first asked you to marry me . . . and now, now I am a pig, huh?"

He banged the window with his hands as he uttered the unspeakable word. Then he turned and walked towards his front door, tears streaming down his cheeks. The young boys selling newspapers on the corner called out to him. He shook his head to indicate that he was not interested in purchasing a newspaper. The youngest of the group called out at him, "Mister, Mister . . . " Ganief threw his hands up in the air in a dismissive manner. This infuriated the boy further. He muttered something offensive then turned his attention to other potential customers.

Gadija was shaking. She felt the warmth of tears melting down her cheeks. They ran down her throat and into her scarf and she had no way of stopping them. She looked back at Ganief and observed how he walked and composed himself. He was a good-looking man: he had a beautiful face with the clearest and softest dark skin framed by thick, black, curly hair, thick eyebrows and a full, curvaceous mouth which bore a neatly trimmed moustache. She looked at him for a few seconds as he turned the knob to his door and swallowed hard. She was furious as she pulled forward to the stop street, quite unaware of pedestrians.

A woman and a child were crossing and Gadija, in her haste, crossed the line behind which she was meant to stop. The woman, who was wearing a colourful scarf over a long plastic yellow raincoat with a hood, the kind worn by men at the dockyard, and the child looked at one another then at her. Gadija rolled the window down.

"Ai, Gadija," Mamma Zila said.

Gadija hastily wiped her face and pulled her scarf up to her forehead.

"Leikom, Bokkie," Mamma Zila added, in the customary Muslim greeting.

"Leikom Salaam," was Gadija's reply.

Mamma Zila held her head down.

"Hello, Rosa," Gadija greeted.

"Leikom, Auntie Gadija," the young child replied.

Mamma Zila tilted her head and bent down close to the window to speak to Gadija.

"Ooh, Bokkie. You better get home. That was quite a spectacle."

"I am sorry. I didn't realize that anyone could hear," Gadija said, still wiping her tears.

"Ai, Bokkie. We all hear what we want to, you know. I don't hear so well myself, but I heard that."

"Ai, what a disgrace."

"Oh, Bokkie. Come on. Don't be so hard on yourself. Life has its moments and men will be men. Besides, can you really expect Ganief to get on with his life when you are the most single married woman around? Come on, Bokkie. Think. It's hard for him."

Gadija was silent.

"You take care of yourself, Bokkie."

"Okay, Mamma Zila."

"Okay, Bokkie. Salaam. Krislaam to Motchie Gafsa, hey. Is she oright?" Mamma Zila asked, all at once.

"Yes, Mamma Zila. Oemie is doing fine."

Rosa tugged at her grandmother's dress. Mamma Zila bent down to attend to the child.

"Ai, Gadija. Rosa missed the dance class today. You know the children have a concert coming up in two weeks. Madam here missed the practice and Mr Jacobs taught new steps today. Can Rosa go home with you and have Amina and Mymoena show her the steps? I'll come and pick her up later.'"

"Ja, Mamma Zila. Come on, Rosa. In you get. The light is going to change."

Mamma Zila helped Rosa into the back of the car.

"Tramakasie, Bokkie."

"Okay, Mamma Zila."

She was furious, as she turned left on Constitution Street to go home. Her hands clutched the steering wheel quite strongly and she shook with anger as she banged her forehead onto her knuckled hands. She looked behind her and was convinced that Rosa was not paying attention to her at all. The young child was looking at the boys selling newspapers and clutched her little book in both her hands.

The rain was so heavy Gadija could barely see in front of her. The youngest little boy selling the *Argus* newspaper ran after her, calling out to her, and for a moment she thought she had hit him. She stopped, and in a second he was at her window banging at it furiously. Gadija moved her scarf and placed it firmly on her head.

"Motchie! Motchie!" he screamed as he banged on the window.

She sighed, wound the window down, and took some change from her purse and gave it to him; he handed her the newspaper through the small space she had left for their exchange. He cast his eyes on Rosa and the young child moved her head back.

"Can I keep der change, Motchie?"

Gadija simply nodded.

"Tell Ludwi . . ." he said, looking at Rosa, then made a fist and held it up against the window.

"Hey! I'll have none of that!" Gadija cried out.

The young boy chuckled merrily and began to call out again, attending to his next customer. Gadija drove off. She looked in the mirror and spoke to Rosa.

"Why is it that you are so often in trouble with these boys, hey, Rosa?"

The child did not answer.

"I'm speaking to you. Who is he?"

"He Moegsien, Auntie," she answered, looking out of the window, quite unperturbed by Gadija's irritation.

"Moegsien gave you a message to give to Ludwi, didn't he?"

"Auntie Gadija, is Uncle Ganief Auntie's boyfriend?"

Gadija gasped and looked at Rosa in the mirror. She momentarily lost control of the car. She swerved, then struggled with the gears since her foot could not quite coordinate her muddled intentions. She used the strength of her body to force the car into second gear and it jerked, reluctant to comply. In a moment, her car had stalled and she pushed hard on the brakes and tried to pull over to the side of the road. Luckily her house was within sight.

"Hasn't anyone told you that you shouldn't ask so many questions, Rosa?" she shouted, her voice loud at first then levelling off.

"No, Auntie," Rosa replied still looking out of the window.

"There are certain things that little children just should not ask adults about. You have to learn that. Some things are just not your business. Do you hear me?"

Rosa did not utter a word. The young child merely nodded her head in reply.

Gadija noticed her younger brother some distance away.

"Boytjie," she called out.

Rashied looked about the street. Her brother Rashied was twenty-one years old and was called Boytjie, the diminutive for "boy," ever since he was born. He was a handsome young man whose manner was pleas-

ant and polite yet firm when he needed to be.   Gadija stepped out of
the car, and glared at Rosa. The child was still clutching her book.

"What is in that book of yours, hey, Rosa?" Gadija asked.

"It's private, Auntie," the child replied.

"Guh," Gadija uttered, half in clearing her throat and half in shock
at what she perceived as the child's impudence. The child seemed oblivious to Gadija's irritation and hummed pleasantly to herself as she
scratched the palm of her hands.

"Cheeky," Gadija murmured to herself.

Gadija waved at her brother with her arm, whilst she held the newspaper to her head.   Rosa was still in the backseat and observed Gadija's
rattled state with great curiosity. Gadija wiped tears from her face as the
raindrops battered against her cheeks.

"Liekom," she called out, yelling her voice above the rain.

"Leikom Salaam, Tietie," he called out in response, using the
respectable term for the eldest girl in a Cape Malay family, as he held
unto his white crocheted fez and tried to cover his face. "What's der matter wit der car Tietie?" he asked, almost squinting.

"I don't know . . . it just stopped," she replied

"Get in der house, Tietie. Doan worry, I'll take care of it."

Gadija pointed to the backseat and Rashied's face lit up when he saw
Rosa. He took his jacket off and passed it to Rosa.   She knew immediately what was required and put it over her head, still holding onto her
book. Rashied simply picked her up then carried her into the house amid
exchanges of laughter.   He pulled faces at her, and she laughed aloud.

Gadija walked ahead and stormed into the house, greeting,
"Leikommmm!"

A joint greeting of "Leikom Salaam" followed. Her two daughters
and her mother made a circle around her, each of them greeting her.

Gadija wiped herself dry with the towel that was in her mother's outstretched hand as soon as she entered the house.   Her mother's eyes
were larger than life, as many said of Motchie Gafsa.   She was a round
and stout woman. Her hair was plaited and hung down her back, and
although only the tip of the plait could be seen since she wore a long
scarf that had a crocheted row at its edge, she made sure that her hair
along with the clothes she wore each day was spotlessly clean. Motchie

Gafsa undid her hair every evening and plaited it afresh every morning. She now scrutinized Gadija's appearance as her grandchildren held onto their mother. Gadija hugged her daughters whilst still holding the towel in her hands.

"Mummy, you're wet," Amina said, moving away from her.

"Yes, second time today. Go into the room. I'll be with you now-now."

"Natalie is here!" Mymoena called out.

"Oh, is that right?" Gadija looked towards her mother for an explanation. Motchie Gafsa rolled her eyes instead.

"Rosa is here too. Boeta is bringing her now."

Amina and Mymoena started to clap as their uncle, whom they called Boeta, entered the house with Rosa on his arm.

"Leikom," Rosa called out as Rashied put her down.

"Leikom, Rosa. Masha Allah, what a nice dress you have on, hey," Motchie Gafsa commented.

Motchie Gafsa grabbed the child and held her close, stroking her hair as she spoke. She dried Rosa with her scarf playfully. Rosa looked about the house, and her eyes soon fixed on the kitchen.

"Natalie is here, Rosa. I suppose you wan someting to eat, hey?" Motchie Gafsa said as she observed the child suddenly chewing her lips. Rosa simply nodded.

Amina and Mymoena looked at their grandmother. At her nod, they ran into the kitchen with Rosa, even though Motchie Gafsa had asked that they leave Natalie to eat her supper without their constant chatter. When mother and daughter were alone Motchie Gafsa filled Gadija in.

"The child came with Galiema. Gmf! The mother must be off to the dockyard again."

"Ja, Oemie. Not the Meisie story again. She does what she does and it's her business, not ours. She's our family, even if it's not on your side. No matter what she does Meisie is still our family. *Here ruh*, do I have to come home to this again?" Gadija sighed.

"Yes, take her side. Dat's right. Take her side, nuh," Motchie Gafsa remarked as she saw the look of irritation on Gadija's face.

Gadija shrugged her shoulders.

"And to think that I raised you all with Islam, hey," Motchie Gafsa muttered.

"Islam does not pay Meisie's bills, Oemie."

"It's geraam, I tell you. Geraam!" Motchie Gafsa raised her eyebrows and widened her eyes, as she always did when she spoke on matters which she regarded as sinful. Her mouth was drawn and she held her right hand close to her face and uttered several words in Malay and Arabic. Motchie Gafsa looked about the house and touched her scarf.

"Oemie, I hope you're not going to put a scarf on Natalie's head again. Meisie doesn't like it."

"What does Meisie know? The child doan even know her father."

Gadija sighed and walked to the bedroom. She put down her bags then sauntered about the dining room drying her hair. Motchie Gafsa mumbled to herself and looked fiercely at Gadija.

"Galiema! Galiema!" Motchie Gafsa called out.

Galiema emerged, a book in her hand, and greeted her older sister. She squinted and scrunched her nose then looked at her mother in search of an explanation as to Gadija's state; none was forthcoming.

"Rosa's here!" her mother called out. Her raised eyebrows and piercing stare indicated that an exchange of words would be forthcoming.

"Galiema, go and serve der child some soup wit bread, kanala."

Galiema crossed the dining room, looking back at both her mother and her older sister. Motchie Gafsa often spoke intimately with Galiema when Gadija was at work. Galiema was the one family member Motchie Gafsa relied on, for she was ready to perform any task requested of her without complaint. Rashied was still walking about the house sorting out his tapes and collecting various pieces of paper, which he had photocopied for the men in his singing group.

"What about der singing tonight? Der children need to practice der ballet steps," Motchie Gafsa said, looking about the dining room.

"I'll be in der back, Oemie. Tell der men to come straight to der back. Der girls can practice here or in Galiema and Gairo's room." He pointed to the room his sisters shared as he offered his suggestions. Motchie Gafsa nodded at her son and still kept one eye on Gadija.

"And what's der problem wit Gadija's car?" Motchie Gafsa asked.

"Is der spark plugs, Oemie. Is not a problem. I can do it tomorrow," was Rashied's casual reply.

Rashied walked towards the backyard where he had built a wooden cabin and took the electrical extension cord with him. He sang for the Ottoman's men's Muslim choir and was now organizing the small space he had available to practice, which was initially built so that he could have some privacy when studying the Koran and practising his singing. The choir had their annual competition during December and January, coinciding with the start of carnival time, and the men practiced throughout the year. They would often sing at weddings and other ceremonies such as baptisms and wore formal grey suits with white shirts accompanied by a navy blue tie and a red fez.

Galiema walked about the house attending to chores. Motchie Gafsa relied on Galiema to keep house when she returned from school, and the young woman did not complain. She regarded her older sister as the one who needed everyone's help in the house, and she took the time and trouble to care for her nieces in a degree many thought unusual for an aunt. All the young girls sat down at the table in the kitchen. Rosa's book was on the table beside her and she kept her eyes fixed on it. Galiema occasionally shook her head at Rosa, whom she was quite fond of, urging the child to stop slurping.

Motchie Gafsa now turned her attention to Gadija.

"What's der matter wit you?"

"Wet."

"No, I mean, what is der matter wit you?" Her mother placed her hands on her hips. Her face had a learned expression and she looked at her daughter as though she knew exactly what had happened, or so Gadija thought, as she shifted her gaze.

"I've had a rough day."

"Dat's not all."

"Oemie, can I just sit down and dry myself?"

"Okay, okay. You doan look oright to me. You look like you have man trouble."

"Ai, Oemie. Genoeg! Just leave it, hey?"

"Hmm, doan hide tings from me. I'm not blind. If I can see what der little children get up to at der crèche and I'm not in der same room den I can see what my own children get up to. You had an argument . . . ah-huh . . . wit a man."

"*Here ruh*, Oemie, I'm tired. I'm wet."

"What do you tink I was born yesterday? I'm not yesterday's child, Gadija. You have man problems. No woman looks like dat, right now, dat colour in your face, your eyes, your mout, everyting, if it isn't man problems they are hiding from."

"Oemie, just change the subject, kanala. Oemie's sounding like a stuck record now."

"Stuck record, gah, my foot. Watch your mout, meisiekind. You are at varsity but I am still der boss in dis house."

"Ja, ja, ja, Oemie. *Here ruh*, Oemie, just leave it now, kanala," she said again, as she looked towards the door.

The girls, accompanied by their second cousin Natalie and their friend Rosa, were in their aunts room and Motchie Gafsa could hear them laughing. Galiema had already attended to the dishes and the kitchen was now, as usual, spotlessly clean. Motchie Gafsa turned to the stove and gathered a few items that were hanging close to it—socks and jerseys mainly. She muttered to herself and gave Gadija, who had now followed her into the kitchen, one of her learned looks.

"*Here ruh*, Oemie, you have all those oil leaves on your head. They smell a mile and the handkerchief looks like it's had its day . . . when are you going to take it off?"

"Escuse me," Motchie Gafsa said, with her hands on her hips. "I doan wear dis for glamorous reasons. Der leaves help me. Wit der amount of nonsense I have to take from little children and my own children." She maneuvered the large folded white handkerchief containing the oil leaves on her forehead. Gadija looked about the kitchen and listened attentively to the sounds coming from her sister Galiema's room.

"Galiema must have put the tape on for the children," she said, as she pulled a face and waited for a response from her mother. Motchie Gafsa had moved toward the kitchen window and looked through it, shaking her head.

"Gairo is late. I wonder when dat child will learn. I hope she's not playing soccer in dis weather. Guh, I never have to worry about man problems wit dat one."

Motchie Gafsa was oblivious to the wave of sorrow that swept over Gadija. Gadija had her back to her mother. Motchie Gafsa turned around and looked at her daughter and touched her hair, then moved away, muttering to herself. Gadija whimpered a little. Motchie Gafsa gasped when Gadija turned around, her hands covering her tear-soaked face.   Her mother went to her side, and led her into the bedroom

Gadija fell on the bed and sobbed. Motchie Gafsa sat at the edge of the bed rubbing Gadija's feet. She had to close her eyes against her daughter's distress.

"Ai, Gadija. What's der matter, Bokkie?"

Gadija shook her head and sobbed into her pillow. Her mother spoke to her in a quiet, soothing voice as she massaged her feet.

"Oh, you know, before I met your boja, I met dis very nice outjie. My friends all liked him.   His brother jus dirin like me. Ai, you know in dose days people interfered in udder people's business all der time. His brother dirint wan us to get married and he even said my family was too low class for dem. Dat man hated me so much dat he followed me all over."   Motchie Gafsa's mouth stiffened.   She drew a deep breath. Her fingers fidgeted with her scarf.

Gadija sat upright as she observed her mother. Motchie Gafsa was breathing heavily. She drew breaths as though they were from a water-well buried deep inside her. Gadija sat upright and crossed her feet.

"Oemie, what happened?" she asked, as one might a young child who had been injured.

"Ai, Gadija.   You are the child and I am der mudder."

"Oemie, tell me what happened?" Gadija asked, her voice tender.

"*Here ruh*, Gadija, I have never toal any of my children dis.   Only your father knew about it."

"Oemie, what is it? Tell me."

"His broder, der man who hated me . . .   he . . . he took . . . advantage of me."

Gadija let go of the pillow and sat there gaping at her mother.   Her right hand moved towards her mother, but Motchie Gafsa soon withdrew from the place where she sat.   She moved to the table and chairs in the corner of the room. She kept her head down and held her back stiff and upright.   Motchie Gafsa lit an incense stick and took the pearly white tasbiem from the railing of her bed. She rubbed soothing words into each bead; the tasbiem, much likethe rosary, was used during prayer and confession.   She held onto the beads and whispered a prayer in Arabic.

The door swung open allowing the sounds of little patters of feet, laughter and giggles to be heard.

"Come and see der new steps we taught Rosa, Mummy," Amina announced as she hung on to the door.

"What's wrong, Oemie?" Mymoena asked, as she stepped from behind the door. Motchie Gafsa ushered the child away with her hand and her perky laughter.

"Noting," replied their grandmother as she wiped her face with the ends of her scarf.

"Go into Auntie Galiema's room. I'll be there now-now," their mother commanded. Gadija raised herself from her bed and straightened out her clothes.

Rosa looked about the room. Gadija gave her a fierce look then raised her eyebrows at her. Rosa read the message quickly yet continued to hover at the door.

"You too, Rosa. Go next door to Natalie and Auntie Galiema." The child complied and Gadija sighed.

The two women looked at each other as the children left. Magrieb had long since passed and the last prayers were now being echoed over the loudspeaker from the main mosque on Hanover Street. Motchie Gafsa pulled her scarf further up until it covered her entire head.

"Oemie, did you tell your mother when this happened to you?"

"Ai, no. In dose days you kept dat sort of ting to yourself. It wasn't like it is today. *Here ruh*, Gadija, I have not set eyes on dat man in years. He married a Christian woman, then left the woman with the children, and I later heard that the woman left the children with one of his uncles. Allah has kept him out of my sight. And his brother, the man I was supposed to marry, I listen to him every day. Can you hear? Gadija, listen, hey? Listen to der Imam. We shouldn't be talking now."

"The man that you were going to marry is an Imam, Oemie?"

Motchie Gafsa simply nodded and held onto the ends of her scarf.

Motchie Gafsa moved closer to the window and heard the prayers louder now as she opened the window. She closed her eyes and held another green tasbiem in her hand, rubbing on the green shiny beads.

Gadija was not able to move.   She looked at her mother from head to toe. Her mother turned suddenly.

"I was wearing more or less der same ting, you know.   Noting fancy. And he still did dat to me. Allah will take care of dat man."

Gadija did not reply. Motchie Gafsa walked towards the window and observed that newspapers had blown to the windowpane, covering the view somewhat.

"Ai, tog. Now what is der meaning of dis?"

Gadija glanced over towards the window.

"It's the wind, Oemie, just the wind blowing papers."

"Oh no, meisiekind, it might look like dat to you. Gmf, with all your studying, you still doan understand dis kind of ting, hey?"

"Oemie, it's the wind. There's nothing else there."

"Ai, tog, and look, the whole pavement is full of newspapers."

Motchie Gafsa gazed further along and looked in both directions from her house.

"Ai, tog, and it's only dis house that has the newspapers by the window hey. No newspapers next door hey, look! Dis is a sign, Gadija, a sign I tell you."

There was a knock on the door. Her mother put both tasbiems down and walked to the living room then towards the front door, patting herself to ensure that her scarf was on her head.

"Leikom, Motchie . . . Leikom, Motchie."   Several men greeted her. She returned their greeting, then indicated that Rashied was in the backyard.   All of the men wore fezes; most of them wore the more common crocheted white ones whilst a few of the older men wore the stiff, red ones, which gave them a dignified look. Motchie Gafsa was particularly keen on one of the men, Shakeem, whom she thought suitable for Galiema. Shakeem was in his early thirties and lived with his mother. His father had died shortly after he was born, from stomach cancer, which his wife maintained was as a result of his unwilling participation in the Second World War. Motchie Gafsa thought it charming that Shakeem took care of his mother. He looked at the floor of the living room avoiding further eye contact with Motchie Gafsa. Motchie Gafsa engaged him, asking him how his mother liked the chocolate cake she had delivered only two days since. Shakeem answered promptly, then turned his attention to the men standing by attentively, their eyebrows raised, aware of his desire to draw Gadija's attention. He kept a watchful, fearful eye on Galiema's room and hoped she would not leave it. She, on the other hand, had the same idea, for she lay there grinning to herself, listening to her mother's attempts at securing her hand in marriage. Galiema was not interested in Shakeem, despite her mother's obvious meddling.

The men now walked into the small wooden cabin in the backyard and removed their shoes upon entering. They started each practice session with a prayer. Gadija waited until she could no longer hear the men in the dining room. She was tired of the looks they gave her and the manner in which they tried to engage her on matters she thought they were intensely ignorant of. Shakeem in particular had taken a liking to her, and upon engaging her on her psychology studies, she proved, without a doubt, that he was inferior in both speech and conception, and therefore not worthy of her attention. It was at this time that Galiema came to his aid, skillfully brushing her sister's comments aside, and he, in an attempt at preserving his manliness, kept his eyes focused on the woman who was bold enough to confront learned words with gallant modesty. Gadija's arrogant display put great distance between herself and Shakeem, and as a result she was now, in her view, happily rid of his sorrowful gaze.

She lifted herself from her bed and walked to her sisters' room and opened the door slightly. Galiema was lying on the bottom bunk, reading her usual Mills and Boon romance novel. She did not take her eye off the book. Gadija observed Natalie and her two daughters speaking very intimately with Rosa whilst Galiema, who was close enough to hear the details of their conversation, seemed unperturbed by her sister's presence. The center mat was fully rolled out and the girls were practicing their steps with the help of a small tape recorder, which Galiema had loaned to them.

"I thought you were practicing," Gadija said as she squinted at the girls.

Rosa looked at the woman, and then turned towards Natalie, Amina and Mymoena.

"We are, Auntie. We're talking orso." Rosa tilted her face as she spoke, giving her words the kind of authority Gadija resented.

Gadija looked over at Galiema, who would not put her book down; Galiema grinned, well aware that Gadija was not keen on the manner in which Rosa took up her elders. The two sisters exchanged little other than occasional glances. Gadija glanced back at Rosa then at Galiema, who refused to participate in Gadija's series of reprimanding looks.

Rosa laughed out loud each time she fell over whilst practicing the jazz combination she was taught, the last steps being new to her. Amina and Mymoena followed suit despite their mother's reprimanding looks. Natalie, on the other hand, always appeared dutiful in Gadija's company and tried not to annoy her aunt; she sat quietly at the edge of the mat with her feet crossed.

"Gadija! Gadija! It's the Boere!"

Gadija froze. Her mother's words echoed through the house. The children stopped their dance practice and the men came rushing into the dining room as Motchie Gafsa clutched her scarf and held onto her daughter.

"Oemie, just calm down. There's nothing here for them to take," Gadija remarked. Gadija looked towards her young daughters, then at Rosa and Natalie, who had their arms folded across their chest. Mamma Zila and Motchie Gafsa trained the children on how to appear in front of the police should the occasion arise. Rashied and the men from the singing group were all standing by.

"It's Van der Merwe," Gadija noted as she peeped through the lace curtain. "Oemie, just stay calm. There are two more people in the car. At least it's not a van. I'll do the talking, Oemie. You men better get back to what you were doing. Just stay at the back. Boytjie, kanala, just go to the back. I will call you if I need you. I am sure Van der Merwe will come and get you if he wants anything."

The men looked at one another, quite taken by the commanding manner in which Gadija spoke to everyone.

"Boytjie," Gadija said, her hands behind her back. She motioned with her eyes and he led the men to the wooden cabin. The men shuffled their feet reluctantly.

"Quickly. Kanala!" Gadija called out.

As the men left, Gadija ushered the children into Galiema's room.

"Stay with Galiema," she uttered, and as her eyes met Galiema's her sister nodded and took her nieces and Rosa with her. Gadija heard the knock on the door and motioned to her mother to wait. At the second attempt at knocking she moved towards it and turned the knob.

"Meneer," she said, geeeting Van der Merwe.

Her sullen face soon grew fearful as she observed her sister Gairo standing beside Van der Merwe and a young constable. Gairo's face was bruised. Gadija was gasping for air; she covered her mouth with both her hands. The two policemen stepped into the house without an invitation as Gadija stared at her sister. Gairo's eyes were frozen and her head hung to one side as though she was irritated rather than ashamed.

"Gairo! Gairo! Gairo!" Motchie Gafsa called out, in loud trembling bursts.

Gairo raised her bruised head and held it high.

"Mrs Ebrahim . . . it appears as though your daughter has been . . ." Van der Merwe paused. He looked at both Gadija and Motchie Gafsa, then towards the door of Galiema's room, which stood ajar. Both Gadija and Motchie Gafsa came to embrace Gairo.

Gairo looked bold enough to walk pass her mother and her sister but the fierce look Van der Merwe gave her assured her that it was not yet her time to depart. She stood there, annoyed at being on display and fiddled with her football bag, which Van der Merwe then took from her. Van der Merwe held the black football bag on the floor between his legs. He lit a cigarette and smirked, fully aware that no one in Motchie Gafsa's house smoked—certainly not inside her house or in her company. He held the flame close to his rugged hands and coughed as he took the first draw.

Motchie Gafsa and Gadija tried to comfort Gairo, but she just shrugged.

"We did not catch the men, but one of our constables has an idea," Van der Merwe continued as he sniffed and pulled on his nose. "We did find her bag, when she showed us where they jumped her and blindfolded he. One of our constables was driving on DeWaal Drive when he saw a van pull away from a side street rather suspiciously and saw your daughter lying close by."

Gairo stood upright with not a teardrop in her eyes. She had a faraway look in her eyes, as though she was not present in the room at all. Her lip was cut and her trousers were ruffled and soiled with sand and mud, under normal circumstances she would have known better than to enter the house with muddy shoes. She chewed her lips as her mother and sister looked on. Her nieces, along with Rosa and Natalie, stood in the doorway of her room, which was now ajar. Gadija's hand covered her face as she leaned against Gairo and Motchie Gafsa sobbed uncontrollably as she held on to her youngest daughter.

Gadija held onto her mother whilst Gairo looked at both the policemen.

"Can I go now?" Gairo asked, looking at the ceiling.

"I always thought you had two daughters and two sons, Mrs Ebrahim. I see that I was wrong. She's tough, she'll be alright," Van der Merwe said, as his younger colleague looked on. "Now, the men at the back there," he asserted as he pointed to the backyard. "I suppose they are quiet because they are waiting for me to leave."

Van der Merwe did not get a reply from anyone.

He walked toward the backyard and Gairo loosened her mother's grip and walked to her room.

"Don't noborry ask me anyting," she muttered as she shut the door. All of the children moved from the door and stood outside, making way for Gairo to enter it.

Van der Merwe indicated to his colleague that he was to going to the back of the house. The young constable looked at Gadija from head to toe. Galiema came to her mother's side and took Motchie Gafsa's hand and walked her to the kitchen. The young children followed on.

Van der Merwe stood in the middle of the dining room and observed the movements of the Ebrahim family.

"I see little Rosa is a regular here too," he commented. There were no words forthcoming. The young child stared at him with a frown on her face. "So Ludwi isn't here then? Not ready to throw stones at the van like he usually does?" he asked, sniffing and coughing as he puffed away, his eyes inspecting every movement in the house.

He walked to the back of the house with his young colleague, who looked uncomfortable. The young constable, who could easily have been twenty-one years old, looked on as the family huddled together around Motchie Gafsa. He stood with his head down and occasionally looked towards the back door, expecting Van der Merwe to appear sooner rather than later. When Van der Merwe made his appearance, he had a sheet of paper in his hand and waved it at his colleague.

"We have all their names written down. They are in the men's Muslim choir, so they say, but who knows, hey, who knows?"

Gadija now came into the dining room and looked sternly at Van der Merwe.

"I have not come here to look for trouble," he said, almost smiling now. Gadija stared at him coldly. "The soup smells very good." Van der Merwe looked towards the kitchen. Gairo had still not left her room; Gadija had turned her back and kept her eyes on the kitchen. Van der Merwe was looking about the dining room, waiting for someone to extend an invitation to him; none was forthcoming.

A knock on the front door, he decided, entitled him to open it.

"Oh, good evening," he said. The two women did not return the greeting.

"Rosa's family, hey? Just as I expected."

"Leikom!" Mamma Zila and Auntie Flowers called out.

"These are the women you should watch out for," he remarked as his colleague nodded at Mamma Zila and Auntie Flowers. Auntie Flowers returned the nod and Mamma Zila walked into the kitchen after sucking the air through her teeth, loudly and with contempt.

"Is everything oright, Motchie? Gadija?" Mamma Zila shifted her eyes between the two women.

Within seconds, she returned to the dining room looking rather fierce.

"Isn't it time for you to go about your business now? You came to do what you had to do, so leave now. Leave people in peace to attend to their families. I am sure you have one too."

Van der Merwe sneered at Mamma Zila, coughed and sniffed a few times as his eyes surveyed her from top to bottom.

Auntie Flower's scornful look may have done the trick, for he hastened towards the door soon after, and pulling his colleague, along with him by his collar. Van der Merwe whispered in the young constable's ear, and his body jerked upon hearing the no-doubt disturbing news. He kept his head down and did not look up again.

Rosa ran onto the field after the whistle had blown accompanied by
Wasfi, Ludwi and Nita, all of whom were now jumping for joy since
their team won. The two drums used by Wasfi and Ludwi as the instruments upon which they made music were now left side aside. They
used it every Saturday afternoon at the soccer field to cheer their team.
They drummed to their heart's delight as Rosa and Nita sang or wagged
their tongues, in the true District Six outcry. Gairo, who played soccer
on the men's team, fascinated the four children. Not only was she a
dashing looking player, in shorts and soccer jersey, but she played the
game beautifully too. She drew many young spectators because she was
skillful and fast of both vision and action, and many of the young children who crowded the soccer field were enamoured of her. There was
no issue with her gender. The young men with whom she played on the
team never ridiculed her because of her femaleness; very little of it was
visible, and many would say that she was more manly than most of the
young men she kept company with. Gairo always wore long trousers
when she was not playing soccer. She smoked with young men of her
generation on corners, whistled at the women they whistled at, and par-
ticipated in discussions on sport and other matters considered suitable
for male company only. They regarded her as one of the boys, so to
speak, and she never corrected their sense of gender when they referred
to her as "him."

Rosa ran ahead of the group and several other children followed on.
Although Gairo was over the age of eighteen, none of the children called
her "Auntie" or "Missus." Gairo ran towards Rosa, picked her up and
threw the young child in the air, then caught her again. The other three
children laughed heartily, Wasfi exhibiting all of his rotten teeth. Several
children watched closely yet kept their distance since Ludwi was quite
fierce and rather territorial when it came to Gairo, for whom he held a
special flame. Gairo swung Rosa around and the child held on with
both her gloved hands. Rosa called out as she straightened her legs and
closed her eyes as Gairo went round and round. Rosa wore a red jersey
and a pair of dark jeans; Mamma Zila insisted that she wear her gloves,
and whilst she did attempt to hide them in her bosom, Mamma Zila
pulled a face and the young Rosa soon followed her grandmother's
orders. Rosa wore two plaits, which hung down the side of her face close

to her waist. Nita was dressed similarly, without gloves, and her thick black hair was tied behind her back with an elastic band. Both Wasfi and Ludwi wore the football jersey of their team, which was dark green and bore the number nine, indicating Gairo's position, center forward. They stuck their tongues out at their peers who supported the opposition, and Ludwi and Wasfi each had their own victory dance, which usually involved them making fists, moving them about rhythmically, thrusting their thumb between their second and third finger and waving it about. Everyone around them read it as they had signalled it: "You've been had." The latter was only one of its meanings; the other more popular one referred to sexual prowess and intention, which the boys, at their age, were very well aware of. Rosa and Nita imitated a carnival dance and the girls twirled imaginary sticks, pretending to be drum majorettes, then went back into carnival mode, each with their own dance. The field was swarming with young children, and they kept their distance from Gairo's exclusive fan club, for they were too afraid of Ludwi's tongue.

"I have to change now," Gairo said, after she had given her victory hugs and swung the children around as they held on. Ludwi, as usual, refused, since he thought he was too old to be swung around by her. He stood back and leaned against the school's wall, watching every part of the performance with a matchstick in his mouth.

"I really have to go now," Gairo said again.

"Nooo, Gairo. Nooo, stay here," they replied jointly, as if orchestrated.

"Motchie is waiting for you, Gairo," Ludwi asserted in a very manly tone as he joined the group.

"Oh yes. I forgot," she said, scratching her head and rubbing her fingers through her short-cropped hair. "I told Oemie I'll take der parcel to Motchie Tiema. I suppose Oemie's fast tongue service oready got word to your grandma, hey?"

The children laughed heartily.

"Oh well. I'll have to go and see Motchie Tiema right away."

Gairo looked about the field as though she was expecting someone. Ludwi's eyes narrowed each time she looked towards the entrance closest to the field.

Gairo did not dress or undress in the boys' toilets, preferring to arrive on the soccer field wearing her uniform under her clothes. After the game she would simply put her jeans and jersey back on. She showered in the backyard of her house with a hose pipe. Motchie Gafsa complained about this on regular occasions, especially when she thought it was too cold, but Gairo did not alter her habits. Gairo pointed to her soccer bag and Rosa handed it to her. It was light in weight and the child took great pride in lifting it. Gairo checked her bag momentarily and took the already wrapped parcel out, held it up to Ludwi and Wasfi, then put it back in her bag. She slipped her jeans on and hastily pulled her jersey over her head. She raked her fingers through her short-cropped shiny hair. Each time she touched any part of her body, Ludwi's face would perk up, both his mouth and eyes would observe every movement. Her actions were suddenly slower as she straightened her jersey out. The children looked about to ascertain whom her attention was now directed upon.

Ganief was standing at the edge of the field. All of the children recognized him and cast their eyes upon him rather unfavourably. Wasfi and Ludwi attended Muslim school with Ganief, much against the boys' better wishes, and although they protested regularly, their grandmother, Motchie Tiema, insisted. Rosa attended the Thursday afternoon class and would then stay after the class with Galiema who made supper for Ganief and his brothers every Thursday. Ganief's mother had abandoned her children when they were very young. Their father left shortly after and lived with his second wife in Mannenberg, on the Cape Flats. They were raised by one of their uncles and only saw their father occasionally; he did not come into District Six. Nita rubbed her spectacles each time she saw Ganief. The young child, unlike her three friends, did not utter a word to Ganief under any circumstances, even though her friend Rosa had asserted that he was a good teacher. Nita, having recently revealed to Rosa what she knew of Ganief in a heated argument, now looked at her friend to see whether Rosa would act upon the information she received. Rosa looked carefully at Gairo's eyes then back at Ganief whilst Wasfi and Ludwi were talking about his legs; although it was not obvious to anyone, one was shorter than the other. This had been revealed to them by a close friend whose family were friends with Ganief's family. The young children were encouraged to have respect for Ganief since he was after all a schoolteacher, and a vice-principal at that. Ludwi in particular had indicated to Motchie Tiema that he did not want to attend Muslim school any longer because he did not like Ganief. The older woman reprimanded him severely and reminded him that when it came to his education he was to do as he was told.

The three children stood aside as they observed Ganief approaching. Rosa, on the other hand, refused to move from her position beside Gairo.

"Is Uncle Ganief your boyfriend, Gairo?" she asked, as she tilted her head and kept her hands behind her back.

"No, Rosa. Don't be silly. We're just friends."

"Hello, Rosa," Ganief said as he approached the child. He greeted her as though she were a mere accessory to Gairo, upon whom he had fixed his gaze.

Rosa returned his greeting but looked at Nita instead. She cast her gaze between her best friend and the teacher, who she had on another occasion remarked was by far the best teacher she had ever had. Ganief wore a big smile, but it began to wear off as he observed the hostility of all the children present, most of whom he taught. Wasfi greeted him before he turned to him and Ludwi grunted. Nita stared blankly at him when he looked in her direction and adjusted the spectacles on her nose. For a moment he could see the reflection of an event that had tran-spired, in her spectacles, and of which he hoped the child, if indeed she knew anything, would remain silent. Ganief was still not sure that Nita had actually witnessed the event. The child, as most people asserted, did not speak much to begin with and thus, like most people, Ganief assumed he had nothing to worry about.

Gairo's brow was sweaty and she took the tip of her jersey and wiped it. Ganief stood looking at her, unable to communicate his wishes, since four pairs of eyes were upon him and scrutinizing every move he made. Gairo's face was flushed, as she stood beside Ganief. She looked awkward since Ganief's presence was one which drew attention to her being intimate with a man in ways quite unlike the children were accus-tomed to. Ganief usually waited for her in his brother's car. Gairo knew, and could tell by the exchanges the children made with their eyes, that they were well aware that this was not just a matter of two buddies enjoying each other's company, but that Ganief had feelings for Gairo which they, as children, clearly decided were unwelcome.   Ludwi thrust his foot into the grass, loosening a patch. He dug his foot deeper and deeper into the earth, creating a rather unsightly hole. The school's care-taker took great care of the football field and would not be pleased on Monday morning to find it ruined.

Ganief moved closer to Gairo and the two adults tried to converse as best they could under the circumstances. Rosa was still standing beside Gairo. Ludwi was pouting and could not look at Ganief.

"Gairo! Gairo! Motchie Tiema is waiting," he finally called out from the distance. Gairo did not reply. "Rosa, go and stand over there with them, I need to speak to Ganief, okay." Rosa looked at Gairo, whose manner was now quite transformed and whose speech was altered, but the child did not move.

"Now, Rosa," Gairo asserted. She laughed uncomfortably as she sauntered reluctantly towards her group of friends.

Rosa joined them and each of the children wore an angry frown.

"What does he want?" Ludwi asked as he looked at Ganief in the dis-tance. The question was intended for Rosa.

"He smaaks Gairo, nuh?" Wasfi asked.   His question was also direct-ed at Rosa. The young child had a faraway look on her face.

"I doan know," she replied, as she stretched her neck and attempted to eavesdrop from the distance she was now expected to keep.

"Gah, you know.   You know everyting," was Wasfi's reply.

"I doan knowwww," she said, looking rather agitated. She rubbed her hands behind her back and made a hissing sound as they clearly itched to unbearable proportions. She brought them to her side then blew her breath over them to cool them down.

The two boys looked towards Nita. Both boys had their hands behind their backs in a fierce and inquiring manner.

"I don't know anything," Nita replied, as she rubbed her spectacles.

"Den why you playing wit your glasses?" Ludwi asked.

"Jaaaa, why you playing wit your glasses den, huh?" was Wasfi's fol-low up question.

"Because I'm hot."

"Uh-uh," Wasfi remarked, as he shook his head indicating that he did not believe her.

Ludwi was still looking over at Gairo and Ganief. Gairo had her back turned towards the children and stood at an angle where they saw the back of her.

"Why is he orways here on der soccer field . . . every Saturday morning wit his short leg standing against his brother's car?" Ludwi spoke without looking at his friends.

"Huuurh! Ludwi! Dat's rude. Uncle Ganief carn help he has one leg shorter," was Rosa's flabbergasted response.

"Ja, he's a cripple. What does he want wit Gairo? Isn't Galiema his girlfriend?" Ludwi asked, as he looked at Rosa. He kicked the grass and was himself green with envy. Rosa's eyes widened and she looked over at Gairo, then at Nita and grimaced as her friend nodded at her.

Ganief was standing closer and closer to Gairo and Ludwi shifted his body occasionally to see what was transpiring between the two adults. He moved away from the circle and shouted out again.

"Gairo! Gairo! Motchie Tiema is waiting."

She stuck her hand out at him and nodded simultaneously, indicating that he had to wait and that she would be coming shortly.

The remaining children from the oppositional team had now dispersed and the field was still warm with the smell of bodies. All of the young men who played soccer were at the edge of the field, about to leave with their friends, and the four children who stood waiting for Gairo with great anticipation could hear their laughter.

Ganief was standing very close to Gairo now, a lover's distance, and the children could not hear what they were saying. Ludwi was kicking the grass and the hole that he dug now looked unsightly; he looked as though he detested it. Moegsien, a boy who lived on Canterbury Lane and who sold newspapers in the evening, was now approaching the field. Rosa had delivered his message to Ludwi on the Thursday morning as they walked to school and had also provided Ludwi with every detail of the events that had transpired at Gairo's house. Wasfi and Ludwi exchanged glances since Moegsien and his group of friends, none of whom were present, did not hold ownership over the field they were

presently standing on. Moegsien was walking with a stick, and he
scraped it along the pavement and continued to scrape it along the soccer field as he entered. Moegsien was ten years old and attended
Trafalgar primary school, exactly where the soccer field was located.
They were on his school property unofficially, for no one had permission to play soccer on the weekend, but young boys and men did it anyway. He spotted Gairo and called out, "Man-vrou . . . man-vrou . . ."
then laughed heartily, beating his stick into the grass each time his vulgar outburst needed more gravity.

Ludwi flew into a fury and ran across the field. In seconds, he had
Moegsien, who was a year older than he, by the throat, and he landed
one punch after another, then pulled him to the ground, where the beating continued. The young streetwise and naughty Moegsien did not see
it coming, and at first thought Ludwi was going to give him a light tum-
ble, that it might be playful even, as boys often held each other in a grip
to suggest a fight but would not carry it out. The grip was a show of
their willingness to fight and a mark of their budding masculinity but
not meant to lead to a fight, which Ludwi now put up in defense of the
insult Moegsien hurled at Gairo. His friends approached and Wasfi was
shouting encouraging words.

"Moer him . . . moer him, Ludwi," he shouted urging his brother on.

Moegsien had a bloody nose and Gairo, who ran over to the fight in
an attempt to stop it, was quite shocked by the fury displayed by Ludwi
in her honour.

"Ludwi!" she shouted as she tried to lift him off the young Moegsien.

"Ludwi, kanala. Just leave it!"

The young Ludwi was now breathing heavily and moving slowly.
Gairo managed to get Ludwi off Moegsien, who was now rolling about
and struggling to get up. He finally managed to do so, and whilst Gairo
held tightly onto Ludwi, and rubbed his head, Moegsien mumbled
something under his breath. Ludwi was ready to fly at him at him again.
He might not have, but Ganief, unaware of young Ludwi's affections for
Gairo, took it upon himself to hold his pupil back, at an event where he
was not a teacher. He grabbed Ludwi.

"Stop it! That's enough now!" he shouted. Ludwi, whose blood had
boiled over during the moments when Ganief had sought to speak to

Gairo so intimately, now let loose on Ganief too. As Ganief held onto him, Ludwi kicked him, and shoved him with his little nine-year-old frame.

"Voetsak! Voetsak!" he shouted between breaths, using the kind of language one might towards an unwanted dog. Ganief was astounded by the young boys' fury and his outburst. Ludwi conducted himself well in Ganief's classroom and only spoke when he was spoken to.

"Ludwi, it's me. Come on, calm yourself now." Ganief clearly thought that Ludwi's fury had clouded his vision.

"I doan . . . wanna calm myself . . . what do you wan . . . wit Gairo . . . Galiema is your . . ." Ludwi stammered, then glanced at his onlookers; he spat on the grass, missing Ganief by a few inches. Upon hearing this, Gairo turned towards him and stared long and hard at Ganief.

"Ludwi, calm yourself." Ganief was now shaking him and holding him by the shoulders.

"You . . . focking cripple," he called out.

He tried to kick Ganief again, who was expecting it this time.

"What is wrong with you? Hey!"

Ludwi let out another blow, which landed on his shin. Ganief lifted the young boy from the ground and held him up with one arm.

"See, what a man you are now, hey? Look at you."

"Put me down . . . put me down . . . you fockin cripple," he shouted. Wasfi came to his aid.

"Put my brother down!" He too started kicking Ganief.

Just then Meisie and Natalie walked across the soccer field.

"Rosa! . . . Rosa!" Natalie called out.

Ganief threw Ludwi down and was himself out of breath. He looked at Gairo, who was taking everything in and not quite sure what to do next. She went towards Ludwi, who seemed calmer once she knelt down at his side. She now had to contend with Wasfi, who was furious too. The young boy shoved Ganief. She had seen the children furious before but not with adults, and certainly not in this manner.

"There's your jintoe . . . why doan you go to her?" said Wasfi as he pointed at Meisie. He stood boldly face to chest with Ganief pushing out his upper frame as far as his body allowed. Wasfi wiped his nose with the edge of his jersey then put both his fists up, as older men did when

they were ready to box in a manly sort of way. Meisie had now joined
the group and was looking to Gairo for some explanation. Rosa and
Nita had carefully drawn Natalie away from the events, even though the
young child wanted to be informed. Nita stood by with her arms folded, her thick bushel of black hair now hanging in the front beside her
left cheek, and she squinted and looked at Ganief with utmost contempt.

"What did you say?" Ganief asked, quite shaken and trying desperately to compose himself as he spoke to Wasfi.

The young Wasfi sniffed, and brought his sleeve to his nose again, as
he answered.

"You heard me. Why doan you go to your jintoe . . . I know you
and your brother play tournament wit her," he said, pointing at Meisie.
Meisie gasped, looked toward Gairo and walked away. She held her
hand to her mouth upon hearing his remark, which betrayed the sexual
nature of the relationship Meisie had with Ganief and his brother Ismail.
Ganief grabbed Wasfi by his neck and was about to shake him, when he
uttered, "I'm not coming to your school no more . . . I'll put my uncle
after you . . . he'll fix you . . . my uncle's a Star 17 and he's a number
twenty-six . . . he'll get you cos you're a twenty-eight, moffie!"

Wasfi's face was red as he kicked Ganief furiously, one blow following the next, quite forgetting that he had a runny nose and that it was
difficult to contain the flow when engaging in such swift head movements. Ganief's dignity was at stake since for a young child to suggest
that he was a twenty-eight, a man who would suffer sexual coercion at
the hands of a twenty-six, a position usually taken up by the leader of a
gang, was completely out of the scope of a child's conversation. It was
the kind of ridicule that men hurled at one another during fierce argu-
ments, and one he had never experienced.

Meisie decided to return to the scene to defend Ganief. Rosa, Nita and
Natalie were now sitting on the steps of the school watching the entire
event. The two young girls filled Natalie in on what they knew of Ganief.

"Give it to him, Ganief, give it him," Meisie called out as she
observed Ganief slapping Wasfi across his face. Wasfi, in a wicked turn
of movement, spat at her, the contents of which, thick and colourful,
reached her feet.

"Jintoe," he called out at her, as he drew his sleeve to his nose again.

Ganief boxed his ears, picked him up by the collar of his jersey and lifted him above the ground and threw him down. "You little snot-nosed moffie," he called out as Wasfi staggered to his feet.

Gairo looked at Meisie, then at Ganief, then at Wasfi, not sure where her attention ought to be. Ludwi was on his feet again and drawing Ganief out, challenging him. Ludwi ran towards Ganief before Gairo could stop him; Gairo moved between the two young brothers as fast as she could.

"Why doan you fight wit men your own age . . . you just wanna fight wit lighties, hey. I'll tell my uncle about you . . . "

Meisie was shouting obscenities at both the boys. They, in turn responded with their share of obscenities, quite outdoing her. She was exhausted as she screamed at both boys and Ganief tried to hold them back, attempting to manage the situation as best he could.

"I'll tell Motchie Tiema when I see her . . . you boys are filty wit you mouts!" she called out.

"Motchie doan like jintoes . . . why doan you go to der dockyard where you belong."

Meisie was beside herself and looked towards Ganief to defend her. Natalie ran towards the fighting pair; she too began to attack Ganief. She kicked him whilst Wasfi and Ludwi moved away and threw stones at him from a distance. Wasfi had removed his jersey and now wore it around his waist. The sleeves of his shirt were rolled up and he did not seem to care that the contents of his runny nose was spread across his face.

Ganief approached Natalie and tried to hug her, but the young girl refused his advances. Her mother took her from Ganief, who stood holding nothing but rejection in his hands, which were now lifted above his head. There were no words exchanged between Meisie and Ganief. Gairo was now sitting on the field with her head down. She had a twig in her hand, and made little drawings in the sand.

Ganief approached her and sat down beside her.

"I'll explain everything to you. Come with me, I'll give you a lift in Ismail's lorry . . . Ismail's car," he said hastily as he looked at it to ensure that it was the vehicle he was making reference to. Gairo did not utter a word. Ganief looked towards the end of the field and all four children were standing against the wall of the school. Ludwi still had his head thrust out, defiant, urging Ganief to come after him. She pushed her hand out at them, to indicate that they must wait for her and that she would be back.

Ganief now moved ahead of Gairo and walked to the passenger side of the car, to let her in first. She looked at him as he showed his gentlemanly ways and opened the door for her. He had performed the same gesture every Saturday morning now for the past two months and smiled as she came towards him. In seconds he was clutching his nose and cupping his hand to contain the blood, which was running all over his clothes. Gairo rubbed her head, and turned around, spat on his brother's car and walked toward the children.

Gairo did not turn to look at him.

It was after three in the morning when Motchie Gafsa raised herself from her bed. The wind rattled her window and she awoke to its tremble as periodic gusts blew old papers against the glass. She stretched and held onto her tasbiem, her eyes still narrow with sleep, as she gazed at the papers clinging to the glass pane. It was too early for her to get out of bed, yet she could still smell the cooked coconut from the previous night, ready for the Sunday morning's koeksisters. Motchie Gafsa was the kind of woman who was raised in the old school of reading and interpreting signs, especially when they came to her window, and she held her hands to her head when confronted with messages she was not sure she could interpret. All her children wore kadoematjies pinned to their undergarments, as assurance that evil spirits would leave them be. "Ai, tog!" she sighed as she lifted herself out of her bed, attempting a reading of the significance of the papers which flew to her window. She squinted at them, knowing full well that messages had to be read and understood: the earth spoke to her, as it did to many who allowed themselves to hear what it had to say. Motchie Gafsa shut her eyes and pondered several possibilities. She stood on the small mat and scratched her head, her thoughts trailing unsolved current events. Gadija and the children were asleep, and she could hear her grandchildren snore. Motchie Gafsa did not turn on the light but could see the open-gaped mouths of her grandchildren. The white of Mymoena's eyes were visible and Motchie Gafsa grimaced as she tiptoed over to her slippers. She slid her feet into her slippers and tiptoed into the living room, clutching her shawl. Rashied lay covered in blankets on the floor; she had to walk across the edge of his bed to get to the kitchen. She rubbed her eyes momentarily as she shut the kitchen door to adjust to the bright light she now expected as she lifted the switch to turn on the light. The light fizzled and the bulb went out. A spitting, hissing sound echoed in the room. Her whole body shook and she was now awake and alert enough to taste the electricity on her tongue. She stood still for a while considering whether to wake her son and ask him for a lightbulb, but turned instead to the kitchen drawer to light a candle.

As she lifted the small white candle to the table, she was surprised by the appearance of a small man. She knew immediately by his demeanour and his grotesque physical features that he was none other than a Tokkalosh. Motchie Gafsa hastened to shoo him away, but to no avail. The Tokkalosh told her of other old secrets she kept, and new ones to be revealed, including something vague about a baby, which Motchie Gafsa could not quite understand. The Tokkalosh, it is said, tells tales, and much of what he says, it is believed to be, is the unspoken truth.

This one too began to speak. "There is a man," he said, "who is living close to you, through your children, and he will appear in your life, and show himself, and you will not know him at first, but he has harmed you in the past and he will try and harm you again. Be careful, for he will come into your life when you least expect it. He has been away but he is back now."

Motchie Gafsa gasped and clutched her heart, and within seconds the Tokkalosh disappeared. She looked about the kitchen, the table, the chairs, the windowsill, and there he was, cross-legged and smirking, his rotten teeth showing every bit of decay that was visible to the eye. Motchie Gafsa staggered to the kitchen tap, her ankle still swollen, and and poured herself a glass of water. She held the glass close to her lips and gulped anxiously, her heart racing. She was suddenly overcome with silence. The Tokkalosh had left, and there was not a trace that he had ever been there.

Motchie Gafsa looked around the kitchen and her eyes fell on her ironing cupboard. She opened it and took from it a small blanket, which she placed on the floor. She knelt down, facing east, and said her prayers, her legs shaking and her mouth quivering at each utterance. Upon completion, she sat upright, and then folded the blanket methodically. She could hear whimpering and sobbing. She placed the blanket in the cupboard, and then sat down at the table to assure herself that the sounds were coming from her house and not her head. She could hear whispering amid the sobs, and she looked over to the dining room floor where Rashied lie asleep. Motchie Gafsa's eyes suddenly bulged: Rashied was not in his bed. The sounds were coming from Gairo and Galiema's room. Motchie Gafsa knocked on the door then pushed against it; Rashied was standing close to Galiema, who was shaking. Gairo stood close by with a blanket, which she draped over her sister whilst holding onto it. Motchie Gafsa did not utter a sound as she lowered her head and observed the bloodstains on the floor. Motchie Gafsa appeared calm as her three children stared at her, not one of them taking the initiative to speak. The blood spoke for itself as the circle grew larger and its onlookers preserved its presence with their silence.

"Can Gadija's Mini take us to der hospital?" Motchie Gafsa asked, looking at her son, her tone cold. Rashied nodded and left the room. Galiema was sobbing, and stared at her mother at the door.

"Make yourself decent," Motchie Gafsa remarked, looking at Gairo curiously.

Gadija was now beside her mother, rubbing her eyes, and looking at both Gairo and Galiema, none of who offered any explanation. Galiema moved to sit down and her mother ran towards her and helped her to the bed.

"Go on, Merem, put some proper clothes on," Motchie Gafsa said as she looked at Gairo. Gairo threw her jeans on and looked about for a jersey. As she pulled it over her head she observed Gadija standing at the door. Gadija did not utter a word. She stood at the door, looked at Galiema and her mother, and left the room.

Motchie Gafsa followed her daughter out of the room. She held onto Gadija's arm and whispered, "You stay here, Bokkie."

Gadija had tears in her eyes. Her mother held her close and wiped her tears with the ends of her scarf. "Galiema needs us now, Bokkie, be strong for her, Bokkie."

Gadija nodded and looked about the dining room. Rashied's ruffled bed was still on the floor. She looked at her mother and nodded, indicating that she would take care of it and that she was fine and would cope, then went into her room.

The children were still sleeping. Rashied had taken Gadija's car keys, and Motchie Gafsa could now hear the car running. Gadija came out of her room carrying a light coat, which she hung over her mother's shoulders. She placed two ten-rand notes in her mother's hand, folded small, then went back into her room. Motchie Gafsa looked down at her feet and the thought of wearing her going-out shoes occurred to her, but she decided against it. Galiema and Gairo were now standing beside her. Galiema did not look at her mother; in one hand she clutched a book, which her mother took from her and flung onto the settee. Gairo's eyes followed the arc of the book. The three women stood looking at one another for a few seconds, then Motchie Gafsa walked towards the door without looking back. Gadija could hear footsteps. She crept to the door, looking at Galiema and Gairo. Gadija went over to Galiema and held her hand. Her sister lowered her sobbing head close to hers, and for a brief moment, they stood with heads locked together in silence. A closeness of this kind was last seen when they were children. Gadija placed her arm about her sister's neck to console her. Gairo kept her gaze away from both her sisters and held her body stiff and upright. When Gadija heard Galiema coughing, she ushered her towards the door. Galiema and Gairo walked through the house towards the front door without exchanging glances. Gadija, realizing that her presence was not requested returned to her room without uttering a word.

The emergency unit at Groote Schuur Hospital was not as busy as expected, certainly not on a Sunday morning. Rashied let his mother and two sisters out of the car in the thick, gray, fog then had to contend with a cantankerous parking attendant who insisted that he park in the visitor's section on the far side of the emergency unit. Rashied refused to state the purpose of his visit to the parking attendant, who he recognized as someone who lived several streets from his. This of course infuriated the attendant. Rashied ignored him and delivered his mother and sisters to the emergency entrance. Motchie Gafsa walked behind her two daughters and relied upon Gairo to do the talking. A young nurse came to their aid. She introduced herself and spoke English rather slowly and with a Portuguese accent, shifting her eyes between Gairo and Galiema. Galiema was still bleeding and the nurse called upon someone, a young porter, who brought a stretcher along for Galiema to lie on. An older man who stood with his arms folded, waiting to hear news of his wife's condition, gave Motchie Gafsa a seat. When the man spoke to her, inquiring after Galiema, Motchie Gafsa simply shifted her eyes and pretended she did not hear. The nurse, whose name was Anna Maria, according to her name tag, whispered in Gairo's ear. Motchie Gafsa raised herself from her chair, expecting that her youngest daughter had some information to share. Gairo shook her head instead. One of the male doctors walked briskly along the corridor to attend to one of his patients. He glanced over at Gairo, frowned, put his folder down on the patient's bed, and walked over to speak to Gairo, who was now standing some distance from her mother.

"How are you?" he asked.

She looked up and down the corridor, not sure where her mother had gone. She moved away from the doctor, and half turned her back to him, but he persisted.

"I'm sorry. I didn't mean to intrude. I was just concerned when I saw you the other night because the social worker told me that you withdrew the charge. It's none of my business really, and I am sorry if I alarmed you. I was just going to let you know that just because you have decided not to press charges, does not mean that you cannot continue with treatment. Counselling is still available to you."

Gairo nodded, looked up and down the corridor, then pulled the collar of her shirt right up to her neck. Her manner was tough and casual. She sniffed in a manly sort of way as she sauntered and held her shoulder in the way she had learned to adopt among men who wished to feminize her. The doctor recognized the gestures directed at him. He bit his lip and lowered his head. Gairo stood a little distance from him and kept her head high. He nodded, and then walked away. Just as Gairo thought the matter was over and done with, he returned again.

"Just one more thing," he said. Gairo did not alter her posture nor did she attempt to convey that she was listening. "When I saw you, you gave me some sort of impression that you might know who this man is . . . and his accomplice. Did you say anything about this to the police?"

Gairo simply shook her head and sauntered along the corridor, ensuring that the masculinity in her step prevented nurses and doctors, those who might venture interaction upon recognizing her, from further engaging her. Motchie Gafsa followed the porter who moved Galiema into the triage unit, where a female doctor was seen popping in and out of the adjacent rooms. She sighed with relief when she recognized the woman. One of the nurses walking by greeted Galiema, who in turn called upon her to come closer. Galiema whispered something in the nurses' ear, and Motchie Gafsa could see the nurse nodding and agreeing to something. She followed the nurse and saw her approach a solid black telephone. She paused and checked her watch before finally picking up the receiver and dialing a number. Motchie Gafsa looked about and found the clock on the wall and saw that it was seven minutes after six.

The nurse whispered suddenly. "Yes, I am so sorry to telephone this early but I am calling from the hospital . . . hello, hello."

The nurse looked at the telephone in her left hand, then shook her head and put the receiver down.

Motchie Gafsa now spotted Rashied hovering about at the entrance. She walked over to her son, who told her that Gairo was somewhere smoking. Motchie Gafsa maneuvered her scarf and placed it firmly on her head. Gairo made an appearance shortly after, smelling of nicotine, and Motchie Gafsa held onto her. The young nurse, Anna Maria, gestured to Gairo to approach and she bent towards her and whispered something in her ear. Gairo hung her head and nodded.

Upon delivering the news to her mother, Gairo carefully walked to the door, accompanied by her brother, and wiped the dewdrops from the bench before asking her mother to sit down. She wiped her wet hands on her trousers. Motchie Gafsa sobbed into her scarf as Gairo and Rashied tried to console her. Gairo explained the situation to her mother, providing little detail as to the procedure but adding that she would be returning to speak to the doctor as Galiema had asked that she be present when she signed the consent form.

"Doan talk to me about Dee's and Cee's and Bee's," said Motchie

Gafsa. "I doan have time for dis modern tings. Your sister is going to have a scrape, is dat right?"

"Well, Oemie, is not like dat . . ."

"Doan mess wit my head, meisiekind . . . is she still going to have der baby, yes or no?"

"They doan know yet, Oemie. If they carn save der baby den Galiema will have der D and C, or what you call der scrape, to clean everyting out."

"Ai, Allah, oh Allah. Did Galiema tell you who the father is . . . tell me, Gairo, kanala tog, tell me," Motchie Gafsa urged, as she held onto her daughter.

Gairo shook her head as her mother looked on. Motchie Gafsa looked intensely at Gairo.

"No, Oemie, Galiema dirint say anyting."

Just then the young nurse, Anna Maria, popped her head around the curtain. She stood still and bit her lip, not entirely sure who to approach as several sets of eyes were now staring at her. A man close by was coughing uncontrollably and a young woman whose arm was in a brace had been asking after her father for some time now. Each time the nurse looked in their direction, she simply shook her head to indicate that no news was available. She gestured to Gairo who was standing whilst her mother sat down. Rashied was walking up and down along the driveway to the emergency unit, convinced that the arrogant parking attendant would have the red Mini towed. Motchie Gafsa raised herself from her chair and held on to Gairo. Gairo looked about the passage hall, then walked towards the door.

"We can talk in one of the rooms, you know. There is no need to talk out here."

"Dis is better," Motchie Gafsa said, as she stood against the freshly painted wall. Gairo tried to brush the chalky white paint off her mother's coat, but Motchie Gafsa hit her hands away. "I am fine . . . ja, now stop all of dis and speak to me like a big woman," she said, her words directed at both her daughter and the nurse. Motchie Gafsa indicated to Rashied that he was not to approach and he wrung his fingers instead and looked about the parking lot, adjusting his fez each time he saw the parking attendant.

"Well, Mrs Ebrahim," the nurse said as she tried to find the appropriate pose to deliver her message. "It seems as though the baby is going to be fine. Miss Ebrahim will be taken to the maternity ward for further observation. You may see her for a little while, the doctor gave her permission, and then once the arrangements have been made with the ward, you know, the bed sorted out and all that, she will be moved over. I would say within the hour since the new staff will come on at seven o'clock."

Motchie Gafsa had a stern look on her face. She looked at the nurse then at Gairo. "Your daughter is on the phone now, Mrs Ebrahim. Her condition is stable, for the moment, and she needs to have some rest. Doctor has asked that you not stay too long."

Motchie Gafsa turned away. She let the teardrops run down her face without attempting to erase them. She did not sob or even cry really. Rashied walked up to his mother, who had now started off towards the main road.

"Oemie! Oemie!" he called out.

Gairo was sauntering then stood against one of the walls herself. She cursed when she realized that she too had gotten the white chalky paint on her jacket.

"Oemie," Rashied said, as he caught up. "Come to der car, Oemie … Oemie! Kanala!"

"I doan wan to go in a blerry car. I wan to walk. Just leave me. I am not a cripple. I can walk. I may be old but I am not stupid. Dis Galiema was pregnant all along, nuh, and she kept it quiet, hey? What kinda mudder does dat make me, hey? What kinda woman does it make Galiema hey? She look at me, she look at Gairo and she doan say who der farder is. She go to work, she come home, and dat's it. So if is not someone at school, one of der teachers, den it happen in my house. My house, Boytjie, my house. . . and I'm at my house or at my work."

Motchie Gafsa sobbed. Gairo kept a safe distance and gestured to Rashied to approach their mother.

"Oemie," he whispered. "Is not Gairo's fault what happened to her, hey, Oemie?"

"No, Boytjie, is not her fault. But Allah, oh Allah, I am going to get to der bottom of all dis family's problems. Some ting is not right, Boytjie

. . . not right, I tell you. So many tings come to me, Boytjie, and I carn see it. I have to find out . . . all dis men trouble."

Rashied put his arm on his mother's shoulder. Gairo had now caught up to them and was standing beside her mother. Motchie Gafsa held her hand to her daughter's face.

"I'm not cross wit you, Gairo, not cross wit you. I wan to walk. I feel so sorry for you. Ai, tog, meisiekind . . . so sorry for you. You go home, both of you. I wan to walk. Der buses will be running soon. I can orso go and see my cousin in Woodstock who reads der cards . . . jus leave me, hey?"

Motchie Gafsa had her daughter's face in both her hands as she ended their talk. Gairo looked at her mother and nodded. She pushed her chest out as she gathered herself to part from her mother's loving embrace. Rashied dangled the keys in his hands, moving them from one to the other, then walked ahead to the car. At the sight of the parking attendant, he took a five-rand note from his pocket and handed it over. Gairo, who observed the exchange, remained quiet. Rashied sat in the driver's seat, not quite ready to start the car, as he watched his mother walk the unpleasant slope towards the main road. The sun was beginning to rise and the quiet of the street urged him to look at his wristwatch more than once to ascertain what the correct time was. It was almost seven o' clock. The thought of sleep appealed to him as he stood still and momentarily pondered the possibility. Gairo urged him to leave and they soon lost sight of their mother, who continued her walk without looking in their direction.

As Motchie Gafsa reached the main road she stumbled a little and feared a horrible fall, but no sooner had she regained her posture then she almost fell again. She felt a pair of hands grab her by the arm just before the expectant stagger.

"Ai, tog," Motchie Gafsa muttered to her young Good Samaritan. She regained her balance, her scarf now awkwardly hanging loosely about her neck. "I wasint looking where I was going." Motchie Gafsa saw that there were two men, one young and the other older. The older man's mouth gaped wide open the minute Motchie Gafsa raised her head.

"Huhh! Huhh!" Motchie Gafsa let out a penetrating cry. "You!" She pointed as she staggered back in horror. "You piece of rubbish, gemoers, nageboorte . . . you cross me on a day like today! Get out of my. . . and you, what are doing wit dis man? Aren't you . . . huhhhh."

Motchie Gafsa had cursed the older man so severely that he was shocked into silence. The younger man frowned at first to hear such vile curses, but horror and disgust soon flushed itself out in his many fearful expressions. He reluctantly moved towards Motchie Gafsa.

"Mrs Ebrahim, I am Ganief . . . remember, Gadija's old school friend from Herald Cressy."

"Huh!" she cried out again, holding her hand over her mouth as she staggered towards an electric pole for help.

"Mrs Ebrahim, I think you've got us mistaken. I'm Ganief Salie . . . I also work with Galiema. I am going to see her in hospital."

The older man stood far back from this encounter between Motchie Gafsa and his son.

"Is dat man your farder? Is dat man your farder?" she asked, over and over again, as she gasped for air.

Ganief's frown grew fearful. He approached Motchie Gafsa, who held her hands out and her fingers up, to prevent him from coming closer.

"Yes, Mrs Ebrahim . . . my father moved back with us a few months back . . . and . . . "

"Doan touch me . . . get away from me. . . doan touch me . . . I dirint see it when you were a young boy, standing at my gate . . . but I see it now . . . your eyes . . . ai, tog . . . what has this family come to." Motchie Gafsa was now beside herself and looked penetratingly at Ganief.

Ganief stood back and held his hands up as though a weapon had been placed to his head. He looked over his shoulder and caught a glimpse of his father walking briskly up the hill towards the hospital.

Motchie Gafsa ran heavily after Ganief's father. Several times she stopped and turned around to look at Ganief. Each time Motchie Gafsa drew a circle around her with both hands, with her thumb and forefinger pinched together, then shaped her fist like a snake's head and hissed. She drew her hand down from the level of her eyes to the ground, as though she was imitating a snake, the curves drawn out as she bent her body to accommodate the shape. She uttered a few words each time she performed the motion. Ganief could not hear what they were, but he knew from the feral expression on her face that they were chilling and that they warranted great caution. When she had completed the sequence of gestures, she stepped out of the circle she drew and called out some distance away. Ganief observed liveliness in her now and the frown on his face grew deeper.

It was then that a fish lorry stopped for her.

"Peter! Peter!" she called out.

The lorry's brakes screeched and the young man leapt out, the entire vehicle shaking at it came to a halt.

"Motchie Gafsa . . . Ai, Motchie Gafsa, what is der matter?"

She leaned against Peter Jantjies as she tried to speak and used her scarf to dry her sweaty face. She looked down the street; hardly anyone was about. Peter followed her lead and looked down the street too, not quite sure who or what he was looking for. He helped Motchie Gafsa to the door of the lorry and spoke to her slowly and calmly.

"Motchie Gafsa, what is der matter?"

"Ai, Peter . . . ai . . . ," she said, breathless.

He opened the passenger door and helped her to the seat.

"Put your head back, Motchie. I have some water in der back." She shook her head profusely. "Motchie, I can take you home, not a problem."

"Ai, Peter," she said again, swallowing hard.

Peter did not wait for her permission to fetch the bottle of water. He opened the back of the lorry and brought her the bottle of water, which was round, made of strong rubber and difficult to open.

"Let me open dis, Motchie. My cousin is waiting for me in Kalk Bay. We go out and do crayfish diving in Simon's Bay, you know . . . and we go wit a coupla guys from Kalkie . . ."

After Motchie Gafsa had gulped enough, she shook Peter's body and interrupted his speech.

"Peter, jus take me to Mamma Zila and Auntie Flowers' . . . kanala, Peter."

Peter shut the driver's door, blew his nose, and started the lorry. He looked about the street as he fiddled with his handkerchief, still trying to ascertain whether anyone walking on the Main Road could provide him with some information as to what had taken place. Peter tucked the handkerchief in the top pocket of his shirt and looked in all directions, trying to catch a glimpse of someone who would give him some information.

Motchie Gafsa now had her hands neatly folded on her lap; she looked out of the window and did not utter a word.

When the lorry pulled up in front of Auntie Flowers' house, Motchie Gafsa looked at Peter and said, "I am very grateful . . . I woan forget your kineness, Peter, Masha Allah, I woan forget your kineness. Thank you, Peter."

Peter nodded and did not say another word. He walked around the lorry to help Motchie Gafsa and could see Auntie Flowers squinting through the curtain.

"I'll be fine, Peter. You better go do your crayfish business wit your cousin. Tramakasie, Peter." Peter moved away reluctantly and walked to his lorry. He stood at the driver's door for a few minutes until Motchie Gafsa waved him away with her hand.

Peter started the lorry when Auntie Flowers came to the door then headed for De Waal drive. He drove slowly, turning left onto Constitution Street. He pulled up in front of Motchie Gafsa's house only to find Gairo and Rashied pushing the red Mini towards their house. After assisting the pair, Peter entered the house and asked to speak to Gadija. Gadija, who was not only surprised but also taken aback that Peter took the liberty of speaking to her, simply looked at him as he attempted to be articulate. Peter held his hands behind his back. He fondled with his jersey then with his handkerchief until Gadija took it upon herself to direct him to the backyard. The air must have aided Peter's speech for he soon filled her in on her mother's whereabouts. Gadija was silent. She walked into the kitchen as Peter stood in the backyard. She returned with four koeksisters wrapped in foil paper and handed them to him, smiling, then she led him to the front door. Peter held the foil package to his nose and inhaled the warm coconut-filled delicacy. Gadija thanked him and Peter, quite aware of his unwelcome presence, hastily dashed off to his lorry. Gairo and Rashied busied themselves in the house and looked to their older sister for some feedback, knowing full well that the contents of her conversation with Peter concerned their mother or Galiema. Gadija stared at them and carried on with her chores, not once meeting their eyes.

It was Gadija who made the much-needed telephone call to Groote Schuur Hospital to ascertain whether Ganief and his father had been to see Galiema. Gadija who, destined to do her third-year psychology practice in the Emergency unit, presumed on the familial connection she had with one of the medical students. He, on the other hand, sought out one of the nurses in the maternity ward, and verified for Gadija that it was indeed Ganief Salie and his father Gamiel who had visited Galiema. He engaged the nurse on as many details as possible. The nurse made a point of telling the medical student that Galiema was rather upset when she saw Ganief's father but that she was willing to see Ganief. Gadija was determined to get to the bottom of the matter. She crunched her knuckles as she paced up and down in her bedroom upon her return home. After Peter's short visit she had walked to DeVilliers Street, where she chatted with her mother, Mamma Zila and Auntie Flowers. Although they assured her that they would take care of matters, she believed that she had better ways of dealing with crisis situations—more modern, she believed, than reading cards, turning Bibles and interpreting tea leaves or incomprehensible Tokkalosies, as the discussion of the generation before her revealed. Motchie Gafsa did not reveal the full extent of her emotional upset to her daughter, nor the reasons for it: only Mamma Zila and Auntie Flowers alone were privy to that information. Motchie Gafsa was particularly distant towards Gadija since she appeared agitated with the women who her mother sought for advice, guidance and comfort. Mamma Zila and Auntie Flowers were not impressed with the way in which Gadija spoke to her mother nor keen on the manner in which she addressed them. Like a modern tempestuous woman, Gadija left Auntie Flowers' house in a huff, her hands sweaty, her scarf draped clumsily about her neck and her pouted maroon mouth pointed with contempt, all the while scheming and planning.

Gadija now sat at the window of her bedroom. Her sister Gairo and her brother Rashied had taken her daughters to the Cape Town Gardens for their Sunday walk, after Rashied attended to her car. Cape Town gardens had water fountains and breathtaking flowers, all of which would keep the girls occupied, she thought, as she brushed her hair. Gairo prepared Sunday lunch, as was expected of her, despite the fact that she had not cooked a full meal before. She had, of course, on many occasions observed her mother and Galiema, and since neither one of them were home, she proceeded with lunch, as her mother and Galiema would expect of her. Gairo struggled throughout, but did not once ask for assistance from any of the neighbours, even though she could have since it was customary for women to assist one another, especially when there was a family emergency.

Gadija ate her food without saying a word to anyone. Her two daughters, Amina and Mymoena, did not utter a word either. Rashied helped Gairo with the dishes and neither one of them asked Gadija for any assistance. Gadija announced to both her siblings that she had urgent business to attend to, although its nature was not made clear to either one of them. Gadija walked about the house in her bathroom robe, looking rather learned since the garment was white and resembled a lab coat, but she realized she had to suppress her exaggerated sense of self-importance and make some decisions. She was accustomed to making decisions without speaking to anyone, and certainly accustomed to ignoring the wishes of those she believed she acted on behalf of—her younger siblings. Unlike her mother and the women of Motchie Gafsa's generation, Gadija did not speak to the universe or consult the earth for guidance—she scoffed at those who believed in such superstition. Her mother, with the help of her friends, had access to this kind of knowledge, but it was she who contemplated the outcome and intervened to assure its result. Gadija thought of herself as alone in her own laboratory, concocting her solutions by herself.

She now sat at the kitchen table eating beetroot out of a glass jar. There was plenty of leftover lunch since Gairo had roasted a chicken with three vegetables and a bobotie, the household favourite, made of spiced sweet and sour minced lamb with a custard topping which was accompanied by yellow rice. Gadija had sought out the beetroot to settle her stomach. She separated out the onions and ate only the vinegary beets. A knock on the door broke the silence of her thoughts. She dashed to the window and saw that the request she had sent out for was

now on her doorstep. She hastily washed her hands and put the beets
back into the refrigerator.

"I'll be there now-now," she called out. "Just hang on . . . hang on."

She took the bathroom robe off and threw on a neat black skirt and
a white shirt. She brushed her hair again, then patted it down as one
might a hairy pet. It was when she was applying her dark maroon lipstick that she noticed her hands, stained with beet juice. There was no
time now to scrub them. She rubbed her hands against her skirt but to
no avail—the stains refused to go. The person at the door knocked
again, this time much louder than before.

"Leikom," she greeted, opening the door.

"Leikom Salaam," replied the visitor, as he introduced himself as
Ludwi's uncle, Gamatjie. He was small in stature and not at all what
Gadija expected. She expected to see someone tall and rugged—someone who, in her estimation, looked like the leader of a gang. He was a
leader, but not the leader of his gang: gang leaders did not frequent the
homes of those who wanted jobs to be carried out. He spoke very little,
and his tattooed face revealed little emotion, let alone expression. He did
not sit down on the settee despite the invitation she extended, several
times, nor did he wish to partake of the tea and biscuits she had prepared in anticipation of his visit. His eyes were cold enough, she
thought, for him to carry out any act; he did not care whether he had
served time in prison and had not been inside in two years despite his
public and rather colourful resume, so he was, in her opinion, a good
choice for the task she had in mind. Gadija made several attempts at
conversation, all of which he ignored. She even made reference to his
gang, expecting that he would say something in response. He simply
shifted and shrugged with indifference. When Gadija made another
attempt at conversation he interrupted her.

"Jus gimme der money, Galatie, and I'll be on my way."

She stared at him for a long time, astounded by his use of the common street term, a form of address street vendors used when pitching
their fruit and vegetables to their Muslim customers. There was some
level of professionalism on his part, she thought, as she stumbled to the
kitchen, annoyed at his unwillingness to converse. Many gangsters made
a pretence of good manners and civil speech. But Gamatjie hardly spoke

to Gadija. He did not even look at her: not at her clothes, her body, her lips, her gestures, nor at her lipsticked mouth as she spoke. His eyes did not follow her into the kitchen, nor did it roam about the house. She did not matter to him and thus, as a consequence, she was willing to go ahead with her plan and for someone as uncaring and unmannerly as Gamatjie to carry it out.

She handed him the envelope and he took it by the tip, ensuring that his unsightly hand did not brush hers. She did not attempt to hide her beet-stained hands for she thought it might arouse his curiosity. Whether he noticed it or not, she didn't know, for he averted his eyes. It was then that she noticed the letters tattooed on the knuckles of his right hand, POES, which was the vulgar term for a woman's genitals. Tattooed on the knuckles of his left hand were the letters LOVE, odd for a man who showed no evidence of the kind, she thought.

"Leikom," he said as he walked to the door and turned the knob. He shut the door fast and hard behind him, preventing her from indulging in further unwanted courtesies. He put his woolen hat on his head the minute he stepped outside, pulling it almost over his eyes, spat on the pavement, then performed his rhythmical, sauntering, slanted-shoulder gangster walk with utmost pride.

Gadija stood behind the door, cracking her fingers, pondering how the deed would be carried out and whether it was possible for her to be witness to it. The mental projection she indulged in did warrant some screening, and she held her string of thoughts on her mental screen, white and bold, as far and for as long as time, imagination and memory permitted. She stared down at the table, with its tray of tea and the plate of untouched biscuits. She decided that a visit to Galiema would make up for the conversational emptiness of her encounter with Gamatjie.

It was now early evening and the rain started on her again. Although she thought it was merely going to be a light drizzle, the heavy downpour now rattled Gadija a little as she stepped off the bus and prepared herself for the uphill walk to Groote Schuur Hospital. The ground was slick and she kept her head down and watched every step she took since visiting hours on Sundays were busier than other times. On her arrival at the Maternity ward Gadija was approached by one of the nurses.

"Excuse me, are you Gadija?"

"Yes, who wants to know?"

"I think that you will find your sister a little quiet. I'm not sure how to tell you this, but she said that she doesn't want to see you."

"What? She said what?" Gadija replied, looking both stunned and scornful.

"Well, she described you to me and said that she did not want to see you."

"That's nonsense. I will go and speak to her myself. Thank you. You may go now," Gadija replied, whereupon the nurse gave her a rather unfriendly look.

"So, it's true then, you do think you're Miss High and Mighty. I work here . . . you don't dismiss me like a servant . . . do you hear me? Gah, full of yourself, hey," she said all at once, as she grabbed a pile of linen from the nearby trolley and walked off.

Gadija walked hastily to the ward, looked about and spotted Galiema.

"So, I hear you don't want to see me?" she said as she flung her hand-bag over the chair adjacent to hers.

Galiema stared at Gadija without saying a word. She did not adjust her lying position in her bed, nor did she make any attempt to sit upright to address or converse with her sister. Instead, she pulled the pink woolen blankets over her shoulder and turned her back to her sister so that she now faced the wall.

"Galiema, what's the matter? Talk to me. At least tell me who the father is. Come on, we are all worried about you . . . Galiema!"

Galiema stared at the wall to her left. Gadija glanced over at her sister's bedside table and noticed a basket of fruit and two cards. Galiema grabbed the cards before Gadija could read them. Gadija was quite unaware that anyone outside their family knew of Galiema's hospitalization, apart from Mamma Zila and Auntie Flowers, whom she knew her mother had informed earlier in the day, and who had indicated that they would visit the following day. Gadija pulled a chair close to her sister's bed and touched her arm. Galiema turned herself around in her bed and Gadija reached for the small card in her hand. In an instant she drew it out and read it. Gadija was so shocked by the handwriting of the writer that she screeched and as a consequence startled all of the visitors in the ward. The nurse who had warned her away was now standing close by with her hands on her hips, glowering. Gadija flung her handbag over her shoulder, almost hitting the nurse, and ran out of the ward. A trail of stares followed her out of the ward and the nurse stood aside, shaking her head as she called upon one of the trainee nurses to attend to Galiema.

On Monday morning, Gairo and Rashied had just left for work and Amina and Mymoena were eating their corn-meal porridge when Gadija emerged from her room and greeted her mother and her daughters. Gadija looked at the breakfast table, which still had on it a jug of milk, cinnamon and a pot of rooibos tea. Gadija shook her head when her mother gestured her to sit down. She kissed her daughters on the forehead and swung her handbag over her shoulder. Motchie Gafsa had asked Gadija to stop by Chapel Street Primary School, where Galiema worked, to inform her principal that she was in hospital. She would telephone her manager from there, she thought, as she pulled her scarf over her head and patted her hair down. Motchie Gafsa did not know how to use a telephone and Gadija did not feel comfortable using the telephone at the corner store. She kissed her daughters and said a few comforting words to her mother. Her friend Shaheeda waited for her in her cousin's car, and Gadija was delighted to see her. Once in the car, Gadija, who was usually reserved, even with her best friend, now spoke quite openly to Shaheeda. Shaheeda turned the car off and pulled over to the corner, where the younger boys were smoking before they departed for school. Several minutes later Shaheeda started the car again and pulled her scarf over her head, much as Gadija did. When Shaheeda pulled up in front of Chapel Street Primary School, Gadija asked her to stay in the car. She walked briskly to the entrance and was met by the caretaker, who carried a mop and a bucket of water. He recognized Gadija immediately and directed her to the principal's office, upon her request. The principal's office door was ajar. After knocking on the door, she peered in and she observed him talking on the telephone. He raised his eyebrows, nodded and gestured for her to wait in the adjacent office, which was the one her sister Galiema occupied as the school's secretary.

One of the senior teachers walked by and nodded. He turned suddenly and asked, "Is everything alright?"

"Yes, thank you. I am here to see the principal," she said.

"I haven't seen Miss Ebrahim this morning," he said, gesturing towards Galiema's office. "You are Miss Ebrahim's sister, right?" he asked. "You look so much alike. Is she alright? I don't know what we'll do without her."

"She's in hospital," Gadija replied.

"Oh. Is it serious?" he asked, stepping quite close to Gadija now.

"No, we don't think so. I am here to inform the principal."

"Oh, well, go inside. I am sure he'll be with you shortly."

"Actually, I was wondering where I could make a phone call?" she asked as she glanced at her watch.

"In your sister's office. Make yourself at home. I'm sure the principal will be with you any minute."

He nodded again, straightened his tie then walked towards the staff room, stealing a glance of her legs. Gadija was well aware of the effect she had on men, and she prudently pushed her scarf back on her head since it had slipped down during their conversation.

She placed her handbag on the chair, then walked over to the desk and sat on her sister's chair in order to make her telephone call. She stopped suddenly when she noticed, on the bookcase, a photograph of her husband Abdul. She was mystified by the presence of the picture, and alarmed. Mechanically, she picked up the receiver and called her manager. Her voice was shaky, and he in turn thought that something was terribly wrong with her. Gadija then looked about the room with mounting suspicion. Her heart was pounding as she began to rummage through her sister's top drawer. There she found a pack of letters, neatly held together by a rubber band, and upon it her husband Abdul's writing. With shaking hands she pulled off the rubber band. A small photograph of Ganief drew her attention to the open drawer. She put the pile of letters down and picked up a neat stack of photos. In it were several photographs of her children, cut out from larger photographs she herself was in. She heaved with anger when she saw several little cards bearing her sister's name, all suggestive of presents and flowers she had received. The little cards bore the name of the sender and the flower shop from which they were purchased. She stared at the name of the sender, which was none other than Ganief, and heaved as she read his name aloud. Several other cards were bundled together and simply read "from you know who." She took the pile of letters and dropped them in her handbag. Then she walked out the door right past the principal's office without saying a word.

Gadija ran towards her house as she waved to Shaheeda, who looked on bewildered. Gadija had not uttered one word on their way back and Shaheeda was now quite concerned, yet uncertain as to what she would do. Shaheeda asked Gadija whether she wanted to be accompanied but Gadija just shook her head. Shaheeda sat in the car and played with her car keys, wracked with indecision, before driving off slowly away. Gadija stormed into the house, took her scarf off, and headed to her room, intending to read the letters sent to Galiema by her husband. She was stopped by the sound of sobbing coming from the kitchen. Motchie Gafsa was home. She shoved the pile of letters under her pillow on the top bunk, then walked into the kitchen. Auntie Flowers and Mamma Zila were at her mother's side. She could see the orange-red rooibos tea in their cups, their smell still strong and fresh.

"Leikom," Gadija said, looking at both Auntie Flowers and Mamma Zila. Both women nodded.

"Ai, Gadija," Mamma Zila remarked, as she put the teacup in its saucer.

"Oemie, what's the matter?" Gadija asked, as she sat down beside her mother.

Motchie Gafsa dabbed her eyes with the ends of her scarf. She looked at her friends and gestured with her teary eyes, urging them to respond to her daughter.

"Ai, Gadija," Mamma Zila remarked again, shaking her head with her eyes closed. Gadija stared at both women rather coldly then rolled her eyes. "That poor man . . . " Mamma Zila continued as she held her hand to her mouth.

"Will someone please tell me what is going on?" Gadija asked, agitated. She folded her arms across her chest and looked about the kitchen contemptuously.

"Gadija, there is bad news," Auntie Flowers said, lowering her head.

"Please, just tell me, Auntie Flowers . . . Oemie?"

Upon addressing Auntie Flowers, Gadija looked towards her mother who in turn looked towards Mamma Zila.

"There is no easy way of saying this, Bokkie," Mamma Zila remarked, as she kept her eyes low and her voice soft.

Gadija was both fed up and annoyed at the suspense she was kept under.

"Just tell me, kanala!" she screamed, her hands in her hair.

"Ganief went to visit Galiema yesterday . . . Oh, Bokkie, this is so sad. He found out that the old man, his father who just moved back with them a few months ago, had taken advantage of Galiema, you know . . . and you know . . . he was so angry last night that he had a fight with his father . . . and the old man had a heart attack and died. Ganief thought the old man was just putting it on so he left. This morning, Ismail, his brother, found Ganief dead in the lane. He had been stabbed."

Gadija did not move. She looked at her mother, who was now sobbing uncontrollably. Motchie Gafsa lifted herself from her chair and started to fall when, in an instant, Mamma Zila and Auntie Flowers caught her. Motchie Gafsa indicated that she was fine and able to get herself up. She held onto the kitchen table as she sobbed and walked the backyard where everyone could hear her sobbing and wailing.

Gadija's face was flush but she remained silent. Auntie Flowers was looking at her rather closely. Gadija looked up, caught her gaze and shifted her eyes again. Gadija looked at the cups of tea which where on the table and shifted her eyes from one to the other. Auntie Flowers followed Gadija's every gesture with her eyes and began to inform her on matters she thought Gadija needed to be aware of.

"You know, Gadija, Ganief's father left them years ago. He's name is Gamiel, he was the one who . . ."

"Raped! Raped! He was the one who raped my mother! Yes, I managed to work that out after I left your house, even though my mother only told me bits and pieces."

Auntie Flowers and Mamma Zila were shocked by Gadija's tone and stared at her in disbelief. Gadija seemed oblivious to her mother's presence and continued.

"Yes! Finally, an adult, a grown woman like you can use the word," she said, banging her hand on the table, her hair flying in every direction and her posture forceful and stiff. Auntie Flowers and Mamma Zila looked at one another; Motchie Gafsa was crouching in the backyard crying into her scarf, which was covering her entire head. "What is wrong with you people, hey? What is wrong with you? Are you all going to go about your business today and just forget to use the word? Rape! Rape!"

Gadija threw her body over the table and cried out loud.

"He raped my mother, he raped Galiema, and his son, my so-called friend, Ganief, probably raped Gairo! Just think about it, for Allah's sake and Galiema is going to have this rapists baby, and I . . . I killed . . ."

She was screaming now, throwing the tea-cups and saucers at the wood-burning stove where a fire was glowing.

The two women just stared at her then lowered their eyes, still attempting to make meaning of her words. Fury was bursting from Auntie Flower's lips, but she held back and looked on. Mamma Zila bore a look of intense inquiry and stared fiercely at Gadija.

"Oh, Allah, Allahhhh!" Gadija cried out. She banged her hands and her head on the table.

Auntie Flowers grabbed her firmly and shook her.

"You had Ganief killed? . . . Answer me . . . answer me!"

"I will make it right . . . I will make it right," Gadija murmured, as she gazed up at Auntie Flowers. She looked about the kitchen, ensuring that her mother had not heard her confession. Auntie Flowers shook Gadija vigorously, and when Gadija lifted her hand to her face, a motion Auntie Flowers may have mistaken, she slapped Gadija across the face, her own hand shaking as a result of the force she used.

"You will do nothing of the kind. Nothing at all! Pull yourself together. Get a grip. You sit here in judgment of us, hey? We don't have your education and you go about doing stupid things."

Gadija was shaking when Auntie Flowers let go of her. She looked at Mamma Zila, who in turn gazed at her with cold eyes; Mamma Zila shook her head, and disappointment could be read in her gestures.

Auntie Flowers rolled her sleeves to her elbows and walked towards

Gadija. Gadija stepped back, and attempted to speak to the two women.

"I was . . ."

"Be quiet! Shut your mouth! You will do nothing. Nothing! You don't speak to anyone because you think you're so high and mighty and you know everything."

Auntie Flowers kept her eyes fixed on Gadija and walked right up to her as she spoke; the younger woman moved back, sobbing, until she was trapped against the wall and could not move.

"Auntie . . ."

"Don't Auntie me!"

Gadija could see Auntie Flowers' tonsils as she spoke, her fierce face was so close. Auntie Flowers continued, raising her voice several notches.

"You don't know a damn thing! Not one damn thing! Ganief could be the father, but even that we are not sure of. You stupid, stupid woman! He was angry because he was a man, and he wanted to be the first and the only man Galiema had been with. His brother says that he was angry because of what his father did to Galiema . . . that he forced himself onto her . . . but that nothing actually happened because Galiema told Ismail. Ismail kept it to himself and when Ganief and his father were fighting, Ismail only knew then that Ganief knew but he did not say anything. Ganief was also angry because he was not Galiema's one and only. You don't understand men, do you? You don't understand men at all. You think they are made of private parts and eyes alone, eyes to look at you, and you alone, and fancy you! Well, Ganief also fancied your sister. Your own husband fancied your sister. So there, you were not the only one. Go to your room, like a child. Stay there. One of us old women will go to your employer and tell him you are sick. Don't look at me like that, because, really, you are. You will stay in your room and do as you are told. These are my orders, and I am sure your mother will agree. Look after yourself and your children, and other than that, keep your mouth shut. We'll take care of everything. Your children have one parent in jail already, they don't need another."

"But what about Gairo . . . the children . . . Rosa, Ludwi," she muttered as her tears fell to the floor.

"Ganief had nothing to do with that! It could have been his father; we are not sure. But never you mind, I will find out. As for the children,

I didn't think you even spoke to them. If you did, you would know that they are angry with Ganief about other things! You're a grown woman and you don't know how to speak to children! They have more sense than you. They know what's going on in District Six. You should have asked them and not drawn your own conclusions!"

Auntie Flowers shook her head and looked at Mamma Zila. She moved away from Gadija; shaking her head, and made a fist as she sat down. She banged her fist on the table, shaking the entire kitchen and its contents. Mamma Zila squinted, a look of contempt on her face, as she looked at Gadija's legs, not her face.

Gadija looked at the two women. Her mouth was open and she was breathing heavily. Her eyes drooped with fatigue. The kitchen was silent as Mamma Zila and Auntie Flowers observed every expression on Gadija's face. Auntie Flowers stood and placed her hands on her hips waiting for Gadija to make her move. Gadija dragged herself from where she was standing. She looked up and saw her mother crouching in the doorway, her face drawn and her eyes still. It was clear that Motchie Gafsa heard what had transpired. She attempted to move her hand towards her mother, only slightly, but the look in her mother's eyes gave Gadija every reason not to.

Motchie Gafsa leapt from her crouched position and grabbed Gadija by the hair. Gadija was so shocked since she first mistook her mother's raised hands as intending a warm embrace. Motchie Gafsa dug her hands into her daughter's head. Since Gadija did not expect it, she staggered back, looking rather surprised. Motchie Gafsa slapped her in the face, and Gadija gasped so loudly that she lost her balance. Motchie Gafsa did not stop; she slapped her again, and again, and again, until Gadija sat huddled on the kitchen floor. Mamma Zila and Auntie Flowers now tried to move Motchie Gafsa away from Gadija, who was screaming and crying at the top of her lungs with both her arms covering her head.

"Oemie . . . kanala tog, Oemie . . .Oemie . . . kanala, Oemie!"

Motchie Gafsa took the slippers off her feet and continued the beating. Gadija's beet-stained hands were redder. and thick welts showed evidence of the intensity of her mother's beating. Mamma Zila held Motchie Gafsa back as Auntie Flowers spoke to her. The women moved

Motchie Gafsa to the window and assured her that she had done enough
and that they were concerned about her health. But Motchie Gafsa continued to shout at her, much to the surprise of her friends, who both
thought that Motchie Gafsa was done talking.

"You're a disgrace . . . all der education, hey . . . and all our time dat
you take . . . all my hard work, hey . . . a disgrace . . . get yourself out
of here . . get out!"

Gadija got up off the floor and covered her eyes. She walked into the
kitchen and tried to turn on the tap.

"You will do nothing of the kind!" Auntie Flowers remarked her
hands still on her hips.

"I . . . need . . . to wash . . . my hands," Gadija said, amid hiccups
and stammers.

"No you don't!" Auntie Flowers insisted.

Gadija tried to turn on the tap again. Auntie Flowers grabbed
Gadija's hand and pushed her aside.

"You will not wash your hands, do you hear me? Over my dead body!
You will not wash your hands!"

Gadija wiped her hands against her clothes. Her body was shaking as
she walked towards her room. All of the women's eyes were on her and
tears were streaming down her face. She walked into her bedroom and
sat on her mother's bed, sobbing and crying as the three older women
huddled around the kitchen table with their teacups.

A loud knock on the door got Gadija up, and she answered it, over
the women's objections. It was Meisie.

"Gah, so I hear Galiema is going to have your husband's baby, hey? I
am the jintoe, I am the one who whores with policemen for favours, but
the favour they gave me was even better. I hear your husband gets treated well by one of the police on Robben Island, hey; so well that they left
him alone with Galiema. So now . . . look at who is the whore. . ."

Gadija slammed the door in her face. She did not utter a word. She
walked into the kitchen and looked at the older women, who sat together, staring at her. They did not utter a word, nor did they act surprised.

Gadija's tears were still warm when her Motchie Gafsa opened the
bedroom door minutes later. A pair of scissors was in her daughter's
hand and all of her hair lay on the floor. Gadija did not recognize her

mother when the woman entered and spoke to her. Her entire face was covered with lipstick, and scraps of clothes were strewn everywhere. Strips of paper from the letters she collected littered the floor. The look in Gadija's eye was of another world, one she had descended into to escape the consequences of her thoughtless actions.

The Bracelet

Carolyn and Nathaniel lived on the upper side of DeVilliers Street. Uppersiders lived along the border between District Six and De Waal Drive. Roeland Street was the lower part of De Waal Drive and met several District Six streets, quite against the better wishes of those who cherished the notion of living on its border. DeVilliers Street had an upper side only to those who named it such, to suit their purposes. This upper side on DeVilliers Street was composed of a row of seven houses, close to Roeland Street, which were occupied by families who carried themselves as though they were not Black and certainly not Coloured, as the latter was more descriptive of the social, ethnic and cultural particularities of District Sixers. Uppersiders were mocked by most of the District Six residents because they put on airs and graces, which many thought completely uncalled for and utterly ridiculous. They carried themselves as though they were White, but their misfortune was that one drop of Black blood rendered them Coloured. This system of classification did not allow them to realize their aspirations and kept them hostage to a reality of blood counts. Thus, as a consequence, they lived among the District Six residents. The uppersiders felt protected enough because their houses were close to Roeland Street, which was linked to De Waal Drive—the highway to the White neighbourhoods. Accordingly, when they went into the center of the city they simply walked straight down Roeland Street and did not venture into the heart, let alone the arteries of District Six. The uppersiders did not show themselves on Hanover Street, the Seven Steps, the Star cinema or even the Avalon cinema: the belly of District Six. They frequented drive-ins, where they remained in their cars and ordered food which was delivered to their car window. On the other side of Roeland Street, the border as it were, lived the "Poor Whites," and many on the upper side scoffed at these poorer people for not living up to the full potential their blood allowed. Uppersiders lived on the border of District Six as it extended itself towards Walmer Estate and the new Zonnebloem—close to Roeland Street, all along De Waal Drive. One could easily spot uppersiders because their noses were stuck in the air as though they only belonged there, away from their bodies, whose smell might remind them of what they shared with those whom they chose to ignore. God had not granted them the inestimable privilege of replacing their body functions with ones they might consider more suitable.

Nathaniel was new to District Six; he was from the Christian quarter of Salt River, where pockets of the population were fair skinned enough to warrant consideration for a White identity. At first glance District Six residents could easily assume that he was much like those with whom he shared close ties but upon approaching him his friendliness soon proved quite the contrary and converted them instantly. He was tall, tan, as many would note, or honey brushed, as others would assert, depending on who fancied to offer the description. His hazel eyes and light brown hair were also detailed during verbal exchanges; some even described him as blonde. It was not unusual for men in District Six to have his complexion and physical features; they, however, conveyed in their posture, mannerism and speech, very clearly, that they were District Sixers. It was difficult for Nathaniel to learn the masculine mannerisms appropriate to his economic status, education and new place of abode: they all seemed rather conflicting.

Carolyn's mother and grandmother had lived on the upper side of DeVilliers Street for many years. District Sixers were not quite sure what the family's true ancestry was, but it was said that the family had "jumped over the rope," that is, they had jumped over the colour line. Such people were usually the product of Black-White couplings that had occurred since the establishment of District Six.

Washing lines were strung with rope, and whilst uppersiders exhibited few items on their lines, District Sixers mocked every custom they performed. Most District Six residents treated uppersiders with contempt; others felt sorry for them because they were caught between two worlds: the White world they wanted to be part of and whose privileges they believed deserved to be extended to them, and the world of the Coloured population of District Six, composed of Muslims and Christians, the children of emancipated slaves who intermarried with the Khoi and the San and with people who were brought from Malaysia by the Dutch—those with whom the uppersiders believed they did not share anything in common. The Muslims, with this Malaysian ancestry, were referred to as Cape Malay, and for Carolyn and her family there was, apparently, no evidence of their blood among those who gladly celebrated their District Six heritage.

The uppersiders ate English and Dutch style food; their palates were not trained to crave the spiciness of the District Six dishes nor desire the saucy, passionate performance of hands scooping curry with roti or tongues licking warm cooked desiccated coconut out of syrupy ginger and cardamom spiced koeksisters. On Sunday mornings the uppersiders would send their children lower down on District Six to buy koeksisters; their children, of course, were wiser, and would ensure that they were accompanied by children who were better known to the residents from whom they purchased these delicacies. Nita, their chosen negotiator, would on many occasions accompany the children from these seven families, but not without her friend Rosa. Her fee, as stipulated by Rosa, was frequent packets of Willards crisps, preferably cheese and onion flavour, and that they not torment Nita by calling her "four eyes," for not only did she wear spectacles, she did, much like her friend Rosa, see events before they actually happened.

In 1970 it was a big accomplishment for someone like Carolyn to be a university-educated schoolteacher. She had gone to the University of Cape Town, where she met Nathaniel's sister, Victoria. Carolyn, who was classified as Coloured on a document she kept hidden in her underwear drawer, had been part of a small group of Coloured people allowed to attend the University of Cape Town under the permit system. The University of Cape Town was, after all, a White university with one priority only: to educate the White population for further superiority and governance. Carolyn now taught at Hewitt College in the English department; not many District Six youth had even heard of Hewitt

College, let alone the University of Cape Town.

Nathaniel was fair skinned enough to work in a bank in the center of town. The selections of fair-skinned men and women to work in public places such as banks were made by their White overseers; the selections were obvious to residents of District Six, who knew well enough that their children would be coached on their employment potential by schoolteachers, based on their skin colour, how well they spoke English and where they lived: few, if any, would be advised on bank work. Parents, whilst aware of the limitations their ancestry, colour and class offered, cultivated within their children a love of life, joy, passion, strength, determination and rebelliousness—all of which were above legislation.

Carolyn and Nathaniel's eight-year-old daughter played with Rosa and Nita when her mother and grandmother were not keeping their watchful eyes on her. Victoria, named after her aunt, was a sweet and soft-spoken little girl who appeared to be socially inept in the eyes of many of her peers who took pleasure in spinning wooden tops whilst barefoot, shooting and trading marbles, tying stockings with stones and flinging them over avocado trees and competitively climbing trees at the Hopelots with little boys who traded and paid the going rate for a girl on their team who would lead them to victory. Victoria was quite unlike her name suggested; she sat at the window most afternoons, whilst her mother and grandmother spoke condescendingly of children in District Six who had runny noses, played barefoot and whose fathers smoked cannabis in broken bottletops. Nathaniel made an effort to speak to his neighbours, but when he was accompanied by Carolyn, he ensured that he stayed a safe distance from the District Six residents, whom he greeted with his eyes; he did not utter a word to anyone she disapproved of in her presence.

On Friday evenings Carolyn and Nathaniel stayed indoors, mostly, and on the odd occasion the family beside theirs would visit and they would drink white wine and eat hard white cheese on dry, unsalted crackers. Carolyn's parents, Mr and Mrs Collingwood, had three daughters and a son. The older daughter, Olivia, lived in Germany and the middle one, Elizabeth, lived in Maitland, some twenty-five minutes away by car. Elizabeth's twin boys, Shaun and Paul, aged twelve, lived with their grandparents because their mother was not allowed to take them to her new home: her new husband forbid her to bring her Coloured children from a previous union into his house. Carolyn, as their youngest, lived with her parents. Carolyn's brother, Neville, lived on Hanover Street with his business partner Calvin because, as was regularly asserted by his parents to those who asked after him, it was easier for Neville to be close to the hairdresser he co-owned and ran with Calvin than to live with them.

The Chamberses and the Collingwoods were getting ready to sit down to their annual evening meal with their select charitable guests. Mrs Collingwood prepared more than one stuffed chicken and boiled several vegetables. The rice she boiled in turmeric, much to the surprise of her family members. It ended up a yellowish colour, and after admiring the dish, which somewhat resembled one she had seen eaten by her lower-side neighbours on the rare occasion when she was privy to their cooking, she sprinkled raisins over it. "That should give it some colour," she said aloud. She was a little nervous as she placed twelve plates on a table, which had not previously supported such a number.

Carolyn Chambers stood idly by and watched as her mother polished silver and moved knives and forks about, measuring the distance between each plate and the accompanying cutlery. "Why are you making such a fuss?" she said. "It's as though you are expecting the queen." "Haven't we done enough already?"

"Look, it won't kill you," her mother replied. "We do this once a year, and it is as little as we can do after Mamma Zila saved Victoria's life." Mrs Collingwood swung the silver cloth over her left shoulder, keeping a safe distance from her daughter. She glanced at her labour and straightened the silver cutlery with her cloth, not once touching it with her fingers.

"That was four years ago. I think I've done my share of being grateful. She happened to be walking past here with that other woman and you called them in. I am sure if you hadn't been so hysterical and phoned Nathaniel at work Victoria could have been taken to the hospital to have the bean removed from her throat . . . curried beans, I'll have you know. What were you thinking? Now, I have to sit at my dinner table with those people and pretend to be grateful."

"Well, that is okay for you to say. I still shudder to think what would have happened if Mamma Zila and Flowers had not walked past our house that day."

"So now you call her Mamma Zila too?" Carolyn pulled a face of scorn and disdain. "And the other woman, doesn't she have a proper Christian name? How common! And coming from you! You become just like those people when you let them into your house once a year . . . Is Daddy expected to eat yellow rice? You've turned our dinner into one of their carnivals."

"Keep your voice down, Carolyn."

"Ooh," she cried out in retaliation.

Mr Collingwood entered the dining room. He looked at Carolyn and grinned as he observed his wife carefully placing table mats on the table. His posture was a little hunched and his wrinkled, freckled face showed evidence of too much exposure to the sun and too little exposure to people. He looked about the dining room and observed, with raised eyebrows, the efforts his wife put into making the table beautiful. Mrs Collingwood glanced at her husband as he placed his hands behind his back and nodded at each place as though he was counting the guests at their seats before their arrival.

"What do we have here?" he asked in a deriding tone. "Table Mountain came down, hey," he remarked. Mrs Collingwood did not look up from her tasks and continued straightening out the tablecloth and putting the plates in their proper order. "Ohhh, so many plates," he said mockingly and with an air of jealousy since Mrs Collingwood fussed over the dinner settings of her guests more than she fussed over him.

"Don't you start. If you insist on making comments you better give me a hand," his wife replied.

"Sit down, Daddy, I'll get the other chairs," Carolyn remarked. Carolyn glared at her mother for attempting to draw her father into the organizing of the dinner table. "I would have preferred for Victoria to eat ahead of time. She shouldn't be here with all the adults . . . and that little girl. I suppose she's coming too."

"Look, Carolyn, we've been over this many times. Mamma Zila and

Flowers come here once a year and they always have their children eat at the same table. These people have taken an interest in Victoria, which I know you don't particularly like, but it is only one day of the year. They prefer for everyone to eat together, and Victoria can go to bed if it gets late."

"Well, make sure that the little girl, what's her name . . . Rosa . . . sits far away from me and from Victoria. Leave this side of the table free for them." She looked about, her eyes jotting down every possible move their guests might make, and she pointed to the side of the table closer to the front door, not the kitchen, as the side their guests ought to occupy. "Who is the other plate for?" Carolyn asked suddenly as she counted. She squinted and shook her head disapprovingly.

"It's for Mrs Hood."

"Oh, don't tell me she's coming too. Argh!" Carolyn's slim, frail, body folded itself in exasperation. Her mother just gazed at her and carried on with her tasks. "That woman's eyes are everywhere. She always looks at me as though she is trying to find fault with me. Oh dear, so now we'll have the little crazy child with that ridiculous book which hangs around her neck like a prison plate with a pencil sticking out from it as though she's deaf or dumb or mentally retarded or something and that strange woman who looks at me as though she is counting my veins."

"Oh, you do exaggerate. It's just her way. She's a very nice woman."

"Please don't tell me her husband is coming here too." Carolyn said, as she held both her hands up to push away the thought.

"No, no, no. He has never been here before. Besides, he walks with a stick and with a lot of difficulty. Apparently he has a gentleman friend staying with him tonight."

"Oh, I see. You do know everything about your neighbours," she said, tauntingly, expecting her mother to further engage her. Mrs Collingwood continued with her tasks.

Mr Collingwood now entered the living room with his newspaper under his arm. His face was a little flushed and his brows were raised to complete the frown of conceited curiosity he held.

"Are you talking about Tuckie?" he asked, touching the flowers in the center of the table. "He's a nice man. We used to greet each other in those days. He used to work in the dockyard and I used to see him almost every morning on my way to work."

Victoria joined her mother and her grandmother. She was small in stature for her eight years and had her mother's slim frame. Her hair was curled into ringlets and they hung at each side with a big blue ribbon curled out to full, frilly perfection. Carolyn inspected her daughter and insisted that she change her shoes. Victoria stood there a little bewildered. She looked at her shoes and then at her dress, not at all convinced that her mother's request warranted her consideration.

"Those ones do not go with that dress, darling," said Carolyn. Her daughter sighed and removed the shoes, then held them both on top of her head to indicate that she was fed up.

"Get the dark blue ones, darling," her mother said. Victoria was obedient, although a silent rebelliousness did surface within her, if only occasionally.

"Okay. All set," Mrs Collingwood called out as she admired the dinner table.

"I wonder what happened to Nathaniel. He's not usually this late." Carolyn looked at her wrist watch and tapped it to see that it was working. She winded it a few times and held it close to her ear. Victoria stood in the doorway of her bedroom observing the interaction between her mother and her grandmother.

It was thirteen minutes later when a knock on the door and a turn of the knob alerted Mrs Collingwood that her invited guests had arrived. She had forgotten that people on the lower side of DeVilliers Street let themselves in. As they opened the door, the sounds of District Six forced their way in. The cocks were crowing, most likely Motchie Tiema's, the sound of goema music could be heard, and the smell of cannabis, although slight, lay fresh and alive, clinging to the clothes of the guests, who often found themselves in close proximity to smokers, many of whom were present in their households. Mrs Collingwood stood there and inhaled it all as she greeted her guests. Their presence soon took over the entire house. Rosa stood beside Mamma Zila, who wore her fancy pink shoes and flowery pink dress whilst balancing a few plates, one stacked above another, in one hand. Peter Jantjies came along too, and

Carolyn staggered back when she saw him.

"Evening, everyone," he said hastily, in the most humble of tones. "I am just der carrier. I am just helping der ladies wit carrying a few tings for der supper." Mrs Collingwood gestured to her husband, who reluctantly relieved Peter from his load. "Good night," he called out as he dashed towards the door, looking almost frantic and relieved that he was not staying.

"Thanks, Peter," Auntie Flowers replied.

Mrs Collingwood and Carolyn were too busy observing the colour-fulness of their guests, the gifts they brought in the form of food, and the manner in which they asserted themselves in their home to pay attention to Peter's departure. Carolyn's eyes darted to and fro, not entirely sure that she had captured everything she was meant to and certainly not swift enough to respond to, as an experienced hostess might. Mamma Zila carried a small brown box which contained several glass jars of pickled fruits and jams; the box was handed to Mrs Collingwood, who accepted it thankfully yet rather clumsily. Auntie Flowers and Mrs Hood each carried a pot of flowers, and the box which Peter handed to Mr Collingwood contained a breyani in a rather large glass dish, fish frikkadels, daltjies, a tomato sambal and a plate of koeksisters. Auntie Flowers and Mrs Hood were dressed in their Sunday best.

They both wore dark blue dresses, differently shaped, accessorized with colourful scarves, and Auntie Flowers, who also brought her big black leather bag along, wore her walking shoes. Mrs Hood had her hair done up, much like Auntie Flowers did, except she looked a lot more glamorous for the occasion. Mrs Hood flashed her devilish smile each time Carolyn looked in her direction. Both of the women wore bras for the occasion, and it was obvious by the manner in which they shoved their breasts from one side to the other with their hands that their breasts were not too happy with the imposed constriction that social gatherings of this kind insisted upon. Auntie Flowers placed her big black leather bag in the corner of the living room, the one closest to her, whilst Carolyn looked on. Carolyn stared at the bag rather suspiciously.

"This is for later. I have to go and see a woman who has a bit of man trouble, you know. Nothing my remedies cannot cure. Her man is straying, so she says, and I will make a mixture for her to keep in the house . . ."

Auntie Flowers noted the frown on Carolyn's face and stopped suddenly. She held her hands in front of her, clasped them together and spoke
gently to Carolyn as she leaned forward.

"I am a voetvrou . . . a healing woman . . . and when there is sickness
or pain, I heal. You look puzzled my dear, but then again, you do not
know our ways." Carolyn simply nodded, half-heartedly, relieved that she
could now place her attention elsewhere.

"Hello, Rosa," Mrs Collingwood said.

"Hello, Auntie," Rosa replied. Mrs Collingwood tottered a little since
the child used the same familial term to refer to her as she used with
women in District Six. She touched Rosa's hair with restraint, not quite
sure how to engage the child. "Oh my, how beautiful," she remarked as
she observed the arrangement of flowers which were draped around Rosa's
head, much like a crown.

"Oh, I did that," Auntie Flowers remarked. "Doesn't she look mar-
velous?"

"Well, you look all pretty at the top . . . but what about this outfit?"
Mrs Collingwood said, as she shifted her eyes from Rosa to Mamma Zila.

"Oh, yes, today she's Maria de la Quelerie, aren't you, Rosa?"
Mamma Zila exclaimed.

"Yes, I Maria and Auntie Flowers did my hair wit der flowers."

Mrs Collingwood frowned and her eyes shifted about. Rosa read
her expression rather quickly.

"Maria was Jan Van Riebeeck's wife!" she called out. Rosa posed and
held her face at different angles as though she had been trained to show
herself off in that manner.

"Yer nuh, Rosa. Genoeg!" Mamma Zila called out, as she observed
Rosa taking the compliments to another, perhaps chancy, level.
Mamma Zila wore one of her Sunday dresses but no bra. Each time she
walked past one of the chairs she would allow herself a lot more room
than was ordinarily expected since she still had her money cloth with the
many knots, which most women in District Six of her generation wore,
pinned to the inside of her undergarment, which was a long white slip.

Victoria, who had been standing behind the curtain when the guests
arrived, now emerged from it. Her mother, still caught up by the

speed of events, some of which she was well aware she missed, stood observing Rosa and looked about to see where her daughter was. Victoria stood beside her friend; her excitable body jumped for joy as she observed Mamma Zila's little cellophane package, which the woman dangled in front of her. It contained sweets and some home-made biscuits, which Victoria had previously been privileged to enjoy— in their home, not hers.

Nathaniel entered the house and everyone turned to him. He managed a beautiful pearly smile as the older women's eyes fixed themselves on his appearance.

"Oh, our boy is here. Don't you look handsome," Auntie Flowers said in a giggly voice as her eyes naughtily surveyed every inch of him. He wore blue trousers and a white shirt, which was brought together rather well by a reddish tie. His jacket was draped over his shoulders and held by one finger, as was the custom with men who cultivated that particular handsome but casual look. Mr Collingwood sneered and looked at the furnishings in the living room as he greeted his son-in-law; his greeting was hardly audible to anyone.

Nathaniel bashfully extended his hand to Auntie Flowers, Mrs Hood and Mamma Zila. He kissed his daughter on the cheek and greeted Mrs Collingwood. She lowered her eyes with a smile and looked about the room, noting the order in which she received the greeting from her son-in-law. He stroked Rosa's head and grimaced when he observed the colourful flowers. She soon let him know who she was dressed as, and as he moved to touch her book she held her hands in front of her body to prevent his attempt. He got the message, grinned, and then looked about the house to see where Carolyn was. Shaun and Paul then came running into the dinning room, their hands still wet. They wiped their hands on their shirts despite the embarrassing stares their grandmother directed at them. They drew everyone's attention as they stood there, almost too tall for their age and certainly too tall for the juvenile treatment they were given. Nathaniel greeted them without shaking their hands. They were not expecting to be greeted in the manner in which he greeted their guests, and whilst their hands were now dry, they kept them behind their backs. The boys looked at each other constantly, ensuring that their actions were coordinated.

"Just excuse me for a minute, ladies," Nathaniel said. He sauntered across the dining room, jacket over his shoulder, in all his manly glory.

Carolyn was in the kitchen with her back towards him. She did not turn to greet him and he did not approach her either.

"Hi!" he exclaimed, waiting for her to return his greeting as he stood in the doorway.

She turned around and looked at him from head to toe.

"Are you done now with receiving compliments?" she asked with raised eyebrows.

He smiled. "How was your day?"

"So-so," she replied, handing him the cotton serviettes.

"I think everyone is waiting for you to start, Carolyn," he said.

"And so they should," was her taut reply.

His face was reddened by the position of superiority and insupportable haughtiness she assumed—without any thought for those around her who treated her with kindness. He ushered her into the living room, his hand strategically placed on the small of her back. Carolyn attached herself to his manly manner, practically serving herself to her dinner guests as though she were on the menu, held high on a golden platter by her much-admired husband.

She walked to her chosen seat and Nathaniel moved it out, then waited until she sat comfortably before he left her side. The women had removed their eyes from the spectacle they were meant to observe and carried on their conversation with Mrs Collingwood and the boys after their own secret communication to one another with their eyes.

"Your uncle is a hairdresser and he can't give you a haircut? Oh, come on, you can't cut your own hair . . . with such a sweetie little face you need a proper haircut."

Shaun giggled with contentment since his grandfather's eyes were not scrutinizing him. Mr Collingwood stared at Nathaniel, who clumsily took the seat at the end of the table opposite his father-in-law. Paul sat with his arms on his lap waiting for Auntie Flowers to turn her attention towards him.

"And you . . . don't even get me started on you. What a lovely young boy you've turned out to be. Now if only you could take care of those flowers in the garden I gave you like you take care of your stomach," she said as she pulled a face and teased the two boys. Paul was gesturing to Shaun with his arm. They both laughed merrily and without hesitation to show how excited they were.

Mrs Collingwood looked at Carolyn, who was moving serving plates about, as if to ask her permission to wait until her brother arrived. Neville was expected and had not made an appearance yet. Everyone sat in silence as Mrs Collingwood looked at her watch then back at Carolyn. It was clear that she was waiting for her son. There was an exchange of awkward stares between mother and daughter. Mr Collingwood did not make any effort with the guests, except when he occasionally stared at Rosa's costume, and sat with his elbows on the table looking at his empty plate. When his stares did not deter Rosa he decided that he would insert himself into the dinner-table conversation. Mrs Collingwood broke the silence by tapping her wine glass with her spoon. The doorbell rang and the doorknob was turned shortly after.

"Aaah," she called out. She fell back into her chair and folded her arms with ease and smiled. Mrs Collingwood beamed from ear to ear.

"Evening, everyone. Sorry I'm late."

Neville strolled in and looked at his mother, then turned his sparkling gaze to the invited guests. He was dressed casually in a white shirt and bluejeans. His father's eyes looked penetratingly at his mother, whose cheery disposition annoyed him greatly. The adult guests were smiling and shifted their chairs to make room for Neville to join them.

"Come in, sweetie. We are all waiting for you," she said.

Mrs Collingwood's eyes sparkled when she saw her son and greeted him but the sprightly nature of her excitability soon turned sullen when Calvin stepped into the living room and greeted her guests by their first name before turning his attention, dutifully and courteously, as his face suggested, to her and her husband and lastly to Carolyn.

"Oh, there you are, Bokkie. I was just saying to Mamma Zila how I saw you today and how I hoped you would come," Auntie Flowers remarked as she raised herself from her chair and looked about the table to ensure that there was room for Calvin to join them. She kissed him on the cheek whilst he greeted the remaining guests with his eyes. He was a lot smaller in stature than Neville and wore clothes many would find rather feminine. His trousers were of a creamy colour and his shirt was loose and flowing somewhat, and also cream. His small-featured face had a certain femininity to it, which he carried with comfort and ease. His hair was longer than most men's in District Six and had streaks of red and blonde, all tastefully done.

"Evening, Mrs Hood."

"Evening, child. How is your mummy?"

"Mummy's fine, Mrs Hood. Thank you."

"Evening, everyone," he said, looking at all the unwelcome adult eyes that laid their gaze upon him.

Mr Collingwood mumbled something when Auntie Flowers looked in his direction; Carolyn could not be bothered to conceal her disapproval. She looked at her mother in search of an explanation, and it soon became clear that none other than Auntie Flowers had invited the unwelcome guest. Shaun and Paul were sniggering and elbowing each other. They were old enough to know that whilst their uncle's love interest was not spoken of, Calvin's presence urged their family to address Neville's relationship with his business partner. The two boys were practically leaping out of their chairs with excitement. Neville walked into the kitchen whilst his father's eyes remained fixed on Calvin. He soon found a kitchen chair and an odd plate and held it in his hand, unsure where to place it. He moved beside Nathaniel, who stood as Calvin took his seat. The two newly seated guests looked at Rosa's outfit, then looked at Mamma Zila and smiled. Nathaniel took the plate from Neville whilst Mrs Collingwood reluctantly got the cutlery and arranged the unmatched thirteenth place setting. Her gestures were deceitful for she had to give the impression to her daughter and her husband that she was unwilling to attend to Calvin. Calvin's face reddened, and Mamma Zila, in observing Calvin's expression, soon drew him out.

"Auntie Flowers did her hair, Bokkie," she said as she leaned across the table to both Neville and Calvin. "Isn't it beautiful?" she asked.

Mr Collingwood nodded when Calvin looked in his direction and kept his eyes fixed on his plate.

Carolyn observed the way that Calvin spoke to Mamma Zila, Auntie Flowers and Mrs Hood. Rosa was chattering to Victoria, and Carolyn did not know where to direct her attention. Her eyes could no longer reprimand anyone; the manner in which the household now functioned was quite contrary to how she maintained it. Carolyn's father was silent; her mother was deliriously happy that her son was present; her daughter was thrilled to be sitting opposite her friend Rosa, a move orchestrated by Mamma Zila, who took Rosa's request quite seriously; her husband was engaged with the uninvited guest who paid her no mind; and he sat merrily, quite comfortably, between her brother and his lover; and her nephews were mesmerized by the attention they received and thrilled that people spoke, and spoke merrily, around dinner tables, quite unlike what they were accustomed to.

Carolyn looked at those with whom she shared her dinner table and was not pleased. Her father sat at the head of the table, her mother beside him, then followed Shaun and Paul, then herself and her daughter, Victoria; her brother Neville sat beside Victoria, enabling that side of the table to hold six seats.

Nathaniel sat at the bottom end of the table facing Mr Collingwood and thus beside Neville, and across from him sat Calvin; Rosa sat beside Calvin and thus opposite Victoria, whom she called Toria; and Mamma Zila, Mrs Hood and Auntie Flowers completed that row, in that order. Auntie Flowers thus occupied the chair beside Mr Collingwood, which she shifted some distance from him so that she could sit facing Shaun. And there they were, thirteen people sitting around a dinner table.

"Daddy, can you say grace?" Mrs Collingwood asked her husband.

Rosa nudged Mamma Zila with her elbow.

"He not her daddy, is he?" the child asked, quite unaccustomed to the manner in which Mrs Collingwood addressed her husband.

"No, he's not," Mamma Zila whispered.

Rosa seemed on the verge of another question as her lips were chattering away and her roving eyes composing one. "Not now, sweetie," was her grandmother's unsolicited response.

Mrs Collingwood was still waiting for her husband to start the prayer. She looked at him, her eyes asking the question again. Mr Collingwood looked uncomfortably at his dinner guests.

"No, someone else can say grace," was his mumbled reply.

He looked over towards his son-in-law, who seemed uncomfortable in his authoritative position at the bottom end of the table. Nathaniel was quiet and steered his father-in-law's undermining stares towards the backdoor.

"Do we not have any gentlemen here who can set the ladies the example?" Carolyn uttered in perfectly enunciated English. The men in the room appeared ill at ease. There was a short pause. A cloud of withdrawn manliness suddenly filled the room.

Auntie Flowers gathered herself together and stood up from her chair. Everyone soon gave Auntie Flowers their full attention. Shaun and Paul looked at their grandparents, both of whom seemed annoyed at one another. The boys were having a jolly good time since it was usually they who were the cause of unease and unpleasantness. They closed their eyes out of courtesy and peeked through every possible crevice to enjoy the full view of Auntie Flowers' bold actions. They folded their hands in front of their chest and waited for the woman to start the prayer.

"Auntie Flowers is taking over," Shaun murmured to Paul, whose entire body was shaking with suppressed giggles.

The Collingwoods, whilst annoyed at each other, appeared stunned but did not protest. Carolyn looked at her husband, then lowered her head disapprovingly. Her brother Neville started a chain of hand holding, which was not a custom they had ever practiced in their household. Her brother on one side and his lover on the other side were holding her husband's hands—and this disturbed Carolyn greatly. Paul looked at his aunt, who refused to hold his hand and kept her own under the table. The two boys nudged one another and glanced over at the end of the table, where their aunt's gaze was fixed. They noticed that Calvin's little finger bore a pinkish nail varnish on a rather long nail. Auntie Flowers held her head high as she faced the heavens—as though her voice was expected.

"Dear Lord. We are gathered here today . . . to give thanks to our friends and family . . . for standing by one another in our time of need. We remember your goodwill, dear Lord . . . and we ask that you grant us your peace . . . and your mercy . . . as we continue to learn . . . to be your humble servants. Bless us, dear Lord, on this day, when our guest Calvin joins us for the first time . . . at this gathering . . . and grant us the wisdom and understanding . . . to see beyond . . . the day-to-day trivialities and unkindness of mankind . . . and to work towards love and recognition of each and every one of us . . . in our individual spirits. Nurture us, dear Lord, and teach us, through your guidance . . . to love one another and to cherish one another . . . for who we are . . . not for who or what we want others to be. Teach us to share . . . and to partake in your glory and your kindness . . . in showing our love to one another openly . . . and without selfish boundaries. Bless us, dear Lord, as we try to live in harmony . . . and try to raise our children with pride and joy. Guide us through the troubled waters of our land . . . and watch over our children, in kindness and in health, and show them, dear Lord, through your mercy . . . that they matter to the world even if the world sometimes shows them otherwise . . . in your name's sake . . . Amen."

Auntie Flowers sat down and folded her hands on her lap. Rosa and Victoria still had their eyes closed, and the two adults on the opposite side of the table appeared rather uncomfortable. Shaun and Paul had their eyes open and their mouths too. Both Carolyn and her mother looked at Calvin and smiled. Carolyn's smile soon turned green when she noticed that Calvin still held her husband's hand.

"I think the prayer is over," she remarked, looking at Calvin, then with a cough withdrew her gaze the minute he looked at her.

Hands were let go, slowly, and serviettes, one after the other, were opened then placed on eager knees, as Carolyn hastened to set the example. She raised herself from the table and folded her serviette and placed it on her chair; she was keen to show, in full and calculated performance, the extent of her training. She assisted her mother with the chicken platter and walked straight to the end of the table where her husband was seated. He had already started chatting to Calvin. Her mother, overlooking her own husband, handed the second chicken platter to the women guests, who each passed it along to one another in an attempt to first serve Rosa. Shaun and Paul were looking at Calvin with great fascination, their eyes still fixed on the pink varnish and the long nail upon which it was painted. As Carolyn fussed over her husband, Nathaniel indicated to her to remain seated. He gestured with his hand, without once looking at her. She flung her hair back and walked to her chair. Auntie Flowers and Mamma Zila attended to Shaun and Paul whilst Mrs Hood kept a watchful eye over Calvin's plate.

"I know you don't always get time to eat at the hairdresser, Bokkie, so eat up," instructed Auntie Flowers. Calvin had his hands beside it and smiled as his plate was decorated. Shaun and Paul were still staring at him and in response he winked at them; this gesture provoked an outburst from all four of the children, each in their own way displaying their interpretation of events. Shaun and Paul folded their hands and placed them, singularly, between their legs. They rocked back and forth in their chairs, eliciting a reprimanding look from their aunt.

"Do you have ants in your pants?" was their aunt's question. The boys shook their heads and giggled at one another. "Then sit still!" was the command that followed.

Rosa was staring at Calvin too. He winked at her and she winked back at him. Victoria leaned forward to request her wink, but when she received it she recoiled into her chair, looking bashfully at her giggling cousins. They lowered their heads and looked at the floor. Rosa joined them in their effort to avert attention, copying their actions.

"There's a kakalak!" she called out, almost leaping out of her chair.

"Oh, don't be silly, we don't have cockroaches in our house," was Carolyn's immediate, irritable reply.

"Is true, Auntie Carolyn," Shaun boldly asserted as he pushed his chair back.

She looked under the table and found the creature scurrying about rather close to her feet. She leapt out of her chair then immediately tried to contain herself. Auntie Flowers raised herself from her chair after observing the little creature.

"There is no need for all this fuss," she said. "Fetch me a piece of paper, Shaun, from one of your school books, and I will put the little cockroach on the paper and put her outside."

"I don't know how that thing got in here," Carolyn remarked.

"Oh, she must have followed us, I suppose. She is one of God's creatures, just like us, and we will simply put her outside since she is not welcome on the floor of your supper table."

Auntie Flowers was casual in her manner and put the children at ease. They now sat rather still in their chairs. Mr and Mrs Collingwood did not utter a word but just stared at one another. Auntie Flowers accepted the piece of paper from Shaun, whilst Carolyn stood back in horror observing the creature being put onto the paper and then carried outdoors. Auntie Flowers did not request permission to walk through their kitchen and into their backyard. She sang merrily as she washed her hands and helped herself to a tea towel to dry them on. Mrs Collingwood was breathing rather heavily and her face was flushed. She was heaving and shaking slightly, and her face was beating to echo the sound of her pulse. Auntie Flowers, Mamma Zila and Mrs Hood chatted merrily among themselves whilst Rosa pulled faces at Calvin, who, in turn, indulged her accordingly. Victoria seemed bemused by the exchange but was elbowed into servitude by her mother. Mrs Collingwood, still shaking, served her husband and looked about the room whilst Auntie Flowers placed generous portions of chicken and rice on the plates of both Shaun and Paul. Their grandparents peered over at them and the two boys kept their eyes fixed on their plates. Mrs Collingwood was still uneasy and looked about the floor in search of unwanted surprises. There was a pause. Eyes were searching for colour-ful, spicy delights, all of which were absent from the table. Mrs Hood looked about the table, then gestured with her eyes to Auntie Flowers. Carolyn and her mother removed themselves from the table and headed for the kitchen, where they then placed the food which Mrs Hood, Auntie Flowers and Mamma Zila had brought on their own porcelain platters.

"I don't want that child with the wolf claw to sit so close to Victoria."

"Stop it now, will you? Carolyn, honestly. You are out of order," her mother replied in a hushed tone as she looked over her shoulder.

"A cockroach? They are just loving it, showing us up like that. They must have brought it with them."

"I don't want to talk about it," her mother said again, this time hold-ing a quivering hand to her mouth.

"They even bring their food here. They can't do without their own food so they have to bring it into our house as well. It just shows you they are criticizing our food."

"Just stop it now, Carolyn. It's not like that. People take food as an offering, a gesture of goodwill. You are taking it all the wrong way."

"What are they going to do about the little girl's problem with her hands."

"It's . . . it's not a problem, it's a condition."

Carolyn had not completed her sentence, when Mamma Zila replied.

"Oh, I'm sorry. I didn't mean to pry. I was just asking my mother . . ."

"You are most welcome to ask me. If there's anything you want to know about Rosa then ask me. Her mother works the night shift, so you only have to ask me if you want to know anything concerning Rosa."

Carolyn was silent.

"So, go on. I'm here now," Mamma Zila added.

"How long will she have this condition for . . . er . . . Mrs"

"I'm not one for all this Missus business, my dear. Zila. Just Zila. And to answer your question, Carolyn, we don't know."

"Isn't it a problem for her, though? I mean, isn't she bothered by what other children say about her hands?" Carolyn asked as she folded hers.

"No, not at all. Nothing is a problem for Rosa. As you can see for yourself. Look at her." Mamma Zila gestured with her hand toward the dining room. "She is well loved and well cared for . . . it's adults one has to look out for. Adults who say inappropriate things, and who are unkind in the way that they relate to children because many of them are ignorant. Children Rosa's age and even older don't have the nastiness yet. Children play together, that's what they care about . . . being friends, enjoying each other's company. They call each other names, but it all blows over the next day and they play together again. Rosa has been taught not to bother herself with other people's comments."

Carolyn held her head back and tossed her long hair from side to side. She looked at Mamma Zila as though she was trying to figure out where Mamma Zila had gotten this superior sense of herself. Her countenance was self-assured and her posture impertinent as she thrust her features in Mamma Zila's face. Her long flowing hair, which she dyed a reddish brown, hung straight down her back and her nose was thrust higher than usual, above the company she clearly thought she had to endure.

Mamma Zila paid attention to every aspect of Carolyn's performance.

"My mother taught us at home, you know. She was a schoolteacher, and she was taught by her mother, informally, you know, on how to be a woman, how to live in the world and how to give to the world. My mother taught me. She only spoke the best English, but only when she had to, you know, for business and government type things . . . but other than that, she was just herself, with no interest in proving anything to anyone." Mamma Zila looked over her shoulder to the dining room. She moved closer towards Carolyn and Mrs Collingwood and whispered, loudly. "She's a little different, our Rosa, but she's not short of intelligence and she's certainly not short of friends. Rosa will go to university one day, of that I am sure. She has good breeding, and that is something a university degree cannot buy."

Mamma Zila spoke with her whole body; her head curved and her eyelids curtseyed; her mouth pouted as she held her sixty-year-old posture together. Carolyn did not say a word. She was perplexed and irritable but contained herself, in silence.

"Let me tell you a secret."

Carolyn and her mother were swept away, unwillingly, into the hailstorm of Mamma Zila's repartee—they hung onto every word the woman uttered. Their bodies moved forward: they obeyed, reluctantly.

"You know, in our culture, many of us can see things. It's a gift. One day, I was sitting with Rosa at the hospital, waiting for the doctor to see us, you know, for her hands. An old lady, who I recognized as someone from Russell Street, you know, further down, just off Hanover Street . . . never mind, you wouldn't know it anyway . . . well, the woman then came to sit next to us and she was watching Rosa. She asked Rosa to open her hand, and it was July, so it was very difficult for Rosa. Somehow she was drawn to this woman. The woman took one look at her hands and told me that the doctors won't find what's wrong with her hands. This is really out of their hands. That her hands were going to bring her goodwill. That she will travel one day . . . and go to university . . . and be a writer . . . and so, yes, we indulge her a little with her book, and she even has it around her neck now . . . but our children is all we have. They are our gifts." Carolyn's impertinence was now dismay, a consternation one might say, for she looked at Mamma Zila as though the woman was from another world. "Shall I take some of these food platters in now. I am sure everyone's waiting to fill their plates," Mamma Zila said, as she swung herself around and helped herself to the platters.

"Yes, thanks, Zila," Mrs Collingwood replied, her lips quivering with fearful contemplation.

Mamma Zila went straight to Nathaniel's end of the table. She laughed aloud as she placed the breyani platter in front of the men on the lower side of the table. They rubbed their hands together as they waited their turn. "Lekker, hey!" she exclaimed as she put the platters down and placed her hands on her hips. The fish frikkadels, the tomato sambal and the daltjies, were welcomed with wide-eyed anticipation. Auntie Flowers raised herself from her chair to serve Shaun and Paul, as Mamma Zila attended to the other children. Carolyn looked on as Victoria chatted with Rosa and enjoyed the daltjies.

"They're not too hot for you, darling?"

"No, Mummy," the child replied.

Mr Collingwood's eyes were feasting on the breyani—in all its colourful splendour, for it had cardamom and cinnamon sticks sprinkled abundantly over it, all cooked within the rice, lentil and mixed vegetable mixture, to bring out the pungent flavour; boiled eggs and tomato quarters were placed strategically on the dish for decoration purposes and brought out the colourfulness of the breyani mixtures, which were all cooked in a well-spiced buttermilk mixture—when his daughter walked over to his side and placed a plate of sliced cucumber beside him. Betrayed by her father's refusal to take from it, who instead served himself a rather generous helping of the breyani, she asked one of her nephews to pass it along to her, and she then passed it further down the table to her husband. Nathaniel ignored her wifely intentions and gladly took the plate of fish frikkadels, which Auntie Flowers handed him. He looked at Mrs Hood as she passed the tomato sambal to Mamma Zila, who passed it to Calvin. Calvin placed two spoonfuls of the sambal delicately at the side of Nathaniel's plate instead of passing the bowl to him. His pinkie was raised higher than his other fingers, as his hand performed the task of serving Nathaniel the sambal rather daintily. Their eyes met for a brief moment. Carolyn would have intervened if she could, to assert ownership, as a claimant, over a pair of eyes, which did not want to be claimed. Her plate revealed little evidence of enjoyment and she sat motionless with her knife and fork in each hand; unlike other guests, she was not harmoniously tangled or engaged in the act of cutting or lifting.

Her brother Neville made sure that for each spoonful of breyani and sambal he served himself, he added his mother's boiled vegetables to his plate. Mr Collingwood was looking at the food from which delight sprang and decided that conversation was now in order. He then attempted to engage Auntie Flowers.

"The flowers you gave the boys are beautiful. It's good to give them that kind of responsibility, they need it."

"Yes, I think so too," was her short reply.

Mr Collingwood was staring at the last frikkadel. He did not ask for it to be passed to him. Aware of its presence and keeping both eyes on it, Mr Collingwood now engaged Auntie Flowers in conversation.

"I would like to know the names of those flowers. I wanted to get the boys a book from the library so that they can learn all about them," he said, looking at the frikkadel.

Auntie Flowers looked at Mr Collingwood with a smile on her face, then looked at the object of his desire.

Calvin asked for something to be handed down the table and upon hearing only part of his request Auntie Flowers remarked, "Would you like the last frikkadel, Mr Collingwood?"

"Oh yes, please, if no one else wants it," he added.

"Oh, someone wants it alright. Your eyes seem to want it more than Calvin, Mr Collingwood," she said as she tilted her head and smiled at him.

"Oh no, let him go ahead," he added, not once looking at Calvin. Auntie Flowers looked at Mr Collingwood as his eyes trailed the route the frikkadel took to Calvin. Mr Collingwood's jaw dropped and his shoulders sagged when Calvin took the plate. Calvin, who read desire in the eyes of his lover's father, was thoughtful enough to suggest a means for each of them to partake in it and thus cut the frikkadel in two, on the plate, and passed half of it along to Mr Collingwood via Auntie Flowers. Mr Collingwood's teeth sunk into the flaked crayfish, snoek and prawns, all brought together by mashed bread, egg, and select roasted spices. Frikkadels were fried and then eaten with a tomato sambal and spices, which merged their individual sensations into one glorious moment, all revealed in that first bite which drew out the different flavours of the seafood. Auntie Flowers slowly and carefully handed Mr Collingwood the sambal and he scooped it all on his frikkadel then ate it like a ravenous animal. His appetite was insatiable. His teeth gnashed and gnawed at the food in a crude way.

"Mmm, mmm," he exclaimed, completely oblivious to the stares he now attracted. His teeth chattered, his body shuddered, almost urging him to enjoy it as though it was the first and most important moment of pleasure he had ever indulged in. Mrs Collingwood regarded her husband with a distant look on her face; she had not seen him like this before. As she watched him closer and observed how his tongue caressed every morsel which sunk itself into his mouth, she could not contain herself. Calvin equally enjoyed the other half. Her eyes looked at both men as though she was watching a tennis match, except an invisible ball of aromatic air was passed between the two competitors. Her eyes drooped, heavy and laden with tears, and before she could partake of another forkful the salty drops flushed themselves out of her face and onto her plate.

"Oh, excuse me," she said as she sniffed and bit her quivering lip. "Something is burning my eyes. All those onions, I suppose. Please excuse me." She kept her head down and could not walk fast enough. She hastened to the kitchen where she quickly grabbed a cotton tea towel and held it to her eyes.

"Mummy, come and have the last bite of the breyani," her son called out. "It's almost all gone."

She burst into tears and held the tea towel close to her mouth as she trembled, almost gagging on it. She could not go back into the dining room. The doorbell rang. No one attempted to answer it. Knives and forks were fencing harmoniously and happy mouths were receiving food and chewing away delightfully. Carolyn looked at her husband who got up from his seat rather reluctantly to answer the door. It was Ludwi.

"Er . . . Mister . . .um . . ."

"Ludwi!" Auntie Flowers called out as she detected the urgency in his breathless and stammered utterance. She raised herself from her chair immediately.

"Auntie Flowers . . . Soot is in der street Auntie Flowers . . . and he's been stabbed . . . dere is a lotta blood, Auntie Flowers . . . a lotta blood. Motchie say . . . Auntie Flowers . . . come quickly."

His chest heaved as he spoke and he brushed his mouth and nose with the sleeve of his jersey. Mamma Zila and Mrs Hood raised themselves from their chairs.

"Oh, dear Lord! The poor man! Let's go, Zila!" Mrs Hood called out.

Mrs Collingwood came from the kitchen; she had dried her tears and stood there quite uncertain as to what to do next. Auntie Flowers grabbed her black leather bag, opened it and shut it again.

"Thanks for the supper," she called as she looked about the dining room for Mrs Collingwood. "Shaun, Paul, Victoria, see you all soon," Auntie Flowers said as she slipped her shoes on, which were placed at either side of her chair. Mamma Zila and Mrs Hood waved at the children and said their good-byes in swift outcries. "I will send Peter for the dishes later," Mamma Zila added as she tidied the area where Rosa was seated.

"Byeeee," Rosa called out. She had jumped from her chair the minute she heard what had happened to Soot. Mamma Zila bent down to collect the little petals, which had fallen from Rosa's flower band. She placed them on the table and looked at Carolyn.

"Thanks for the supper. I am glad we had the chance to talk."

Calvin was still uncertain as to what was happening. Neville did some explaining to Nathaniel, who frowned yet continued chewing. Calvin knew Soot and he was eager to leave with Auntie Flowers, Mamma Zila and Mrs Hood. He remained at the dinner table as the Collingwoods and the Chamberses looked bewilderedly at one another.

Shaun and Paul were having their own private conversation.

"Do you have it?" Shaun asked his brother

"Ja, in my back pocket."

"Did Grandpa see you?"

"What, do you think I'm stupid?"

"Where are we going to smoke it?"

"In the Hopelots, moffie."

Shaun punched his brother.

"We'll smoke it later Grandma will clean up and they won't really miss us," Paul added.

As soon as dinner was over, Calvin excused himself and remarked that he had to visit a sick aunt on MacKenzie Street. Neville saw him to the door and the two parted by casually exchanging keys and ascertaining the time of their return, each on their own. Carolyn and her mother busied themselves in the kitchen whilst her husband spoke to her brother about his hairdressing business in the backyard. The window was open and she heard every word that was spoken.

"What are your overheads for this month?" Nathaniel asked in true business form.

"Well, I can show you the books," Neville replied as he looked over his shoulder towards the kitchen window. "We've had a little difficulty and Calvin and I are wondering about someone taking money out of the till." He looked over his shoulder again, holding his cigarette close to the edge of his fingers. "We have been short every week now, and my calculations show that we are only short on Thursdays and Fridays, which is when this one apprentice is in. I can't prove anything, so I want you to come and have a look at the books and our system of taking cash."

Nathaniel glanced up at the window and observed the sullen look on his wife's face. Neville followed his gaze and looked at his sister as he spoke.

"No," Nathaniel continued, "I would bring the books here. I want to get a new till and devise a new system. We are very busy on Thursdays and Fridays and we all use the till, the new apprentice and our older girls as well."

Nathaniel was looking at his watch as Neville spoke.

"Are you going somewhere?" he asked.

"No. Well . . . actually, I was going to go for a walk."

"It's quite windy out there."

"Ja, my back is sore though. I have been sitting all day and then I get back home and I sit down again."

Nathaniel looked up at the window again. Carolyn was now drying the dishes. He excused himself casually, then joined his wife in the kitchen.

"Anything I can do?" he asked.

"No," she said. "Well, you could go and check on Victoria and make sure she's getting ready for bed."

Mrs Collingwood was fussing over her husband, ensuring that his chair was comfortable on the stoep. As soon as she was done fussing and he seemed content, she dashed over to the backyard and sat beside her son. She stopped sniffing and seemed a lot more relaxed after Calvin's departure.

"Hi, sweetie. Don't you want any bread pudding?" she asked as Neville walked about the backyard with his cigarette.

"Yes, I would love some. Put some idle milk over it, Mummy, please."

"Sure," she said, as she observed the two men in conversation.

He smiled, slightly embarrassed because his mother looked at him so adoringly. She ran her fingers through his short-cropped hair as she left for the kitchen. Nathaniel stood in the doorway, scratching his head, wringing his hands and touching his chin repeatedly.

"I'm going for a walk," Nathaniel finally said.

"Again," she replied, without looking at him. "It's very windy out there." She looked up at the clouds from the kitchen window.

"Yes, it is windy. I promised a friend I would go and see him tonight."

Neville frowned as he observed Nathaniel and Carolyn's interaction.

Nathaniel greeted Neville who was busy scooping idle milk over his warm bread pudding, and took off.   Mrs Collingwood was hovering about and looked over her shoulder repeatedly to ensure that her husband, who had now entered the house, kept his usual distance from their son.

Sundays were days when Carolyn went to church in the morning and prepared her lessons. The family attended the Catholic church at the bottom of Roeland Street, close to the city center, and sat far away from Nita and her mother, Biebie. Nathaniel appeared to be restless. He walked in and out of their bedroom and lingered at the door each time Carolyn looked in his direction. Victoria had taken to being highly active and ran in and out of the rooms banging doors. Shaun and Paul had accompanied their grandparents, and the eight-year-old girl appeared to be rather bored.

"I want to go to the beach," Nathaniel remarked abruptly.

"In this kind of weather? It's May. It's almost winter," Carolyn replied.

"It's still warm. My body is tired from sitting down all day."

"Well, why are you asking me? I told you that I have a lot of marking to do and I can't possibly go to the beach."

He stood and looked as though he was about to say something when suddenly her face perked up.

"Actually, if you went to the beach you would take Victoria off my hands. I have to get all this marking done."

Nathaniel nodded.

"Just so that you know, a couple of guys from my work also mentioned this beach so I might see them there."

"Who exactly are you talking about?

"A new guy who's just started at the branch on Long Street. You don't know him. Actually, I think the old crowd might not even be there."

"You know how I feel about the company that Victoria keeps."

"Carolyn, I know how you feel. Please don't lecture me. I think we agree on Victoria's upbringing in most regards. I just happen to think that you're a little harsh on Neville; he is her uncle, you know, and she has to learn to accept him for who he is."

"Accept him? She doesn't have to accept him! What, do you want . . . her to accept his lifestyle? She knows he's her uncle, and that is all that she needs to accept, nothing else."

"I don't mean to criticize you, but it seems as though you are turning Victoria against him."

"Meeee? Me? Turn her against himmmm? Have you lost your mind? You have seen how my mother breaks her back for him. People around here go out of their way to be nice to him. He's entertaining, I agree, and for sure, people do want to be nice to men like him. Why? I will never know. I mean, what has he ever done? He cuts hair, for crying out loud. Women have to be nice to him because they want favours, but you, you have no reason to defend him."

"I'm not defending him, I'm just saying that Victoria is my daughter too and I have seen the way that you look at her when Neville is here. Neville is her uncle. She is afraid of you and afraid of what you'll do when you see her too close to him."

"And so she should be. What do you want? . . . for your daughter to be around people like that?"

"Well, there is no arguing with you on this. I am sorry I raised this."

"Well, I am sorry you raised it. You have no business telling me how to treat my brother or to question how I bring up my child."

"Okay. Apology accepted?" he asked, looking at her pleadingly as she continued to fold the sheets and merely stare at him as she shelved them. "Carolyn, I'm sorry. I didn't mean to upset you."

She sighed. "I just wonder whose side you're one."

"Carolyn, it's not a matter of sides. There's no one on my side of the family for her to call uncle. I have five sisters. Neville is Victoria's only uncle."

Carolyn did not respond. Nathaniel looked to her for further engagement.

"Yes, why do you have five sisters? Your parents had six children, God knows why. Why do people breed that much? It is very low class."

Nathaniel folded his arms and stared at her long and hard.

"I thought you were leaving," she said, without looking at him.

"Yes," he replied as he looked about the room and got his bag together.

It was early evening and the house was quiet; Carolyn's parents and nephews had not yet returned and she was collecting her papers from the dinning table, after having spent a good few hours marking them, when the telephone rang.

"Hello! Hello! Hello!" she called out, again and again.

There was no reply.

Just then she heard the doorknob being turned. Nathaniel called out, followed by Victoria. The young girl was jumping about and brought her bag filled with shells and sand into the kitchen.

"Hi, you're back. Go to the toilet, Victoria, you'll get sand all over the kitchen."

The child sighed but ran along obediently.

"Where did you get that bracelet?" Carolyn asked as she looked at Nathaniel's arm. Nathaniel did not reply. She grabbed his arm and inspected it thoroughly. "A silver bracelet?" she asked as she looked murderously at him.

"A friend gave it to me," he said, as he nervously brushed his hair back.

"A silver bracelet from a friend. Take it off! Take it off now! Since when do men give each other bracelets like that?"

Victoria came running into the dining room when she heard her mother's raised voice.

"Go to your room, Victoria, and stay there!" The child looked at her father then returned her gaze to her mother.

"Now, I said!" Victoria darted into her room and stared at her father, who did not speak out in her defense.

"You! Get outside into the backyard."

Nathaniel appeared frazzled.

"What?"

"You know what I'm talking about. Go into the backyard now!"

"What? What are you making such a fuss about? I am going to have a shower."

"Don't mess with me. Just don't mess with me. In the backyard now, I said."

"You're being silly," was his nervous yet casual reply.

Nathaniel left for the backyard. There was a shower beside the toilet and he removed his clothes whilst Carolyn spoke to him.

"Don't pretend you don't know what's going in. I can't believe that you're doing this. Do you think I'm a fool? Do you take me for a fool?"

He left the door open and turned on the shower.

"Turn that off right now! Turn it off! How long has this been going on?" She pulled the shower curtain open as she spoke.

"What?"

"When are you going to stop pretending?"

"What are you talking about?"

"Do you think I don't know!" she shouted at the top of her voice.

"Just calm down."

"Turn that damn shower off!"

He moved her hand away again.

"Now, I said!"

"Carolyn!"

"Move out of the way." She pushed her way through into the shower. "Move out of the way," she asserted again. "This is the same reason why you were late now the other night. You think I'm a damn fool.

Don't insult me."

Nathaniel did not say a word.

"Do you want me to go to your parents' house now?"

Nathaniel did not utter a word. Instead he poked the inside of his cheek with his tongue.

"Okay, stay in the shower and I will leave to go to your parents. Your sister should be there. I want to ask her why she didn't tell me you're a damn moffie!"

His mouth was making all kinds of shapes and he still did not utter a word.

"Get out of the shower, now!"

"Carolyn, control yourself," he said as he trembled. He turned the shower off and she threw a towel from the washing line at him.

"How long has this been going on?"

"What?"

"Answer my bloody question?"

He stared at her blankly.

"How long has he been your boyfriend for?"

"He's not my boyfriend."

"So, you just have sex with him, but he's not your boyfriend."

"It's not like that." Nathaniel began softly. "You've been saying over and over how you just want us to be Victoria's parents. How you don't want to be intimate with me. Yes, I have been out with him a few times . . ."

She slapped him across the face.

"He has a name, then? Now! Tell me now!"

"Matthew."

"Matthew who?"

"What difference does it make?"

"Matthew who the hell who?"

"I don't know his surname."

"You don't know his surname? You've had sex with him but you don't know his surname?"

"I was going to tell you."

"When, when were you going to tell me?"

"In a few weeks . . ."

"In a few weeks! Liar!" She hit him again and he grabbed her hands. "So, you were planning on more weeks?"

"Well, this was just the beginning stage. I like him . . ."

"What do you think I am? Have you noticed that you haven't tried to correct me? You haven't corrected me . . . you haven't said that you did not have sex with him?"

Nathaniel was silent.

"How many times?   How many times?" she asked, at the top of her voice.

"Does it matter?" he asked, looking from behind the towel.

"Of course it matters. Where? Where?"

"Well, the other night when we went out we went to the park . . ."

"The one in Tamboerskloof on the left of . . ." She let her words trail off and slowly shook her head. "I know which one. My God, the gayest place you could find. Are you out of your mind? What if the police caught you having sex with a man . . . in public. They would have come knocking on this bloody door . . . I would have to answer questions about my moffie husband . . . I would have to bail you out . . . I would have to save your bloody moffie ass from jail."

"Don't be so dramatic."

"Did you have penetration sex?"

Nathaniel did not answer.

"Answer me!"

"No," he said as he looked at her. His head was now at the level of hers and he was no longer looking at the paved backyard.

"So you were there pulling at each other? Ha, ha, ha," she laughed sarcastically. She looked at him and mocked him in the only way she could, with words. "Pulling at each other's private parts . . . how pathetic!"

"Interesting how the English teacher who teaches Christopher Marlowe . . . how does it go again, 'come live with me and be my love and we shall all the pleasure prove,' is that how it goes? Your part in all of this is that you are quick to point out to your students the assumptions . . . Go on, . . . you tell me . . . I am not the one who has read all those books and talk about being so open about sexuality . . . and not being homophobic like other people, yeah, that's the word, see, I've remembered. I'm a good listener. And there you are teaching all that stuff and you don't even speak to your own brother. Lifestyle, you call it, now that is a joke. And to think, you are the teacher who boasts that you make your students think and then you can't even talk to me without being homophobic yourself."

She laughed again and clapped her hands together.

"Well done, Nathaniel. Oh, aren't you clever. I see my university education has served you very well. So, you didn't just lie in bed with me, lie there and cheat about who you are, you have actually learnt something from me. And here I was thinking that the only use I have been to you is as a cover-up. Gha! Don't try to be clever with me. You've learnt my words very well ha! I'm not homophobic, I was just trying to provoke you. I was just trying to get you to speak. And now I have. I'm good, don't you think. Very, very, good."

He was silent again.

"So, when can I meet him?"

"What?"

"You heard me. When can I meet him."

"Are you serious?"

"Of course I am serious. Invite him over. I want to meet him. If you are so keen to have our daughter in his company, why not invite him over here. I can arrange for your in-laws to be out of the house. Those two little brats are hardly here anyway."

"I don't feel ready yet."

"You were ready to pull on his penis . . . how many times?"

"Why do you want to know everything?"

"What do mean, why do I want to know everything? You'll need my support. I know that and you know that. You just expect to get my support. How long were you going to keep this from me?"

"It's just starting. I don't really want to invite him over. I don't want to give him the wrong impression."

"I think it's a little too late for that."

"You're pushing me now."

"How many times?" she asked, narrowing her eyes.

"Three times," he replied, reluctantly.

"Ah huh, just as I thought." She began to list the number of

occasions to him. "Two weeks ago on a Saturday . . . that Friday night .
. . last Wednesday. Is that right?"

Nathaniel nodded half-heartedly.

"And today was your day to play happy family with our daughter.
What were you thinking? She's not stupid, you know. And here you
are defending my brother when it's really yourself you are defending.
How noble of you. You will invite him to this house. I will make sure
that my parents are out. I want to meet him. I'm not having some moffie
run around thinking that he has outsmarted me . . . that he is seeing my
husband whilst the little wife knows nothing."

Nathaniel stared grimly at the wall and did not say anything.

After a difficult and painful night of revelations, Nathaniel went to work
the following day full of anxiety. He arrived at his workplace just shortly after 8:30 and had to make his apologies to the manager

"You've been slipping up lately, Chambers. It's Monday morning and
you are already late. I expect you to be here at 8:15."

"I'm sorry, sir. I do apologize."

"We can't have that sort of thing here, not with the reputation we
have as a main branch. If you need to take unpaid leave, just say so and
it can be arranged. If you're having family troubles . . ."

"Well, yes, actually, sir, it's been a little uphill lately . . ."

"If you'll let me finish."

Nathaniel stood with his hands behind his back.

"I was just going to say that if you're having family troubles, I
don't want to hear about it. You need to take unpaid leave and sort it
out. This is the last time that I am having this conversation with
you."

"Yes, sir."

"Is that a bracelet I see under your cuff?"

"Yes, sir."

"Well, as long as you do not roll your sleeves up."

"The women wear jewelry all the time, sir. Why should my bracelet
be a problem?" he said.

The manager remained silent. He removed his spectacles and looked
at Nathaniel long and hard.

"Yes, that is true. Besides, you do not have contact with many clients."

"Even if I did, I would not take it off."

"You know, Chambers, apart from coming in late a few times, I really like the way that you have handled yourself lately. You seem to be a lot more assertive. You're standing your ground a lot more."

Nathaniel was preparing to get the cashiers ready for a short meeting before they opened at nine o'clock when he was called away by one of the secretaries, who whispered in his ear. He placed his hand in front of his body to indicate that he would attend to the matter shortly. When the cashiers left his office, they collected their cash balances and walked straight to their numbered cubicles. Nathaniel looked over to the secretary and she pointed to the front door. Standing there was Neville, leaning against the glass door, waiting for it to be opened. He was wearing sunglasses, his hair had been dyed black again, and he was dressed in black jeans and a black woolen, polo sweater.

The security guard checked his watch and opened the door promptly at 9:00 a.m. Neville sauntered in and walked straight towards Nathaniel.

"Hi," Neville said, in a slow, deep, drawn-out voice.

"Good morning," Nathaniel replied, finding it rather difficult to read the expression on his brother-in-law's face since Neville wore sunglasses. "Is anything the matter?"

"Where can we talk?" Neville asked, his voice sounding deeper.

Nathaniel looked at his watch.

"We can go into my office for a few minutes."

Nathaniel shut the door after allowing Neville in.

Immediately, the secretary knocked on the door and popped her head in.

"Morning," she said as she looked at Neville. He simply nodded his head; he had still not removed his sunglasses. "Can I get you some coffee, sir? . . . Something to drink for the gentleman?"

She looked first at Nathaniel then at Neville as she spoke. She wore the branch's uniform, which was a jacket and skirt suit in light blue, and her eyebrows were plucked into a thin line; it gave her face an expression of overeagerness. She stood there with her mouth and eyebrows smiling.

"Yes, coffee would be great, thanks," was Nathaniel's reply.

Neville nodded and said, "Make it two, please."

She nodded at Nathaniel and shut the door.

Nathaniel sat back in his leather office chair. Neville sat back too and began stroking his chin reflectively.

Nathaniel now appeared quite pale.

"My, my, my . . . There you were with that little slut, Matthew, and here I am thinking that you are happily married to my sister." He slid his sunglasses up onto his forehead without taking his eyes off Nathaniel.

Nathaniel was taken aback. He had not heard this tone in Neville's voice before.

"Didn't you know that all gay men go to the same beaches? I mean, honey, tell me you didn't know."

Nathaniel narrowed his eyes, bit his lip and looked at Neville as though he did not recognize him. Neville's eyes and mouth were coordinated in a smooth, suave, pose.

"Not only is Matthew gay . . . he's a moffie . . . a bloody queen, a big woman, you know, if you catch my meaning . . . Mister I-work-in-the-bank, huh." Neville was now speaking with his eyes, his hands, and his whole body, in ways Nathaniel had never been spoken to. His eyes punctuated every word, and with it, he pouted his mouth in a taunting, tantalizing manner. He folded his arms and continued. "You should have said that you like moffies . . . I mean, I live outside of my parents' house, come and get fresh clothes every few days or so, and there I was, walking away from what could have been a very cosy situation."

Nathaniel jumped up from his chair.

"It's not like that. You have no right to speak to me like that."

Nathaniel's face was stern and the look of shock was now soon vanishing, as he looked deeper and deeper into Neville's eyes.

"Please, honey, sit down. Don't talk to me about rights. You are beginning to sound just like my sister."

Nathaniel did as he was told.

"When you service someone like Miss Mathilde—you do know that is what she is called by the girls, hey, even though you call her Matthew. You're not unboxing her, honey, because madam has been round the block a few times. She's probably unboxing you." Neville walked over to Nathaniel's chair and leaned forward then he cupped his hand and placed it on Nathaniel's crotch.

"And why should that little bitch have all the fun?"

Nathaniel pushed him away.

"Oh, so you like a little rough, hey. Miss Mathilde must have taken you to one of her favourite rough clubs."

"Just get out!" Nathaniel shouted, brushing his hair back with his fingers.

"Oh no, mister, not so fast. This is not the way to speak to me."

Nathaniel sat down in his chair again. He brought both his hands to his face, like a child might who under pressure sits and ponders the scope and nature of the punishment dealt by a parent. Neville went back to Nathaniel's desk and patted him on his face.

"We are all part of the same club, honey. This is no way to speak to a sister. You're a moffie now. You have to learn the rules."

"I'm not a moffie, you are!" he said, as he moved away from Neville, who now sat on his desk.

"Oh, oh, oh, a matter of the pot calling the kettle black, hey."

Nathaniel walked to his door cracking his knuckles with agitation. Neville followed him.

"You may sleep next to my sister, and you may have a gold band on your wedding finger, but we both know its a piece of the ass that you want. It's men that you're after. Don't fool yourself, honey. It's okay. There are many, many moffies in this town. The Six is full of them; full of men who spit in the street when they see a moffie, but when the lights are out, honey . . . after they've been schushed by a moffie there's no going back . . . they swallow that spit and use it for you know what and scream for that lunch. But when the sun comes up its back to wifey. You're no different, honey. The only difference between you and them is that they are not that dumb to go and lie on a moffie beach, like roast beef . . . in your case, roast pork . . . in broad daylight and be seen by their moffie brother-in-law."

Neville chuckled as he spoke. He folded his legs in a rather feminine way, sealing his words by rapidly dusting his hands.

Nathaniel looked at Neville with narrowed eyes.

"Miss Thing has taught you to gail . . . you know, speak the moffie language. Oh, come on, she must've. She's a fast mover and there's no use pretending. I mean, she must have complimented you on that nice lunch of yours," he said, as his eyes focused on Nathaniel's crotch.

Nathaniel then raised himself from his chair.

"Are you finished? Are you quite done?" he asked, with a calmer look.

There was a knock on the door. Before either one of them could say anything, the secretary stepped into the door with a tray; the cleaner had opened the door for her.

"Sorry it took me so long, Mr Chambers. There's a problem with the plug and I didn't want to disturb you. I got some boiling water from the bookstore across the road." She placed the tray on his table.

"Oh, you should have said something. Do you need me to fix it?" he asked as she placed the tray on the table.

"No thank you, Mr Chambers. Mr Pearce has already taken it to the hardware store."

"Thank you," Neville uttered as she moved away from the tray. She nodded as she turned the knob of the door to let herself out.

"Mmmmm, butch, huh! Very butch. So, you fix electrical wires, huh, like a real man."

"I have had quite enough of you now," Nathaniel said as he brushed his clothes, pulled his tie straight and walked to the door. He opened it with Neville looking on.

"Leave!"

Neville looked him up and down, racing his eyes from the start of his trousers right down to his shoes.

"You heard me. Leave before I call security."

"Ooh, you're calling Priscilla, hey? So you do like the rough stuff. Does security handle you too, huh?"

"You think I'm joking, don't you?"

Nathaniel grabbed Neville by the arm and walked him through the entire bank, with everyone's eyes fixed on him and went to the front door and released Neville's arm with a push.

"Don't put your foot back into this door. I don't care how good a customer you are."

Neville leaned against Nathaniel and whispered in his ear.

"What are you going to do? Get Priscilla? Nothing they haven't done before. Beulah as you are, I would come back here with the loud moffies, all my girls, and stand outside here and call you moffie . . . make sure we make skandaal . . . make sure everyone knows you're a damn moffie. So don't think you're clever. I like a man who knows how to take charge. So, for today, I'll forgive you. I don't want you to go on your knees, not here, not in front of all these people, only when we are alone. So, mmm, mmm, see you later."

"Nobody threatens me. Nobody! I don't want you here, ever. I'll explain to my manager, but don't think you can threaten me. You can say whatever you want about me, I really don't care."

Nathaniel turned around and walked back to his office. Neville was at a loss for what to do next. He simply shuffled away slowly, half expecting Nathaniel to come after him.

Nathaniel sat in his chair and immediately the telephone rang.

"Nathaniel Chambers." He noticed that the reciever was shaking in his hand.

There was no reply but he could hear someone breathing on the other line.

"Good morning. Nathaniel Chambers."

There was a sigh on the other end the line. He knew immediately who it was.

"Well, I just had your mother on the phone. She wants us to come over next Sunday for their wedding anniversary. I'm not going. I cannot look at her or your sister knowing what you're doing."

"Good morning to you too, Carolyn," he said as he moved to the edge of his chair and rearranged the pencil case on his desk. "What am I doing again? Please tell me."

"I'm at college. I'm not going to go into details here. I've just had my morning break and I have to answer your mother when she asks how I am, how you are, how our child is doing, and you, you don't have to answer to any of this. All you do is run around with your moffie boyfriend."

"Carolyn, he has a name. We've already been through this. You told me over the last year that there was no chance of us getting back together and that you were waiting for me to move on. Well, I have. I am not going to sit around and wait for you to decide whether you want to be with me or not. I don't want to simply live in the same house as you, I want an intimate relationship, a sexual relationship, one based on love and respect. You told me that you did not love me. You can't have it both ways. First you say you don't want me then you try to ridicule me for having a relationship with someone else. Yes, he is a man. First I was a homophobe for not being able to discuss sexuality openly, but of course, this was only for your benefit; so that you could have someone to bounce ideas off and look and sound superior to not so that I could also think about myself and my own sexuality."

"I am at work," Carolyn said wearily, "I am in no mood for this . . . in no mood for your sudden use of the English language. I see you are very articulate when you want to be—when you need to insult me and provide justification for your behaviour. How dare you? How dare you speak to me like that? You were nothing when I married you. Nothing. You could hardly hold a decent conversation. You could hardly look people in the eye. You'd better change your attitude and your tone. If you want me to lie to your mother, then you'd better shape up and shut up. You need me for your lies. Why am I suddenly the bad person here? I have always understood that you have those tendencies, always understood your insecurities, except I did not think you'd be stupid enough to act on them. Yet, according to you, I am the bad person here."

"Oh, here we go again . . . back to the chapter where you start to list the many things you have done for me."

"I want to talk about this tonight. Sort this mess out once and for all."

"I told you I was going to our branch's braai . . . the barbecue."

"I know what a braai is. Don't patronize me."

"I'm not—"

"You know what, next time your mother asks me how you are, I will tell her to ask her moffie son herself. How about that?"

"Well, why don't you do that then?"

She gasped.

"Go ahead, knock yourself out. You do want to embarrass me, so go ahead. Tell my mother whatever you like."

Carolyn slammed the phone down.

It was a chilly May evening, especially for someone who had been sitting in a car with the ignition off. Carolyn rubbed her arms and looked about. She was afraid to stray far from her car. She pondered whether people stood around fires when it was so cold. With nipped fingers and toes, she maneuvered her way through the bushes, to see for herself who her husband was with. The parking area was small and cars were parked in rather odd positions, not leaving much room for someone who, like herself, did not want to be noticed as she slid between the small spaces allowed. Her elasticized trousers were cutting off her circulation, and she could not possibly squat like most men and women did when they were in the forest. She stood still for a few seconds, crossed her legs, waiting for the urge to urinate to subside, then slowly walked towards one of the trees. Moving slowly and peering through the branches, she spotted Nathaniel's car and noticed that two women were sitting in it talking intimately. She recognized one of the women as someone she had met at a dinner dance some years ago. The other woman had several scrunched-up tissue papers in her hand to wipe away her tears. Seconds later the two women laughed and the younger of the two placed both her hands on her belly, which was not entirely visible to Carolyn's eyes, but which she took to be their hand movements. Seconds later, the two women screamed and both of them leapt out of the car.

Carolyn saw a huge flame flicker just behind their vehicle. She took cover behind the tree, fearful and hesitant as to what to do next.

Her husband was somewhere in that crowd as she cowered behind the tree. She peered around the trunk and saw Nathaniel surrounded by men and women who were now helping him to extinguish the flame. She could hear patches of conversation.

"I threw too much petrol on it . . . Sorry . . . it will calm down, don't worry," one man said as he stirred the contents of the huge barrel in which the fire burned. It was not uncommon for fires to be made in such barrels or for flame worshippers to gather around and sing traditional Cape Town songs. The pregnant woman smiled at her friend, who nodded back at her to reassure her that all would be well.

Most of the men held beer bottles in their hands whilst others simply rubbed their hands together and stared at the fire. The worshippers jumped every time the fire crackled drawing them out of their mesmerized state. Laughter followed as the fire spluttered into the evening air. Carolyn peered around the tree looking for Nathaniel. She recognized some of the people around the fire from occasions when she had met them, although she did not remember many of their names, but no one seemed to be with Nathaniel. Someone had to be attending to the meat; Carolyn could smell Boerewors distinctly. Carolyn moved about stealthily, hoping that her clothes would not reek of smoke. She patted herself on occasion and sniffed her hands. She could not help but sniff and cough as she walked about to see where the cooking fire was, which would be closer to the ground.

Suddenly she caught sight of the most beautiful woman bending over the fire, illuminated by the yellow flames. Carolyn was intrigued by this young woman, who seemed to be the most stylish of the group. She wore a fashionable pair of jeans, unusual in shape and design, high heels, clearly, for she tottered on them daintily as she tended to the meat, and a hairstyle that only a very good and expensive hairdresser could accomplish. The beautiful young woman stood with her back to Carolyn. She wore an angora jersey much like the one Carolyn had discovered in her wardrobe. She figured Nathaniel was hiding it and would present it to her as a birthday gift.

Carolyn gasped as the woman turned slightly to face her. Seen from a different angle, her beauty was now rather masculine.

"Mattie," someone called out. "Hey, girl, is everything ready?" the same person asked.

The woman in question now pranced around, and it was clear that her walk, her gestures and the way she flapped her arms were exaggerations of femaleness. Thus, in Carolyn's summation, this woman was a male.

Nathaniel soon made his appearance and put his hand on the crossdresser's shoulders. Carolyn saw the sparkling silver bracelet on his arm, and as the angora-clad moved towards her husband, she saw that he was wearing a bracelet identical to Nathaniel's. She watched in horrid fascination as the two men embraced and kissed tenderly.

Carolyn turned away from this scene and ran off. She stumbled and sobbed from one tree to the next. Back at her car her breath was laboured and she thought her chest might give in. She brushed her hair back and looked in the mirror, looking at her face from different angles. She stroked the skin of her cheeks, then looked at her teeth. Tears flowed down her cheeks and into her mouth. All she could see in front of her was the beautiful face she had observed illuminated by the fire.

She removed the wedding ring from her finger and sat holding it. She rubbed it now for comfort, as the tears rolled down her neck and onto her clothes. She noticed the headlights of an approaching car and realized that the driver might be intending to park close to her. Fearing discovery, she hid under the seat, raising herself only when the lights of the approaching car were turned out. When it was dark again, she started her car and drove off.

It was late on a Wednesday afternoon when Nathaniel drove up Long Street to one of the branches of his bank. The bank was now closed and Nathaniel nodded at the security guard to let him in. Matthew stood there motionless when he saw Nathaniel. He was not sure whether Nathaniel knew that he wore makeup to work. It seemed too late now to take it off. Both the women beside him knew that the exchange, which took place between the two pairs of eyes, was not quite a working matter. To make matters worse, Nathaniel walked right up to Matthew and smiled at him.

"Hey," he said in a low and husky voice and with the same look in his eye as when they were alone.

Matthew looked about, to both sides, and smiled nervously. He did not reply.

"I'm here to see your manager. Wait for me. I won't be long." Nathaniel winked at him.

Matthew pursed his lips; he was beaming from ear to ear. Both the young women beside him had heard rumours but were absolutely flabbergasted when Nathaniel stopped at Matthew's cubicle to acknowledge his presence. Matthew was preening, touching his hair, stroking his face as if to boast that a man as good looking as Nathaniel, who was so admired and sought after by women, would acknowledge their relationship in public, without hesitation, and whilst he was wearing all his makeup.

"Psst, Matt. Are you guys an item?" the woman to his right asked.

"*Here ruh* girl, mind your own business," was his noncommittal reply.

"Matthew!" the woman to his left called.

Matthew moved his head, slowly yet dramatically, and fluttered his eyelashes at the inquiring woman.

"So its true, hey? Is he your bag? I've heard rumours . . . and now Mr Chambers is here speaking to you like you guys are an item.   Oooh, lucky girl. Very nice for you, girl . . . oh, oh, and he has the same bracelet as you . . . very nice."

Matthew simply raised his eyebrows to further draw out their envy and rolled up his sleeves in order for his bracelet to be fully revealed and marveled at.

"Oh, so it's true then," his colleague to the right said.

"Does his wife know?" was the young woman on his left's question.

"Do I scratch in your affairs? Don't be so bis, hey. Do your cash up. I don't want you to be short because then we'll all have to stay here and wait for you to count it all over again."

Both the women stepped back and glanced over at one another whilst Matthew had his back to them.

"Okay, I'm done," he said, as he placed his cash bag on the counter.

"Coo-ee! coo-ee" he called out, to the security guard. The bold man acknowledged the call and fetched the bag from him. Matthew then bent down and busied himself in front of his little mirror.

It was minutes later when Nathaniel walked through the manager's door smiling. He looked at Matthew and winked, then leaned forward and whispered, "Are you ready?"

"Yes," Matthew replied.

"What happened to your makeup?" Nathaniel asked.

"I took it off. If you walk with me in the street you're outed. That is just the way it is."

"I don't care. Do you want to wear your makeup?"

"Ja. I wear it all the time."

"So, go and put it on. I'll wait."

"Are you sure?"

"Sure," Nathaniel replied, as he licked his lips.

Matthew emerged looking ever so pretty. Nathaniel had all the eyes of his colleagues on him. He casually collected Matthew's womanly handbag, and other parcels and carried them to his car. They walked side by side to Nathaniel's car. Nathaniel opened the passenger door of the car for Matthew, who proudly seated himself whilst hastily pulling down the mirror which was placed in the inside flap of the shutter.

When Nathaniel got into the car he threw the parcels on to the back-seat and kissed his lover. Clearly some of their colleagues were still about. Matthew looked about then looked over toward his lover.

"You're adorable," he said.

"So are you," was his lover's reply.

"Where are we going?" Matthew asked as Nathaniel started the car.

"We're going to my parents' house."

"What?"

"I told you I wanted them to meet you."

"But so soon? You're joking, right?"

"No, I'm not. Why wait?"

"But what about Carolyn?"

"What about her?"

"Does she know that I am going there with you?"

"No. I don't care. I could tell her if you want me to."

"Nat, you're not out to your parents. They'll take one look at me when I walk through their door and they'll know I'm a moffie. No man walks with a moffie if he's not the father or the brother. You'll be outed just like that."

Nathaniel laughed. He pulled up his sleeves, one at a time, as he held the steering wheel with his right hand then his left.

"So what."

Nathaniel shrugged his shoulders. He offered Matthew some of the gum he had in the car and chewed away as he observed his lover.

"You look so sexy when you chew gum," Matthew commented.

Nathaniel smiled and winked at Matthew.

"I can't go like this. Why dirint you tell me at work. I mean, I would-n't have put my whole face on. I wouldn't have worn all this founda-tion."

"This is who you are, isn't it? How many times have I heard you complain about friends and family who still expect you to take off your makeup when you visit them. And those who say silly things like, 'not in front of the children.' If I am going to tell my parents about me then I want them to meet you too. If they react badly, then that's it. I'm not going to do this whole thing of breaking it to them gently as if I have done something wrong, then have them go all soft on me, then when they finally meet you they freak out."

"Don't you want to give them some time, at least. I mean, your family is high society. Mummy is okay with me and you know my father just tolerates me because I pay the rent."

"Your father's not that bad, though."

"No, not in front of you. I think you should give your parents some time to get used to the idea."

"Listen to yourself. This is not an idea, it's my life. I've wasted enough time pretending to be straight and pretending that marriage is what I want. I'm not going to live a lie."

Matthew shrugged his shoulders and let out a loud sigh.

Nathaniel stopped the car.

"So, either you come with me or you don't. You can leave if you want to. I'll drop you off at home if that's what you want."

Matthew remained silent.

"Matthew, I have to say that I am a little surprised by you. So many contradictions, hey, like there's one rule for moffies and another for gay men who don't wear makeup and dress up in drag. How many times have you told me that none of your previous boyfriends wanted to take you to meet their parents? You would even make clothes for their wives."

"You're right," Matthew said with tears in his eyes.

"What's wrong?"

"Nothing."

"Come on. Tell me what's wrong."

Matthew grabbed a tissue from his handbag.

"I just don't want to lose you," he murmured as he sniffed into the tissue.

"You don't want to lose me? I don't get it. Here I am wanting you to accompany me to my parents and you are concerned about losing me?"

"Nat, you don't know how people treat moffies. I think you are very naive. You have an innocence about you, which I love, but then there's a part of you that I think is completely naive. You have no idea how I am treated even when I try to be butch. People are only okay with moffies because we form part of the entertainment, we play netball, provide fun and laughter, do women's hair. Even for those of us who can't do hair, we have to learn because it is what earns us favours, and we are left alone, not beaten or humiliated, that often, because we provide a service."

"Okay. Yes, you are right. I am naive. And you know, so what. A part of me doesn't want to know what people think or what goes through their minds when they see us together and look at your make-up. I don't care. I know how I feel about you. I don't want to see you unhappy and I definitely don't want to spend my life waiting for people to accept me. I really don't care. I have accepted myself. I can live with being gay. I can live with who I am and with how you are, and no matter what you say to me about other people, it will never matter to me."

"Nat, you've only been gay a few weeks."

"But I've been a man all my life."

Matthew stared at Nathaniel and lowered his eyes. He had a faraway look about him and he kept his head close to the headrest of the passenger's seat. His lips were quivering as Nathaniel continued.

"A few weeks . . . yes, because I have been with you for a few weeks, and that's enough to know that I will not let anyone treat me like a cliché. Why give anyone that choice? I am not going to ask my parents to accept me, nor am I ever going to ask anyone else to accept me because I am gay. If I ask to be accepted then I deserve to be rejected. Me, I'm not asking anyone for anything. I am not going to ask my parents for anything. I am simply going to tell them, and they can like it or lump it. I am not going there to make a speech or to cry and beg them to accept me or my relationship with you."

Matthew still looked at him with tears in his eyes. He touched Nathaniel's face gently.

"I never ever thought I'd say this . . . but . . . you're my hero."

Nathaniel bent towards him and kissed him.

"I love you, babe. That's all that matters."

Nathaniel pulled up in front of his parent's house. His mother came running down the cement path to the gate to greet him. The movement of her excitable body moving about made her look sprightly. She was slight in build and had short-cropped hair, which she put in curlers. Her hair was smooth and stylishly curly and the style demanded that regular maintenance was kept. Her face was round and friendly and she wore the neatest frock imaginable for a woman her age; the big red bow, which folded above her buttocks, made her look quite young and frivolous. Her hands were small and she appeared very energetic as she ran to meet her son. There was a strong resemblance between mother and son; Nathaniel had her smile and her shiny eyes.

"Everything okay?" she asked as she drew her hand to his face and brought it down to her height and placed a kiss on his cheek. "Your mother-in-law dropped Victoria off here with her friend, Rosa. They are in the back with Daddy."

Nathaniel frowned.

"Come in, come in," she said as she gazed at her son then at Matthew. Matthew fussed over his appearance whilst Mrs Chambers stood to the side to let him into the house. Nathaniel did not move, and neither did Matthew. She looked at her son and the frown which was still on his face.

"Your in-laws had to take Carolyn's nephews to some function because their mother was rushed to hospital. Carolyn left straight from school, apparently, and went to the hospital to see her sister."

Nathaniel tilted his head somewhat and did not say a word. His lips were pursed and he nodded to himself.

His mother moved closer to him and spoke rather softly.

"There is something strange going on."

Mrs Chambers was now looking at Matthew.

"Oh, look at me, not minding my manners. Do come in. Make yourself at home."

"Oh, Mom, this is Matthew."

"Pleased to meet you, Matthew. Have a seat."

Matthew observed that the furnishings in the house were all tasteful and understated. There was a settee, rather old and in good condition, and a couple of armchairs, a large wooden long-player, which also had a radio, part of it stood boldly in one corner and above it stood a rather large hanging clock. A small drinks cabinet was placed right beside the long-player, where a few glasses were placed on the dark blue marble top. There were few photographs, and the room, unlike most dining rooms Matthew had seen, was not cluttered at all. He turned around, the full three hundred and sixty degrees, and saw the table and six chairs in the corner of the room. The curtains were light in colour yet heavy since they were velvet; they suited the living room well. A few doilies were placed on areas where there were ornaments, and these too were sparse. Mrs Chambers smiled at Matthew, who seemed to take it all in as he sat down.

"Let me go and check on Victoria."

Just then Victoria and Rosa came running in.

"Daddy!" Victoria exclaimed.

Her father approached her gently and kissed her on her forehead.

Matthew stood looking at the exchange between mother and son then between father and daughter.

"Hello!" she said as she stood behind her father and greeted Matthew.

Matthew returned the greeting. Rosa moved towards Nathaniel.

"Hello, Uncle."

"Hello, Rosa. How are you? Why are you wearing a black ribbon in your hair?"

"I fine,Uncle. Der black ribbon is for Soot who died. Soot was stabbed last week and he died. Der funeral was today, Uncle."

Nathaniel was still frowning and looked at Victoria then back at Rosa.

Toria's Mummy go wit her auntie to der hospital cos der husband hit her . . . huh, Toria?"

Victoria pulled a face, then shook her head at Rosa. The children each had a jar of blowing bubbles in their hand, which Mrs Chambers had bought for them at the corner shop. Rosa's hands were sticky and she still had the plastic blower in her hand as she spoke to Nathaniel.

"Victoria?" Nathaniel now frowned and tilted his head again; he looked at both the children to gauge some sense of what they knew. "Did Grandma say something? Did you hear anything?"

Victoria pointed to Rosa.

"Toria in der toilet, Uncle, and Toria's mamma say to her mummy on der phone dat her auntie was beaten be her husband. Den Toria's mamma start to cry, huh, Toria?"

Victoria stood beside her friend now. Her father lowered his head, then lifted it slowly and looked at his mother, and then at Matthew.

"I don't know what to do about this situation. Every time I ask I get told all kinds of lies. Carolyn and her mother will make up all kinds of stories to prevent the truth from being told. What can I do, Mom?"

"There's nothing you can do. If they want to hide this and lie about it, and they don't want you to know, then there's nothing you can do. I am sure that if they needed your help they would have asked. Which section of the hospital does Carolyn's sister go into?"

Victoria moved closer to her father and grabbed his arm, urging him to bend down. She proceeded to whisper in his ear.

"Toria . . . is not nice to do dat in front of udder people . . . hey, Auntie?" Rosa now looked to Mrs Chambers.

"She goes into the Coloured section," was Nathaniel's reply. Nathaniel looked at his daughter who, much to his surprise, supplied the answer to the question when she whispered in his ear.

"Come on, you girls come with me. Let me make that fish paste sandwich that Rosa was after and your peanut butter sandwich, Victoria. I didn't know you were mourning, Rosa. I saw that black ribbon but I didn't know you were mourning."

"Auntie, can it be Redro fish paste on der Deuns bread?"

"Oh, you like whole wheat bread, hey, Rosa . . . and the special kind too?"

"Yes, Auntie."

"And you, sweetie?" she asked as she turned to her grandchild.

"I want the same as Rosa, please, Grandma."

Mrs Chambers took both their hands and led them into the kitchen.

Matthew took some time to observe the decorations. Matthew appeared tense and Nathaniel rubbed his shoulders.

After Mrs Chambers made the sandwiches she instructed the two girls to play in the backyard. Mrs Chambers turned her attention to Nathaniel immediately as she entered the dining room.

"Some coffee with a bit of brandy?" she asked as she chuckled.

"Mummy, you're incorrigible."

"No, just checking if you still fancy your evening favourite, which I know you don't drink in your own house."

Nathaniel looked at Matthew as he spoke.

"Mummy always reminds me of what I am missing when I come here."

"Let me put the kettle on and get your father."

"I'll call Dad," was Nathaniel's bold reply. Matthew just looked at him and motioned with his eyes. "She won't bite you," Nathaniel whispered then stroked Matthew's head.

As Nathaniel moved towards the kitchen door he could hear his mother speaking to Rosa and Victoria.

"You girls are being naughty now . . . you shouldn't listen to adult conversation."

Nathaniel almost walked into his father.

"Ah, I thought I heard voices."

His wife handed him a cloth then dried his hands for him as he stood there. Mr Chambers was a tall man and good looking for his nearly sixty years. He was fair of complexion, had dark green and grey eyes and his plentiful hair was still a light grey. He had a good frame for a man of sixty years. Father and son then walked into the dining room. Mrs Chambers followed on.

"Good evening," he said as he moved towards Matthew. "I thought I heard voices." Mr Chambers extended his hand to Matthew.

"Good evening," Matthew said, keeping his voice coarse and steady, as he extended his hand to the man who requested his. Mr Chambers looked at his bracelet momentarily, and tilted his head.

"Mr Chambers has Alzheimer's, my dear," Mrs Chambers whispered to Matthew as her husband walked about the dining room. Father and son were now greeting each other, rather lovingly, Matthew thought. Nathaniel walked along with his father, who seemed intent on pursuing Matthew.

"Sit down, Charlie. Sit down, Charlie," his wife insisted.

"Dad, this is Matthew."

"Hello . . . er . . ." Mr Chambers said again.

"Matthew, Dad, Matthew." Nathaniel was now repeating his words much as his mother did when she spoke to his father.

"Hello, Matthew."

"Good evening," Matthew said again, looking at Nathaniel and keeping his braceletted hand awkwardly hidden under his chair.

"Dad, I want you and Mom to sit down. I need to speak to you about something."

"Does anyone want any biscuits? I mean, it's a little early for supper. Can I get you some biscuits, dear? Or a sandwich?" Mrs Chambers asked as she looked at Matthew.

"No, thank you, Mrs Chambers."

Mr Chambers sat down, then got up and walked about the dining room. His movements had a rhythm to it: as though he was dancing to music only he could hear.

Mrs Chambers looked towards her husband and started explaining his condition to Matthew.

"His day-to-day memory is not so good, you know. His mind is a little gone. He is fine most of the time . . . he just blurts things out sometimes but does remember things."

"The biscuits will be fine, Mummy," Nathaniel said as he tried to get one of his parents to engage him as they both were occupied with Matthew.

Mr Chambers was still staring at Matthew and walking about the dining room.

"She looks familiar, hey? What a pretty girl you are!" Mr Chambers remarked.

"He! He, Bokkie. His name is Matthew," Mrs Chambers asserted as she jerked her body forward and in her view corrected her husband's sense of gender.

"Did you give her some tea?" Mr Chambers asked with a broad smile on his face, completely oblivious to his wife's comments.

Mrs Chambers was silent. She looked a little uneasy as Mr Chambers sat beside Matthew on the armchair.

"You're very pretty, my dear."

"He, Bokkie. Heeee!" she bellowed again. "His name is Matthew."

"Oh, hello, Matthew."

"Matthew, who?" Mr Chambers asked as he leaned to speak in Matthew's ear.

Nathaniel was standing and moving about, running his hands through his hair. He was quite beside himself and looked at his mother, then at the door, since Rosa and Victoria were set on taking part in some of the events.

"Dadddd! Dadddd! Come over here, Dad."

Nathaniel was sighing and blowing into the dining room, but his father did not cool down. His movements were faster and he moved about, jerking his shoulders now, and sidestepping the air around him as though he was dancing with a partner.

"Let me go and get the biscuits then," Mrs Chambers remarked. She indicated with her eyes for her son to keep a watchful eye over his father.

Nathaniel followed his mother into the kitchen.

"Mom, what is going on? Dad is behaving very strangely. Maybe if you didn't treat him like a child. He still has a mind that works fine, you know."

"Really?" she said as she placed her hands on her hips and looked at her son. "When he washes himself, he also eats the soap. He always wants to eat soap. And, by the way, your father is calling your friend 'she,' so his mind is fine then, hey?"

Nathaniel tilted his head to one side.

"Mummy, I would like for us to sit down and talk. I don't want Dad to feel awkward, like we are treating him like a child."

"Your father blurts things out sometimes. I don't want Matthew to be embarrassed," Mrs Chambers replied.

"Matthew is not embarrassed. You are making matters worse by speaking for Dad."

"Oh, excuse me, please."

Nathaniel moved back a little and as his mother brushed past him carrying the biscuits on a platter.

Mr Chambers was still sitting close to Matthew.

"What's your name again?"

"Matthew. Matthew Michaels," he replied, as he sat uncomfortably in his chair.

"Dad. Come on. Come and sit over here."

"It's our custom, Skattie. Don't mind him. You know, people always like to ask your last name and where you come from. Don't mind Nathaniel."

"Oh, I don't. It's fine."

"Dad. Come and sit over here," Nathaniel asked again.

Mr Chambers did not move at all.

"Has my father been bothering you?"

"Nat, it's fine. People always ask questions about family and sur-
names and that sort of thing all the time; I don't mind."

"Yes, there's nothing wrong with it. Cape Town is really a small
place and we all know one another," Mrs Chambers remarked as she
assisted Nathaniel with his father and helped him into a chair.

"Oh, don't worry, Mrs Chambers. My mom does the same thing,
and my gran. They always want to know who my friends' parents are,
their grandparents, their uncles and so on, and then my gran starts to
tell them about 1932 or something like that and how they look like their
second cousin's brother."

Mrs Chambers was quite attentive and her eyes lit up as Matthew
spoke. Matthew communicated with his eyes, his limp wrists, his whole
body. He gestured with his shoulders, making every word that he spoke
seem utterly danceable. Mrs Chambers looked at Matthew's bracelet
then at Nathaniel's; she looked at Matthew again then at her son and
smiled, as though she was about to ask a question—but refrained from
doing so.

"You and Dad have never really done that, though. I know that
other people ask about relatives and relations, and when someone first
asked me I thought it was really odd because I grew up not knowing
that. Mom, and you, Dad, you both didn't really talk about yourselves
very much, I mean of your younger days."

Both his parents looked at one another and grinned.

"Actually, why is that?" Nathaniel asked, folding his arms. The question echoed in the silence of the room, itself now warranting discussion.

Mrs Chambers served the coffee meticulously.

"Oh, so much to say, really. Daddy and I just kept to ourselves.
People do gossip, you know, and some people fall out for the smallest little thing."

Nathaniel looked at both his parents and handed Matthew the cup
of coffee his mother had poured. Matthew already had the saucer tilted on his lap.

"You are so pretty," Mr Chambers said again.

Matthew smiled.

"I had one just like you when I was a young man," he said, all at once.

"What, what did you say, Dad?"

"Oh, your father is just being silly."

"You are very pretty," Mr Chambers said again.

"Thank you," Matthew replied.

"Can I hold your hand?"

"Dad, I am trying to tell you and Mom something. Please, leave Matthew alone. I need to talk to you and Mom."

"I had one just like you when I was a young man."

"What . . . what are you saying, Dad?"

"Nothing, nothing. Argh,your father is just being silly. I am listening Nathaniel. You were going to tell us something."

"Nathaniel, is she your girlfriend?" Mr Chambers asked.

Nathaniel was stunned.   Matthew tottered a little and spilt some of his coffee on his lap as Mr Chambers spoke.

"Oh, I am so sorry," Matthew remarked, as he tried to dab the coffee on his pants and on the carpet.

"What did you say, Dad?"

"Is she your girlfriend? You have a girlfriend now, hey?"

"Er . . . er . . . Dad . . . er, I really need to talk to you and Mom."

"We are talking. Ha, ha," he laughed.   "And your mother tells me I'm losing my mind." Mrs Chambers pulled an awkward face as she looked at her son.

"We are talking, aren't we, luvvie." Mr Chambers was referring to Matthew and looked adoringly at him. Matthew was smiling nervously since Mr Chambers extended his hand towards him and rested it on his lap.

"Auntie, Auntie . . . here Auntie."

Rosa had entered the dining room with Victoria walking behind her. She handed Matthew a wet cloth. Matthew smiled and thanked her.

"Don't I know you?"

"Yes, Auntie . . . I come wit Mummy to der hairdresser where Auntie's friend work."

"Oh, yes. That's right. I thought I recognized you. You are Maria's daughter."

"Yes, Auntie," Rosa replied.

"I thought the two of you were playing in the backyard," Nathaniel remarked.

The two girls looked at one another and shrugged their shoulders, each with their set of smiling eyes.

"Yes, we are, Uncle. . . we saw Auntie spill der coffee."

The two girls hopped and skipped out of the dining room. Nathaniel sighed out loud again and pulled his hair. Mr Chambers sat in his chair smiling from ear to ear.

"I had one just like you when I was a young man." Matthew looked at Nathaniel. Mr Chambers followed suit. "Nathaniel, come on. Tell me. Is she your girlfriend?" Mr Chambers asked as he lowered his biscuit into his tea.

"Eat some more," Mr Chambers said, directing Matthew to partake in the biscuits placed before him.

Matthew just stared at him.

"Ha, ha, got you. I mean the biscuit. It's called an Eat-Sum-More."

Mrs Chambers just smiled. "Charlie has always had a sense of humour . . . he means no harm, Bokkie."

"Dad, I didn't want you to hear this from anyone else."

Nathaniel clasped both his hands together and stood upright as he addressed his mother and father. He was pulling his hair and had somehow developed a twitch.

"After being married to Carolyn for nine years I have decided that it's not . . ."

"Oh, save the speech. I knew she was your girlfriend when you walked in here with her. She's so pretty."

Mrs Chambers looked at her son and started to cry.

"That's it. I'm leaving."

He looked over to his father, who was very carefully watching his wife.

"Why is everyone crying? And all in front of this pretty young girl. Nathaniel, you did well, hey. She's a pretty girl."

Mrs Chambers was sobbing quietly. She stretched her hand in

Matthew's direction; Matthew was ready to hold hers as Nathaniel stood there tight lipped and twitching.

Nathaniel was dumbfounded. He looked at his father, then at Matthew. His father had tears in his eyes as well but was smiling ever so cheerfully.

"Dad, please tell me what is going on."

"Oh, sit down, Nathaniel."

Mrs Chambers got up from her chair.

She wiped her tears with the tissue that Matthew handed her. Matthew's face was flushed and he was nervously rocking in his chair.

"This has nothing to do with you, Bokkie," Mrs Chambers remarked, as she leaned forward to address Matthew. Nathaniel still looked puzzled. "Mr Chambers and I should have spoken to Nathaniel a long time ago."

"Can someone tell me what is going on? For crying out loud what is going on?" Nathaniel called out.

Mr Chambers got up from his chair and walked over to their long-player. "Let me get my favourite record out," he said. He bent down and rummaged through an orderly box of vinyl long-playing records. "Do you like ballroom, Matthew?" he asked as he placed the needle gently on the record. Nathaniel started to cry, holding both his hands to his face.

Mrs Chambers had her head buried in her hands. She still had tears in her eyes, but she beheld her husband adoringly.

"I am a foxtrot man. Always loved it. There is nothing better than a tango, though, to get the juices flowing. She doesn't like to dance the sexy numbers anymore." He pointed to his wife and seemed rather oblivious to her state. Mrs Chambers still had her head buried in her hands

"Dad, what are you doing? Argh!"

Mr Chambers danced by himself, extending his arm to an invisible partner.

"This is a waltz, Matthew; a really wonderful waltz. Are you sure you don't want to dance this one with me?"

Matthew did not reply.

"Dad, please. Stop this."

"Oh, don't be such a spoil sport, you. I want to dance with Matthew."

Matthew sat with one hand over his cheek, moving it to his mouth occasionally. He looked at Mrs Chambers, then at her husband, then at Nathaniel. Nathaniel was pulling at his hair. His father now started moving furniture about.

"There, that's better," Mr Chambers remarked as he placed the chairs against the wall.

"How about a little vastrap, Matthew? I can skip all the other stuff and go straight to the foxtrot . . . hey, leave that."

Nathaniel took the needle off the record as his father reprimanded him.

"Mom, what is going on?"

"Shall I tell him, Charlie," she said, as her husband danced past her.

"Tell him what? Oh, come on, someone dance with me." He moved towards the long-player again and kept the record above his head so that his son would not take it from him.

"Dad. Please. Stop this dancing now."

"Just leave it, Charlie. First things first, hey?"

Mrs Chambers bent down to speak to Matthew.

"It's the Alzheimer's. He says whatever comes into his mouth. He just blurts things out. He means no harm, you know."

"Come on, Dad, please."

Mr Chambers was dancing away and Mrs Chambers took her son's arm in an attempt to speak to him; Mr Chambers intervened.

"Your mom probably wants to tell you that Chambers isn't our real name." Nathaniel moved away from his father and sat beside Matthew.

"Please don't tell me that I'm adopted, because I look like both of you."

"Oh no, it's not that," Mrs Chambers said, stroking the air.

"Now, how about goema? I have those records too, you know, Matthew."

Matthew smiled nervously.

"So, you don't fancy me then, hey, Matthew? Gee, I was better looking than this guy over here in my heyday. Gah, you should've seen me. Hey, Sarah, tell her."

"Goema, goema, goema . . ." He started to sing and dance in front of Matthew.

"Mom, speak to him. Dad! Please!"

Matthew was now clutching onto Nathaniel.

"Goema, goema, goema . . ." Mr Chambers started to sing again. "That is how we used to do it in District Six in those days, hey?"

"District Six!" Nathaniel called out.

His father was still dancing on the spot.

"Oh, yeah, Mummy and I are both from District Six." He spoke to his son yet looked at Matthew throughout. He did not stop dancing once, and spoke as he danced, merrily. "My father . . . was a September and . . . Mummy's was an April."

Mrs Chambers started sobbing. Nathaniel looked at both his parents, as though he was listening to someone else's life story. Mr Chambers seemed rather calm. He was not overexcited, except dancing on the spot, and enjoying himself. He spoke plainly, and with no affectation. He started to speak at each pause of the song and with the rhythm.

"I don't have to tell you . . . that history of our names . . . because you know it. Our ancestors . . . were made slaves . . . by the Dutch, and when they were set free . . . they were named after the month . . . of their freedom. Some people say . . . that they were named . . . after the month . . . of their arrival . . . into a particular bay . . . or port along the Cape coast.

"Dad, please sit down. Dad, please. This is very upsetting for me, Dad." Nathaniel started to sob.

Mrs Chambers had now dried her tears. She stood beside her husband and he tenderly placed his arms around her waist.

They stood with their arms locked together rocking back and forth, dancing in slow motion, with no music except for Mr Chambers' hum.

"Oh, yes," he said, as he stopped and Mrs Chambers stood aside. "I met Cedric during the war when we were all shipped off to Egypt."

"Let's sit down, Charlie," Mrs Chambers said, calmly and politely.

She managed to get her husband to do so. He sat in one of the armchairs and she sat herself on his lap.

"Those were the days, hey, Sarah?" Mrs Chambers nodded.

"We were rounded up, the Cape Coloured Corps, and forced to fight on the side of the British, in the days when South Africa was a British colony. This is before I met your mother." He looked at his wife again.

"After the war, Cedric and I were still seeing each other; he was also from District Six. Then one night, we were on the stoep of his house, on MacKenzie street . . . remember that stoep, Sarah."

She nodded again and stroked her husband's hair as he spoke.

"One of our friends came to see Cedric and found us together. We were doing our thing, you know."

Nathaniel lowered his eyes. He sighed out loud.

"Oh ja, you wanted to make a speech. I forget. What was I going to say again?"

Nathaniel sighed louder.

"You were telling Nathaniel about Cedric and how a friend found you and him on the stoep.

"Was I? What about the children and their sandwiches? Weren't you going to make Victoria and Rosa their sandwiches, Sarah?"

"I already made them, Charlie. The children are in the backyard."

Everyone was now silent . . . but not for long.

"This guy who found us together that night made it very difficult for us. Cedric and I were laughed at from that day on, we were told not to come to any of the events or parties the soldiers had, you know. Everywhere we went, people would say terrible things. Our parents were not the problem. They begged us to keep it quiet. Cedric eventually lost his job because the strain became too much. One day, I went to his house and found out that he killed himself. I had no one to turn to. His parents were devastated. I met your mother three months after that and she consoled me. I am not very proud to say this, son, but because your mother and I are light-skinned and we got treated differently in our workplaces, we took advantage of that and decided that we would get married and move away from District Six."

Mrs Chambers stroked her husband's hair and kissed him on the forehead.

"Matthew, this woman is my life. I can only hope that my children will be as happy as I have been for more than thirty years."

"Your father and I always danced in the house when you children were out," Mrs Chambers said, rocking on her husband's knee as she addressed her son.

"She still has rhythm, hey? Once a District Sixer, always a District Sixer." Mr Chambers looked at both his son and Matthew.

Nathaniel was distraught. He looked as though the blood had been drained from his body.

"You don't look so good, you know, son."

Nathaniel sighed and moved his body about uncomfortably. He was rubbing his head and Matthew tried on several occasions to hold his hand. He looked towards the door to see whether Victoria and Rosa were anywhere near the kitchen.

"So, tell me, then. Where does Chambers come from?"

"I worked for a judge for a short while. He is dead now. I asked his advice one day after Mummy and I decided to be married. He was in his chambers and he told me that the best thing for us to do was to move and change our names. He was going to do it right then and there. I telephoned Mummy at work and she came down to the courthouse. I had to think quickly. Mummy and I couldn't decide, but we were in his chambers and I guess we decided to go with that name.

"How could you? How could both of you lie to your children like that? Do you know what you've done? You've robbed us of our name, of our blood."

"Oh, don't be silly. You still have your blood. Blood is thicker than water, as the saying goes . . . Blood is even thicker than history, hey, Sarah?"

Nathaniel was now crying uncontrollably.

"At least with a slave name . . . you would have every reason to . . . be proud because you know . . . who you are. I don't know who . . . I am anymore. I don't even know who you are."

Nathaniel wiped the tears off his face, then turned and vomitted, "Let's go, Matthew." His mother moved towards him. "No. Stay where you are, Mom."

Nathaniel ran quickly through the kitchen. The minute he reached the backyard, he hurled furiously. In a moment, Victoria and Rosa were at his side. His head was hanging down and his face was red.

"Go inside please, darling," Nathaniel said to Victoria. "I need to be alone. You too, Rosa. Go inside, please."

Both children looked at him with sympathy written all over their faces. They stroked each other's arms and held on to one other as Nathaniel gestured for them to leave. Nathaniel gestured with his hand and the children moved back. He shut the back door and bolted it from the outside.

Nathaniel hurled several more times. His bracelet was now covered in the remains of his afternoon lunch. He took it from his arm and washed it under the tap for a long time. The backyard was fairly spacious and he leaned against the wall as he dried the water from his face. He wiped his face dry and stood there. Nathaniel put the bracelet back on, then took the bucket and washed the excretions down the drain. He kept his face under the running water and held it there for a while, as the water ran over his face.

Mr and Mrs Chambers were dancing to goema, the fast-beat District Six rhythm. Rosa joined them in no time, and she clicked her fingers and gyrated to the music without hesitation. Her friend, Victoria, stood by and observed every move—her eyes larger than usual. Mr and Mrs Chambers soon formed a circle with Rosa, and each then took their turn to dance in the circle. Matthew sat close by and encouraged Victoria to join the goema circle. Rosa managed to persuade her, and while she had less rhythm she managed to participate and enjoyed herself. Matthew sat with his hands folded; he rubbed his bracelet since there was little else for him to do with his hands. He was, momentarily, preoccupied with watching two adults and two children dance one of District Six's favourites: the goema.

The cool autumn evening was filled with periodic hisses. The crickets were out and their sound portended a rainy day. The wind was now at rest, and the mist rose above the heads of those who were still out on the street. Grayness foamed over the blackness of the night. Carolyn had asked her mother to watch Victoria and ensure that she went to bed promptly. Her husband had brought their daughter home, packed several bags, and left without informing her as to his intentions. Carolyn was wearing a light coat, with a hood, which she threw over her head. She was unrecognizable and sauntered pass her neighbours, many of whom she did not know and did not care to know. She sat in the cold, in the shadow of a bright streetlight, like a common beggar. She was observing Auntie Flowers' house but did not have the courage to go towards it. Her eyes were red and her mouth dry. She sat, and waited—with no clear idea as to what her next move might be. A stray dog ventured towards her and for a brief moment she thought he might bark at her and alert the neighbours as to her presence. He lifted his leg and urinated against the pole quite oblivious to her presence. He stood beside the pole as though he owned it. He then sniffed Carolyn, and upon deciding that she was not a threat, went about his business sniffing and rummaging through garbage in the cold gutters.

There was a little girl sitting in a window with a black ribbon in her hair, watching Carolyn, who did not look up at the child for fear of recognition. Rosa did recognize her. The young child had her little book out and she wrote in it as she observed the hooded woman in the shadow.

Glossary

Agamdrila: Bless you!

Ai, tog: Oh, dear! Oh, what a bother!

Anerkind: A little girl or little boy, a form of address like the term "child"; *aner* from the shortened Dutch form, *ander* meaning other, another.

Barakat: A gift, presented in the form of a basket, offered at weddings, funerals or baptisms (religious ceremonies and festivals). It is an offering which the hostess provides, and it is meant to be taken home to share with the rest of the family. The basket is wrapped in cellophane paper and consists of cakes, pastries, fruit and a selection of snacks which were offered at the ceremony or festival.

Beulah: Beautiful A particular vernacular has been developed by trans-gendered peoples (man to woman) referred to as moffies, which was in regular use in District Six and within Cape Town. There is a particular subculture surrounding the vernacular, and words that are chosen to replace others are usually kept within the range of the first letter of the actual word replaced.

Bioscope: Cinema.

Bis: from the term "busy-body," somebody who is inquisitive.

Bloodcloth: A cotton cloth used for menstruation.

Bloomers: A female undergarment with elasticized waist and legs; the elastic of the legs is just above the knee. During the 1970s school-going children were required to wear bloomers, in the chosen colour of the school to accompany the rest of the uniform.

Bobotie: A well-known dish in Cape Town, usually made with minced meat, which is sweet and sour, although it can be savoury; the topping may consist of mashed potato with a custard top which is usually baked. The custard top is made with eggs and milk.

Boeber: A dessert which is rather like a drink. It is made of fried vermicelli, which is then boiled together with sugar, rosewater, milk, cinnamon, cardamom seeds and sago and served in a cup or bowl.

Boere-van: A vehicle used by the South African police. As was customary at the time, most policemen were of Afrikaner heritage and were thus referred to as Boere.

Boerewors: A Dutch style sausage which is made and eaten among the population at large. The spiciness depends very much on where the sausage is made and by whom. In Cape Town it is much spicier than in other parts of South Africa.

Boeta: A term used to refer to the oldest brother in a Muslim household; also used to refer to a [male] Muslim elder.

Boetatjie: Often used as a diminutive of "Boeta"; diminutives are oftentimes used sarcastically and/or condescendingly.

Boja: A term used to refer to a man who is a father and head of the household within Muslim families.

BoKaap: The upper region of Cape Town, mainly Muslim, which was also considered an extension of District Six.

Bokkie: A term of endearment. An expression derivative of buck, (like deer, pet) and the Afrikaans usage of buck is bok; hence bokkie, which is the dimunitive.

Bollas: A dessert, much like a doughnut, made out of butter, flour, eggs, milk and baking powder, then fried. After bollas are fried, they are dipped in syrup and rolled in sugar or coconut then filled with apricot jam.

Bredie: Meat and vegetables stewed together. The most common meat used for bredie is lamb or mutton. Within Hindu households and many Muslim and Christian households, it was common to find vegetable bredies without a trace of meat.

Breyani: A rice dish with spices which are cooked together in either buttermilk or yogurt in a pot or in the oven. Depending on one's preference, chicken breyani, fish breyani, lamb breyani and vegetable breyani are all eaten. Breyanis are known for their aromatic flavour and usually contain cardamom seeds, cinnamon, oftentimes saffron and other mixed curry spices. The wonder of a breyani is the fact that it is layered: the parboiled rice mixture, the parboiled lentils, then the layer of marinated meat or vegetables. This is then cooked together and sealed until it is ready to be eaten, when it then tossed together in a colourful ensemble.

Buju: A herb many use in tea or on its own for its calming properties.

Chht: An expression to indicate that one is fed up or had enough. The sound is usually accompnied by rapid sucking of air through the teeth.

Constantia: The grape-growing region of Cape Town; also a wine-producing region.

Dagga: Marijuana, cannabis

Daltjies: A savoury snack made from chickpea flour, grated apple, onion, ginger, chili powder and other spices which are then mixed with water; spinach is dipped into this mixture and then spooned into hot oil. They resemble onion bhadjis in shape, texture and flavour.

Dela: a word used to describe the genitalia of women; this would include clitoris, labia minor, labia majora. The term is used fondly by older women, less so among the younger generation.

Deurmekaa: From the Afrikaans/Dutch word, *deurmekaar* means troublesome, bothersome, difficult.

Drakensberg: A range of mountains in the eastern region of South Africa, operating as its geographical border.

Eina: An expression used when one is hurt, as in "ouch!"

Frikadel: A mixture, much like a meat patty, which contains onions, eggs, and herbs and spices mixed with either fish or meat; small round balls are made, slightly flattened, then fried in oil.

Gail: The name given to the language spoken among moffies (transgendered people).

Galatie: A term used for a Muslim woman; the term is usually used when referring to a woman who is unknown; it can also be used respectfully.

Gemaningal: Someone has died.

Gemoers: Rubbish! A derogatory word, used when referring to someone in an unkind and demeaning manner.

Genoeg: Enough!

Gestamp and Gechap: Signed, sealed and stamped. (With reference to official documents).

Ghienna: The term "henna" is used in English-speaking countries, although it is of the same ingredient. Muslim and Indian girls and women use Ghienna to colour adorn their hands and feet.

Graaf Reinett: A small town, inland, located to the east of Cape Town, closer to the city of Port Elizabeth.

Halaal: This refers to the eating of meats which have been prepared and approved by a Muslim Judicial Council. Animals are slaughtered by someone of the Muslim faith, and the killing is swift, with all of the blood being drained from the animal at once.

Here: (Italics in the text). *Here rer!* An Afrikaans and Dutch term used to refer to "The Lord" or "God." "Dear Lord" or "Dear God" would be a reasonable translation.

Hoer: Whore.

Hopelots: A wooded area designated as part of the "Poor White" section located on the opposite side of De Waal Drive; thus, not officially part of District Six, although frequented by children of District Six.

Imam: A Muslim priest.

Inshallah: (translation) "If Allah permits." Often said with reference to an understanding of "God willing" or "all in good time."

Jan Van Riebeeck: Sent by the Dutch East India Company [DEIC] in 1652 to build a half-way station at the Cape, he sailed around the Cape of Good Hope and was, along with his men in three ships, swept into the Cape by a storm on the 6th of April.

Jintoe: Whore, prostitute.

Kabeljou: A type of fish, scaly, and commonly used since it is generally quite cheap.

Kadoematjie: A piece of cotton filled with earth, herbs, plants, and indigenous mixtures. The cloth is sewn together and worn around children's (and sometimes adults') necks and most times pinned to their vests or any piece of underwear. It is meant to protect people from harm and colonial evil.

Kak: Considered foul and vulgar, it is an expression akin to "nonsense" or "rubbish." The official translation gives it an equivalency to "shit" with reference to animals.

Kalkie: Kalk Bay; along the Muizenberg coastline.

Kanala: Please. This expression is used when one asks a favour. It is well known that the Muslim community, in particular, used the word kanala interchangably: both as please and to ask for a favour. District Six was also referred to as Kanaladorp (meaning, Kanala Town; the place where everyone says, "kanala").

Kee Feit: A Muslim funeral

Klaverjas: A rather sophisticated card game.

Kloofnek: A direct translation would read "Neck of the Cliff." This is located to the east of the center of the city and, much as its Afrikaans/Dutch name reveals, it is situated at the neck of a cliff, all of which forms part of Table Mountain.

Koeksisters: A dessert usually eaten on Sunday mornings by both the Muslim and Christian community. It is made of a dough which consists of flour, eggs, milk, fine ginger, aniseed and yeast. It is then fried and sweetened in a syrup of sugar water which also contains cinnamon and cardamom seeds. Depending on preference, certain households will place cooked desiccated coconut in the center whilst others may simply choose to sprinkle the syrupy koeksister with desiccated coconut.

Krislaam: Greetings.

Lekker: Tasty, delicious, tasteful; also used much like, "good and solid," or "well." The word is used in many expressions which refer to a state of being, in response to being asked, and also to a way of being; in the latter case, it also means "cool," "groovy" and "well."

Lieberstein: A local, fairly cheap white wine.

Lighties: Youngsters; with reference to someone who is considered a "lightweight," thus young.

Lunch: The word used by moffies to refer to penis or crotch.

Meisie: A girl

Meisiekind: A girl child, used as one word.

Meit: a term used to refer to a "woman"; the term "meid/meit" is derivative of Dutch and has historically been used to refer to a "freed slave," a woman roaming about and available, and certainly available to Dutch men at the time when the Cape was under Dutch colonial rule. When used by members of the District Six community it is used to refer to a loose woman, also a lover.

Meneer: The exact translation means "sir"; Also used to refer to a male teacher or male authority figure associated with the government and/or law and order.

Milnerton: A White suburb a short distance to the East of the centre of the city; also one of the locations for horse racing.

Moffie: From the word "Hermaphrodite," thus "Hermaffie," which then became "Maffie," and later "Moffie".

Motchie: A term used to refer to a Muslim woman, usually one who is older, much like the term "Auntie."

Nageboorte: Afterbirth. A derogatory term; a term which is used to demean someone and inflict pain.

Oemie: The Malay, thus Muslim, term used for mother or grandmother, similar to the Ducth/Afrikaans term, Ouma, which means grandmother.

Ospavat: A factory, on DeVilliers Street, where wooden furniture was made.

Pakuit: Unpack; to speak oneself "out," so to speak.

Salomi: A roti which is filled with a minced (ground) beef, mutton or lamb curry mixture.

Skattie: Dear. The term "scat" is used as the reference and "skattie" as the diminutive.

Slangetjies: A mixture of chickpea flour and spices is put through a sieve then into hot oil; it is eaten as a snack and often has spiced peanuts in the mixture, depending on preference.

Sjambok: A thick wooden stick, mainly carried by the South African police at the time, used for hitting people and animals.

Skollie: From the word "scallywag," meaning troublemaker or rascal.

Skoot: Let's go! Go quickly. To leave in haste.

Snoek: A silver-gray fish, firm and white inside, indigenous to Cape Town. The texture is soft with few scales. Regarded as highly delicious.

Strandloper: Beachcomber. In Cape Town, this refers to someone whose nature is to romb endlessly. The best known Strandloper is "Harry the Strandloper."

Tokkolosh, Tokkalosie: Difficult to translate; not a spirit or a ghost. The Tokkalosh or Tokkalosie is usually seen by women who are in trouble; he comes to the aid of women, reveals himself, and speaks to matters which they are seeking answers to. Perhaps the Tokkalosh is a manifestation of the unconscious. The existence of the Tokkalosh is not questioned but treated as part of the world of speech and the imagination.

Tossed out: A term used by children to indicate that they are no longer on speaking terms. Children would agree not to speak to each other, put their thumbs together, lock them, then release them. Alternatively they would put their thumbs in their mouths and propel them forward when released, pointing at the person with whom they no longer wish to speak.

Twenty-six: A prison term to denote a man who is considered weaker than others or effeminate. It is a derogatory term used to refer to a man who looks like someone who would be raped or sexually asaulted by another man.

Uit die blou van onse hemel: The national anthem prior to the Mandela government. When Mandela became president, "Nkosi Sikelele" was added. South Africans now sing both.

Vasco da Gama: Da Gama was a Portuguese sea captain and explorer who sailed around the Cape of Good Hope to India in the late 1490s.

Vertel: To tell; to tell off; in other words, to reprimand or scold.

Voetvrou: A woman who delivers babies and who is known for her knowledge of traditional herbs and medicines. The term also comes from "voet" which means foot in English. It therefore can also mean a woman who walks or uses her feet.

Vuilgoed: Rubbish! Dirt! Garbage!

Wellingtons: A shop located in the center of Cape Town which many District Six residents frequented, since it was within walking distance, to buy cheese, nuts, chocolate and other dried fruits and grains. The prices were usually lower than at the local supermarkets or corner stores.